In a Glass House

Nino Ricci

M&S

Cloth edition published 1993
First trade paperback edition published 1994
This trade paperback edition published 1999

Canadian Cataloguing in Publication Data

Ricci, Nino, 1959 –
In a glass house

ISBN 0-7710-7505-7 (trade pbk. ed.)

I. Title.

PS8585.I12615   1999   C813'.54   C93-094445-3
PR9199.3.R5215   1999

We acknowledge the financial support of the Government of
Canada through the Book Publishing Industry Development
Program for our publishing activities. Canadä

We further acknowledge the support of the Canada Council for the
Arts and the Ontario Arts Council for our publishing program.

All of the characters in this book are fictitious, and any resemblance
to actual persons living or dead is purely coincidental.

Cover design: Ingrid Paulson
Cover illustration: Eric Dinyer
Set in Sabon by M&S, Toronto

Printed and bound in Canada

McClelland & Stewart Inc.
The Canadian Publishers
481 University Avenue
Toronto, Ontario
M5G 2E9

1 2 3 4 5   03 02 01 00 99

BOOKS BY NINO RICCI

Lives of the Saints (1990)
In a Glass House (1993)
Where She Has Gone (1997)

for Jan and Gary Geddes
and for Peter Day

"And we shall all come forth without shame and shall stand before Him. And He will say unto us, 'Ye are swine, made in the Image of the Beast and with his mark; but come ye also!' And the wise ones and those of understanding will say, 'Oh Lord, why dost Thou receive these men?' And He will say, 'This is why I receive them, oh ye wise, this is why I receive them, oh ye of understanding, that not one of them believed himself to be worthy of this.'"

> – Fyodor Dostoyevsky
> *Crime and Punishment*

Cristofiru Culumbu, chi facisti?
La megghiu giuvintù tu rruvinasti.

Christopher Columbus, what have you done?
You've ruined the best of our young.

> – Calabrian saying

I

The town of Mersea rested on a small bluff that looked out over the shores of Lake Erie; and had the waters of that lake not reversed their flow from the Mississippi to the St. Lawrence when some cataclysm of nature opened up the Niagara Gorge, the few acres of raised land on which Mersea sat might have remained an island, cut off from the mainland by ten or fifteen miles of shallow lake. Even still, much of the land around Mersea had had to be reclaimed from the marshes, the country roads that lined the lakefront on the eastern side of the township, toward Point Chippewa, raised up on twenty- or thirty-foot dykes; and after the thaw and heavy rains of spring you could drive down those roads and have the strange, thrilling experience of seeing the lake on one side higher than the land on the other, only a man-made ridge with sides sloping at smooth forty-five-degree angles holding back tons of water from seeking their own level.

Highway 76 formed the spine of the township, St. Mary's, over which Mersea presided, known despite its muddy winters and springs as the Sun Parlour. It came down from the big divided highway to the north and cut through the centre of town, intersecting Highway 3, the old Talbot Road, to form the town's four corners before ending finally at the lake, where it was extended a few hundred yards into the water by the Mersea dock. The concession roads came off Highway 76 with a Euclidean regularity, as if some giant had merely taken a great pencil and ruler in hand and divided the wilderness into a tidy grid. In Italy the roads had snaked and curved to the rhythm of the land like a part of it, but here it seemed the battle against nature had been fiercer, the stakes higher, the need to dominate more complete. Only two roads broke the pattern – the old Talbot Road, which weaved in and out among the concessions, sometimes following at a distance the curve of the lake, sometimes veering suddenly north or south without apparent reason, conforming to some forgotten agenda of its original builders; and the lakeshore-hugging Highway 13, which from the west connected up a string of lakeside communities before dipping down into the Point and ending abruptly at the entrance to Point Chippewa National Park.

The first Italians in Mersea, from before the war, had bought up farms on the lake, along the stretch of highway known as the Seacliff because of the fifty- or sixty-foot rise that ran along the shore there. Other Italians had settled around them as around a nucleus, along the lakeshore itself or north of it where the Talbot Road, coming west out of town, rose up along the Ridge, the remnant of a former shoreline that followed the Seacliff at a distance like its shadow. But my father had bought a farm further north and east, on the 3rd Concession. We were the only Italians then who lived east of Highway 76, until the Massaccis, a year or so later, bought a farm on the 12 & 13 Sideroad; and though by road we were only four or five miles out of town, could see from our back field the weathered wall of the Sun Parlour Canning Factory, with its ad for Caporal cigarettes, the pink brick and white clapboard gables of the houses on the town's outskirts, the stucco tower of St. Michael's church, still the farm seemed remote and forgotten, like a place cut off from the world. It was strange to see so many houses spread out across the countryside the way they were along those concession roads, each one separate and discrete, set off in its own tiny realm as if in enmity; and in that flat landscape, with no point from which you could hold the world in a glance, you got no sense of where things stood in relation to one another, only of endless, random repetition, the openness pressing down on you, holding the world back. When visitors came to see us during my first weeks on the farm, it seemed in my seven-year-old's dim imagining that they could not have reached us by anything as simple as a road but must have bridged a strange chasm as wide and blank as the sea.

Those first weeks in Mersea were like a journey through fog – objects seemed to emerge like phantoms, shimmer briefly into focus, fade away. People too: the strange half-familiar faces of the *paesani* who came to visit us, sullen and restrained as at a funeral; my father. When he'd come for me in Halifax after the crossing, the two of us face to face then on the long train ride in, while the baby sat apart in its hamper like some parcel to be delivered, he had seemed after his five years' absence from my life like someone who had nothing to do with me, who was outside of me like a stranger, who I had to think about, be awkward with, only because I was sitting beside him. But more and more it began to seem that some shadow surrounding him took me in too, that he was not just outside but inside me somehow, so I could not see how things were now except through his shadow.

3

Sometimes, during those first weeks, I would wake suddenly in the middle of the night and for a moment, in the darkness, feel a disorientation so complete that I might never have known what a world was, or a bed or a chair. My mind in that instant seemed to mirror exactly the darkness of the room around me, seemed to contain no thoughts, no past, only a sudden panic and terror; and it was only when I could put together a little story in my head, a boat, a train, until I arrived finally at the bed I was lying in, that the room around me slipped into dim focus, and the panic passed. I thought then that the blackness I fell into on those nights must be like death, that I had dreamed of being dead, because sometimes, afterwards, I could remember an image of myself closing my eyes and sinking into a sleep as dark as the sea; though it was never the moment I closed my eyes that frightened me but the moment I opened them, when I emerged again into everything strange and new and forgotten, as into the sudden horror of being born, or born again.

II

My father's land, about thirty acres in all, was split part way up by a creek that wound its way through the farms on the 3rd Concession, the land on either side sloping gently down to it to form a tiny valley. Beyond the creek was open field, indistinguishable from the other fields that flanked it, whatever private history it might have had revealed only in the occasional arrowhead or fossil that the plough churned up in the fall. But the front part of the farm, with its strange buildings and variations, the cavernous barn and kiln, the irrigation pond, the greenhouses with their white wooden frames and their weed-choked alleys, the coal-dust-filled boiler room, was its own little world, as compact and multifaceted as the tiny villages, often merely the centuries-long elaborations of single families, that had clung like outcroppings to the rocky slopes around Valle del Sole. When I first arrived at the farm its tidy arrangements, the trees that rose leafless in an orderly row along the edge of the driveway, the little courtyard formed by the house and garage and kiln, made it seem like something in a picture, without dimensions, unreal; it might have been set out by some titan child, who had simply placed this tree here, this house, this red barn, like so many giant toys. The roofs of the greenhouses then were covered with a thin crust of snow that made me think of sugar, though here and there the snow was cut away in perfect dark squares – I thought the squares must form some kind of pattern or code, but they were only spots where the glass had broken, and the snow had fallen through.

Our house, of white clapboard, appeared to stand in those first days like an object frozen in a moment of time and then forgotten, with an air at once of abandonment and preservation. My father had preceded us there but whether by days or weeks or months wasn't clear, only the barest evidences of him scattered here and there, a few dishes in the kitchen cupboards, a dirty towel on the rack in the bathroom, as if he had come like an intruder, feline, ready for flight, the house still seeming to await some small crucial act that might shatter its chill calm. There was a modernness to it that I thought of as what was foreign, not Italian, the preternatural gleam of the kitchen with its chrome table and chequer-board tiles, its porcelained fridge and stove, then the living room with its picture-book decorum, the sofa and armchair there, faded and worn but imposing, a different order of things than what I'd known in Valle del Sole; a hundred mysteries seemed to shelter there, the radio above the fridge whose insides slowly warmed to a glow as it came on, the telephone with its distant buzz like insects mindlessly churring. But if the house had any informing spirit it didn't seem to reside in its objects, which despite their novelty gave no feeling of welcome to the rooms that held them, refusing to give up their histories, sitting stubborn and mute in their separate spaces like things that had turned their backs to you. The only thing that betrayed them in this was a smell, a faint odour of mothballs and sweet rot and something else, not as simple as sweat or the smell of a breath but definitely human, lingering on the furniture, in the cupboards in the kitchen and pantry, in the chintz curtains left at the windows, and stealing over me sometimes to leave an odd hollowness in me like a gloom, the creeping intimation of whatever unknown lives had gone on there before us.

The day after my arrival a girl named Gelsomina came to live with us to look after the baby. On the train my father's awkward ministrations to the baby had seemed to draw attention to it as to a magical thing, women in the seats around us bending to coo to it in their senseless languages, slowly taking it over for its feedings and changes while my father sat darkly by. But now it was brusquely turned over to Gelsomina like something to be quietly disposed of. Gelsomina was the daughter of my father's cousin Alfredo – I remembered the visit he'd paid my mother in Valle del Sole the previous fall after her troubles had begun, come back from America then in his fancy suit, though now he spoke as if he hadn't seen me since I was a baby.

"*Ma guarda cuist*', do you remember your Uncle Alfredo? Look how big you are, I remember when you were as small as a cabbage."

But his friendliness seemed forced, almost bitter, put on more for my father's benefit than for mine.

Gelsomina, thin-limbed and moody, dark like the back-country urchins who'd come into school sometimes in Valle del Sole from their distant homesteads, was strange with me as well. I was sure we'd known each other in Italy, could call up images of her from the gatherings of my father's side of the family in Castilucci; but she gave no sign now of this past between us, as if we could no longer be the same people we'd been once, now

7

that we were in Canada.

"I'm only helping here until I can work at the factory again," she said, making it seem as if she'd been in the country a long time already, though her father had brought the family over only the previous fall. "I was there before but I had to leave because one of the *inglesi* told the boss I wasn't sixteen yet and it was against the law. But it's just they can't stand to see the Italians make the same money they do when they've been in the country a hundred years."

Tsi'Alfredo and his wife Maria brought things for the house, pots and pans, a washboard, jars full of tomato sauce, a stack of diapers. Other *paesani* came by as well, people who called me by name but who I recognized only vaguely or not all, couldn't connect to a place or a time; but if they had gifts they'd quietly turn them over to Gelsomina, as if shielding my father from the shame of their generosity. My father would tell Gelsomina to bring glasses and wine, and sometimes he'd talk with these visitors in such a casual way that the shadow around him receded and he'd seem transformed, different from the man who had sat beside me on the train, from the one who in some painful way was my father; but other times he sat silent at his corner of the table and the guests talked only among themselves.

There were two bedrooms in the house, one off the pantry and one off the living room. My father slept in the first, in a bed with a headboard of slim metal tubes like the bars of a cage; Gelsomina and I shared a double bed in the other with the baby. For all this compelled closeness, Gelsomina and I hardly spoke to each other – the house seemed to impose its own silence on us, to police and enforce it. Even the baby was quiet, its blank eyes probing the world with what seemed an unnatural calm, though often in the middle of the night it would begin to whimper and

8

I'd watch through a haze of sleep as Gelsomina soundlessly rose out of bed to make up a bottle. I'd go into the kitchen with her sometimes, taking comfort from her cool efficiency, the way she moved through the room undaunted by its porcelained strangeness, the chrome taps, the dark coils on the stove that slowly melted to red as the heat fed into them. The milk she used came in large thick-lipped bottles that the milkman left every morning on the steps inside the back door; before warming it she'd mix in a cupful of boiled water into which she'd stirred a few pinches of sugar. When the bottle was ready she'd touch the nipple against her wrist to check its heat, then nestle the baby with practised ease in the crook of an arm, her movements so certain and smooth they seemed instinctual; but there was an edge in them too, an urgency, one that seemed less protective of the baby than of the silence that ruled over the house.

My father was working shifts at the canning factory then, on top of the hours he spent on the farm. To me it seemed only that he came and went like a spirit, his presence never certain but somehow lingering around us always, like the house's strange smell. In my sleep I'd hear his truck starting up in the middle of the night, its lights flashing past the bedroom window a moment later like a dream, but then in the morning I might be awakened by the sound of his hammer and rise to see him already stooped on a catwalk atop one of the greenhouse roofs, home again though I hadn't heard him return. Gelsomina, at least, seemed to make some sense of his movements: once a day, sometimes in the morning, sometimes in the afternoon, sometimes at night, she'd fill a big silver lunchbox with sandwiches wrapped in wax paper and set it out on the back steps, from where it would disappear each time my father's truck pulled out of the driveway and appear again, empty, several hours later. But then often at mealtimes Gelsomina would set a third place at the table that wouldn't be filled. Sometimes a day passed when my father didn't come into the house at all; and then at night we'd see the boiler-room light still burning when we went to bed.

The worst times were when my father was sleeping. He slept, as he worked, in erratic fits, without apparent pattern, perhaps asleep when Gelsomina and I awoke in the mornings, or coming suddenly into the house in the middle of the afternoon and disappearing almost at once into his room; and each time he closed himself behind his bedroom door he set the seal on a second order of silence. Gelsomina and I would take the baby out to the front porch then, which was separated from the living room by a thick door with a heavy latch we had to remember to click back so we didn't lock ourselves out, and there we would sit out our exile on chairs we'd brought out from the kitchen, the baby set on a mattress of blankets on the wood floor. The porch had windows all around, pleasant and warm when the sun was shining, with an air of dreamy indolence that made me think of summer days out tending the sheep in Valle del Sole; but almost every day now was cloudy and wet, the April wind rattling through the windows then and our breaths hanging in the air with the damp cold. After a half hour or so the baby would begin to whimper, its little fists reddening and its nose beginning to run; but Gelsomina would merely wrap it more tightly in its blankets and rock it in her arms to silence it.

The baby didn't have a name then, seemed too small somehow to merit one – at night, tucked between Gelsomina and me in bed, its body looked so tiny and frail I was afraid I'd roll over and crush it in my sleep. It hadn't grown at all since it had been born, only its eyes showing any change, clearing slowly from murky grey to a pellucid blue till it seemed some spirit had crawled up inside it and was peering out now from its hollow sockets.

"It's a bastard," Gelsomina said. "My mother says your father should put her in an orphanage."

But instead we merely kept up our careful avoidances, the baby closed away in the bedroom whenever my father was in the house, at meals Gelsomina sitting sideways in her chair to be ready to rise if it should begin to cry. A line seemed to divide the house in two at the living-room door, Gelsomina seldom bringing the baby into the kitchen and my father, for his part, seldom crossing beyond it. Every day I half expected that some-one would come to take the baby away from us, and that our lives would assume then some more normal course; but the weeks passed and still the baby remained.

Then one night I was awakened by the baby's cries, unusually insistent and loud. Beside me Gelsomina was already up, rocking the baby in her arms with a troubled urgency.

"*Calmati*," Gelsomina hissed. "*Calmati!*"

But the baby only cried more fiercely, in the moonlight her face seeming gnarled like an old woman's.

"Here," Gelsomina whispered, setting the baby in my lap. Its thin hair was dank with sweat from the spring mugginess of the night, the first warm one we'd had since I'd arrived. "Hold her while I make a bottle. If she wakes your father he'll break both our heads."

So my father was asleep, then – Gelsomina must have heard him come in after we had gone to bed. I tried to silence the baby by rocking her, clutching her close to me hoping to smother her sound with my body; but her small fists hit out against me to push me away. I panicked and clamped a hand down hard against her mouth; but in an instant her chest had begun to heave so wildly that I pulled my hand away in fright.

Gelsomina returned now with the bottle. The baby resisted it at first, seeming too intent on her crying.

"Oh, *basta!*" Gelsomina whispered.

Then finally she took the nipple and grew quiet again, instantly transformed by her silence, made suddenly toy-like and harmless again when a moment before she had seemed so monstrous.

Gelsomina's eyes flashed to mine.

"Go back to sleep. Anyway it's not our fault."

But it seemed some demon had got into the baby now: over the next days she grew more and more unmanageable, sleeping fitfully, crying at all hours, as if she had only just overcome the shock of her early birth and was suddenly bursting on the world with all the energy and rage of a newborn. My father said nothing, only grew more shadowy, more elusive, sleeping less often, coming in less often for meals.

"She must be sick," Gelsomina said. "My sister cried like this when she had the colic."

"Do we have to take her to a doctor?"

"A doctor! Who'll pay to send her to a doctor? If she dies it'll be better for everyone."

But the baby did not die, only continued for days her incessant crying. Gelsomina kept placing a palm on her forehead but could feel no fever there – except for her crying the baby seemed normal, her limbs beginning to thicken, her hair filling in, her cheeks puffed out with what looked like ruddy health.

My father had stopped coming in for meals entirely now. Then one night, while Gelsomina and I sat wide-eyed in bed trying to quiet the baby, we heard the back door slam, saw my father's shadow pass outside our bedroom window, saw the boiler-room light go on, then off again; but my father didn't return. The next day was Sunday, when we usually had lunch at Gelsomina's house; but well past noon my father still hadn't come in from the fields. Finally Tsi'Alfredo called on the phone.

"Tsi'Mario said I should tell you we can't come today," Gelsomina said. "He has to get the field ready to plant."

Tsi'Alfredo's voice crackled loud an instant from the other end.

"He told me to call," Gelsomina said, "but I forgot."

But she was making things up – she hadn't spoken to my father at all.

"Why did you say that?" I said afterwards.

"Mind your own business. Do you think I want to go back to the factory again?"

My father switched back to the night shift at the factory that week. But he didn't come into the house any more to sleep, the rotations of his lunchbox on the back steps the only evidence that he had come into the house at all, at night his footsteps sounding from the boiler room when he came to collect it. Then one afternoon Gelsomina made me go out there with her while my father was in the back field.

"I just want to see," she said.

"See what?" I said.

"Never mind what, just come."

It was the first time I'd been out to the boiler room. I had thought it must be a kind of house, with its glass windows and false-brick walls, but it seemed merely a storage place where so many odds and ends had been heaped haphazardly over the years. A boiler rose up near the entrance like an outsized bull, a tangled web of pipes and shafts and cables leading away from it;

then beyond it the room was all dark clutter and filth, wooden storage niches along the walls crammed with strange implements, switches and fittings, lengths of pipe, coils of wire, a workbench littered with oily tools and tin cans and with a mess of gears and metal shafts that looked like the remains of some great engine. A film of coal dust covered everything like a pall, the windows so powdered over with it they let in only an eerie twilight. Along one wall, though, was a bank of niches that looked newly built, unpainted and fresh, its tidy slots seeming hopeful somehow in their empty newness.

Gelsomina led me to the back of the building toward a room whose walls rose up only part way to the ceiling, its roof forming a loft. An old calendar, 1957, was tacked outside the door, yellowed with its four years' lingering, a few dates circled in red and cryptic messages written beneath in a foreign hand. Inside the room, a small mullioned window looked out from a dimness that smelt of mould and something else, a faint animal scent like the smell of a stable. A massive wood desk, its surface blotched and pitted, filled most of the space; but on the floor against the inside wall, spread out as far as the foot of the door, was a narrow stretch of straw, a blanket heaped at one end of it. A rawboned cat raised its head from the blanket's folds as we came in, yellow eyes shining; it stared for an instant, stiffly alert, then sprang up suddenly and disappeared through the doorway into the boiler room's shadows.

"See," Gelsomina whispered, jutting her chin toward the straw as if it were the final proof of some argument she'd been making. "That's why he isn't coming inside any more."

I made out now the hollows and contours there – they followed the shape of a human body like a mould, as if the body still lay there, invisible, silently impressing its weight into the straw.

14

There was an oily bag on the desk. Gelsomina found cheese inside, a half loaf of stale bread, then a half jug of wine on the floor between the desk and the wall.

"I told you," she said, though to me it seemed that whatever mystery it was we were solving only loomed larger now.

She had begun to try the drawers of the desk. The three on one side were jammed or locked, but the top one on the other opened easily. Inside was a handful of shotgun cartridges, and then, at the back, a pile of old photographs. Gelsomina began to leaf through them.

"God, look how big he was then," she said. "He looks like an ox in those clothes."

"You shouldn't look in there," I whispered. "We should go."

But I'd edged closer to her to see the photograph she held – it showed a group of soldiers scattered pell-mell across a hillside as if caught in mid-action. But they were playing a game: one in the forefront had his hand drawn like a pistol while another a few feet away was pretending to die as in a child's game, his knees buckling and his hands clutched over his heart.

"That was before your father was married," Gelsomina said. But it took me an instant to realize that he was the man in the centre of the picture, the one pretending to die – it was a kind of shock to think of him like that, playing like a schoolboy, to see the smile urging itself like a ghostly afterthought just beneath his look of mock pain.

That night my father returned from work well before the end of his shift. We heard his truck door slam, his footsteps outside our window; then in the morning there was no lunchbox on the back steps, and no sign of my father in the greenhouses or the fields. Gelsomina went out to the porch once or twice to stare toward the boiler room, then finally went out to the garage to my father's truck. She came back with his lunchbox – inside it his sandwiches sat still intact in their folds of wax paper.

The sandwiches seemed an accusation, a final evidence that the fragile normalcy of our household had been shattered. All day we were silent as if awaiting some threat to overtake us, whatever doom it was that had been stalking us since we'd first come to the house. The spring sounds through the window screens, the birds, the rustle of leaves, seemed magnified, unnaturally loud; way off in the distance some neighbour's tractor churned steadily on, a small quiet hum in the afternoon stillness.

There wasn't much food left in the house. Ordinarily my father bought groceries once a week, supplemented by the vegetables and preserves Gelsomina's mother gave us on Sundays; but it had been a long time now since we'd got any new supplies. Gelsomina began to ration out what was left as if preparing for some lengthy dearth – for supper that night we had only an egg apiece and fried onions. Then afterwards she discovered we'd run out of the red tokens she put out every night for the milkman. After rummaging a dozen times through the kitchen drawers she turned finally to where I sat watching her from the kitchen table.

"You'll have to go get some money from your father," she said.

But I pretended not to have heard.

"Are you listening to me?" She'd come to stand over me. "You'll have to go, there's no other way."

I didn't dare look up at her.

"I don't know where he is," I said finally.

"Don't be an idiot, he's in the boiler room, he's been there all day."

"The light wasn't on when I looked before."

I caught a flicker of movement and flinched, thinking she was about to strike me; but at the last instant she seemed to check herself.

"Go on," she said, more gently, leaning closer, "it'll only take a minute. If you go I'll give you five cents from the change the milkman gives me."

But I hunched away from her, inching toward the edge of my chair.

"It's your fault he's angry," I said. "You shouldn't have looked in his desk."

"*Ma 'stu stronz' –*"

She'd raised her hand against me in earnest now, but before she could strike I slipped from my chair and ran toward the bathroom.

"*Scimunit'!*" she shouted, coming after me. I slammed the door against her, fumbling in the dark for the key and turning it hard. Gelsomina began to pound against the door's thin panels.

"Open the door or I'll break it!"

And afraid that she would I leaned my back into it, could feel the weight of her fists reverberating down my spine.

"Do you want the baby to die, is that what you want? You're just a mama's boy, that's all you are. But your mother's dead, don't you know that? She's dead!"

The baby, asleep before, had begun to cry. I heard Gelsomina move away from the bathroom door, heard the back door slam, then her footsteps on the driveway beneath the bathroom window. Still in darkness I climbed onto the toilet seat and made out her silhouette moving down the driveway in the evening gloom. At the boiler-room door she stood blankly for a moment as if waiting for someone to answer a knock, then moved toward a high window nearby, gripped her fingers on the sill, raised herself up to peer inside. But in the end she turned away and started back up the drive. I ducked.

"Don't think I can't see you there, idiot."

I heard her footsteps in the house, kitchen sounds; then finally the baby's crying died down. When the silence had stretched on for several minutes I reached into the cupboard at the end of the tub where we put our dirty laundry and pulled the laundry onto the floor in a heap, spreading it along the edge of the tub to make a bed and then stretching out there to sleep. For a few minutes I seemed to float in the room's comforting darkness as in some tiny windowless vessel, invulnerable, lost to the world; but then Gelsomina was at the door.

"Vittorio, you can come out now."

But I lay perfectly still, thought that if I stayed quiet enough, inconspicuous enough, she would go away.

"Don't be a fool, you can't stay there all night. I'm not going to hit you."

Silence, then a sound of metal against metal. I remembered suddenly that all the keys in the house were the same, Gelsomina forcing out the one on my side now with one of the others. The bolt clicked back and the door swung open, Gelsomina haloed an instant against the kitchen's light like an apparition.

"Look at you!" she said, laughing. "Like a cat!" And she bent to take me up from my bed, hugging me to her with such force that I burst into tears.

"*Dai*, what's the matter now, what kind of a little man are you?" But she was crying too.

"He's angry because we looked at his pictures," I said.

"Don't be stupid, he's angry because of your mother, it's not our fault. Because she went with another man. You're too small to understand."

But in the morning there was no milk on the back steps, only my father's lunchbox, which Gelsomina had set out as usual the night before, though when we opened it we found the old sandwiches from the previous day still untouched there. Not wanting to waste them Gelsomina had us eat them for breakfast, though by now the bread was stale and the meat had a metallic aftertaste. Afterwards Gelsomina said we shouldn't have eaten any meat at all because it was Friday. But it didn't seem like Friday or any day to me, every day the same, with no way to tell one from any other.

Gelsomina made up the last of the milk for the baby's feeding.

"I'm going to call my father," she said.

But she seemed unable to get the number right, painstakingly dialling several times but then each time hanging up as soon as a voice came on at the other end.

"Damn him! Doesn't he know we have to eat? God knows what he's doing in there, probably picking fleas off the cats."

Well before midday the baby began to cry. Only a few fingers of milk remained now from her first feeding, Gelsomina mixing what was left with a few cupfuls of boiled sugar water. The baby took to the cloudy liquid without complaint but Gelsomina sat grim-faced during the feeding, holding the baby with a stiff carefulness as if she had become something dangerous.

Gelsomina gathered together what food we had left from the cellar and cupboards. There was sauce but no pasta; for lunch Gelsomina made up a thin soup from it that we dipped stale pieces of bread into. Afterwards Gelsomina retreated into the bathroom to do laundry, her back and shoulders working with a restrained violence as she scrubbed. I followed behind her to hand her clothespins when she went outside to hang it, the clothes billowing on the lines like a strange portrait, each of us represented in odd fragments. On a back line, behind the cover of sheets, Gelsomina hung a long row of newly white diapers, perfect squares of cloth that slanted and warped in the wind like gliding birds.

For the rest of the afternoon Gelsomina kept the baby quiet with feedings of sugar water, but toward evening she began to grow restive. The liquid seemed to pass straight through her: by nightfall she had wet her diapers several times, and Gelsomina had begun to replace them with ones still damp from the wash. With the constant wet the baby's thighs grew chafed and red, as evening wore on her sporadic crying merging into an almost constant wail. Gelsomina left her crying in the bedroom while we ate what remained in the house of the bread and meat normally used for my father's sandwiches; but afterwards the baby wouldn't take to its bottle at all.

"Stop it, for the love of Christ!" But the baby only cried louder. One of her fists shot out against the bottle and knocked it from Gelsomina's hand onto the bed.

"Oh! *Basta!*"

She cracked a hand hard against the baby's cheek.

In an instant the baby's wails had grown so intense they were almost soundless, her chest heaving so wildly it seemed she had emptied her lungs with her cries and was unable now to refill them.

"*Addíu*, what have I done," Gelsomina said, and she had begun to cry as well. She clutched the baby to her and sobbed into her shoulder, her body seeming to melt suddenly, to lose all its straight-backed authority and brazenness. For the first time it occurred to me that perhaps she couldn't take care of us, that she didn't always know the right thing to do.

"*È niend'*, it's nothing," she kept saying, like a chant, "*èniend', poveretta. È niend'*."

But when we were awakened the next morning by a call from Gelsomina's father, Gelsomina made it seem as if nothing was wrong.

"Tsi'Mario's not in the house," she said. "I think he went out to the boiler room."

Her father's voice crackled briefly from the other end.

"He doesn't go to the factory any more," Gelsomina said, after a pause. Then her father's voice again, louder; Gelsomina grew defensive.

"How should I know why? Maybe he has too much work to do on the farm. He's always in the boiler room."

Before long Tsi'Alfredo's truck pulled up in the drive. He stopped first at the boiler room but emerged alone a few minutes later and drove around to the back door, coming into the house red-faced with anger.

"Where is he?"

"Isn't he in the boiler room?" Gelsomina said.

Tsi'Alfredo struck her hard against the back of her head.

"*Stronza!* Couldn't you see that his truck is gone?"

Tsi'Alfredo made us get into his truck. The baby had been crying all morning, Tsi'Alfredo grimacing in irritation now as he pulled the truck onto the road.

"Can't you keep that thing quiet?"

Tsi'Alfredo lived on the town line just beneath the Ridge, a trip of several miles along backroads and highway before the sudden slope his own road dipped into, from the top of it the lake briefly visible in the distance like a mirage. His house, narrow and weathered and tall, was covered in the same false brick as our boiler room; but his own boiler room was built in concrete, and his greenhouses in frames of metal. Gelsomina had taken me inside them once, the plants there filling the space like a fairy-tale forest with their prickled cucumbers and yellowing flowers, the air alive with the hum of bees and the smell of earth.

Tsia Maria was waiting for us at the back door. I noticed that the fields around the greenhouses had been planted since the last time I had been there, pencil-thin rows of green stretching away toward a distant line of trees.

"And Mario?" Tsia Maria said.

"Ah, *sì*, and Mario. That idiot, your daughter –"

Tsi'Alfredo's son Gino had come out beside his mother, towering over her in his oversize adolescent mannishness, his face still puffy from sleep and his hair falling in unruly tufts across his forehead. Tsi'Alfredo made him get in the truck when Gelsomina and I were out, then drove off back toward the highway.

Tsia Maria had taken the baby from Gelsomina.

"Why is she crying? Didn't you feed her?"

We had gone into the kitchen, drabber than the one in my father's house, the tiles worn away in spots to the wood beneath and the walls yellowed with grime. There was a washtub now in one corner with clothes soaking in it and a pot of sauce cooking on the stove, its smell filling the room.

Tsia Maria handed the baby back to Gelsomina and began to prepare a bottle.

"Why was your father angry?" she said. "What happened to your uncle?"

Gelsomina's two sisters had huddled around her at the table, silently staring at me as if I'd become a kind of curiosity.

"How should I know what happened to him?" Gelsomina said sulkily. "He wasn't there, that's all."

"Is it possible you couldn't see that something was wrong? Why didn't you call us? Half the town knew he'd lost his job at the factory, and like fools nobody thought to tell us. And with me and your father working every night to finish the planting, and then the greenhouses –"

But I didn't sense any anger from her. She seemed always outside of the way other people were thinking or feeling, as if the world didn't impress itself as deeply on her as it did on others; yet I took a kind of comfort from her easy ramblings, so even-tempered, so devoid of any sudden swells or crags, that they made the world of events seem a wide plain where nothing stood out as more important than anything else, as more grave or portentous.

When she'd finished preparing the bottle she took the baby back from Gelsomina to feed her.

"And then this baby," she said. "If that woman her mother had never set foot on the earth she would have made everyone's life easier."

"*Mamma* –" Gelsomina said.

"Ah?" Tsia Maria glanced toward me. "He doesn't know what I'm talking about, eh, Vittorio? When you're older you'll understand what your father had to put up with."

When Tsi'Alfredo returned later that morning he was alone. But the back of his truck was laden with trays of young plants, their leaves forming a carpet of green that shimmered and waved in the wind like water. Tsi'Alfredo made us all get into the cab, only Tsia Maria and the baby left behind, and in a few minutes we were at my father's farm again, bumping down the lane that led to the back field. There were cars parked in the lane between the barn and the pond, and then in the field itself more than a dozen people were already at work, men unloading trays of plants from a trailer that Gino was slowly guiding across the field with my father's tractor, while others, mainly women, followed behind on hands and knees, setting the plants into the furrows that had been dug for them. But my father wasn't among them.

"The holiday's over," Tsi'Alfredo said. "You'll have enough work now to keep you out of trouble for a while."

He showed me how to plant. Getting down on his haunches he scooped a handful of dirt out of a furrow and lifted a plant into the hole he'd prepared. The plants were held in sleeves of thin wood, open at the bottom, that had to be torn away.

"Like this," Tsi'Alfredo said, sticking two fingers of each hand into the sleeve on adjacent sides and giving a quick tug. The sleeve came apart neatly at the corner, a square of wet earth still intact around the plant's roots.

"It should look exactly like that when you're finished. If you let the dirt come off the roots the plant will be dead in half an hour."

With a swift circular motion of his hands he levelled the ridges of dirt that flanked the furrow so that finally the plant sat firmly embedded in the earth.

"Don't leave it at the bottom of a valley – just a little down, the way I did it, and fill up the space between each plant as you go. Understand?"

"Sì."

He went through the process again a few times, using a short stick to measure out the distance between each plant. His hands moved swiftly, each plant finding its place with the same smooth precision. Still on his haunches he watched me as I tried to imitate him, Gelsomina and her sisters, already at work in the rows next to me, stopping to watch as well. But I couldn't get the wooden sleeves to tear apart neatly as Tsi'Alfredo's had, with each failure Tsi'Alfredo reaching over impatiently to finish the job himself, grimacing at my awkwardness.

"Like that. No one taught you how to work back in Valle del Sole, eh?"

But when he saw that I couldn't get it right he sent me up to the barn for a bucket and then set me following behind the women to collect the wooden sleeves they left discarded in their rows as they planted.

"Oh, Vittò! Look at the way he's dragging that bucket, you'd think he had all the sins of the world inside it!"

"You never saw fields like this back in Italy, eh, so flat? You can plough a field like this in the morning, and plant it in the afternoon. Not like there."

"What does he know about it? When did the children have to go out and work in the fields the way they do here? At harvest, maybe, that's all. But here men, women, children, it's all the same – if it's not the fields it's the greenhouses, if it's not the greenhouses it's the factory."

We worked for what seemed a long time. Tsi'Alfredo's truck came and went, carrying more loads of plants. I made piles of wooden sleeves at intervals along the edge of the laneway that flanked the field, trying to measure the time by the spaces between them. But then Tsi'Alfredo saw what I was doing.

"You don't have to make so many small piles like that, what were you thinking?"

We ate lunch at the edge of the field. It was warm now in the noon sun, though the air had a crispness like the spring air in Valle del Sole. Tsi'Alfredo had brought water and wine, a few loaves of bread, some meat and some cheese. The women sat on the ground or on overturned plant trays; the men leaned against

25

Tsi'Alfredo's truck or sat on its tailgate. Gelsomina sat away from me, with the women, seemed not to want to be seen as one of the children. One of the men cut slices of cheese and meat with a jackknife he pulled from his pocket, offering the slices around to the rest of us on the knife's blackened tip.

"And Mario?" one of the men said to Tsi'Alfredo.

"Nothing."

"*Mbeh*, maybe he just took a little trip," one of the women said. "To clear his head."

"*Sì*, a trip, what are you saying?" someone else said. "And his fields not planted yet at the end of May."

"Anyway he would have had to leave the factory, sooner or later. With the farm and no one else to look after it –"

"He would have left when he wanted to," Tsi'Alfredo said, red-faced. "Those damned foremen there, when it's one of their own they look the other way, but one of ours, for every little thing –"

Later, when we were working again, I overheard some of the women talking.

"Someone told me they let him go because he fell asleep."

"Ah, *sì*, fell asleep, does that sound like Mario? Now if you told me he broke someone's skull –"

Tsi'Alfredo kept carrying trays of plants, and by mid-afternoon the men setting them out had reached the line of trees that marked the end of the field. They went back with the tractor and trailer to collect the empty trays left behind by the planters, driving up to the barn to unload each time the trailer was full. But Tsi'Alfredo had gone away again in his truck, and hadn't returned by the time the men caught up to where we were planting.

"And now?" one of the men said. "What do we do, *senza boss*?"

He gave the word "*boss*" an extra energy, as if making a joke.

"*Mbeh*, when *lu boss* is away," another said, "you stretch out under a tree and have a nice sleep."

But this time when they came back from the barn from unloading, the tractor was pulling a narrow trailer that I'd seen before buried in weeds at the edge of the pond. The trailer was stacked high with long silver pipes that the men began to set out in rows along the field, each pipe ending with a tall T that looked like the head and neck of a strange bird. While they were working, Tsi'Alfredo came back in his truck and stopped to help them, and before nightfall they had again reached to where we were planting.

It had begun to turn cold. The men got down on their knees to help plant, doubling up in rows that had already been started; but Tsi'Alfredo drove back down the lane in his truck, Gino following on the tractor. Some minutes later an engine echoed to life from the direction of the barn, sputtered and died, then started again, building this time to a steady roar and then faltering suddenly like a bus grinding up a hill. A hissing sound rose up from the pipes laid out along the field, and then gradually the heads on the T's started to twirl until finally long jets of water had begun to shoot out from them, filling the air all along the field with splaying arcs that glinted like silver in the dying light.

By the time we stopped work it was truly dark. Tsi'Alfredo and Gino had come back, their clothes drenched from walking up and down the rows of pipes to check them. About a third of the field still remained to be planted.

"So, Alfrè," one of the men said. "What'll it be in the morning, church or the fields? It's the same to me, either way I'll be on my knees."

"We can finish up ourselves."

Gelsomina and I went back to Tsi'Alfredo's for the night. I rode with Gino on the back of the truck – he didn't seem to mind the wind, sitting in the brunt of it on one of the wheel humps, his scruffy hair blown back and his damp clothes billowing and cracking like laundry. But I had huddled up against the cab with the cold, my muscles aching as if from fever. I nodded off for a moment, imagined that I was back on the ship that had brought me to Canada, reliving the dreamy roll and swell of the storm we'd passed through. Then a sudden jolt of the truck woke me. Gino was grinning.

"Tired, eh?" he said, shouting to be heard above the wind. But his voice had no sympathy in it.

At Tsi'Alfredo's I heard the baby crying from some upstairs room.

"She's been acting like the devil all day," Tsia Maria said. "I spoke to Letizia down the road and she said it's the milk, you can't use it here, you have to buy a special powder or something. What do I know about it?"

We had a large supper but though I'd been hungry all day the first few bites seemed to fill me now. Afterwards we were sent directly to bed, Gino and I sharing a narrow cot in a small room off the kitchen. Gino fell asleep almost at once, but for a long time I lay in awkward wakefulness, pinned between Gino's broad undershirted back and the wall. I could hear Tsi'Alfredo and Tsia Maria talking in the kitchen.

"Maybe you should call the police," Tsia Maria said.

"Don't talk nonsense, what are the police going to do?"

"*Mbeh*, who knows where he's gotten to? Maybe he's lying in some ditch with his head broken."

"*Grazie*," Tsi'Alfredo said. "And what are you going to tell the police when they ask you why he's gone?"

"Tell them the truth, what's happened."

"*Sì*. We might as well just publish it in the newspaper, and then everyone will know."

"Everyone knows as it is."

"Don't be an idiot. You know how they are here – every little thing they know about us, they make up some story. We'll take care of our own problems."

Later I heard Tsi'Alfredo's truck drive away. I drifted into sleep, but was awakened again some time afterwards by Tsi'Alfredo's voice from the kitchen.

"Enough with your stupid questions! Is it possible you can't keep your mouth shut for even a minute?"

"And what will we do, then? If you'd done what I told you in the first place –"

"*Ma chesta stronza –*"

Some object hit a wall or cupboard with a crash.

"Have you gone crazy?"

Tsia Maria's voice was strangely altered now, tense with a panic that made me want to close it out. A door slammed, and the house grew eerily calm; then from the kitchen came a sound of sweeping, the clink of broken glass. I noticed suddenly that Gino was awake, was lying open-eyed beside me staring up at the ceiling; but he turned finally and hunched his shoulders away from me without a word.

It was barely dawn when Tsi'Alfredo brought his children and me back to my father's farm to begin work again, the sun just a streak of orange along the horizon and the air frosty with cold. But someone had preceded us: my father's truck was parked at the edge of the field, and already from a distance I saw him stooping in one of the rows, a small dark speck against the grey line of trees behind him. When we'd come even with him Tsi'Alfredo jumped from the cab.

"Where in Christ have you been?"

Tsi'Alfredo was moving toward him, stepping over empty trays in the row in long quick strides.

"Mario, for the love of Christ what got into your head?"

The rest of us had gathered in a group at the end of the row, watching now as Tsi'Alfredo came up to him. But my father remained hunched over his tray.

"*Dai*, Mario, what's happened?" His voice carried strangely clear in the morning stillness. "It's nothing, *dai*, don't be like this."

My father was crying. Tsi'Alfredo got down on his haunches beside him and put a hand awkwardly on his shoulder.

"It's better to be dead than to live like this," my father said; but his voice had the tremor of a child's.

"*Dai*, what are you saying. *È niend'*, Mario, it's nothing."

III

For several weeks after the planting my father and I were alone on the farm, Gelsomina coming by on Saturdays to do laundry and cook up soup and sauce for the following week, and the baby staying at Tsi'Alfredo's. But though we were together more often now, my father's presence seemed still merely a kind of gloom that surrounded me, my body tensing against him like a single hard muscle when he was near, taking in only his animal scent and then the shape he cut like black space in a landscape.

For a week or so he had me clean out an old chicken coop in the barn, leaving me alone there the whole day in the barn's dim mysteriousness. Bits of dust hung like gold in the slits of light that passed between the wallboards; from the shadows of the upper rafters came a constant cooing and flapping of wings. In the chicken coop there was a nest of some hard clayish substance against one of the ceiling beams, and every morning a swallow would swoop out from it in a swift arc when I came in, slashing a quick hieroglyph in the air like a secret signal before disappearing in the branches of a mulberry tree across the lane.

The coop was crammed with all manner of refuse, busted packing crates, hoops of thick wire, old farm implements with decayed leather harnesses, rolls of rusted chicken wire. My father would give me a few terse instructions, sullen and precise, when he left me there in the morning, but then as soon as he'd gone everything he had said became a haze. When he came back to check on me he'd see my mistakes at once.

"I told you to pile those crates against the other wall, where they'd be out of the way." And in fifteen minutes of swift, silent work he'd redo what I'd spent a whole morning on.

After the barn he set me to work collecting broken glass in the alleys between the greenhouses. But it seemed now that it was exactly the mistakes he warned me about in advance that I invariably fell into.

"Don't fill the wheelbarrow too full," he said, "or you'll spill it."

But I did pile it too full; and even feeling its weight begin to lean as I lifted its handles, already seeing in my mind how it would spill, watching the image unfurl there like a premonition, still I tried to push it forward. There was a tremendous crash when it tilted, the glass splintering through the wall of one of the greenhouses. In a moment my father was standing over me, his face flushed.

"*Gesù Crist' e Maria.*" It was the first time I had seen his anger so plain and uncurbed, so ice-hard. "Is it possible you can't do anything the way I tell you?"

I had steeled myself instinctively against a blow. But the blow didn't come, and afterwards, when he bent quick and silent to pick up the glass I had spilled, he seemed chastened by his outburst as if he had been the one who had suffered some humiliation.

He left me less on my own from then on, often keeping me beside him to be his helper. He'd make comments sometimes while he worked, or curse some problem in a way that was strangely intimate and frank, as if he'd forgotten I was merely a child. But usually he was silent, the work taking him over, bringing out in him a hard-edged concentration that seemed somehow to free me from him even though it was exactly then that I was most aware of him, the tawny muscles of his arms and neck, the patches of sweat on his clothes, his ghostly familiarity then like a mirror I looked into.

At noon he'd send me home ahead of him to put soup on the stove or set the water heating for pasta for our lunch. If we ran out of the food Gelsomina had left he'd fry up onion and eggs, scraping the eggs onto our plates with a casual violence, a mash of grease and broken yolks and scorched whites, though I preferred them to the porcelain-smooth ones Gelsomina used to prepare. He listened to the radio while we ate, odd music at first and then a voice, the same one every day, my father turning the volume up when it came on.

"*Mbeh*," he'd say afterwards, "maybe we'll get a little more sun after all, if you can believe all the stupidities they say on that thing."

Once when we were hoeing beans in the front field someone came to visit us, a grey-haired man in a checked suit and dark glasses. He pulled up in the courtyard in a large blue car and came toward us smiling broadly, his hand outstretched.

"Mario," he said. "Mario, Mario, *como stai, paesano?*"

But after his greeting he and my father began to speak in what must have been English. They talked for a long time, and it seemed from the way my father was laughing and smiling that speaking in English brought out some different person in him, one more relaxed and good-humoured. But then when the man had gone my father grew canny.

"That was the guy I bought the farm from," he said. "Those Germans – *paesano* this, *paesano* that, everyone's a *paesano*. But the old bastard just wanted to make sure I don't forget to pay him."

But he was smiling – the old man's visit seemed to have heartened him somehow.

He took me into town with him that night to a sort of bar, a long gloomy room with a counter on one side and a row of rickety tables on the other. There were several men talking around one of the tables at the back, a few wearing the striped grey-and-white uniform that my father had worn when he'd worked at the factory. My father nodded in greeting toward them, but his good mood seemed to pass from him suddenly. He ordered an ice cream and a coffee from the man behind the counter; but one of the men at the table had turned to him.

"*Dai*, Mario, let's get a game going. We need a fourth, these others here are too afraid to put a little money on the table."

My father stared into his coffee.

"Maybe they're the smart ones," he said. "Nobody gives you something for nothing."

"What are you saying, for the fifty cents we play for you couldn't even buy a whore in Detroit."

The other men laughed.

"*Sì*, fifty cents," my father said, still talking into his coffee though his energy seemed drawn to the men now. "It took half a day to make that, when I came here –"

"Oh, always the same story! *Dai*, sit down, you'll be a rich man soon, when the cheques start coming in from the farm."

34

"The farm, at least what I made before I could put in my pocket. Now I'm just working for the bank. And then that damned German, still worried about the four cents I owe him –"

"What does he have to do with it? Didn't he get his money from the Farm Credit?"

My father had turned to face them. With the mention of the German his good humour seemed to be returning.

"*Mbeh*, we kept a little back because of all the work that had to be done, he'd left the place to rot like that. So today he comes around, in his suit and his new car, still thinking about those few pennies, though the contract says he doesn't see another cent until October –"

"*Che scostumat'*. What did you tell him?"

"Don't think he was stupid enough to say a word about the money. You know how they are, always smiling, *amico, paesano*. But the whole time he was looking around, checking to see how things were, asking about the crop, about the prices. So I smiled too. I told him if he wanted to see how the crop was, he could come back in July and I'd give him a bushel of beans."

The other men laughed.

"And he'll be back for those beans, too," one of them said.

My father stayed to play cards.

"You can be my banker," he said, pulling up a chair for me beside him.

"That means every time he wins," one of the others said, "you take five per cent."

"And if he loses he gives you the farm."

They played until late, making laconic conversation at first but then becoming more and more involved in the game. At the end my father gave me some change from the money he'd won.

"What are you doing, Mario," one of the men said, "you want to spoil him? That's half a day's wages."

A few days later Tsi'Alfredo's truck was parked in the courtyard when we came in from work, Tsi'Alfredo waiting for us at the kitchen table while Tsia Maria prepared supper.

"So? Are you keeping out of trouble?" But his good humour seemed forced, as if he'd come to bring bad news.

There was a sound from the bedroom, and then Gelsomina emerged with the baby in her arms. I felt a kind of outrage well up in me – it didn't seem right that the baby should be in the house again. I thought someone, Tsi'Alfredo or my father, would stop Gelsomina from bringing her into the kitchen, but there was only an awkward silence when she came in.

"She's been an angel all day," Gelsomina said.

Tsi'Alfredo turned to her red-faced.

"Is that how you come into a room? And your uncle, *stronza*, did you think to say hello to him?"

Tsi'Alfredo and Tsia Maria left after supper, but Gelsomina and the baby stayed behind. The group of us sat unmoving a moment in the lull left behind by Tsi'Alfredo's departure, till finally my father got up without speaking and went into his room. Afterwards Gelsomina began to prepare a feeding, humming to herself as she moved about the kitchen. But her gaiety seemed put on, couldn't hide the familiar gloom that had settled over the house again.

In bed that night Gelsomina was distant and cool, adult.

"I shouldn't be sleeping in the same bed as you," she said. "It's not as if I was your mother."

She'd grown more moody and unpredictable during her absence. Around my father she talked to me only to reprimand

me, grown-up and brusque, seeming to imply some new understanding between the two of them, asking him questions about
the farm in an informed, offhand way, lingering a strange
instant beside his chair when she served him. But then if my
father was out she might sneak a deck of cards from his room to
play with me on the living-room floor, sitting cross-legged there
with her dress tucked indecorously between her legs and shriek-
ing girlishly every time she took a trick. If the baby cried then
she'd drag herself up from the floor with an exaggerated look of
exhaustion.

"Everyone says he should find another family that wants it,"
she said. "That's how they do it here, not like in Italy – the *inglesi*
do it all the time, they don't care for their children the way
Italians do. But my mother says if someone tells your father to
do something he always has to do the opposite. It's his own fault
then if people laugh at him."

But she made little effort any more to hide the baby away
from him, somehow taking her own re-entry into the house as a
kind of licence, feeding the baby in the kitchen while we ate,
making faces at her to get her to smile, seeming to treat her like
any normal child. There appeared something provocative in
this, and yet my father continued simply to blot the baby from
his mind, never referring to her in any way, as if he saw in her
place only an irrelevant shadow or blur.

We were well into summer now and there was much work to
be done on the farm, the beans to be picked, the tomatoes to be
hoed, the days seeming to blend into each other without distinction. I thought the work couldn't go on like that, without stopping, but every morning Gelsomina would wake me at dawn
and it would continue. In the first hours there'd be the morning
breeze at least, the air seeming laden with some uncertain

promise and the plants crisp with dew; but by noon the fields would be smothered in a wet, oppressive heat, all the world unnaturally dead and still for as far as the eye could see.

My father seldom worked with me any more, moving shadowy through his other mysterious projects and obligations. When the beans began Gelsomina came out to the fields sometimes in the afternoons, leaving the baby in a bean crate for a crib; the time passed more quickly then, Gelsomina forever criticizing my work but helping me to keep up with her and afterwards lying in my favour to my father about how many crates we'd picked, attributing to me some of her own. But usually now I worked with the people my father brought out to the field each morning on the back of his truck – matronly, dark-eyed women in black, mainly, with aquiline noses and wiry hair tied back in kerchiefs. They hung together in a tight group, talking constantly in a harsh, guttural language but swift at their work, picking three or four rows while I finished one. They'd offer me fruit from their lunchboxes sometimes or pieces of strong white cheese, trying to joke with me in their strange speech. But often my father would argue with them, coming behind them in their rows to point out plants they had damaged or picking half-rotten beans from their crates.

"Make sure you count all the crates you pick," he said to me. "Those damn Lebanese will rob you blind if you don't watch them."

After that I stopped accepting the food the women offered me, watching them while they worked hoping to catch one of them out in some deception. But when once I told my father that one of my crates seemed to be missing he was oddly dismissive.

"Did you see them taking it?" he said.

"No."

"You probably just counted wrong."

After the beans there were the greenhouses to be planted and then the tomatoes again, another weeding and then the first pick. The rows there stretched so long I couldn't finish one on my own in a day. All day long I worked in counterpoint to the sun, measuring out the hours by its slow movement – mid-morning break, when Gelsomina would bring out a jug of water, then lunch, then another break in mid-afternoon. The afternoons were the hardest – the other workers would be far ahead of me by that point and I'd be left alone in the silent heat, the sky so endless and blue above me it hurt my eyes to look at it. I couldn't bear the thought then of all the work that still had to be done; if no one was around I'd stretch out in my row sometimes and close my eyes, letting myself drift a few moments near dreamy sleep. Toward evening I'd get a second wind, knowing the day was almost over, pleased at the long string of red-filled bushels stretching out behind me in the setting sun; and then the dead fatigue at night, back to our house's strained silence with only sleep to look forward to and then work again.

Then as the end of summer approached Gelsomina told me she would be going back to the factory soon.

"Is the baby going away too?" I said.

"Don't be an idiot, where is she going to go?"

"Who's going to take care of her?"

"How should I know? Maybe your father's going to sell her to the gypsies."

"Maybe I'll have to take care of her."

"You?" she said. "She'd be dead in a week. Anyway you have to go to school."

All the same, in the next days Gelsomina began a sort of clandestine instruction, turning jobs over to me whenever my father was out.

"You don't have to be afraid of her. There, like that, keep the pins in your mouth so you have both your hands free."

She made me do things over and over till I got them right, standing by unflinching though the baby was crying and I myself was close to tears. Then other times, unpredictably, she'd lose all patience.

"*Dai*, you'll never learn how to do it, idiot. *Maledetti* both you and your father, who thinks he can leave one baby to look after another."

Then at supper one evening she somehow mustered the courage to confront my father.

"Who's going to take care of the baby when I go?"

My father's eyes lit with what looked like anger but also something else, a sudden flash of interest – it seemed the first time he'd ever really noticed Gelsomina, hadn't taken her for granted like a part of the house's furnishings.

"*Che scema*," he said, strangely mocking. "You'll have your own too, don't worry about other people's."

Gelsomina seemed put out for the rest of the evening. Then at bedtime she behaved queerly: instead of changing in the bathroom she flicked off the bedroom light and began to undress in front of me. I tried not to watch but she seemed to be willing me to look at her, stood for a moment completely naked in the window's moonlight like an awkward statue, all stiff angles and knobby protrusions. Her breasts, small and vulnerable and pale, were capped with dark circles the size of 500 *lire* coins.

"Do you think I'm beautiful?" she whispered, fierce, daring

me to contradict her though I felt only the shame of seeing her like that.

Headlights flashed past the window: my father, returning from bringing a load into the factory. In an instant Gelsomina was cowering in a corner, arms clutched over her breasts.

"If you tell anyone about this," she said, "I'll cut your little bird off."

Three days later Gelsomina had gone, my Aunt Teresa come from Italy to replace her. I knew nothing of her coming until I actually saw her descend from my father's truck one evening at the back of the house, simply there like an apparition, suitcase in hand, picking her way inexpertly across the courtyard in her high heels; in the moment of recognizing her I had the sense for an instant that I myself had somehow brought her magically into being, that an image from memory had leapt across some chasm to suddenly take solid shape before me.

"*Ciao*, Vittorio! Look at the little man you are! Were you waiting up for me? What's the matter, don't you remember me? Mario," turning now to my father, "didn't you tell Vittorio I was coming? Look at him, you'd think he'd seen a ghost!"

I had last seen Tsia Teresa at my grandfather's funeral service in Castilucci, when she'd been the only one of my father's siblings who'd come over to greet my mother and me. On the rare occasions when my mother and I had gone to visit my father's family back then, Tsia Teresa would take me to the square and tease a few *lire* from the young men at the bar to buy me candy or walk with me in the pastures near town, taking my arm in hers and joking that she was my girlfriend. She'd seemed from a different family then, the coddled youngest daughter, the only one who'd been allowed to go on in school; and she'd been pretty, an angular, sharp-boned prettiness, with her pale skin and her dark eyes, that she'd parade at once brash and awkward before the men in the square like a prize she wasn't yet sure was hers to award.

But now her energy had nothing tentative about it, seeming to spread out around her like heat from a fire. In a few minutes she had finished a tour of the house, coming out of my bedroom finally with the baby in her arms.

"*Ma com'è bella!* She was lying there wide awake, quiet as a mouse. What's her name?"

But no one had thought to name her yet.

"Mario, don't tell me you haven't given her a name! You can't treat her like an animal."

I felt embarrassed for her, thought she had misunderstood how things were with the baby, expected some sign from my father that would put her right; but my father's silence, this shutting down in him when the baby was around, seemed lost on her.

"We'll call her Margherita," she decided finally. She held the baby close and pronounced the name slowly, offering it to her like a gift. "Mar-ghe-ri-ta. That's the saint all the mothers pray to when they're going to have a baby. You say it: Mar-ghe-ri-ta. Look, she's smiling, see how she understands?"

With my aunt's arrival things began to change, the mood of the house, the careful eggshell order that had established itself. I thought the household couldn't bear her blind energy, that it must shatter, and yet somehow it shifted to accommodate her. She referred to the baby as my sister, a strange thing, so intimate; what had been unthinkable before, these plain declarations of what we all were to each other, seemed in her to become merely commonplace. It was odd to have someone in the house

42

who didn't simply capitulate to its gloom, who so openly carved a space for herself there. Within a few days she had moved me out from the bedroom to the couch, within a few more had asked for a crib for the baby.

"I don't think I can go another night in the same bed," she said. "It makes me think of what we used to do when the pigs had babies, remember that, how we had to make a little house for them in the stall or the mother would roll over and crush them."

"One bed was fine for three people," my father said. "Now it's not enough for one."

"*Dai*, it won't cost you a thing. Mauro's wife has a crib they're not using, I spoke to her on the telephone."

But my father flushed with anger.

"I'm going to crack your skull with that phone, then you'll learn to stop bothering other people with your stupidities."

"Let her sleep with you then," my aunt said, undaunted. "What a sight you'd make, I'll bet you've never held a baby in your life!"

I thought my father would fling something at her, so furled did he seem with his anger; but then he faltered.

"*Sì, va bene*, everything's a joke to you. Like a chicken. We'll see if everything's a joke."

Already he seemed merely to be grumbling to himself, to have made some concession; and a few days later when we came in for lunch there was a van in the courtyard and a blond-haired man in overalls in my aunt's bedroom putting together a small bed with high, barred sides.

"*All-set*," he said when he'd finished.

I didn't know what to make of my aunt, couldn't understand what things looked like from inside her, how she missed their gravity. And yet my father seemed diminished somehow since she'd come, his darkness become merely private and small, no longer taking the world in – around her he seemed to draw his anger back into himself as if to guard it from her, deferring it in his vague muttered threats to some uncertain final vindication. Tsia Teresa took to calling him Giovanni Battista, John the Baptist.

"As if every little thing was the end of the world."

She spent her days in the house looking after the baby, but with an air of leisured repose like a town woman; outside now we were picking tomatoes every day, hardly able to keep up, but it never seemed to occur to her to come out and help us. Sometimes we'd come home at night and find her on the phone, and supper not ready, and the rage would seem to rise and fall again in my father, precipitous.

"You should spend less time working with your mouth and more with your hands."

But my aunt always had an answer.

"I don't think it's right, that there's people here I haven't seen for five or six years and I shouldn't even say hello to them."

But what seemed to irk my father was not so much that she didn't get things done as the languid air with which she did them, still managing despite it to make time for herself, for her phone calls, for her little projects. She had taken to listening to the radio, writing up lists of words from what she heard and repeating them over and over as if the sound of them might give up their meanings; but my father would darken with irritation at the sight of this.

"That's all they taught you with all your years of school, how to waste your time on this nonsense."

Then once when we'd fallen behind with the tomatoes my

father had us pick all day under a steady drizzle. But when Tsi'Alfredo and Gino came by the next day to help load we discovered that the tomatoes that had been picked in the rain had started to rot. We had to sort through the whole load bushel by bushel to pick out the bad ones, toward nightfall still hunched over our work in the courtyard.

"Why isn't Teresa out here?" Tsi'Alfredo said finally.

My father sent me in to call her.

"You should have said something before," she said, standing at the back door in her apron and slippers. "I'm just starting supper."

"Forget about supper," Tsi'Alfredo said. "If we don't finish here nobody's going to eat. These tomatoes have to be in by ten."

"Can't you bring them in tomorrow?"

"*Sì*, tomorrow. If he misses his turn tonight it'll be three days before they let him bring in another load. And in three days you can make a nice sauce for the pigs with these tomatoes."

"Well you'll have to wait, I'll be out in a few minutes."

But by the time she'd come out we had almost finished, my father already gone to take the workers home.

"See, you didn't need me after all. Anyway what do I know about this kind of thing?"

"You'll learn," Tsi'Alfredo said. "If you were my sister you'd have learned already."

"It's true, you're worse even than Mario, I remember what you were like."

When my father came home he left again at once to bring the load into the factory; he hadn't returned yet by the time my aunt and I went to sleep. But when he woke me in the morning for work I could sense the rage still heavy in him from the previous night. He was already on his way down the back steps when my aunt, her face still lax with sleep, came into the kitchen. Without a word he came up behind her as she bent to a cupboard and cracked a hand hard against the back of her head.

"*Ecc' la signorina principessa!*"

"Oh!" My aunt had turned swiftly, alive suddenly, holding a pot slightly raised at her side like a weapon. "Have you gone crazy?"

"They didn't teach you how to work in Italy, ah? I'll teach you how to work, by God, even if I have to stand behind you every day with a whip!"

But my aunt held her ground.

"If you ever lay another hand on me I'll break your skull, I swear it."

"*Dai*, try it! We'll see if you'll always have things your own way. Not in this house, by Christ, not if you want to live under my roof!"

"Ah, *grazie!* Do you think I asked to come here, to this god-damned America? To wash your dirty clothes like a servant, to take care of a baby you wish your wife had taken with her to the grave? I had my life there, did you think about that when you called me here? What life do I have now, tell me! What life will you give me?"

For days afterwards they didn't speak. The house assumed again its familiar gloomy silence – even my aunt seemed unable this time to bring us out of it, had defeated my father but went about the house irritable and brooding as if burdened now by her victory.

She began to grow impatient with the baby, perfunctory, almost clumsy. Perhaps she had always been, had merely hidden this awkwardness beneath her glow of good humour; but now suddenly everything she did for the baby seemed flawed somehow. When she made up a feeding, with the powder we used now, her measurements seemed more haphazard than Gelsomina's had been; when she gave her bottled food she seemed to stop before the baby had had her fill; when she held her she seemed unable to settle her comfortably against her, struggling with her as with some bulky inanimate thing. These signs of deficiency in her disturbed me, made her seem to lack something crucial in her character, some important instinct, like the sows who'd roll over and crush their own newborn.

Then once when I was helping with a change, the old diaper came away stained with a small patch of dried blood.

"The head broke on the pin, it must have pricked her," my aunt said. But she slipped the pin into the pocket of her apron before I could see it.

I began to watch her more closely after that.

"Look how curious he is," my aunt said. "As if he'd never seen a baby before."

But she seemed to understand now that some contest was going on between us. As if to put me in my place she turned the baby over to me one evening for a feeding, mockingly, indulgent; but I could tell she was quietly impressed then with my small, careful efficiency.

"You learned all that just by watching me?"

"Gelsomina taught me."

"Not bad," she said, but she seemed put out. "She did a good job."

She began to come out to the fields suddenly, diffident at first, prying carefully among the vines as if not to dirty her hands, but then growing quickly more expert, some new resolve taking shape in her. She left the baby at first in a playpen of bushels at the end of her row, sending me now and then to check on her; and then gradually more and more of the care of her began to devolve upon me, till finally I was being left alone in the house the entire afternoon to tend to her while my aunt was out in the fields, my father silently acquiescing to this new arrangement as to something he neither approved of nor could oppose. I'd come to call my aunt still for feedings and changes, not certain yet what I was allowed, how far my dominion extended. But as my aunt saw I could manage these things on my own her interest in the baby seemed day by day to diminish.

"*Dai*, you don't have to come running to me for every little thing, you know how to do it."

What I never told my aunt was the agony for me of these afternoons alone. There was something so unreasonable in the baby then, the dangerous awkward weight of her, her obliviousness. I was never free of her, her sweaty heat, her spit, her smell, seemed not to exist at all, become merely the thinking extension of her animal need. She'd cry and cry inconsolable sometimes, make me hate her, make me wish for her death – the world seemed reduced then to her cries, the brawling chaos of them. But then when they had died into sleep I would see her curled in her crib and feel solemn with responsibility for her, understanding that she was mine in some way, that that had been decided now, and wondering then at the strangeness of her, the soft feathery feel of her skull, vulnerable as a melon, her tiny fingers and toes.

The household seemed to shift again, its shadowy intricate web of alliances and emotion. The tension between my father and aunt had quietly become something new, an understanding: there was a rhythm now in how they spoke to each other, my aunt with her authority, her belligerence, my father with his sullen condescension, that seemed hermetic, almost intimate, a delicate weaving of their stubbornnesses into a kind of collusion that excluded me. I was aligned not with them but with the baby, who didn't belong in our house, was awkward and unnatural there like the baby goats that farmers in Valle del Sole put with their ewes if they'd bought them before they'd been weaned.

It was not until the first frost, into October, that the tomato season ended and I began school. Tsia Teresa set out clothes for me, packed sandwiches in my father's lunchbox, sent me out to the end of the drive to wait for the bus. The trees had begun to lose their leaves by then, all around the landscape preparing for its alien winter; and always there were the few moments then as I waited in the October cold when I seemed to belong to no one, the life going on in the house, my aunt in her morning clothes, the sleeping baby, seeming tiny and strange as through the wrong end of a telescope, and I myself, alone there at the roadside, like an aberration in a picture, the thing when all else was accounted for that didn't fit. There was a smell in the air once, a crispness like the sun-cleared chill of mountains, that stirred something so deep and well-known in me, so forgotten, that I felt my body would burst with the pressure of remembering; and for an instant then the past seemed a kind of permanence I might wake into suddenly as into another country, all the present merely a shadow against it, this country road, this farm, this house.

IV

St. Michael's Separate School, and the church attached to it, sat on Highway 3 at the eastern edge of town, just across from the old folks' home. The school itself was a plain, two-storey rectangular building with walls of white stucco, long rows of metal-framed windows looking into the classrooms, like the ones that lined the walls of the Sun Parlour Canning Factory, and a glassed-in passageway at one side connecting it to the side steps of the church. The church was in white stucco as well, with a squat, arch-windowed bell tower, a slate roof, and a façade whose only ornament was a small circle of stained glass near the peak of its gable. In the patch of lawn in front of the rectory, on a three-stepped pedestal, stood a stone statue of the archangel Michael, his body clad in the short, girded tunic of a Roman soldier and his hands holding a rusting metal cross-staff whose tip was plunged into a strange winged serpent at his feet.

From the back of our farm the stark white walls of the church and school were partly visible across the mile or so of flat field that separated us from Highway 3. But the bus that carried me there and then home again took over an hour in each direction, winding me each way through nearly the whole of its erratic journey, up countless concessions and sideroads in a jagged circle that stretched as far as Goldsmith to the north and Port Thomas to the east. In winter the sun would just be rising when the bus pulled up in the morning and setting when it dropped me off in the afternoon; and on overcast days it seemed that the world the bus passed through was one where the sun never rose at all, where grey-limbed trees were forever shifting in the wind like ghosts, and the fields were always puddled over or covered with dirty patches of snow. Through this landscape the bus moved like a cabin ship, cut off and separate, sealed tight; but it was pleasant then, at the beginning or end of the bus's run, when the bus was nearly empty, to be sitting safely inside, the heater sending a warm shaft of air under the seats while outside the rain poured or the ground was rimed with frost.

After I got on in the morning the bus continued up to the 12 & 13 Sideroad and then doubled back along the 4th Concession to the highway again, following it for a stretch and stopping at some of the new yellow brick houses there. But finally it swung back into the concessions and lost itself in their maze-like grid, and it would seem then as if we had suddenly entered a new country, with its own different unknown customs and average citizens. The land here stretched flat and clean, the horizon broken only by the occasional dark island of pines or maples sitting strangely in the middle of a field, by the red or silver curves of silos, by the tall, steep gables of wooden farmhouses that stood, far from their neighbours, like lonely watchmen, their narrow windows gazing out over the endless fields that surrounded them. Toward Port Thomas the landscape changed again – we came out onto another highway and then entered at once into the town, smaller and meaner than Mersea, with only a few false-fronted stores at the four corners and then the houses growing gradually more weather-beaten and ramshackle until we came finally to the port, where dozens of fishing boats would be moored against the dock, some small and white and new, others with their paint peeling and strange names etched in red or black on their hulls, *Silver Dollar*, *Mayflower*, *The Betty Blue*. From Port Thomas we would follow the lake down into the black farmland of Point Chippewa, where the houses were more ramshackle still, their windows covered sometimes only with gritty plastic, and old farm machinery rusting outside barns and storage sheds like the remains of rotting animals.

Our driver was a man named Schultz, a big grey-eyed German with the rough swollen hands of a peasant and the large round face of a child. In the curved mirror that gave him a view to the back of the bus we could watch his movements as he drove, the way his face screwed into a grimace each time he ground up to a higher gear, the way his tongue strained against the side of his mouth when he turned a corner or rounded a curve. The older boys did imitations of him: sometimes, on cue, six or seven of them would begin squeezing imaginary clutches and shifting imaginary gears in tandem, their voices imitating the whine of the engine. At the noise, Schultz would raise his eyes to his mirror, his face darkening.

"Hey-you-boys," he'd say, in his thick, slow monotone, and one of the grade-eight boys would call out, "Sorry about that, Schultz."

Otherwise Schultz usually didn't take much notice of what went on on the bus; though sometimes, if a girl shrieked or if someone threw something out a window, he'd pull up to the side of the road suddenly and jam his emergency brake up hard, crossing his arms and leaning them into his steering wheel with an air of finality and intention. For a moment the bus would go silent; and then the boys at the back would begin their entreaties.

"Aw, we didn't mean anything by it, Schultz."

"Yeah, Schultzy, give us a break, we promise we'll knock it off."

And finally Schultz would purse his lips and shake his head slowly, and we'd set off again.

When I first began riding the bus I made the mistake once of sitting in the back seat, not knowing then that only the older boys sat there. A tall, lean, black-haired boy who got on at one of the brick houses along the highway sat beside me, flashing me an odd, exaggerated grin and whipping his head back with a practised swivel to bring a long lock of hair up out of his eyes. When he'd settled into the seat he made some comment to me that I couldn't follow, that I hoped had simply been some sort of greeting. But when I didn't respond he spoke again, his face twisted now, mocking or angry. Then suddenly he seemed to understand.

"*Deutschman?*" he said. "*Auf wiedersehen? Nederlander? Italiano?*"

"*Italiano,*" I said, clutching at the familiar word.

"*Ah, Italiano!*" He thumped a hand on his chest. "*Me speak Italiano mucho mucho. Me paesano.*"

When other boys got on the bus and came to the back, the black-haired boy said they were *paesani* as well, and each in turn smiled broadly at me and shook my hand. They tried to talk to me using their hands and their strange half-language. One of them pointed to the big silver lunchbox Tsia Teresa had packed my lunch in.

53

"*Mucho mucho*," he said, holding his hands wide in front of him. Then he pointed to me and brought his hands closer together. "*No mucho mucho*." The other boys laughed.

The black-haired boy took the lunchbox from me and held it before him as if to admire it. Then finally he opened it and unwrapped one of the sandwiches inside, split it open, brought it to his nose to sniff it. He screwed up his face.

"*Mu-cho, mu-cho*," he said, thrusting the sandwich away to one of the other boys and pinching his nose.

The sandwich began to pass from hand to hand. The other boys sniffed it as well, clutching at their throats, pretending to swoon into the aisle. Finally one of them glanced quickly up to the front of the bus, then slipped the sandwich out through an open window. From where I sat I saw it flutter briefly through the air and then fly apart as it struck the road.

They began to pass the second sandwich around. I tried to leap up to pull it away, but the black-haired boy's arm shot out suddenly in front of me and pinned me to the seat, and then his fist caught the side of my head hard three times in quick succession, my head pounding against the glass of the window beside me.

"*No, no, paesano.*"

I avoided the older boys after that, but I carried my humiliation with me like an open sore, always aware of it; and that awareness, more than the humiliation itself, seemed to be what gave the persecutions by the boys on the bus their meaning, what marked me. I thought there could be a way in which what they did to me, then and after, could stay outside me, have nothing to do with the kind of person I was, that I had only to find the right way to act. But each time it was the same, I'd fill with the same anger and hate, and my humiliation seemed then no longer simply a thing they did to me but something I always carried inside. The boys who picked on me had found the right way to act – they were perfectly detached, indifferent, didn't pick on me because they hated me or were angry but only because they could see the humiliation already inside me, as if I were made of glass, and if I'd been different they'd have left me alone or been friendly.

After school the boys would stake out seats for themselves and choose who they'd let sit beside them, and often then I'd have to sit with one of the girls or with George. George lived out near Goldsmith, in a rambling, broken-down farmhouse where in the fall and spring chickens and sometimes even pigs could be seen scavenging on the front lawn and in the laneway, roaming without restraint, as if they'd taken over the farm; and he had the unkempt, wild-eyed look of an idiot, his teeth gapped and protruding and his hair always awkwardly crew-cut, some patches longer than the others, some shaved too close to the skin. From up close I could see he was strangely large and robust, his hands almost the size of a man's and the muscles of his arms bulging against his sleeves; but the way he hunched himself made him seem shrivelled and deformed. When he boarded the bus in the morning he'd lurch up the aisle and fling himself into one of the centre seats with a kind of satisfied violence, then huddle up tight against the window and stare out it the whole trip like someone seeing a landscape for the first time, his head turtled down into the collar of his coat.

"Hey Georgie," the older boys would say, "tell us about the time your face caught on fire and your father beat it out with a crowbar."

Sometimes then he'd glance furtively toward the back of the bus. But his face would be screwed up in what seemed like a grin, as if he were shyly pleased that the boys were paying attention to him, or as if he hadn't understood them at all, had only turned at the sound of his name. The girls and the younger boys made fun of him as well, crossing their fingers and drawing away from the aisle when he got on the bus and passing on Georgie-germs if he should brush against them. Usually George seemed not to notice them; but once when a girl drew away as he was coming up the aisle he lunged toward her suddenly and made a face, and afterwards he seemed strangely pleased at what he'd done, settling into his seat with an air of impish self-satisfaction.

My own feeling about George was simply that I didn't want to be like him, didn't want other people to think I was like him; but whenever I was forced to sit beside him I'd feel a kind of rage build in me at his stupidity and strangeness. When other kids had to sit with him they'd call attention to themselves by making fun of him or by touching other people in the seats around them to pass on his germs. But I couldn't do these things, didn't have the right feeling inside to do them, and I knew my failure made me seem more like George to the others, even made me, in a way, more despicable than he was, because George was protected at least by the severity of his strangeness, had no one beneath him whom the others expected him to make fun of. I'd cross my legs under the seat sometimes the way the others crossed their fingers, furtively though, so that not even George would know I'd done it. But this useless concession made me feel worse than if I'd done nothing at all, made me think that it was only fear that kept me from making fun of George, fear that George too was stronger than I was, because of the way he flung himself into his seat each morning with a force that wasn't angry or bitter but almost carefree and gay, or the way he hummed quietly to himself sometimes as he stared out the window as if even he guarded some secret place inside him, a place that was his alone and could not be touched.

At school we went from the bus to the church, a sudden shift from the bus's strange containment into the wider containment of St. Michael's, the little world it formed with its huddled white buildings, its chain-link fence, its special logic and rules. Sister Jackson, the vice-principal, presided over our arrival from the bottom of the church steps; two other sisters stood at the fonts at the foot of the aisle. The girls sat in the left-hand pews, the boys in the right, in order of class, our heads rising in a gradual slope toward the back of the church. During the service the sisters on duty hovered in the side aisles like sentries; some of them, the older ones, carried long wooden pointers, and reached out quick and silent to rap you on the back of the neck if you whispered to your neighbour or fell asleep.

The church rose up to a high, arched roof that gave it the sense of an emptiness that couldn't be filled, that hung over us during the service as if we'd made no impression in it. In the church in Valle del Sole the pews had stood so close to the altar you could see the beads of sweat on Father Nicola's upper lip as he preached; but here the chancel was raised up four steps from the nave, separated from it by the low marble rail where people knelt for communion and by the wide expanse of the transept. The altar, of green and brown marble, was flanked by two ceiling-high mosaics of sworded angels, one clad in purple and the other in blue, staring out at us each morning like stony sentinels; for a long time I thought that the purple one, his feet wrapped in the coils of a serpent, was not Michael but Lucifer, so stern did he seem, so defiant, that he was challenging Michael

57

across from him as in the primal battle of the angels in heaven.

The services alternated between Father Mackinnon, the school principal, brisk and nimble and efficient, and Monsignor Phelan. With the monsignor the service seemed to go on forever, because he was old and spoke in a slow monotone, and because there were long pauses between each portion of the service while his finger scanned the lines of his great red missal. At the end, when he etched a sign of the cross in the air with a trembling hand, the church seemed almost to hum with suppressed energy. But I didn't mind those morning services, the crackly thin drone of the monsignor's voice over the loudspeakers, the high, arched hollowness of the church, because the church seemed the one place where my language wasn't held against me, and I could relax into the familiar sounds of the Latin responses like a fist slowly opening. Sometimes when we sang or recited together I'd feel that I'd crawled up out of myself and into the sound of our voices, that I was floating inside them above the pews as pure and unburdened as air; and then in the hush afterwards a pleasant aloneness would settle around me, make me feel for an instant as if everything inside the church existed only for me, the tall stained-glass windows that the sun lit up like candy and that dappled the pews with coloured light, the stations of the cross that hung like tiny sculpted worlds along the walls of the nave, the candle-glasses for the dead that flickered red and blue on their tiered metal stands in the transepts. There were always some candles burning there when we came in for morning service – perhaps the sisters lit them, though it was odd to think that the sisters, too, might have their own dead to remember.

Afterwards we walked single file to our classrooms, past the glass showcase in the main hall housing ribbons and silver trophies, past the portraits of Queen Elizabeth and Pope John that hung near the principal's office like a benevolent mother and father, past the big bulletin board that the sisters and the older classes did up every month with pictures and art, on religious themes or on topics like Switzerland or Christopher Columbus. It always made me feel strangely warmed to see these things, as if they could protect me somehow, and to see how the sun glinted brightly off the floor and varnished desktops of our classroom, how the blackboards had been scrubbed clean and fresh pieces of white and coloured chalk had been lined up in the ledges. There seemed a mystery in things then, a sleepy morningtime promise, beautiful and frail as the stillness that settled over the school after a bell had rung; but it teased me like a remembered smell and then passed, seeming to hold itself from the day.

I'd been put back two years, to the first grade. Every morning our teacher, Sister Bertram, stood before us as we sang "God Save the Queen" as tall and straight-backed as the angels on the chancel wall of the church, then clapped her hands twice when we'd finished to make us sit and stretched her thin lips into a smile that held no warmth in it. For the first week or so that I was in her class I spent the first lesson of the day in the corner for failing her morning inspection of ears and hands, my own hands still cracked and discoloured from working in the fields; and after that I seemed to become that first person she'd seen me as, perpetually delinquent, always the example of error. I'd track dirt into the classroom, let my attention wander, went so far once as to fall asleep at my desk; and then suddenly Sister Bertram's voice would ring out with the strange name she had for me.

"*Vic-tur!*"

And her anger would seem to focus in on me like a light beam, as if she were inviting the other children to see how different they were from me.

If I'd been more intelligent, more myself somehow, Sister Bertram might have been kinder; but everything about me proclaimed my ignorance, from my stained hands to my awkward clothes to my large hulking conspicuousness amidst the other children in the class. When I talked I couldn't get my mouth around the simplest sounds, felt my tongue stumble against my palate as if swollen and numb; when we did assignments my exercise book was always filled with the same hopeless errors, though Sister Bertram had explained a dozen times, so that sometimes she'd take a ruler in hand and simply rip out whole pages from it with a single swift jerk. And I didn't pay attention: even though I knew that Sister Bertram would catch me out, that I wouldn't learn if I didn't pay attention, still I couldn't stop my mind from wandering, because the moment Sister Bertram began to talk I'd feel the classroom slipping away from me the way a dream did in the first moments of wakefulness, and I couldn't force myself then to hold the world in focus, to try to get inside the meaning of Sister Bertram's words. I'd stare out the window sometimes at the old folks' home across the street, drawn there perhaps merely because it was different from the school, with its dying ivy and coloured leaves, its tall, spired turret like a tower in a fairy tale, the old people who came out stooped to the gazebo and benches; sometimes a face would be etched in a window against a whispery curtain and I'd imagine the lives inside, this other world going on beyond us, the old women and men stretched out on their beds with their tired faces and withered limbs.

Then in the spring Sister Bertram fell ill and was replaced by someone new to the school, Sister Mary. Sister Mary was not much taller than the grade-eight boys, with a pale round face that seemed held in the circle of her wimple like a moon; yet she gave the impression of being larger somehow than Sister Bertram, transforming the room with the simple bright force of her energy. Her first day she taught us to sing "He's Got the Whole World," coming around to each of our desks and bending to hear if we'd got the words right. When she came to my own I thought she would simply shake her head at my garbled English and move on, as Sister Bertram had always done; but instead she paused and crouched down beside me, with a smile that seemed so friendly and well-intentioned, so misdirected, that I flushed in embarrassment.

"*E di-fficile, no, parlare in-glese,*" she said.

I thought she was trying to trick me in some way or that she didn't know she shouldn't speak Italian in the classroom because she was new; but the class had fallen silent.

"*Sì,*" I said, still awaiting laughter that didn't come; and in the reverent silence afterwards it seemed the first time in that classroom that the air itself hadn't felt malevolent and strange, something set against me.

I began to spend lunch hours with Sister Mary studying English. With her lessons and explanations English began to open before me like a new landscape, and as it took shape in me it seemed that I myself was slowly being called back into existence from some darkness I'd fallen into, that I'd been no one till I'd had the words to be understood. Later on, when I saw how I continued to make mistakes, how my tongue still refused to form around certain sounds and how my brain still fought to make sense of the things people said, it seemed that I hadn't learned English at all, hadn't got inside it, or that I could never see any more than a part of it, would always feel lost in it the way I felt in the flat countryside that surrounded Mersea; but that initial surge of understanding was like a kind of arrival, the first sense I'd had of the possibility of me beyond the narrow world of our farm.

For reading practice Sister Mary gave me a book called *The Guiding Light* that told the story of the bible in pictures and captions. At home I'd sit with it at the kitchen table and slowly sound out the captions, its English easier for me now than the long-worded Italian of the *Lives of the Saints* I'd brought from Italy, and its stories seeming more important because they came from the bible and were in English. Scattered throughout it were colour pictures by famous painters, gloomy and strangely rendered and harsh, the beheading of John the Baptist, the blinding of Samson, the judgement of the woman who'd sinned. But I couldn't pierce their mysteries, preferred the more rustic pictures that went with the stories, the sense they gave of a world that was magical and benign. I read the stories through and then I went back to some of them, the story of creation, with its double-paged picture of Eden, the story of Jonah, of the young Christ in the temple; and I took a special furtive pleasure at making these stories my own, at entering into them as into some secret private world.

That pleasure seemed to draw something at first from the lunch hours I spent with Sister Mary, from the quiet closeness the empty classroom took on then, the warmth that lingered in my shoulder after she'd placed a hand there, the way her clothes rustled intimately when she leaned in beside me as if she were about to whisper to me some secret about herself. But after a few weeks students from other grades began to join us in these lunch-hour sessions – a yellow-haired Belgian girl kids teased because she never talked, a boy who'd failed grade three and been expelled once for smoking, a boy from grade eight, Tony Lemieux, who was taller than Sister Mary and who'd been to reform school – till finally there were more than a dozen of us, even George from my bus route, Sister Mary moving among us all with a democratic efficiency, assigning us each our separate tasks; and I began to nurse a small resentment toward Sister Mary then, angry that I'd been grouped with people like George and the Belgian girl, that Sister Mary didn't see how we all hated each other, hated having our strangeness multiplied and reflected back at us. Even Tony Lemieux, who was tall and broad-shouldered and whose nose was set back in his face so that his nostrils stared out like second eyes, appeared awkward and small among us, coming into class every day with the same defeated lope, as if being put in with us had stripped his infamy of its distinction; and I didn't understand why the other teachers thought he was bad or why he'd been to reform school when he didn't seem strong enough inside to be mean like some of the boys on the bus were, seemed merely crippled and out of place like the rest of us. Because he was too big for the grade-one desks Sister Mary had him sit up at hers while he worked; and occasionally she'd have him help her put things up on the bulletin board, standing beside him then and handing him things one by one with an odd intimacy and trust. But whenever Sister Mary was near him Tony would twist his shoulders awkwardly like an animal trying to shake off a yoke, and it seemed that Sister Mary didn't understand how things were with him, how her attention humiliated him. She'd make me think then of my Aunt Teresa, whose energy appeared to wrap her so safely in its tight space sometimes that it held other people out like a wall, and of Father Mackinnon the school principal. Father

Mackinnon came to the grade-one class about once a week to talk to us and ask us questions, smiling even when we got the answers wrong, his trim greying hair and blue eyes giving him a look of infinite compassion and wisdom. But in the schoolyard I saw how he'd laugh and joke with the same boys who picked on me on the bus, because they played on the school teams he coached, and his kindness then seemed merely a sort of stupidity, something that kept him from seeing the things that were most important about people.

Or perhaps I was the one who missed what was important, the simple goodness of Father Mackinnon, of Sister Mary, a way things were that my own contamination kept me from understanding. There seemed a realm of things other people took for granted that I couldn't enter somehow, that appeared to reside in the school's ordinariness, the mystery of it, the bulletin boards, the varnished desks, the games children played at recess, some normal life unfolding there untroubled and pure that remained as foreign and unknown to me, as inaccessible, as the first dull sounds of Sister Bertram's English; and it was my own failure to enter it that accounted somehow for the casual insults in the schoolyard, the sudden quick elbows in my ribs on the bus, the fear I carried always now that behind every simple gesture was the threat of some new humiliation. But still sometimes the same small bright hope would surge in me that everything could magically change, be different, that all these things that held me out could finally offer up their essences, reveal some secret about themselves that would take away my humiliation and hate, that would bring me up into the warm, sure sphere of their goodness the way Jesus cured the lepers in *The Guiding Light*, and brought Lazarus back from the dead.

V

In October of my second year in Canada my Uncle Umberto and his family came from Italy to live with us. The house took on a different smell then, with so many people crowded inside it, a smell of staleness and sleep. I slept with my cousins Rocco and Domenic on a bed in a corner of the living room; the others shared for a time the two bedrooms, Tsi'Umberto with my father and Tsia Taormina and her three-year-old, Fiorina, with Aunt Teresa, till finally we walled up the porch as a bedroom and my uncle and aunt moved in there.

In Italy my uncle's family had lived out in the countryside near Belladonna, where Tsia Taormina came from, a tiny village far from the high road in the valley beyond Castilucci. Their distance from town had seemed to me then to mark them like a physical deformity; I'd thought of them always as backward, thickheaded, and felt a kind of revulsion now when they moved in with us. Tsia Taormina was the worst, with her strange lumbering dialect – she seemed a cipher to me, a blank, a person without form or substance, as though something crucial had been left out of her and all her actions were only mimicry of what real people did, with no power to make an impression on the world. She was kind to me, and yet in her kindness I never felt any comfort – she'd give me candies sometimes out of a bag she'd brought with her from Italy, but the wrappers were sticky and yellowed with age, and the candies had an odd sickly-sweet liquid inside. In the house she quickly became a kind of drudge, no one taking her into account, Tsi'Umberto speaking to her only to insult her, and even Aunt Teresa, though she was much younger, assuming from the start a blatant condescension: within a few weeks she'd gradually turned over to her all the housework, and then when the new bedroom was built she insisted the baby be moved in there as well, saying it was easier for Tsia Taormina to look after two children than for both of them to look after one. But Tsia Taormina gave no sign of noticing these affronts, merely continued on in her simple-minded good humour as though she had no sense of her own humiliation. It was this blindness that seemed most unforgivable in her, even in the impartiality she showed the baby, the way she treated her with the same plodding efficiency and care as she did her own Fiorina as if she saw no distinction between them, looked after them both merely out of the blind instinct of a mother; I kept waiting to catch her out in some oversight or mistake, though she was the only grown-up in the house now who ever showed the baby the least affection, who didn't treat her as if she were invisible.

Tsi'Umberto, more heavy-set than my father, with a wide round face that gave him an air of expansive good humour, seemed to make up for Tsia Taormina with his own unfailing self-assertion. Yet in him as well I sensed no centre finally, no way of pinning down what was true in him. He appeared oddly

66

anxious to please us at first, even the contempt he showed toward his wife and sons somehow intended for our benefit, to show us he was a part of us and not of them; but through the winter he grew gradually more irritable and grim, seeming to lose interest in us, putting on his good humour then only for guests and beginning to show the same disowning toward the rest of us that he showed his family. In the spring, when he gave up his job at the factory to help us on the farm, the arguments started – clandestinely at first, in short quick bursts directed mainly at Aunt Teresa and usually having to do, perversely, with some perceived slight against his wife. But since Aunt Teresa always answered him with the same off-hand manner she had with my father, was like a smooth surface Tsi'Umberto's anger couldn't take hold in, by the summer the longer arguments had begun, the ones with my father, arguments that went on some-times for days or weeks and from which we had no respite until Tsi'Umberto and his family finally moved out of the house some two years later.

One of the first of these was over a Portuguese man, Vito, whom my father hired that summer at the beginning of the bean season. Vito had worked for us the previous year before my uncle had come, seeming to transform the farm then, rattling up our drive every morning on his old CCM bicycle, his legs working like pistons, and then the day taking shape around his manic energy as if impelled by it. My father told the story one night at supper of how Vito had killed the neighbour's dog, had seen something moving through the field and run to get the shotgun from behind the seat in my father's truck.

"*Pom!* before anyone could stop him. He must have got it into his head he was going to have a nice roast that night – who knows what he thought he'd seen. Then when he saw it was the neighbour's dog he didn't come to work for two days. I brought him a few pounds of meat after but he wouldn't eat it, he said I'd got it from the dog."

Tsi'Umberto laughed at this story with the rest of us, smoking at his corner of the table with the pleased, languid air he sometimes put on after supper.

"*Mbeh*, we'll keep him until the beans are finished," he said finally, as if simply adding to the story a logical conclusion, "and then we'll find someone else."

"What are you saying?" my father said. "You'll never find another worker like him."

"*Dai*, you see the way he is. Anyway there's lots of Italians who need work, I don't see why we have to go hiring strangers."

"Italians, they're the worst – all you'll find now are the old women who can't get work in the factory. They talk nonsense all day and then if you try to tell them anything you never hear the end of it."

But already it was as though Tsi'Umberto wasn't listening. He seemed to discover his opinions himself only the moment before he uttered them, yet once he'd found them he'd retreat into them as into a fortress, sitting inside them with a self-righteousness that allowed no guilt or doubt to weaken them, as if his stubbornness itself was its own justification, something he could hold before us like a trophy at the end of every argument.

"It's not right," he said, and there was the hard finality in his voice that showed he'd found his place and was ready to set there now like cement. "I'm not going to have people say we give work to foreigners before we give it to our own."

My uncle's accusals would seem to close around my father like a cage, make him lash out with an uncontrol that then gave my uncle the upper hand, that added the force of indignation to his stubbornness. Yet it was my uncle's anger that surprised me, continuing to build as if it had no limit, for all its theatricality remaining raw in him many days after an argument, his wife and his sons bearing the brunt of it then in his insults or in the sting of his belt, while my father's by then had already long retreated, drawn inward as if it had turned against him. In the end it was always my father who made some concession: after the beans Vito was let go, though in the fall Tsi'Umberto said nothing more about hiring Italians, seeming content instead when we fell behind to let Rocco and Domenic and me miss the first month of school.

It was a source of disgrace to me to start school late, those terrible first moments boarding the bus, going into class, especially now that I was saddled with the added disgrace of Rocco and Domenic. I'd had to bring them into the office when they'd arrived from Italy the October before, Sister Bertram, drawn and pale after her illness, talking there with Father Mackinnon when we came in.

"I don't see how these people expect them to learn anything if they keep them at home to work half the year."

Rocco and Domenic had both been put back two grades as I had, Rocco into grade five and Domenic into grade three. Their first months at school I spent bitter with the shame of them, couldn't bear sitting with them on the bus, always got on after them so I could choose a place away from them, couldn't bear the sounds of their voices or how they walked or how they looked, their wide-legged corduroys and button flies and the crooked haircuts their mother gave them. They seemed oddly misproportioned to me, Rocco muscled and wide-shouldered but with his mother's tiny weasel-like head, Domenic broad-faced like his father but his body spindly like a comic-strip character's; and I held their awkward looks against them as if their own thick-headedness had caused them, held against them the way they remained stolid inside their strangeness like things unaware of themselves or of the impression they made.

In his first weeks Rocco threw up several times on the bus. His vomit had the stench and consistency of soured corn meal, puddling in the aisle and beginning to run under the seats until Schultz finally stopped to clean it. But Rocco seemed put out only by the fact of his getting sick; the rest he took as a kind of joke, making comebacks in Italian to the other boys when they insulted him and afterwards laughing at home about the uproar he caused. Everything was like that for him – he continued to make his sandwiches with our crusty homemade bread instead of the store bread I made Aunt Teresa buy, said he preferred it, continued to sit where he pleased on the bus without regard for the hierarchies and insults of the older boys. When the Massaccis had first moved to the 12 & 13 Sideroad and begun to ride the bus I had avoided them, setting my lunchbox on my seat when they got on so they wouldn't sit next to me; but Rocco made friends with them at once, talking to them in the crudest dialect though the older boys harangued them, he and Domenic closing themselves off with them in their own small oblivious world. For a while the older boys simply stopped paying them any attention; and then gradually they began to engage them, almost curious, almost friendly.

"You know what wop means?" Rocco said when he'd begun to pick up some English. "It means nice Italian boy."

After that the word became a running joke between him and the other boys; one of them, the ringleader of sorts, took to calling Rocco his good buddy, draping a beefy arm around him then like a protector. But Rocco seemed merely amused by this new friendliness, as if it only proved how foolish the other boys were.

In all this I was left with nothing, no reward for trying to follow out what seemed the careful, ruthless logic of fitting in. In the first month or so of school after Rocco and Domenic arrived my mind would twitch like a nerve each time I found Domenic waiting for me at the back doors at recess, sullen and expectant there in his awkwardness and aloneness; and unable to bear him once, I simply pushed him hard against the wall of the school to be away from him, feeling a lightness as my hands shot out against him as if something caged in me had been set free. But there was a look in his face just before he crumpled to the ground, a grimace like a soundless scream, that seemed not so much pain as the sudden understanding of how things were between us. I felt betrayed somehow, in that instant and then afterwards when other kids sided with him when the teacher on duty came, felt I'd been tricked into thinking he was nothing, that I could release my hate on him without consequence. Later, when he'd begun to make other friends, to avoid me, every small success of his seemed an accusation. In the spring he gained a kind of notoriety at marbles, devising special games for them with shoeboxes and tin cans and collecting Mason jars full of them, steelies, boulders, peeries, trading them sometimes for chocolate bars or bags of chips that he'd bring home for his sister or himself. He won a peery once with a tiny bird frozen into the centre of it as in mid-flight, though he simply turned it over to his sister as if to show how easily things came to him now.

At home we worked together in the greenhouses after school, leaf lettuce during the fall, tomatoes during the winter; but then in the summer I was left home again to look after Fiorina and the baby while the others went out to the fields. The house took on a torpor with only the three of us there as if time were suspended, every hour interminable; cut off like that I seemed to have no way to judge what was normal, wavering always between a childish boredom, resentful at being left behind, at having to do girls' work, and the fear of some catastrophe. The baby disturbed me sometimes, with her eerie passivity and silence, seemed to have taken into herself the blankness with which others regarded her. She could hardly be called an infant now, could walk, could speak, yet there remained an inattention in her like a newborn's; if I tried to get her to talk she'd ape things I said but with a mumbling distraction, turning them inwards like a private conversation. I took to calling her Rita, the only syllables of her name she was able to manage, whispering them to herself sometimes like an incantation; but often she'd fall into moods like trances, lost in her secret games with the toys, a doll, a beaded cushion, that Tsia Taormina had made for her, oblivious then to any attempts I made to get her attention.

With Fiorina she was more responsive – Fiorina acted the mother with her, rocking her, combing her hair, played hiding games that brought out in her sometimes the ghost of a smile; and yet there was something off in all this, a hint of pretence. I caught Fiorina hitting her once, not in anger but with a kind of deliberation or righteousness, as if she were administering a punishment, and though I myself had often come to the point of hitting one or the other of them, still I felt a kind of rage at this presumption in her. After that I noticed her growing increasingly bullyish and manipulative, condescending as if she'd understood finally the difference between herself and Rita; and yet Rita continued to respond to her in a way she wouldn't to

72

me, caught up somehow in this strangely subtle dynamic Fiorina had established between them. I had no control over them: when they were getting along, lost in their private games, a calm settled over the house like sleep; but then some sudden petulance in Fiorina would disturb the balance and leave Rita crying sometimes with a fierceness that frightened me.

I emerged from these days, the isolation of them, as from a soundless dark, dazed somehow by the return of the others, the complex mundane world they brought back with them. Day by day they grew more alien, seemed to share the same strange features that made them different from me, that set us apart as surely as if we'd come from different countries or spoke a different language – they made me think how in Italy I'd regarded people from Castilucci as backward, peculiar, their features then always seeming to bear the proof of their strangeness, their lumbering gait or flattened faces, the watery, muted sound of their speech as if their throats were clogged with mucus. And yet I was no longer certain what choice I'd made to set myself so apart from them, whether my exclusion was something I'd willed or that had simply come about by a kind of inertia. Whole evenings began to pass when I didn't exchange a word with any of them; and the longer my silences went on the more impossible it was to break out of them, to make the simplest gesture or utter the simplest sound without feeling a hollowness at the centre of me. I wanted to sit inside my difference and shelter myself there as if to protect it, wanted them to feel some punishment in it that would show up their own hideousness, this crippled family we formed. But then sometimes they appeared so at ease with themselves, lax with fatigue as they were, good-humoured, solid and real in a way I wasn't, each of them finding their place so instinctively in the mysterious shift and flow of their conversations, that it seemed I had nothing to put against them finally to show I was better than they were, that there was nothing inside me that was true, not even the silent hate I bore against them.

VI

The Italians held parties from time to time at the Rhine Danube Club, sudden distillations of us from out of the wide anonymous landscape we'd been scattered through into the crucible of the club's barn-like hall. It was odd to see all the half-familiar faces from Valle del Sole gathered together there as in some old photograph, people still carrying on with their air of village unconcern though it seemed out of place now amidst the starched tablecloths and careful place-settings, the blue-eyed servers in their tight bodices and flowered dresses. Now and then some boy I'd known back in Italy would catch my eye with a newcomer's furtive hopefulness, whatever divisions there'd been between us back then seeming levelled in the diminishment of being together here in someone else's country; yet finally nothing would come of these past connections, always the lingering shame in me of what my mother had done and then some larger disjunction I couldn't account for, the not remembering somehow who I'd been in that other life.

Aunt Teresa, though, seemed to thrive at these parties. Once the music came on she switched from partner to partner through to the end of the night, her laughter sometimes bursting into the sudden lull between songs so that for an instant the whole hall seemed to focus on her. She was our ambassador, her own normalcy somehow washing away some mark from the rest of us, the thing that excused my father's reclusion, Tsi'Umberto's menacing friendliness when he drank. I'd watch her sometimes from the edge of the dance floor, retreating there after the other boys my age, most of them from Our Blessed Virgin School on the other side of town from St. Mike's, had sifted into their gangs and cliques; and sometimes she'd see me sitting alone there amongst the old women and take my hands suddenly to dance, waltzing me around the floor with the same air of girlish abandon I'd known in her in Italy.

Then finally at one of these parties she spent the whole evening with a single partner, tall and boyish and lean, with a long wave of blondish hair he'd run his fingers through awkwardly after each dance to brush it from his eyes. Though I'd never seen him before there was already the air of casual familiarity between him and my aunt of some longer acquaintance. Tsi'Umberto seemed to know him as well, coming up to him at one point and clapping an arm around his shoulder, his voice booming with drunken heartiness.

"Colie, *figliu miu*, you're the one that gives us the headaches with all the work you bring in for us."

It seemed he and Aunt Teresa must have met him at Longo's Produce, where they'd been working over the winter; and I began to notice now how my aunt prettied herself in the mornings with lipstick and blush before going into work.

The next party we attended was Gelsomina's wedding – she had married an older man just arrived from Castilucci. In the reception line she hardly noticed me, absorbed in conversation with Aunt Teresa when I passed; but I thought she looked pretty and self-assured and adult in her billowing white dress, was envious of the way she held her husband's arm locked in hers as if she'd taken possession of him.

Then toward the end of the meal Colie appeared suddenly at the entrance to the hall and made his way toward our table. He offered a hand to my father, awkward and deferential, introducing himself as Ercole though the Italian sounds of the name seemed foreign on his tongue; but an aura of well-being emanated from him like a tangible warmth, making his awkwardness appear merely a kind of innocence.

"Here, pull up a chair," Tsi'Umberto said, half-rising as if ready to offer his own.

"No, no, I'll just grab a Coke at the bar. I just came to have a few dances with your sister here, I don't want to make it seem like I'm trying to get a free meal."

Tsi'Umberto stared after him with an air of appraisal.

"You should see the loads he comes into Longo's with," he said. "Two hundred crates a day, every day, like a factory."

Afterwards Aunt Teresa brought me to sit with them at a table at the edge of the dance floor.

"In the old days when there was a wedding all the Italians were invited," Colie said. "*Ciociari, abruzzesi, parenti, forestieri*, it was all the same. But now already there's too many of us to fit in one place."

"The old days," my aunt said. "You make it sound like you've been around since the beginning of the world."

"You're just jealous because I was born here."

"You're the one who's jealous, the way you speak Italian, picking every word out of your mouth as if it was made out of glass."

"Let's ask Victor, then. Where's it better, here or in Italy?"

But I didn't know how to answer him.

The bridal dance began, Gelsomina and her husband slowly making their way around the dance floor to a shower of confetti and coins.

"That little fool," Aunt Teresa said. "He probably only married her so he could stay in the country."

"I dunno, they look like a nice couple," Colie said.

When the bridal dance was over I thought they would join the other couples moving onto the dance floor, but they remained talking at the table. Colie thought my aunt should go back to school, learn English, become a teacher as she'd intended; but Aunt Teresa said she was too old already.

"Too old!" Colie said. "Now who was born at the beginning of the world. My grandfather went back to school when he was forty."

"*Dai*, you're just making a joke," Aunt Teresa said.

"You can ask him about it when you meet him, he'll tell you himself."

But when my aunt pressed him it came out his grandfather had been arrested during the war when the police had found an old photo from Italy of his sons in their *balilla* uniforms.

"They thought he was a fascist or something, they didn't know every kid in Italy wore those things back then. So they locked him up for a year or so. He always says that was the time the government sent him to college."

But he told the story as if it were merely an anecdote, safely cut off from him in the past, so different from how other Italians talked about Canada, their stories always seeming intended to call attention to themselves, to impress.

One Sunday not long afterwards Colie came to the house, driving into the courtyard in a long blue Biscayne. It was a warm spring day and Tsi'Alfredo and a few others had come by to play *bocce*, Colie sitting down to have a beer with them at the picnic table on the side lawn. He told a joke about an Italian who had just got off the boat.

"So the first thing he sees when he gets off is a ten-dollar bill lying on the sidewalk. But he walks right past it. When his friend asks him later why he didn't pick it up he says, 'Well, I didn't want to start working yet.'"

The other men laughed.

"*Sì, sì*, if only it was like that," Tsi'Umberto said. "Lucky for you that your grandfather's been in the country for forty years. The rest of us have to work for a living."

When the men started to play, Colie stayed behind to talk to Aunt Teresa. Tsia Taormina came out a few minutes later with Rita and Fiorina, Rita breaking away from her grip and toddling across the courtyard toward Colie.

"Whey, what have we here?" Colie said, taking her up in his arms. "Who does this one belong to?"

But the question seemed to take Aunt Teresa by surprise.

"It's mine," she said abruptly, and Colie laughed. "*Dai*, let's take a walk up the road, since you don't know how to play *bocce*."

Afterwards he began to come by every Sunday for supper. He never asked about Rita again; I thought Aunt Teresa must have said something to him though perhaps he'd just assumed she was Tsia Taormina's, seeming ready now simply to accept her as part of the family.

"She's such a quiet one this one," he said. "So serious."

"We're all serious in this family," Aunt Teresa said.

But Colie laughed.

"You should have supper with some of the Canadians I know, it's like a funeral sometimes – you get the feeling people have to force themselves just to find something to say. It's never like that with Italians."

For several weeks we went on like that, his visits, our suppers, the imperceptible shift to beginning to think of him and my aunt as a couple. It seemed a kind of wonder that things could proceed as simply as they were, that we had only to await now the inevitable conclusion. And yet with each of his visits some apprehension in us appeared to grow larger, as if we could not quite believe our good fortune, couldn't believe this innocence in him wouldn't finally be shattered.

Then gradually Aunt Teresa began to find things to criticize in him, his clothes, his hair, with her usual badgering good humour at first, but then with a growing cynicism, seeming almost to will him to take offence. Colie didn't appear to notice any change, still laughing her off; and yet in conversations now he'd slowly turn his attention away from her toward my father and uncle like a plant bending gradually toward light, the job of courting him seeming as much theirs now as hers. Tsi'Umberto, at least, always saved his best face for Colie, even in the midst of some lingering family argument still all staunch hospitality and attentiveness the moment Colie arrived; and though I thought less of Colie for responding to this ready good humour as if it were real, still there was something in it to be grateful for, the way my uncle could fill the room with it when he wanted to. But my father had none of Tsi'Umberto's skills at dissembling. In a good mood he could be as excessive and loud as my uncle was, laughing too hard and repeating the punchlines of jokes, seeming in a way then less clever than my uncle, less controlled, giving in to his own energy as in to a kind of drunkenness, not seeing there was something in it intended to impress. But his bad moods blunted his words and gestures like a screen, Colie turning from him then with the same unthinking instinct with which he turned from Aunt Teresa. My father would lapse into English sometimes, retreating into the formality of it as though to guard from Colie his truer self; but Tsi'Umberto then would have to strain to understand, his silence seeming to suck the air from the room.

The tension surrounding Colie's visits grew more palpable. The days and hours before them were filled with a grim expectancy; the visits themselves grew more awkward. We seemed to have lost all spontaneity, unable somehow to make a place for him any more, even my aunt's sarcasm grown feeble as though she were merely struggling to play her role. I expected an argument, something to break through the tension and show what lay beneath it, and yet we merely continued on as always, the tension like a thing without source, that couldn't be fought against. It was as if the house itself was rejecting Colie, was slowly turning him out simply because he didn't belong to it.

"I guess I won't be coming by much for a while," he said toward midsummer. "There's the planting in the greenhouses and all that, we'll be pretty busy."

"It's just as well," Aunt Teresa said. "We have the tomatoes coming on outside now."

"Yes, of course."

He seemed to want something more from her, some sign, some way back, but she wouldn't relent.

"I guess maybe I'll call you or something," he said.

But already it was as if he had never been part of us, even then before the weeks had passed and we'd heard nothing more of him. A sullenness settled over our house as after a death, no mention made of him and yet our silence only seeming to keep him constantly before us, to prevent us from simply getting on with our lives. We attended a party on the Labour Day weekend, an inauguration of the new club the Italians had built on the lakeshore, all pomp and circumstance though we appeared to sit the whole meal in brooding expectation, awaiting the person who didn't come; and afterwards Aunt Teresa sat out the dance with the older married women at the back tables, what we had not yet been ready to admit seeming made plain now in her evening desertion.

In the next weeks we passed through a kind of penance for what had happened, in the arguments that flared up at the slightest thing between my uncle and father; and in the midst of them Aunt Teresa herself seemed almost forgotten, closed off in her own private hurt as if she'd withdrawn suddenly from the family. The arguments followed the usual pattern, my uncle's provocations, my father's blind lashing out: it was as if my uncle had been the one who had suffered some affront for which he wanted retribution now, trying to extract it somehow from my father as the wellspring of all our troubles. Yet these squabbles seemed to bring my uncle no solace, left him merely irritable and grim as if he were in the grip of some emotion he couldn't quite find a way to turn to advantage; and then finally we had settled back again into what seemed our usual bearable calm, with only a lingering throb of failed hopefulness and then silence.

In the New Year a salesman came by the house one evening to talk about building another greenhouse. My father and Tsi'Umberto and Aunt Teresa sat around the kitchen table while he spoke, a family again, plotting the contours of our future.

"The way he talked you'd think it was like going to the office," my father said afterwards. "I'll bet he's never set foot in a greenhouse, with that suit of his. He probably sleeps in it."

But Tsi'Umberto kept coming back with a grimace to the figures the salesman had written out on the back of a catalogue.

"I don't see where we're going to get that kind of money," he said.

"*Mbeh*, if it comes to that," my father said, "you can tell the Farm Credit you want to buy into the farm, they'll give you twice that much. Any kid with fifty cents in his pocket can get money from them, there's no reason you can't."

Tsi'Umberto nodded gravely, seeming filled for the moment with a sense of his own importance, and it appeared the matter was settled; and for the next week or so there was a vague, pleasant mood of anticipation in the house, of impending change. But perhaps all along my uncle had merely been biding his time: he had taken on again the dangerous, contented air he had whenever he held my father at a disadvantage.

"There's that *inglese* on the lakeshore trying to sell off his greenhouses," he said one evening, bland, conversational, not seeming to implicate us in any way in what he was saying. "He's asking almost nothing for them, he just wants someone to clear them off the property so he can sell it off for houses."

"If he's asking almost nothing," my father said, "it means they're worth less than nothing. I've seen those greenhouses, they're half rotten as it is. He'd have had to tear them down in a year or two anyway. I doubt anything would be left of them if you had to take them apart and then put them together again."

"*Mbeh*, if you could get them for nothing like that," Tsi'Umberto said, with an air of authority, though he was probably just repeating something he'd heard at Longo's. "For someone starting out it's not a bad idea."

"I wouldn't do it. It's just taking someone else's garbage."

"*Sì, sì*," my uncle said, but with a petulance now, "you always have to have the best."

"What, you're not seriously saying *we* should buy them?"

"Why not?"

"Don't be a fool. Nobody builds in wood any more like that."

"*Sì*, I'm always the fool," my uncle said. "I'll tell you why I'm a fool, because I didn't see from the first how you're dragging me into your big ideas just to get your money from the bank."

"*Ma 'stu cretin'*, is it possible anyone can be so thickheaded? Do you think I needed your money? You're worse than your father, idiot that he was, working like a slave all his life on those few acres of stones, and you'll die and rot poor like him, the way you hold all your stupid pennies in your fist like a schoolboy!"

"Ah, *grazie*, now I understand how you see things!" my uncle said, springing his indignation on my father like a trap. "You always want to be the big man, ah? The big man who married the mayor's daughter, the big man who came to America. And now you thought you would use your brother to get your money so you could be a big man again, isn't that it? But I won't have any part of it, by Christ, even if I have to break my bones in a factory the rest of my life!"

My father and my uncle didn't speak to each other again for the rest of the winter. For months we lived under the shadow of their suppressed anger, and in the charged silence that settled over us the household appeared to split in two, my uncle's family on one side of it, policed there by a violence that seemed intended in its excess as a reproof to my father, and the rest of us shifting like counterweights to the other. A careful pantomime worked itself out like a long wordless argument, separate meals, separate outings, separate work; even Rita had to be claimed now, no twilight space there to hold her in our sudden division. In the past, Rita had always been left at home with one of us whenever there was some party to go to, Fiorina often left as well though almost as if we used her to hide from ourselves the truer reason for Rita's not coming. But at carnival that year it was Tsi'Umberto's family that stayed home, Rita instead, as though to make clear whose side of the family she fell on, bundled up in her coat and hat and brought along with my father and Aunt Teresa and me, awkward and shy in the new dress my aunt had bought for her, hanging near me the whole evening in frightened wonder at the world's sudden largeness and noise. My father hardly spoke, appearing injured by every glance, retreating at once after the meal to a back table to play cards; but still the silence when we drove home that night had nothing foreboding about it, for an instant the group of us seeming held together in the car's dark, tight warmth by our own strange loyalty, an odd silent family joined in its awkwardness and injury.

This time my father did not back down. When the ground thawed in April a bulldozer arrived to level a stretch of field alongside our greenhouses, then a few days later a truck delivered a load of metal trusses and rafters and posts. There seemed no adequate response my uncle could make to the mute fact of this hill of metal that lay glinting in our side field. But one day, taking with them a few suitcases and a wooden trunk, all they'd brought with them from Italy, my uncle and his family simply moved out of the house – as suddenly as that, as if my uncle had reached the decision only hours before. When we came home from school to find my aunt packing the trunk, I imagined they were returning to Italy; but it turned out they moved only next door, into a small clapboard house connected to a broken-down greenhouse and a few acres of land that my father had usually rented for his tomatoes.

Oddly, their departure left no sense of relief in our house, only a strange lethargy, a torpor thick as sleep. The new trusses and posts remained lying where they'd been heaped as if my father had lost interest in them; Tsi'Alfredo came by and warned him to build while he had the time and the weather was good, but the spring planting began and still the trusses and posts lay untouched.

Then Rocco came by one day to borrow our tractor and planter.

"We'll see if he thinks he can make it on his own," my father said.

But when Tsi'Umberto himself came by a few days later it was with the air of bland self-satisfaction he'd put on whenever my father had yielded to him in some argument, an air that seemed to deny there'd been any argument at all.

"That old Ukrainian there, I don't know what he cooked in that house, the whole place smells like cabbage."

He began to come by often then, to borrow tools, to use our equipment; we had to go looking for things, my father grumbling, making threats, but then saying nothing to my uncle. When we finally got around to starting work on the new greenhouse he came by to help raise the trusses, affable and expansive, almost claiming a share in my father's accomplishment now that he had nothing to do with it; and my father put up with this as he did everything else, seeming somehow to have gained less by his victory than Tsi'Umberto by his defeat.

It appeared only a matter of time by then before we'd be back more or less where we'd begun, a single family, bound by some twisted allegiance that infected us like an illness, that made sure there could be no new arguments among us, no new solutions. Aunt Teresa would stand at the kitchen window sometimes now with her face so emptied it hurt me to look at her, etched there against the light as at some threshold she wouldn't cross, that she would turn from finally to wipe the table, rearrange a chair. And yet in all that had happened she was what we'd protected somehow, found a way to hold within our element as if around us we felt the pressure of a world that wouldn't let us spill into it, that held us in the way the dykes at the Point kept the lake from seeking its level in the spring.

VII

With my uncle's family gone our household seemed stripped down again to its essence, all of us suddenly dangerously visible, lacking the spectacle of Tsi'Umberto's arguments to distract us from the awkwardness of one another's presence. We retreated to our separate rooms, the one wealth my uncle's departure had left us with, the rest of the house become just a passageway we moved through uneasily, with no sense of ownership or comfort. The living room took on an air of abandonment, the bed removed so that only the threadbare armchair and couch remained; in the day no one bothered so much as to draw the curtains there, the room like a recess at the centre of us awaiting the family we couldn't be.

Work on the greenhouse didn't go well. First the men who sank the posts set the last three on one side out of plumb and they had to be redug; then afterwards two of them settled lower than the others beneath the weight of the trusses. Those first mistakes seemed to spoil the whole project for my father.

"You'll see, for the next forty years now those two bays will be a pain in my ass, while those bastards just get their cheque and go home. The idiots, a child could have seen the mistake."

"They were probably in a hurry to get to the hotel to drink," Tsi'Alfredo said.

My father would bring his grievances to Aunt Teresa, with a peevishness that was a sort of clumsy sleight of hand, an appeal for sympathy and a denial of any need for it, like a child's false stoicism. But my aunt always said the thing that seemed most calculated to irritate him, allowing herself to see into his need only enough to use it against him.

"You should have let Rossi do it," she said about the posts. "At least he's Italian."

"What does Rossi have to do with it, idiot, he doesn't have the equipment for that kind of thing."

She'd gained weight since Colie had stopped coming round, looked aged beyond her years, a shadow of dark veins beginning to appear on the fleshy surface of her calves. She seemed always at one remove from things now, uninvolved in some core of herself with their small daily unfoldings. At home she let house-work lapse, the floors going gritty, the bathtub rimmed with scum; at work, back full time on the farm now after her one winter at Longo's, she carried a small transistor radio with her always, lost to us then in its static hum. There was a program she listened to faithfully that came on in late afternoon on one of the Detroit stations – it seemed a kind of news show, talked about the riots in Los Angeles, the war in Vietnam, though in a tone charged with a strange urgency, at once sure and deeply troubled. Eventually the magazines began to arrive, with articles about God and the bible, Aunt Teresa reading them from cover to cover in her slow, careful way; but if she ever referred at all to the program or to the things she read it was only to bring up some fact about how bad things were in the world, as if every small, private problem were proof of some general malaise.

Rita's care fell mainly to me again. We shared a bed in the converted porch my uncle and aunt had slept in, at night Rita a tiny ridge beside me beneath the excess of blankets Aunt Teresa covered us with to make up for the room's damp cold. In the mornings I'd wake her when I got up for school; but beyond that she was on her own, seeming to have fashioned for herself a small, quiet life with its own child's logic and order, the meticulous care she took to wash and dress, the private games she played. There was something disturbing in this, in her self-sufficiency, the way she could close the world out as if only the little of it she needed was real. She'd spill long strings of words sometimes as she played, in mixed English and Italian, rolling them out as over a hilly landscape, racing them into a blur and then gradually slowing them to a strenuous clarity, cryptic declarations that moved in and out of sense; but then she might ask some child's simple question or make some child's observation and seem suddenly normal again, unremarkable.

She was four now, her baby fat long gone, melted from her to leave a willowy angularity that seemed at once sickly but somehow natural to her, as if her tiny intricate hands, her bony limbs, the pale oval of her face, had all assumed some perfect final proportion. She might almost have been pretty, with her child's delicacy and her limpid eyes, as brightly blue now as a primary sky in a drawing; and yet there was always an air of slovenliness about her, her hair slightly oily and limp though she brushed it every morning with a slow solemnity, her clothes, mainly hand-me-downs from Fiorina, always shabby and ill-fitting. Fiorina would parade before her conceited and prim in her new school clothes and I'd see the veiled longing in Rita, the knowledge of what she couldn't have, how she'd balk sometimes at the clothes I set out for her in the morning.

"I don't like that one."

"That's all there is, you have to wear it."

But I'd begun to pick out always the shoddiest things, wanting somehow to display the injustice of them before Aunt Teresa.

"Why do you always have her wear those old rags?" she said finally. "She must have other things."

"She needs something new," I said.

"We don't have money to go wasting on clothes like that. She has all those things of Fiorina's to wear."

I decided to take matters into my own hands, slipping downtown after school one day to Schwartz's clothing store on Erie Street with a few crumpled bills in my pocket that I'd taken from Aunt Teresa's purse. The Italians shopped at Schwartz's because you could bargain with him, referring to him as "the Jew" though the label conjured for me only scanty, contradictory facts, that the Jews had suffered during the war, that they'd crucified Christ though he'd been the king of them.

"You're Mario's son," Schwartz said when I came in, mournful and slow, seeming to sort my image from his mind like a photograph. "On the 3rd Concession."

It disturbed me to be recognized like that, to be noticed, but when I'd told him what I needed he nodded conspiratorially as if he'd gathered up in an instant all the circumstances that had brought me there and was prepared to guard them for me now like a secret. His shop was all dizzying disorder, the walls piled with dusty half-open cartons and the gloomy aisles crammed with clothes carousels and racks, hats and cellophaned shirts, tie stands, pleated trousers; but Schwartz manoeuvred his way through it unthinkingly, stopping at a rack at the far corner to pull a frilled, pink dress from it, displaying it for me with a tiny flourish against the bare dappled flesh of his forearm.

"Maybe something like this?" But he saw my eyes dart to the price tag dangling from it and nodded, considering.

"Yes, perhaps you're right," he said. He had an odd lilting accent, pausing a split instant before syllables as if afraid he might injure them. "You need something more sub-stan-tial for a girl that age."

He found a dress in blue corduroy in a bin in a back room.

"Maybe this is more what you want."

At the counter he winked at me, avuncular, as he handed me my parcel. For an instant he was no longer simply the Jew who sold clothes but a man who might have some secret other life, who would close up his shop at night and walk slowly out along Erie Street toward some house on the edge of town, who might have children, a wife, who ate meals at some kitchen table and listened perhaps to the radio. I wanted to ask him that suddenly, if he had children, but it seemed too strange a thing, too out of keeping with my own role as a child.

I walked home along the highway and then up our concession road, my shoes crunching strangely loud against the gravelled shoulder in the late-afternoon chill. My father gave me a dark look when I came out to the greenhouses to work.

"Where have you been?"

"I had to stay for an extra lesson."

"*Bravo*," my father said, immediately assuming some infraction though my reports were always good. "If you don't want to do what you have to there, don't come looking to me after."

I kept the dress from Rita till Sunday, wanting to save the secret of it, the expected still, silent moment of her pleasure;

but then when she came out wearing it Aunt Teresa noticed it at once.

"Where did that come from?"

I hadn't considered this, hadn't thought anyone paid this much attention to Rita, paid any attention to her at all.

"I got it from Tsia Taormina," I said.

"*Ma come*, she brought over all the clothes she had just the other day, that wasn't with them. It looks almost new."

My father was eating breakfast. He stared at Rita strangely for a moment, Rita seeming to shrink beneath his gaze with the sudden intimation of guilt, of some violation; but I sensed no anger in him, no understanding, only a blank curiosity as if he were seeing her for the first time.

"What's wrong with it, it looks fine," he said finally.

There was a moment of silence, of suspension, a sort of gap we wavered in for an instant, but then it passed and the matter seemed dropped. Then when my uncle and aunt came over for lunch, Tsia Taormina, with her typical blundering good intentions, made a big show of praising Rita for how pretty she looked.

"*Ma guarda*, where did this come from, ah? Someone must have bought you a little gift."

But Rita seemed traumatized by now with her confusion, shying away from her in timid silence.

"*Dai*, Taormí," Aunt Teresa said, letting Tsia Taormina's comments fade into the usual indifference people showed her, "give me a hand with these dishes."

Afterwards Aunt Teresa took me aside.

"Tell me the truth, Vittorio, you bought it for her, didn't you, you took the money from my purse. *Dai*, I won't say anything to your father."

But the thing had got so out of hand now that I burst into tears.

"What a crazy thing, did you think we'd let her go naked?" she said, and took me in her arms, the first time in years she'd done such a thing. Yet I didn't understand this forgiveness in her, the unreasonableness of it, felt robbed by it somehow of whatever had been right and true, had been defiantly my own, in what I had done.

From then on Aunt Teresa began to pay more attention to Rita, coming for her in the morning to look after her, taking her out with her when she went to work. But though this was what I'd thought I'd wanted, now I resented the implication that we hadn't managed all right without her. She got me to bring children's books home from the school library, sitting with Rita at the kitchen table sometimes after supper and sounding out their stories to her in her awkward, ill-sounding English; and Rita would sit silent and still, the patient student, staring up wide-eyed at the pictures my aunt showed her or watching her face to see how lips formed around words. There seemed an element of subterfuge in Rita's attentiveness, a careful stifling of herself as if she'd understood that my aunt's ministrations were a kind of performance she had to be grateful for; and I cherished this small resistance in her, glad that I saw it when Aunt Teresa did not, simply forged on with her lessons until she herself grew tired or bored. But then gradually some more instinctive bond began to take shape between them. I'd come into the greenhouses sometimes after school to find Aunt Teresa silently at work while Rita played at the end of her row, the two of them lost in their own thoughts but still seeming always aware in some animal way of each other's presence; and I felt cheated then by Rita's not seeing how easy it was for Aunt Teresa to be kind to her, how little she risked, began to look always for the small oversight or cruelty in my aunt that would betray the fragile trust Rita had begun to show in her, hated that meanness in me but knew with the stubborn sureness of childhood that Rita was the only thing that truly belonged to me.

But in the end even when my aunt's small betrayals did come, her fits of irritation, her inattentiveness, her beginning to treat Rita as if she were any normal child, there was no atonement in them for me. I'd watch Rita's spirits fall at some refusal or reprimand, Aunt Teresa simply carrying on oblivious, though for Rita, who had experience neither of scolding nor of forgiveness, each of these little slights was like a catastrophe. But she'd be inconsolable then if I tried to reach her, warding me off in her stubborn silence as if even the slender, precarious love of Aunt Teresa was worth more to her than the whole of my own.

VIII

When by the winter the new greenhouse was finally built and planted, my father seemed to give in at last to a grudging satisfaction, relaxing into his accomplishment now that the threat of it had passed.

"You're a big shot now," Tsi'Alfredo said.

"*Sì*, a big shot, when the bank owns even the screwdrivers I used to put the damn thing together."

But I saw how he'd look up and down the greenhouse with an air of ownership, contented and grave, how he'd fiddle with valves and switches to make sure everything was perfect.

As part of his new expansiveness he bought a television, at long last bringing us into modernity, a squat, peg-legged General Electric we set in a corner of the living room. It seemed to shift the house's whole centre of gravity, always there as a presence, full of potential, holding more life in its tiny screen than all the empty rooms it ruled over. Within a matter of weeks it was already hard to imagine what we'd done without it, how we'd ever managed to fill in the hours between supper and bed;

and in the new window it provided on the world we seemed at once brought out of ourselves and yet made more intimate, gathering around it every night as around a fire, sealed off in the living room's sheltered space as if nothing existed beyond us, or was real.

My father exercised an unthinking tyranny over what we watched, seeming to use the television simply as a kind of soporific to ease himself into sleep after work yet showing an odd discretion in his choice of programs. Some logic governed these choices but one that appeared to have little to do with the shows' storylines, was more a matter of their tone or of the certain colouring they gave things, the police shows with their grim seriousness, the westerns with their laconic gunmen and their spare, remote worlds. Often he'd come into a show half-way through or fall asleep before the end of it as if attracted merely to its flow of images, like a cat to a moving object; but then the following week he'd have me search it out for him again, already seeing special value in it simply because it was familiar. Gradually each night of the week took on its schedule, its inevitability, one that within a few months had begun to order our time as tightly and precisely as the bells that marked out the day at St. Michael's.

In Rita this control my father had seemed to become the focus of some hard, child's resentment. She had quickly developed a proprietary attachment to the TV, settling in front of it after breakfast and still there before it when I returned from school, ignoring me then as if to make the point that she had something of her own now, didn't need me; and then in the evening she'd hover in the living room in silent protest, stubbornly protecting her claim against my father's temporary usurpation.

Sunday afternoons, though, Rita and I had the television to ourselves, my aunt and my father usually out and the two of us settling furtive in my father's recliner to watch it, the afternoon stretching before us in dead Sunday repose. I took a guilty pleasure in these afternoons, some wariness between me and Rita seeming briefly to fall away then, the television a sort of point of neutral contact that brought us together exactly by freeing us of each other, Rita beside me neither affectionate nor not, simply there in her small unmindfulness. We watched the afternoon movies on Channel 4, tearjerkers mainly, with always some wrenching parting or separation, an accident, a death; Rita followed them with a quiet absorption yet remained also canny somehow, merely curious, even when my own throat was tight with suppressed tears seeming always outside the emotion of them as if she'd understood better than I had that the things we were watching weren't real.

These movies led on into the first shows of Sunday evening, "Lassie," "The World of Disney"; but there was always the tension then of my father's imminent return from the club. We'd hear his truck come up the drive, hear the back door slam, his footfall on the steps; then in the kitchen he'd linger absently a moment watching Aunt Teresa preparing supper, make some gruff, perhaps almost good-humoured criticism or complaint, his way of greeting her. But since Aunt Teresa usually simply ignored him or made some dismissive response he'd turn finally toward the living room, his air of tired contentment at once falling away because Rita was there; and then with the same instinctiveness with which he drew around himself his sudden grimness he'd have me change the channel, seeming thus to empty us from the room, to reclaim it from us.

Rita would sit in silent resistance during all this, shutting out my father as surely as he did her. But then once he'd come something would crumble in her and she'd withdraw into her hurt as into a tiny fortress. All evening then I'd be aware of her sullen aloofness, its rebuke of me for my own failure to prevail against my father in some way. She seemed to understand how I betrayed her: I wanted to think of my father as someone who could not be opposed, whose will would forge on against any resistance from me like a juggernaut; but it was my resistance that wasn't sure enough, that was blunted every time I saw the grimness that came over him in Rita's presence, some part of me then always siding with him over Rita.

In the end it was Rita who prevailed against him, simply pressing herself up against the television one Sunday when my father told me to change the channel. By the time I'd understood that I ought to have pulled her away at once, made her invisible, it seemed her presence there had already become too undeniable.

"What's the matter with her?" my father said.

But he seemed to regard her with an odd detachment: she might have been merely some strange inanimate thing that had blown up against the television by chance.

"She wants to watch 'Lassie,'" I said, emptying my voice of commitment. "It's a story about a dog."

"*Dai*, change it, she has all day to watch television."

But Rita held her ground, her shoulder pressed into the dials and her back to us in sulky stubbornness, closing us out. She seemed so vulnerable there in her child's gargantuan wilfulness, so pathetic, that I couldn't bring myself to oppose her. For an instant we seemed suspended as in a dream, all possibilities open.

"*Mbeh*, tell her to get out of the way then, we can't see anything like that."

This was as far as he'd ever come to ceding anything to her yet he seemed to relax into his concession as though some threat in her had been diminished by it.

"What a stupid thing," he said afterwards. "That a dog can do all that."

But Rita had won her point: he'd been forced to see her, to react, and yet the world hadn't come apart.

"Always that damn dog on the television," he'd say coming in now. But then he'd settle into his chair and watch the show through with us to the end, boyish there in his masked sceptical absorption.

"You're worse than the kids, glued to that damn thing," my aunt said. "And then you complain that the supper's cold."

"Why don't you just make it earlier, you know they always watch that show. Six o'clock is when other people have supper – there's no reason we have to eat in the middle of the night on Sundays."

"Who, other people? I think that television is starting to rot your brain."

All the same she took him at his word, spitefully scrupulous, calling him at the club now if he wasn't home by six. It was an unheard-of hour for us, the sun then still out when we sat down to eat – after years of living by its rhythms there seemed something oddly luxurious in resisting it, some shedding of our habitual immigrant unrefinement.

We seemed to enter then for a few months, on through that fall and into the winter, a period of uncommon stability in the family, a kind of attenuation or truce as if after years of holding ourselves in rigid defence it was no longer clear what enemy we faced. On the surface nothing much had changed – we had our habits by then, the careful balancing of avoidance and engagement, our ways of talking, the things that were never said; and yet something had gone, some sense of threat. There was a calm in us that seemed to reach a kind of pinnacle on Sunday evenings, our early suppers, the long evening of television that stretched before us, and I had a sense then that perhaps things could be all right with us, that we could live in a kind of protective normalcy like a television family. It was almost possible to ignore in all this how Rita still hovered at the edges of us, more accepted now and yet for that perhaps more truly forgotten, for the moment claiming no special attention from us and yet seeming thus to be merely continuing some silent protest against us.

Rita turned six in the spring. It was a kind of shock to think of her aging, having to go to school, requiring things outside us like any regular child.

Then one day not long after her birthday I returned from school to find her playing with a collie on the front lawn, a ghostly double of Lassie like a gift some fairy had brought.

"Where did it come from?"

"A man brought her in his truck."

"What man?"

"A man with glasses. He said I could keep her."

But the story sounded so improbable I thought Rita had made it up, that the dog had simply strayed from a neighbouring farm.

My father thought someone must have been trying to get rid of it. That was the usual way of getting rid of a dog, by driving it out to some distant concession road and abandoning it there.

"Oh, *Leh-sie*!" he said when he saw it. He checked to make sure it was male – he didn't like females because of the trouble with litters.

"*Mbeh*, we'll see how long he sticks around."

But Lassie showed no signs of wanting to leave us. His first days with us he slept right up against the back door, as if afraid we might try to steal away from him in the night; and then in the mornings he'd be waiting for us there when we came out, manic after his long deprivation, bursting with his need for us. When it grew clear that he planned to stay my father finally built a doghouse for him from some scraps of old plywood, even took the trouble to paint it and to cover the roof with some shingles he found in the barn. He set the house in the courtyard against the back wall of the kiln, where it looked, with its fresh white walls and shingled roof, like a tiny mirror image of our own.

We all seemed to expect some crucial flaw to reveal itself in Lassie to explain his abandonment. Yet he took to the farm as if he'd been born to it, understood at once where he was allowed and where not, didn't bother the chickens or the cats, didn't chase cars or burrow in the fields or get in our way when we worked, his sudden appearance like a kind of miracle, as if he'd somehow leapt from the television into life. Only Rita seemed to see nothing unlikely in his having come, taking to him with a child's unthinking acceptance that what was normal was simply whatever happened.

"Did you see the man who brought him? What did he say to you?"

"I don't remember."

Then when Lassie had been with us only a few weeks he was hit by a truck. From the boiler room I heard the long hard blare of a horn, a screech of brakes, came out to see Rita racing from across the road toward our lawn and Lassie a blur of motion behind her. The truck caught Lassie broadside and flung him a good dozen feet into the grass at the side of the road, where he lay unmoving, his head twisted unnaturally to one side. For an instant we seemed to remain frozen where we were, Rita on the lawn, me at the boiler-room door, the truck at its odd angle on the road; and then finally the truck's driver climbed down from the cab. He was an enormous man, the fat layered so thickly around his belly and thighs he swayed like a water-filled balloon when he moved. He came over to Lassie and shook his head slowly, one hand wiping sweat from the back of his neck with a dirty handkerchief.

"She just came out like that," he said, in a throaty monotone. But I wasn't sure if he meant Rita or the dog.

My father had come out by then. He stood over Lassie and grunted with a kind of knowing grimness, as if he'd expected all along that Lassie would have a bad end. I was afraid he had seen what had happened and would blame Rita, but Rita had vanished.

"These damn dogs," he said. "One is stupider than the next." He'd taken on the special tone that he used with non-Italians, forcedly casual and authoritative, though it seemed oddly misplaced on this mountainous, thick-voiced man.

"Nice dog too," the man said. "It's too bad."

My father and I carried Lassie into the orchard, his body still warm but limp as a sack.

"Dig a hole for it," my father said, "or it'll stink the whole place up."

When I'd come back with a spade Rita had appeared again, was sitting in the dirt next to Lassie petting him and murmuring like a lullaby some lines from a nonsense song Tsia Taormina had taught her.

"Stupid, it's dead," I said. "Can't you see it's dead? Anyway it's your fault."

But Rita kept up her chant. I started digging, filled suddenly with an unfocused anger, then noticed a twitch in Lassie's back leg. I thought it must be an after-death spasm of the sort animals had when they were slaughtered; but the leg began to paw the air slowly with the control of something alive, and then as casually as if he were simply rising from a sleep Lassie lifted his head, blinked, and rose unsteadily to his feet, whimpering and bobbing his head toward me with a guilty mournfulness.

"Can you believe that." My father was standing suddenly at the edge of the orchard. "I never saw a thing like that before."

Afterwards it was hard to shake that first sense of wonder at seeing Lassie rise up again as he had, even my father growing animated whenever he retold the story.

"He just got a knock on the head, that's all," Aunt Teresa said.

"*Sì*, let's see if you get up again after a knock like that."

But Rita seemed to accept Lassie's reawakening as unquestioningly as she'd accepted his arrival, all that mattered being the fact of his return, as if it hadn't occurred to her at all that death could be some final, absolute state, beyond any redemption.

Summer began with a torrid heat: by midday the air hung so heavy and still that time seemed suspended, poised like a calm before a storm that would never come. My body appeared to have bloated with the swelter, to have become a dull, dead weight I'd been strangely burdened with, waited to shed now like a cocoon; at night sometimes it shifted against Rita's and the muggy heat of our closeness made me dream this dead casing around me was slowly expanding, was threatening to swallow me in its folds of thickened flesh.

The weather made us all irritable; because of it we had to wake at five so we'd be finished our work in the greenhouses before the heat there became unbearable. Afterwards there were still the beans to be picked, the tomatoes to be hoed, the days stretching on infinitely, separated only by the dead sleep we fell into almost at once when we'd finished supper.

But Rita spent her days with Lassie, wandering the farm, lolling in the sun on the lawn. They were inseparable now, Lassie hanging on her with a blind solicitude, perhaps imagining in his animal's version of things that Rita after all had somehow called him back from the dead.

"*Ecco la principessa!*" Aunt Teresa said to Rita. "You're not a baby now, you should be out there working like Fiorina."

But there seemed an acceptance that Rita had a kind of immunity from work, that to have expected her to take a role in our lives would have been an admission that she was part of the family.

Because of the heat we'd begun to take siestas after lunch, stretching out on the strip of lawn that flanked the courtyard under the shade of the maple trees there. My father played lazy games of fetch with Lassie or wrestled with him, good-humouredly aggressive, Rita sitting apart then, hunched in resentful silence at my father's roughness. But during one of these bouts my father crossed some line and Lassie snapped suddenly at his hand. My father was outraged: he struck a full-handed blow against Lassie's head, then another, Lassie bolting in cringing, yelping shame to his doghouse.

"*Brutta bestia diavolo!*"

A drop of blood had formed at the joint of my father's thumb.

"Next time I'll crack his skull."

For days afterwards Lassie hung close to his house, approaching my father only in cowering repentance. My father teased him, seemed to have put his anger behind him; but there was an edge of contempt now in his baiting, a kind of disowning. I had the sense that some balance had been subtly altered, that Lassie had become contaminated by what had happened, like a charm or spell suddenly broken or gone awry. Even Aunt Teresa, who didn't like animals much to begin with, was constantly shooing cats from between her feet and had always refused to help my father with his chickens, had begun to lose patience with him.

"Oh, *frustilà*." And she'd swat him away like a fly.

More and more now the perception seemed to be that Lassie was not so much our dog as Rita's, was a kind of indulgence she'd been allowed. Rita herself brazenly colluded in this shift: after my father's outburst she began to conspire openly to keep him from us, leaving the table early after lunch to lead Lassie away from the courtyard before we came out.

"Is it possible she can't help around the house sometimes?" my father said. "Her and that damn dog –"

But he said nothing to Rita.

Then he noticed how in Lassie's absence the cats had begun to gravitate toward the leftovers Aunt Teresa or I set out for him after lunch.

"We'll see, we'll see if she goes on like this. And then after she brings him food from the house as if nobody sees what she's doing."

I was surprised my father watched her closely enough to detect such small delinquencies in her, that she could matter that much to him; yet still he said nothing to her, seemed walled up so surely in the silence that separated him from her that his anger couldn't do anything more than relentlessly feed on its own impotence.

"My father's angry at you," I said to Rita, wanting the words to be adequate, to cut into her. But I saw from the fear in her eyes that she didn't understand at all the power she had over my father, remembered that she was merely a child, that her mind could only work with the twisted, uncertain logic of one.

"It's because of the cats," I said, relenting. "Because you let them eat Lassie's food and then bring him stuff from the house."

But Rita, as if she'd understood only that the cats, somehow, had been the cause of my father's anger, began now a silent war against them, keeping up a constant vigil around Lassie's food dish and not suffering them to come close to Lassie at all. The cats, for their part, having early got over their suspicion of Lassie, learning to respond to his own overtures of friendship with a languorous nonchalance, now seemed to grow wary again. There were as many as a dozen of them on the farm at the time, part of a dynasty left to us when we'd taken it over – my father bred them like a kind of livestock, to keep down the rats, searching their litters out when they gave birth and setting one or two aside to carry on the line before drowning the rest; though where before they'd been as ubiquitous as air, now they grew strangely reclusive, could only be seen fleetingly rounding the corners of buildings or staring unfriendly from their dark retreats in the boiler room and barn.

But it turned out that some other terror had begun to conspire with Rita against the cats, one turning up dead one day in a corner of the barn. His corpse was so matted and stiff it might have been lying there already for weeks or months; but then another turned up a few days later in the bushes near the irrigation pond, this one still fresh, its neck showing teeth marks from an attack.

"Some damn fox or something," my father said, and he reinforced the fence around the chicken run behind the barn.

But he'd begun to watch Lassie, noting the wide arc the cats made around him now whenever they passed. When we found a third cat dead in the boiler room my father carried it out to Lassie and flung it in front of him. Lassie stooped toward it warily, sniffed, whimpered, stepped back to bark, whimpered again.

"Always playing the innocent," my father said. "We'll see if you're so innocent."

The next-door neighbour, Mr. Olson, said he hadn't seen a fox in our parts for fifteen years or more; the neighbour across the road, Mr. Dyck, had seen a racoon around his place in the previous weeks, but my father said he'd never heard of a racoon killing a cat. There were the other dogs on the concession, a vicious German shepherd the Kohls owned, a few others, but most had been around for years and had never come near our farm.

"He's a smart one, that one," Tsi'Umberto said. "He's just playing with you, you'll see he's the one."

Then a couple of weeks passed without any more killings, and in the flurry of work we had then with the end of summer it seemed the matter had been forgotten. But one morning my father returned to the house from his egg run to the barn redfaced with anger – something had broken into the chicken coop in the night. Some of the chickens had got out through the hole that had been burrowed under the outside fence and were wandering bewildered in the orchard behind the barn or scavenging among the bushes at the edge of the irrigation pond.

"Maybe it was the racoon that was at Dyck's," I said.

"*Sì*, a racoon was going to dig a hole like that."

When we began to round up the chickens, we found one dead in the weeds at the edge of the pond, its neck broken.

"*Cchella bestia*, I'll send them both to the devil, her and that stupid dog after her."

In the evening, still raw with his anger, my father drove off with Lassie in his truck. Rita kept vigil by the back window till he returned, alone, an hour or so later, then closed herself away in our room without a word. I expected to find her crying there when I came in but the room was quiet.

"Are you okay?"

But she didn't respond, merely lay there staring into the dark in unfathomable silence.

For several days afterwards she didn't come out of the house at all, didn't speak, simply sat watching TV the whole day with an air of entranced withdrawal.

"All this *commedia* about a dog," Aunt Teresa said, not to Rita but to me, seeming to try to put some more normal cast on Rita's strange mourning. "She should learn that she can't always have her own way."

But we had come full circle now, had retreated through what had happened back to our separate glooms, to the familiar tension in the house, my father's familiar shutting down.

On the Sunday before Labour Day I took Rita to a matinée in town to try to break the spell of her bereavement; but the entire time she kept up her eerie silence, withdrawn into some private world, so empty of curiosity or desire it seemed she might crumble at a touch. Walking home we cut across a corn field, zig-zagging up its long gloomy rows, cut off then from the landscape by a thick wall of browning stalks and leaves; and for an instant I felt a peculiar self-consciousness at being alone with her there in that musty, becalmed silence, had a sudden awareness of her in her unknownness, heard her footsteps behind me like my own shadow suddenly taken solid shape and become a stranger to me.

IX

Some curse seemed to linger over us in the next weeks, an early frost leaving blistery lesions on the tomatoes and then two of our pickers quitting because of the trouble sorting the bad from the good. My father's black mood grew blacker, something we had to accommodate now like another person living in the house. He'd begun to have stomach pains of some sort, eating special meals of milk and Campbell's soup, the empty tins beginning to spot our garbage like odd bits of decoration. I imagined some tiny fire burning relentless in the pit of him, his inward-turned anger slowly beginning to feed on his own flesh.

From this darkness Rita and I set out for school every day like fugitives, standing rigid in the September chill to wait for the bus, our worn, unstylish clothes appearing to mark us as brother and sister. For the first week or so Rita clung to me like a frightened animal, the world, the newness of it, its enormity, seeming to panic her like sudden sight after blindness. Outside the unquestioning habitualness of home, what we thought of as normal there, she seemed a misshapen thing, as palely vulnerable and frail as a plant grown in insufficient light, ruined perhaps by the strange hermetic shadow-life we'd given her. Fiorina – Flora, she was called now – shunned her, had her own friends, her tiny world, flaunting it before Rita even as she ignored her; I could see the veiled understanding in Rita of how things were, felt repaid now for my own first contempt for Flora's brothers years before.

But then Rita began to make friends. There was a girl named Elena who had assumed a kind of responsibility for her, at recess taking her down with her to the front end of the schoolyard where the other grade-one girls played. She seemed an unlikely match for Rita, tall and pretty and well-dressed, with blonde, picture-book hair that cascaded down to her shoulders in long, tended curls; I expected some cruel streak to reveal itself, some town girl's bullyish condescension, but she remained simply protective, without guile, using the quiet authority she had over the other girls to make sure Rita was included in their games. I'd see the two of them wandering alone through the schoolyard sometimes, looking oddly intimate and mature, Elena's arm locked in Rita's in a way that made me think of the young women who in the evenings would stroll conspiratorial through the streets of Valle del Sole.

On one of these walks Rita and Elena came up to where I played field hockey with the other grade-eight boys, Elena approaching me during a lull in the game, gravely formal and polite.

"My mother said to ask if Rita can sleep at our house on the weekend."

I felt a familiar shame, the sense of confronting a custom we'd not been initiated into, that couldn't be evaded without making clear what sort of family we belonged to.

"I dunno. I have to ask at home."

The question had been put so officially I felt obliged to bring it to Aunt Teresa. I thought she'd object, with an immigrant's narrow view of what was acceptable, but she seemed to share my own fear of appearing not to know how things were done here, seemed uneasy about denying Rita anything when we gave her so little.

"Who is this girl?"

"I dunno, she's just a girl. Her name's Elena."

"What's her last name?"

"Amherst or something like that."

She seemed to waver an instant.

"Then just make sure she has some extra clothes to take with her."

And on Friday Rita and Elena set off hand in hand up the school driveway toward Elena's house in town, Rita with her plastic bag of clothes like some street urchin Elena had taken in.

No one, though, had told my father about this arrangement. I'd somehow imagined Rita's absence would go unremarked but when we sat down to supper Friday evening her empty place was like a hole in the room.

"Where's the girl?" my father said.

"She's at some friend's house."

"What friend?" The anger rose in him as his mind took in the full force of the outrage. "Who told her to go there? That's what we need now, to have her running around to other people's houses like a gypsy!"

"Always the same story with you!" my aunt said. "What did you think, that we could keep her locked up in the house all her life like an animal?"

And she managed to stave him off for the moment, setting his guilt before his rage like a wall.

The bad luck that had begun with the early frost hadn't yet run its course: toward mid-October I awoke one morning to the wail of a siren to find the boiler room was burning, one side of it already a mass of gnarled flame in the morning dark. For an instant it seemed unthinkable that the fire could be real, that I wasn't still in bed asleep and dreaming, couldn't somehow simply clear the fire from my window like a television image. But a dozen firemen had come, their engines glistening red under a drizzle of rain, lights flashing, and it was their presence that started the panic in me, as if they had made the fire real by believing in it. They were working in rough formation around the fire's periphery but seemed dwarfed by it like playthings, with their toy-yellow firemen's suits, their tiny engines and tools, the jets from their hoses arcing into the flames ineffectual as air. Some of them, oddly casual, were milling around the end of our driveway or leaning against their engines as though simply waiting the fire out.

Aunt Teresa was standing in her housecoat on the front lawn, her arms hugged to her chest, her hair falling in wet strands in the drizzle; but my father was nowhere to be seen. I opened my window, a burst of hot air mingling strangely with the chill of rain, and Aunt Teresa glanced toward me without speaking. Then for a long time we stood staring at the fire joined by the silent awareness of each other's presence. There seemed nothing to be done, nothing but to watch with a horrified fascination the damage fire could do. It seemed to blot out the world, to still time somehow, as if we'd remain forever caught in the endless moment of it as in a photograph. I could make out details in it now, the mesh of pipes and charred beams, the elephantine outline of the boiler; in the force of it the ends of the three old greenhouses had collapsed, further up their roofs glowing eerily orange from refracted light.

Across the road Mr. Dyck and his wife were huddled beneath an umbrella speaking with Tsi'Umberto, their faces flashing red from the engine lights. Their muted voices reached me oddly resonant above the sound of rain and the dull roar of the fire.

"I guess he tried to go in there but there wasn't much you could do by then."

Rita had awoken. She stood beside me staring out silent at the fire.

"Why don't they stop it?" She seemed to be trying to gauge its enormity, what responsibility she might bear for it.

"Stupid, what do you think they're trying to do?"

When the fire had begun to subside an explosion sent great tongues of flame shooting upward again. The firemen drew back; one of them came toward my aunt.

"Ma'am, why don't you go on inside," he said. "And you might ask your husband if there's anything else in there likely to blow up."

But afterwards the fire began to burn itself out. The world seemed gradually to take shape again, the lightening dawn, the spare, grey stillness of the skeletal wreckage slowly emerging from the dying flames. I wanted to hold off this re-entry to things, didn't want time to move forward again or the firemen to be gone. Already they'd begun to reload one of the engines, the truck slowly gathering round itself its hoses and men; and then finally it backed into our driveway to turn itself around and pulled away with a heavy crunch of gravel.

The rain had stopped now, a rim of orange sunlight pushing up against a filament of cloud that had spread itself along the horizon. In the boiler room's wreckage a few wisps of steamy smoke were still rising from a heap of charred wood where the coal room had been, but the rest of what remained sat in damp torpor, unreal against the morning light, the boiler, with its umbilical network of pipes, hunched stolid amidst the ruins like a brooding monster. Only the far end of the building, where my father's office had been, was still partly intact, the wall there left standing like a false front in a western, blackened beams banked up against it and its windows, shattered now, simply passages from open air to open air.

One of the firemen had come up the driveway toward the back door and returned now with a slow gait to the remaining engine.

"I don't know what he's crying about, he'll get the insurance," he said to one of the others. "Half the time they set these things themselves anyway."

When they'd gone I went out to the kitchen. Aunt Teresa was at the table there, her hair still wet with rain.

"Should we go to school?" I said.

"What are you going to do here?"

When Rita and I went to leave, we found my father sitting on the basement steps, his face in his hands. He looked like a character in a movie, James Dean or Marlon Brando, sitting out on some tenement fire-escape in some nameless American city; but he was sobbing, almost silently, just a hint of a thin wheezing like someone struggling for breath. I thought of the bus coming, of people seeing somehow in the boiler room's yawning ruins our humiliation, my aunt sitting blankly in the kitchen, my father crying on the basement steps.

For the next several days Tsi'Umberto's family came to help us with work on the farm. With no way to heat them the plants in the greenhouses had to be stripped; we salvaged what fruit we could, picking it green and setting it on a bed of straw in Tsi'Umberto's small greenhouse to ripen. Our new greenhouse had been almost completely spared, the plants there still fresh, only the corridor that connected it to the boiler room damaged, the glass shattered and the grape vines my father had planted there charred black. The others, though, had felt the full blast of the fire, the plants singed to the far end of them from its tunneling heat and heaps of glass even yards from the boiler room bubbled and twisted like melted plastic.

But we never spoke about the fire, seeming to feel in it not so much tragedy as disgrace; and the mess it had left, the shattered glass, the half-fallen walls, remained as it was, festering there at the front of our farm like an untended wound. For a few days some of the cats wandered the ruins as if they could not understand how something solid and permanent had simply vanished, how whatever memory or image they held of some familiar nesting place could find no correlation now in this charred wreckage. But gradually they migrated to the barn, Aunt Teresa setting their meals out now in the abandoned dish that still sat in front of the doghouse.

With no more greenhouse work to be done after the plants had been stripped our lives appeared broken somehow, without routine, without purpose. Aunt Teresa got work at Longo's Produce again but my father couldn't seem to form any project, spent his days working alone at useless jobs in the barn as if trying to shore up what remained to him. He seemed to regard the fire as a personal affront, flushing as at an accusation when someone mentioned it to him at the barber-shop a couple of weeks after it.

"We were just asking," the barber said, in English. He was a man from Valle del Sole, gregarious and worldly, though the look of him, the thickness of his hands, the strange tight ridges of flesh around his neck, always conjured for me, with the immediacy of a smell, all the village's hard peasant crudeness. "Anyhow the insurance it's gonna pay for it, you were gonna have to tear it down yourself one of these days."

"Maybe that's how some people think about things," my father said.

And he retreated further into his gloom, seeming to feel in this casual public scrutiny some last stripping away of his dignity.

Then like a twist in a movie, the unlikely circling back to some crucial half-forgotten thing, Lassie suddenly reappeared on the farm: he was simply there in the courtyard one Saturday morning, spectral, rummaging without conviction in the food dish near his old house.

"That damn dog, *per la madonna* –"

But it was almost a relief to see my father's anger finally find a clear object.

"If you're going to get rid of it," Aunt Teresa said, "at least do it before the girl sees it. We don't want all that nonsense again."

My father went out to the garage and came out a moment later with his shotgun, Aunt Teresa and I watching him from the kitchen window. He seemed ready to shoot Lassie on the spot, had already cracked open the barrel and was slipping in a cartridge. Lassie had begun to come toward him, tentative, but when my father pointed the barrel at him he seemed finally to understand what was happening and bolted toward the corner of the kiln. My father fired, recoiled; the shot seemed to graze Lassie's backside, leaving him cowering half-prostrate against the kiln's side wall.

But Rita had come to the window at the sound of the shot. Before we could stop her she had run out to the courtyard, reaching Lassie before my father had had time to reload. My father stood not a dozen feet from them, the gun half-poised in his hands. He said something to Rita that I couldn't make out, but Rita remained where she was, her arms clutched to Lassie's neck.

Aunt Teresa opened the window.

"Mario, for Christ's sake, leave them!"

My father struck Rita hard with the back of a hand. One of us should have gone out then, done something, but we seemed paralyzed; and then everything happened very quickly. There was a sort of scuffle, Lassie suddenly lunging, teeth bared, toward my father with Rita still clutched to him, and then somehow my father's gun fell away and he'd pulled off his belt, was lashing out with it, at Lassie, at Rita, everything happening in an eerie soundlessness, only Lassie's low growl, Rita's truncated gasp each time the belt struck her.

Aunt Teresa had bent to the window screen again, her face flushed.

"Mario, stop, for the love of God, you're going to kill her!"

And there was such hysteria in her voice I thought that he would, felt my stomach churn as if the house had abruptly pitched forward like a ship in a storm.

Aunt Teresa was outside. Rita had fallen to the ground now and Aunt Teresa scooped her up and away while my father was still fighting back Lassie, finally landing a kick to his ribs that sent him scrambling down the lane toward the back field.

Aunt Teresa had come inside, Rita clinging to her seeming mangled like some doll that had been left out in the elements, her clothes smeared with dirt and blood and one cheek purpled and large, the swelling there twisting her mouth into a freakish half-smile.

She was sobbing, a low animal moan, the only sound we'd heard from her.

"That damn dog and the curse he brought with him," Aunt Teresa said.

She began to tend to Rita, dabbing iodine on the welts on her back while I held a cold cloth to her cheek to keep down the swelling. Rita's shoulders twitched each time the applicator touched her but the movement seemed disconnected from her, merely her body's reflexive shudder.

My father had gone. Through the window I'd seen him cross to the back field with his gun, and now the morning seemed to deepen its stillness as if in waiting. Finally a shot rang out, followed hard by a long animal cry, dying in waves; then a second shot, this one echoing off into silence.

X

My father drove away in his truck that morning and by the following day still hadn't returned home. Aunt Teresa made phone calls, to Tsi'Alfredo, to Tsi'Umberto, held muted conferences with them in our kitchen late into the night; but still my father didn't return. The sight of Rita brought out a grim distraction in Tsi'Alfredo.

"I hope you're not letting her go to school like that," he said, though in a tone that suggested he blamed her for what had happened.

Then on Wednesday, my father still not back yet, there was a police car in the courtyard when I came home from school. Two officers were talking to Aunt Teresa at the back door, one holding at his side my father's shotgun.

"I was telling your mother the border people took this when your father crossed into Detroit," he said, turning to me with a kind of relief, seeming to expect from me some level of understanding he hadn't been able to get from my aunt. "I guess when he didn't come back for it they thought we might want to check if there was any problem."

But Aunt Teresa remained oddly wary and unyielding, standing in half-retreat at the doorway as if to bar any entry.

"He gotta friend in Detroit," she said to him, her deficient English making her seem hopelessly backward, thickheaded. "He be back day after tomorrow."

The policeman wavered an instant.

"I guess we'll leave this with you then," he said finally, handing the gun to my aunt. "Sorry to be any bother."

As soon as the policemen had gone Aunt Teresa called Tsi'Alfredo.

"He went up to Detroit. He's probably with that guy from Rocca Secca up there, what's his name, Marcovecchio, the one he was in the army with."

Tsi'Umberto and Tsi'Alfredo came by again that night. Tsi'Alfredo had phoned Marcovecchio – yes, my father was there, had shown up Saturday night and asked Marcovecchio to help find him a job.

"And Marcovecchio, that idiot," Aunt Teresa said. "He might have tried to call us."

"*Mbeh*, who knows what went through his head when Mario showed up like that," Tsi'Alfredo said. "He probably thought he'd killed someone. Marcovecchio would know all about that, he's some big shot in the union up there. Who knows what he's got his hands into."

"It's a bad business, getting mixed up in that," Tsi'Umberto said. "Someone should go up and talk some sense into him –"

"And tell him what?" Tsi'Alfredo said. "To come back to the hell he's living in here? He's better off up there, if Marcovecchio can get him work. What will he do all winter here, go work in someone else's greenhouses like some *disgraziat'* just off the boat?"

All the same it was Tsi'Alfredo who said he'd drive to Detroit to speak to him. He went up the next day, but afterwards came back to our house alone.

"Get some clothes and things ready for him, he'll come for them on the weekend. And send the girl to stay with your brother for a couple of days."

But when Tsi'Alfredo had gone we had a phone call: it was Elena's mother. I thought it was a wrong number at first, the voice so foreign to me, my mind scrambling to account for its air of resolute familiarity.

"You must be Victor," she said, with a high, forced friendliness, chilling somehow, unreadable. "It's just that Elena's been wondering about Rita, she'd hoped to have her over again this weekend."

"She's just been sick," I said.

"I hope it's not anything serious."

"No, I think she's almost better now."

"Well I do hope she can come."

The call was so far outside the realm of how we did things in our family that I didn't know what to make of it.

"What business is it of hers?" Aunt Teresa said when I told her about it. But she seemed to feel the same unease as at the last such request, as if unable to find the clear line of logic that would allow her to impose on Rita the family's usual closed tyranny.

There were still the scratch-thin welts on Rita's back, the faint half-moon of blue beneath her eye.

"Take her with you to school tomorrow, she can go from there," Aunt Teresa said. "Anyway she's better off there for a few days with your father the way he is."

And it was as if she was sending her out like a signal of our failure, no longer trusting us to look after her.

Oddly Rita seemed the least blemished of us by what had happened, after a day or two shedding the first humiliation of her injury and putting on a child's false forbearance, sensing the shame in our furtive glances, in Aunt Teresa's brisk attentiveness to her as to a guest we had offended. Waiting for the bus the next day she seemed aware only of the reward her hurt had earned her, another weekend away.

"You shouldn't let Elena's mother see you when you're changing."

"You see me sometimes."

"That's different, I'm your brother."

And by afternoon she was gone again, retreating up the school driveway toward the high, friendly voice on the phone, the untroubled television world I imagined Elena lived in.

My father came home that night, Aunt Teresa and I steeling ourselves for his return, stripping ourselves down to a blank emotionless silence.

"If he asks where your sister is," Aunt Teresa said, "just say she's at your uncle's."

But he didn't ask. Whatever rage there'd been in him when he'd left was gone now, seemed sucked out of him, his whole body drawn and limp as if under-inflated. I worked with him for a while the next day in the new greenhouse, draining steam pipes and water lines so they wouldn't crack in the cold.

"Go on home," he said finally. "I can finish."

But he held me a moment in uncertain silence, his hands working on independent in their slow, clumsy precision.

"How's your sister?" The question seemed so hard-won that I flushed with embarrassment, felt as if he'd had to crack himself open to ask it.

"She's all right," I said.

But he was gone again before she'd returned.

My father spent the rest of the fall and then the winter in Detroit, working in one of the car plants there and boarding with his friend Marcovecchio. Every second weekend he came home, bringing laundry, workshirts, soiled overalls, all we knew of his other life, and taking back Aunt Teresa's preserves and vegetables from Tsi'Alfredo's greenhouses. Gradually a pattern developed, unspoken but somehow sanctioned, Rita's continuing stays at Elena's beginning to correspond more and more with my father's returns. I overheard Aunt Teresa sometimes on the phone in her broken English, her voice loud with the forced brightness she put on for strangers; and then Friday morning she'd have a bag ready again with Rita's clothes for another visit, my father clearly put out by these absences yet saying nothing about them, seeming to relinquish in his silence any right he had to object.

Then over Christmas Rita was allowed to spend most of the vacation at Elena's. We appeared to have surrendered an important illusion in this, that we formed a family Rita was part of. But when my father came home for his own week or so of holidays there seemed not so much anger in him at her absence as a shame, a humbling as though he were home only through our good graces. All through his stay there was an air in the house of a general unburdening, our constant awareness of Rita's absence seeming the thing that then allowed us to forget her.

Rita came home after the holidays bearing boxes of gifts the Amhersts had given her, a doll, a tinselly bracelet, a white blouse, a pleated skirt. Aunt Teresa looked them over with frowning displeasure but couldn't bring herself to tell Rita to give them back.

"You don't have to take anything from them after this, it's not right."

But there was a carefulness in how Aunt Teresa spoke to her, as if Rita held now a stranger's rights that our treatment of her would be judged against. Rita seemed to sense the shift, lording her stay at the Amhersts' over me with a childish authority.

"They had a tree, that's where we put the presents. And then we went to a different church because they're not Catholic, only Elena is because she's adopted."

She seemed merely to be repeating something she'd been told and yet toward some end, an impression or fear she wanted to plant in me.

"What happened to her real parents?"

"I dunno, she doesn't have them any more."

I began to see Elena differently after that, more dangerous somehow, more like Rita, imagined some whispering conspiracy between the two of them that they'd been slowly unfolding since their first coming together. They had friends at school, seemed to fit in, had a group of girls they played with whom they seemed the leaders of; and yet there was something not quite right in this, an apartness as if they were merely feigning their normalcy. Rita was almost bullyish with these other friends, so different than at home, playing with a reckless aggression that left her covered in bruises and scrapes; but then she and Elena would be off on one of their walks putting the others behind them like indulgences they'd grown tired of, joined then in what seemed an ominous complicity.

Their walks sometimes took them to the back of the school-yard where Johnny Elias and his group hung out, sneaking cigarettes there behind the shelter of a workshed. I'd suffered a hundred humiliations from Johnny over my years at St. Michael's, the one time we'd actually come to blows Johnny overwhelming me in an instant, his body unleashing itself on me with a single sudden blow of skilful violence. But Rita and Elena seemed drawn to him, hovering at the edges of his group as if weighing its promise against its threat.

"Hey girls," Johnny would call out, seeming amused by them, by the couple they formed. "How's your *zubbrah* today?"

I saw them linger sometimes half the lunch hour with him, always in half-retreat and yet held there by his teasing badger-ing, resented this power they allowed Johnny over them, the ammunition they gave him to hurt me.

"Vic-tore, my son, that's some sister you got there. She's going to be a real looker."

But still Rita and Elena continued to gravitate toward the back of the yard, seeming to be fleeing a boredom, with their games and other friends, with their put-on six-year-old lives, the things inside them that found no place there.

In February I was called down to the principal's office. Rita and Elena were there, Rita sitting demurely in a chair by one wall, contrite or feigning contriteness, Elena straight-backed beside her like a chaperon. The principal, Mr. Pearson, held his hand out to me as to an adult.

"Please, have a seat."

Mr. Pearson had been with the school three years or so, taking over after Father Mackinnon had been transferred. With his sharper features, his narrow eyes, the slight hook of his chin, he had seemed then to replace Father Mackinnon just as the stern portrait of Pope Paul had replaced John in our hallway a year or so before; but under him we'd entered a period of odd leniency, the strap eliminated, the sisters increasingly replaced with lay teachers, the posts in the schoolyard that divided the girls' side from the boys' removed.

There was a package of cigarettes on Mr. Pearson's desk, Rothmans, my father's brand.

"It seems your sister and her friend were found in the school-yard with these," Mr. Pearson said. He swivelled toward Rita and Elena, frowning down on them. "A serious offence, very serious indeed. Normally it would require at the very least a week's suspension."

But it was clear already from the forced drama of his tone that Rita and Elena were in no real danger. Even they seemed to have understood this, sitting there in their careful attitudes of repentance.

"Do you understand, girls, what a serious thing it is you've done here?"

"Yes, sir," Elena said.

"Rita?"

"Yes, sir."

He let them off with a week of detentions, to be served during lunch hour, threatened no meetings with parents, no letters home. But when he dismissed them he asked me to stay behind.

"I'd like to have a word with you."

Some energy seemed to pass out of him when they'd gone. He paced the room a moment and stopped to stare out his window, looking oddly forlorn there against the desolation of the empty schoolyard.

"You know, Victor," he said finally, "I should tell you this isn't the first time I've had to speak to your sister. She's very disruptive in class, it seems. I thought I should talk to you about that."

I tried to guess what he wanted from me, what I might have done wrong.

"She's not like that at home, sir."

"I see."

He sat again, removing his glasses an instant to rub the bridge of his nose. Something in his eyes then, suddenly bared like that in their startling blue, gave me the sense that he was about to betray me in some way.

"Victor, I should be honest with you, Elena's parents have spoken with me. They think there may be some problems at home for Rita. What I mean is that your father doesn't treat Rita the way he might treat – well, the way he might treat you, for instance. Does any of this make any sense to you?"

He appeared genuinely troubled now, wanting an answer. The air in the room seemed to thicken.

"You see Elena's parents seem to feel that your father is, perhaps, well – *mistreating* her in some way."

His voice had grown strained, almost whispery. It seemed to reach out and touch me like a hand, dangerous, insistent.

"Victor, do you understand what I'm asking you?"

"My father isn't home much any more. He's been working in Detroit and stuff."

"Yes. I see."

He leaned slowly back in his chair, seeming to draw away with him for the time the painful intimacy of a moment before.

"Victor, does your father ever object when Rita stays over at Elena's?"

"No, sir." The question relieved me, as if it somehow cancelled out the one before it. "He doesn't say anything about it."

"And how would you feel if Rita were – well, if she were to stay at the Amhersts' from now on? I mean, if she were to always stay there, if she didn't come home any more?"

I stared at the floor, my mind blank as static, straining to measure the gravity of my response.

"I don't know, sir," I said.

There was a long silence between us. He rose and stood at the window again.

"You've been a very good student," he said finally. "We ought to have moved you back up with the kids your own age."

I'd expected some little talk from him, some adult's attempt at consolation or advice. But he offered only this compliment, generous, superfluous, seemed to have understood how little he could do to help me.

He took up the pack of cigarettes on his desk.

"I guess you better put these back wherever Rita got them from."

Rita's stays at Elena's lengthened. I said nothing to Aunt Teresa yet it seemed she was aware of this slow defection, had capitulated to it as to something no longer within her control. It was to our house now that Rita seemed to come as a visitor, our routines shifting briefly to accommodate her, her remaining hangers of clothes in the bedroom closet kept there like things in storage. Between us there was an awkwardness like the forced intimacy of strangers, our silent morning preparations for school, our shared bed.

The house seemed held in a state of waiting, for something to change, to be over. With no work to be done on the farm I spent afternoons watching TV, the endless sitcoms that played on the Windsor station, the afternoon then merging seamlessly with the evening; I had only this awareness of home now, the long hours of television that filled my time there, the small hollowness that took shape in me every day and then its guilty relief in the living room's darkness. I stayed up for the late movie sometimes, sneaking cigarettes from the cartons my father kept in his room and drinking half-glasses of watered-down wine. There were always the women in these movies, tight-dressed and sly or innocent, their untouchable closeness, the longing they left in me like fever; and afterwards, if Rita was home, I delayed going to bed, aware of her sleeping there, of her body, its pale unknowing slenderness and heat. There was a careful protocol now around our dressing and undressing, a charged, unspoken avoidance: we seemed to see ourselves suddenly as others might, to have the sense of some audience gauging our normalcy.

There was no certain moment that marked Rita's departure from us, only her lengthening visits to the Amhersts, Aunt Teresa's silent complicity in them, supportive or submissive, I was never sure which. But then finally one of her absences stretched on a week, then two, until all our house still held of her, her lingering smell on her pillow, her few remaining clothes, seemed merely remnants, no longer able to hold the shape of some impending return.

XI

My father came back from Detroit for good in early May. The day after his return Aunt Teresa enlisted Tsi'Alfredo to come by to tell him what had happened. The task seemed to irk him, set as he always was on keeping problems within the family.

"They want to keep her," he said. He referred to Rita as "*cchella catrara*," "that girl," never by name. "I don't know, maybe it's the best thing."

Aunt Teresa kept silent. My father showed Tsi'Alfredo a respect he would never show Aunt Teresa or Tsi'Umberto, seeming to see in him the closest thing he had in his life to a friend.

"I wish to God she and her mother before her had died and rotted in the womb."

But he seemed so tired suddenly, so worn out with remembered pain.

He went through a sort of grieving afterwards, going about his work on the farm hunched like a sojourner, seeming made fragile by this unexpected resolution of things. I'd expected anger, a sense of betrayal; but some childishness in him seemed to have fallen away, his fraught, complex need for blame and recrimination. Perhaps all along he had wanted no more than to do the right thing, had always held out for that though it was the very thing that was impossible for him, that he could never see his way clear to.

Yet it seemed no real decision was ever made about Rita, by him or by any of us, that we'd merely given ourselves over to what had happened as to an act of fate, never daring, in our immigrant helplessness, to question what rules such matters were governed by here; and now that she was gone we seemed to fold ourselves over her absence like water rushing to fill a gap, the only proof she'd ever been with us our guilty silence and then the small evidences of her left scattered through the house like pricks of conscience, the clothes in my closet, a tooth-brush, an old pair of shoes left greying with dust on the basement shoe rack. At school she seemed by now a stranger, someone I had no claim to: she made a pretence for a time of ignoring me, childishly, hurtfully obvious, turning loudly away to her friends if I passed or staring through me as if I weren't there; but then even this language between us began to falter, grow strange, giving way finally to simple awkwardness and then to silence.

The end of the school year was approaching, our grade-eight class preparing for confirmation. But it was as if some veil had been stripped from my eyes over the previous weeks, everything I had taken for granted till then seeming suddenly called into question. At confession I couldn't get beyond the first ritual phrase, lapsing after it into hot, awkward silence.

"You know, son," the priest said finally, "it's a mortal sin to receive a sacrament while your soul is unclean."

But there seemed no place inside me to speak from, no word in me that was true. I couldn't understand how the world had come down to this, this futility in things, what mistake I had made.

"Perhaps you can do your own confession," the priest said.

Then finally school was over, my last year at St. Michael's. People lingered at the front entrance when we were let out, drifting into their cliques. I saw Rita and Elena come out and huddle secretively a few minutes with a group of their friends, Rita's laughter suddenly ringing out from among them falsely childish and exuberant.

"Kooky, kooky!" she said. "You're a kook!"

But when our glances met, her exuberance melted from her, only that message passing between us, our instinctive sibling shame and then our turning away.

At home whatever unease remained over Rita's departure was layered over now by a wave of new activity, the farm beginning to undergo a great transformation. The ruins of the old boiler room were finally cleared away, the old greenhouses repaired and extended to the road; and work was begun on a new boiler room, back beyond the garage, and on two new greenhouses to come off it, stretching from the road nearly as far as the creek. It seemed almost miraculous, this transformation, this new farm rising phoenix-like from the ruins of the old; and yet in a sense we'd merely returned to the old order, Tsi'Umberto gone into partnership again with my father as if the past several years had been merely a digression, a slow excising of the flaw at the centre of us that had kept us from being a family.

We'd contracted the work on the boiler room to a man from Castilucci, Tony Belli. He and his men seemed a second family to us, with their noise and activity, their constant presence. We joined them for breaks sometimes, the coffee and sweets Aunt Teresa brought out, the slices of cheese and meat, the men pulling up crates and sawhorses and overturned wheelbarrows for seats, jocular, rugged with work.

"Oh, Vittorio, how's *la gallufriend*?"

But my father seemed wary of them, grim still with inchoate emotion, hovering furtive around their work as if awaiting some expiation, some disaster. Then when building up one of the outside walls one of the masons forgot a window. My father was livid.

"Is it possible you couldn't notice a thing like that? A child could see it!"

But Belli seemed embarrassed less for himself than for my father.

"*Dai*, Mario, it's nothing, we can cut a window in there in five minutes," he said quickly, then issued terse instructions to his men in a clipped, precise English.

"He hasn't changed a bit," I heard one of the men say afterwards. "I still remember the fights he used to have with his father, you could hear them half way across the valley."

But it struck me as strange that people talked about my father's temper as if it defined him, reduced him to it when what seemed more important, more true, was the shame that came over him afterwards, the way now, for instance, he avoided the work site for several days and spoke to Belli with a gloomy thick-tongued awkwardness.

But then as the work progressed some weight seemed to lift from him. It was a gradual thing, like the slow, unthinking relief of escaping a punishment, the realization that nothing would go wrong, that he had called this new work into being and could

allow himself now to take pleasure in it. I noticed a new deference in the workers, the subtle acknowledgement of his enterprise, then the way my father responded to it with an almost
tangible warmth, a bodily ease like the first pleasant relinquishment of drunkenness. It was as if some sense of well-being that
had always lain just beneath the surface of him had finally
reached the moment of its incarnation. Yet something seemed
dulled in him as well, some perceptiveness: I had the sense that
he'd ceased to see the world clearly, could only project himself
onto it, had become with his too-loud voice and his too-hard
laughter as blind and self-willed as Tsi'Umberto. I was surprised
that others were taken in by him, missed this falseness, this easy
forgetting of what he had been, something I myself couldn't
forgive in him.

When the main structure of the boiler room was nearly complete, the large work crews gave way to groups of two or three,
carpenters, plumbers, electricians. In the sudden lull of activity
our world seemed to become small again, unpeopled, all our
projects resolving themselves finally into merely private things;
and I was secretly pleased then to see a tension arising between
my father and uncle, their exchanges marked more and more by
the familiar parsimoniousness of emotion, by their unthinking
need to blame, to contradict, to dismiss, to hold themselves
forever hard against the other as against some uncertain insult
or threat. Already the deforming pressure of habit was weighing
down on us again, the lines being drawn, something in me
feeling vindicated in this reversion as though it were my deep
monstrous wish now to see our family destroyed, to watch its
slow fuse burn to some pure and final violence.

To help with the work on the greenhouses we'd rehired Vito,
the Portuguese man who had worked for us a few years before.

The others condescended to him, seeming to see in him merely the person he presented himself as, still unmarried after all these years, still working his seasonal odd jobs, still speaking his rapid mix of English and Italian and Portuguese. But there was more to him, what he saw, what he held back, the way he worked himself invisibly around our moods and schisms. He'd told my father about a woman, Maria, whom he wanted to bring over from Portugal to marry, about a greenhouse farm on the 4th Concession he hoped to buy; and though he'd joke with my father about these plans as if he himself didn't take himself seriously, when the two of us were working alone together he'd talk about the future sometimes with such fond boyish hope that I knew he held a vision of it whole and clear in his mind, that for all his rambling and clowning he was possessed finally of a sure, quiet strength of purpose.

He drove a car now, a low-slung Impala that sat back on its rear axle like a great lizard sunning itself. After work he'd let me drive it from time to time, never seeming to imagine there was anything reckless in this, as if his simply wanting me to learn, expecting me to, ensured that I would; and sometimes he'd lean back into the room-sized intimacy of the front seat to roll a cigarette or veer off into some anecdote as if he'd forgotten entirely that he was teaching me, that I was merely a child, the two of us rolling up and down the concession roads then like travellers, through a landscape made strange by the falling dark. There was always the instant pulling away from a stop that seemed a kind of magic, the surge of the engine as I eased my foot down on the accelerator and then the car's slow heaviness giving way finally to effortless, weightless flight.

It was Vito who discovered one day while we were weeding tomatoes in the back field what must have been the wasting remnant of Lassie's carcass, impressing a hollow for itself amidst a patch of nettles and Queen Anne's lace like something that had stretched out secretly in a field to sleep. Vito grimaced at the sight of it as at some unexpected ill fortune.

"I think it's the dog my father shot," I said. "Because it used to kill the chickens."

But Vito didn't feel it was right to leave the corpse there in the weeds, said it was bad luck. He sent me up to the barn for a spade, and when he'd dug a makeshift grave and buried the corpse in it he made me scratch Lassie's name across the humped surface of it.

"But the rain will just wash it away," I said.

"It doesn't matter," he said, made mysterious now with his peculiar rites, "the dirt will remember."

My father and I came home from church one Sunday to find an unfamiliar car in the courtyard. There was a man sitting waiting at our kitchen table, tired, middle-aged, vaguely familiar. When my father caught sight of him from the doorway he nodded darkly and stepped outside again, the screen door banging behind him.

Aunt Teresa had set out a cup of coffee, stood silent against the kitchen counter.

"Hello, Vittorio," the man said, sombre, but speaking as if no chasm of years had ever separated us. I strained to remember what he was to me: one of my mother's cousins, a twin, Virginio or Pastore, I didn't know which. I'd never seen him in Canada, hadn't even known that he'd come.

I stood across the table from him, not knowing if I should kiss him in greeting.

"*È morto nonnote*," he said finally.

My grandfather. I tried to call up an image of him, to feel now the news of his death, could remember only his narrow room, his pale withered limbs. His death seemed an anachronism, unduly delayed, the abstraction of an absence already long complete. I bowed my head, trying to feign emotion, afraid of betraying my lack of it.

But when my cousin spoke again it was to Aunt Teresa.

"They said there were some things in the will, for Vittorio, some property –"

I thought of the medals my grandfather had given me: I'd misplaced them years before, had hidden them away at some point in Aunt Teresa's dresser but then had lost all track of them.

"You can't really expect him to go back for a few acres of vineyards," my aunt said, oddly peremptory. But then, relenting: "Anyway we can look after these things later, now isn't the time."

But no mention was made to me afterwards of my grandfather's death; there was only the others' silent deference to me, the solemnity it forced on me for a time, not so different finally from my usual exclusion from things. And yet his death remained with me, the irreducible lump of it: I seemed dirtied by it somehow, by its imperfection, the insufficiency of my response. I thought of the funerals in Valle del Sole, the keening processions to the grave, the desolation of them, and felt chilled somehow to think of the life still going on there without me.

The summer rolled on toward its end. The new greenhouses had taken skeletal form, the trusses raised and Rocco and Domenic and Vito and me working in teams to clamp the rafters in place, making our way like tree animals through a glinting angular forest of purlins and braces and girders; the boiler room, cavernous and imposing, was nearly complete, all straight lines and concrete and steel, a great Cleaver Brooks boiler, a massive cylinder of gun-metal blue, presiding over it like its god. Yet oddly now when the work was nearly done it seemed instead most provisional, still the hills of dirt to be levelled, the greenhouse roofs to be covered, the steam pipes to be laid; and then all the small intricate work to be done, the starting from scratch, and beyond that only endless work still. It would go on like that, year after year, and this would be our lives; already Tsi'Umberto had decided Rocco wouldn't be returning to school in the fall, drawing him into this vortex as its next logical victim.

Sunday afternoons I roamed the farm sometimes in aimless exploration. Searching once amidst the rubble that had been dumped down the bank of the pond from our old boiler room I discovered the remnants of the desk that had sat in my father's office, jammed beneath a ragged section of scorched wall and a slab of uprooted concrete floor. One side of it was charred and smashed but the other was almost intact, the top warped and discoloured but showing familiar scratches and stains, the drawers battered but whole and in place in their slots. The top one opened easily though it seemed a tiny storm had whipped through it, its inside a chaos of pens and old fuses and swollen envelopes and curled stamps; at the back still sat the pile of photographs Gelsomina and I had once looked through, but ruined now, clotted into an uneven lump as if they'd remained fixed as we had left them years before.

The bottom drawer, a double one, was locked or jammed shut, refusing to yield. I banged at the frame around it with a chunk of concrete to free it, then realized I had only to pull out the drawer above to be able to reach into it. Inside, jumbled into a heap, were a dozen or so bundles of paper tied round with string, my father's erratic system of filing; like the photos they'd been reduced to a solid mass, heavy and mildewed with moisture.

I began to sort through them, coming at the bottom to a smaller bundle of what seemed like letters. As I peeled away its rotting outer layers I discovered an old Italian stamp decaying on an envelope's corner and then the ghost of a familiar script, urging memory on me like a smell: my mother's script, its long spidery loops, though in the instant I recognized it it seemed to lose all its nuance, become only itself, these pale watery scrawls of fading ink on rotting paper.

I brought the letters home. They were too damp for me to be able to pull the envelopes safely apart, to pry out from them whatever thin slips of paper might be folded inside. But instead of leaving them out in the open air to dry I hid them in a shoe-box that I then tucked into a box of old clothes at the back of my closet. For several days the thought of them lingered at the edges of my awareness like some put-off obligation: they seemed a kind of wealth I'd accumulated but that I didn't know how to spend. Then when finally I took them out again, my mind strangely blank, empty of expectation, they remained clotted still with damp; I could make out only the blurred faces here and there of envelopes, my father's name on them and his old address, R. R. 1, the careful block capitals of CANADA at the bottom. But I couldn't attach these things to a person, to a hand writing them out, to a room and a place in the past where it may have been possible to conceive them.

I hid the letters away again, thinking I might dry them in the oven at some point when my father and aunt were out. But later that week I noticed that Rita's remaining clothes had been taken out of the closet, then that the box of old clothes at the back had been taken as well.

"It was just rags," Aunt Teresa said when I asked about it. "I put them in the trunk in the basement."

I found the clothes box empty beside the trunk, found the clothes piled neatly inside, but no shoebox.

"There was another box," I said. "With papers."

"Oh, that," my aunt said, suspiciously casual. "I threw them out, I thought they were garbage."

She said she couldn't remember where she'd thrown them. I looked for them in the garbage pit between the apple trees, then in the drum nearby where we put garbage to burn, then along the bank of the pond. But my search for them lacked conviction: I felt only the guilty relief of being free of them, of their uncertain burden, was left again with the sense that something crucial was missing in me, normal human emotion, the way I reacted to things with only this emptiness at the centre of me.

I dreamt sometimes of Rita. She appeared obliquely, palely inert, as if under water or under glass, an icon the dreams seemed to circle but not involve. I dreamt of her once in a field, simply there at a distance: I was picking some fruit, yellowish-orange, pulpy and bloated and frail, found a robin's nest under a vine, its still-warm pastel-blue eggs. I dreamt of her on a beach, for once simply a child like any other, turned from her imagining the shore would taper off to a trailing spit though it merely went on and on without end. When I awoke from these dreams I'd feel a lingering sense of incompletion, of some task not attended to, some duty not fulfilled. But then in the light of day I felt only a blankness where the thought of Rita should have been, couldn't have called up now any certain feeling for her except the familiar deadness in me, and beneath that the small guilty thought that her leaving us was simply what I'd wished for all along.

XII

I entered into high school as into a limbo, no sudden making over there as I'd hoped, no stepping out of the darkness I'd fallen into, merely a sort of perpetual furtive waiting without promise or purpose. The school, a citadel of pink brick amidst the old stone and clapboard homes of Talbot West, seemed a labyrinth after St. Michael's, with its wings and outbuildings, its dizzying symmetry, its unfixed world, the thousand nameless faces that moved unconnected through its dozen halls. I had dreams of wandering lost in it, of being late for some crucial test and then discovering it was in a language I couldn't decipher, all senseless hieroglyphs and scrawls.

What friendships I'd had at St. Michael's seemed to fall away. It was the disconnectedness I couldn't bear, being with people yet having nothing to say to them, not finding the simplest word that was true, exposed to them then in their uncertain threat. There were the other Italians at the school, the shadowy self-contained world they formed, Domenic and his friends from St. Michael's, others from Our Blessed Virgin, lingering in their groups in the high-ceilinged gloom of the technical wing. But with them it was the same, whatever relationship I had with them through the various Italian gatherings over the years seeming somehow suspended at school, only the dark nod of recognition if we passed each other and then we moved on. I began to search out circuitous routes from class to class to avoid the groups that formed outside classroom doorways between periods; I took to sitting alone during lunch. In the minutes then that I sat in hunched silence over my meal the cafeteria took on a painful clarity, every sound and image magnified, the clatter of plates, the bright flash of a dress or blouse, the dull, excruciating monotone of conversation; and then afterwards there was the great dead stretch of time to fill before the next period. I took to closing myself in a cubicle in the washroom to await the bell, sat staring at its scratched walls trying to blot out my thoughts, be nothing, not wanting the time I spent there, the shame of it, to be part of any memory of myself. Groups of boys would filter in, joking, mock-wrestling, thin slices of them flickering past the door slits.

"That kid must be a regular," one said once, and stooped suddenly as if to look under my door.

Then two boys from one of my classes began to be friendly with me, sitting beside me one day at lunch, seeming to pick me out in the room like some project they'd decided to take on. But in the aloneness I'd retreated into by then my first response was only a resistance at their intrusion, at having to work now to present some acceptable version of myself.

"It must get kind of lonely sitting by yourself every day."

"It's all right I guess."

Already they seemed diminished somehow, coming to me when my humiliation lay so plain on me; and each persistence in them, their seeking me out between classes, their coming over every day now at lunch, seemed to diminish them further. There was an innocence to them that made me feel I had to protect them from me somehow, to hide at all costs who I was, how I saw them. This was true especially of one of them, Terry, with his blind too-insistent good nature, his corny humour like a family sitcom's, his body bulging girlishly at his thighs to give him a slightly ridiculous air. The other, Mark, stylishly long-haired and slender and tall, was more canny, bland and unblemished like some new thing still fresh from its wrappings but seeming able to shift to fit in with whomever he was with as if he had quietly, undetectably willed his normalcy into being; and there was something familiar in this that made me feel sometimes that I was merely his deformed underside, capable perhaps of some simple transformation that would make me as flawless as he was, as inconspicuous.

The two of them formed part of a group called the One Way Challenge. I went along with them to one of the meetings, had got the sense from their explanations of a social club of some sort but then had to grope as the meeting unfolded to find what focus held it together, the oddly private revelations, the oblique, sudden references to religion and Christ. Four or five people spoke in turn, volunteering themselves at once tentative and sure, a girl who talked about the death of her father, a boy who'd spent two years in reform school. The last to speak, an older boy, his neck mottled with blood-coloured blotches like hickeys, spoke about a group he'd belonged to when he'd lived up north.

"We used to get drunk or stoned and then sit around in a circle staring at a candle. After a while you'd forget about everything except the flame, that's all you'd have in your mind, and the feeling would get so strong you couldn't take your eyes away even if you wanted to. I guess it shows how powerful Satan can be when you let yourself be taken in by him."

But in each case the stories were told in tones so plain and matter-of-fact and the group was so staid in its response, so quietly accepting, that I thought I'd misunderstood them, couldn't reconcile their easy explaining away with what seemed the cryptic underside of things that had been revealed in them, what one might imagine existing but never actually being talked about or lived through.

Within a few weeks I'd begun to attend these meetings regularly. It was never clear to me what had drawn me into them, perhaps the uncertain allure of those first stories I'd heard, the hope of crossing over into their strange, familiar territory, perhaps simply the petty fear of not going along with Terry and Mark, of losing them, of having nothing else to fill the blank space my life seemed then. But even when the meetings had become predictable, suspect, the testimonials and their inevitable conclusion, the acceptance of Christ, even when the rebellion at this bright, forced certainty had grown large in me, still something brought me back to them. It struck me how wilful and hard-won religion seemed in these meetings, how transforming, wasn't merely a given as it had always been in my life, pervasive and unquestioned as air – I felt something truthful in this, defiant, the group of us seeming hidden away in our upstairs classroom like early Christians in the catacombs.

Yet outside these meetings Terry and Mark seldom spoke about them, neither according them a special prominence nor disowning them, neither different than they were during them nor the same; and with the others, too, there seemed this balancing, this secret they carried within them and yet nothing about them betraying it, the way they looked or dressed, the other friends they had. I wanted their faith to mark them in some way, to charm their lives or simply make them outcast, anything that would test them, couldn't reconcile this mundane ordinariness with their other, altered selves. Yet the marvel of it was how they seemed to live within this contradiction without tension, as if all the while merely feigning their normalcy, going out into the world as though part of some slow, quiet infiltration. Even Mark, who often hung out with some of the more popular boys, matching their rowdiness then with his own, could still move from that other self with perfect equilibrium into the complicit intimacy of our meetings, silent but then suddenly adding some comment or story, his doubts, his small confirmations, that conformed exactly to those of the others.

"I didn't want to go but something inside me said I should, and that was the day I accepted Christ. After I thought it must have been the Holy Spirit that made me go."

For my part I never spoke a word at these meetings, couldn't find the place in me from which to enter into them, into the past tense of the struggles they charted; I was too far from these struggles or too close, had never believed enough or never been free enough from belief to feel it bursting on me in its newness. Yet I continued in my silent acquiescence, not feeling I had the right to reject the redemption being offered, what Terry and Mark after all had seen the need of in me when they'd picked me out sitting alone in my lunch-time desertion.

I began to attend bible classes at the New Testament Church, Terry and Mark coming by for me Monday nights in an older friend's dusty Polara. The church sat a mile or so beyond St. Michael's on Highway 3, modern and spare like an auditorium, inside it blond wooden benches tiered down toward a kind of dais or stage that held only a simple lectern. Off the church was a small-windowed meeting room where our classes were held, in the same spare style, low couches and armchairs grouped round a coffee table as in a living room but the walls completely unadorned, the sense there of a pure, generic comfort, without eccentricity or waste.

We were led by a man named Tom, thirtyish perhaps, blue-jeaned and loose-shirted but always immaculately trim, with the burnished energetic air of a television host. Each week we went over a few passages from the bible, Tom strangely literal in the interpretations he offered of them, seeming to see in them some simple code like a rule book we could follow. He read us an article once by a man who'd escaped from the Soviet Union, how hard it had been to begin to believe in God when he'd been taught all his life that God didn't exist; but I was struck by the awesome freedom of that, of being without belief through no fault of your own, by the possibility, the monstrous hope, that the opposite might be true, belief itself no more than a learned thing, a lingering habit of mind.

Then early in March a Billy Graham crusade came to the church. Terry and Mark and their friend came by to collect me, the church nearly full when we arrived, with an air of casual expectation as before a performance. The service got on with little fanfare, a hymn and then someone from the church introduced the night's speaker, a smallish man in a black suit and white shirt, spindly like a caricature, his body tapering up to the high, black fullness of his hair.

"It's good to hear those raised voices." But he seemed genuinely pleased with us. "I want to know you're enjoying yourselves tonight."

He eased into his sermon, his voice carrying us with its gravelly resonance, bearing down from its first slow casualness toward a hard urgency as he circled various subjects, probing them strangely worldly and undogmatic; and then the subtle swerving, almost undetectable, into religion and Christ. At the end the choir struck up "Lamb of Jesus" and several other men came out onto the dais, taking places on either side of the minister; and finally people in the pews began to file down to them. The action seemed so orderly, so premeditated, that it took me a moment to understand what was happening, that they'd been converted: I felt I'd missed something, some crucial instant in the evening's comfortable sobriety that had given rise to this outpouring of sudden faith.

The minister was talking above the music, inviting people to come down, a cordial exhortation.

"Don't be shy, there's room enough for all of you."

The friend who'd driven us to the service slipped past me suddenly to join the line. I was aware of Terry and Mark beside me, their careful unpressuring composure, their expectation: this was the moment they'd chosen for me, what the past months had been the prelude to, yet all I felt now was the familiar sundering in me, felt desperate with my failure even while I wanted to cling to whatever it was that made me different from the those who'd joined the line. But then suddenly I was there among them: I seemed to have stepped out of myself, saw myself standing there amidst the others as if my body had moved of its own strange accord. An usher directed me to a grey-haired man at the end of the dais, sombre and dark-suited and heavy-set; in an odd monotone he asked if I accepted Christ as my personal saviour.

I would say the words only, test to see if saying them made them true.

"I do."

But there was no breaking open of the heavens, no sudden flash of glorious light.

Afterwards I felt hollowed out by my lie, had the sense there was nothing constant in me that held me together. For a few weeks I continued attending my meetings and classes but then began to make excuses, and gradually the first blithe, enigmatic pleasure that Mark and Terry had shown at what I'd done gave way to an awkwardness, one that seemed to have less to do with my lie than with some sudden understanding of what we were to each other, of our simple failure, after all, to become friends. Perhaps from the start that was all they'd been offering me, all I had wanted, the hardest thing exactly in being so precarious and small.

For a time, though, Terry continued to invite me to various church functions, hayrides and singalongs, a Saturday barbecue, a Sunday picnic; and I went along, even beyond the end of the school year and into the summer, still resisting and acquiescing, still distantly hopeful of fitting in. What always struck me about these gatherings was the normalcy of them, the complex, ordinary humanness that stretched out like a web just beneath their bright surface, the prankishness between boys and girls, the conversations about school or sports or cars, the jokes and the horseplay; and it seemed at bottom that what joined people together was not their belief but something deeper, both more and less important, exactly this casual mundaneity they moved through so unthinkingly. In the end what I feared was not the religion, the testimonials and the prayers, familiar rituals by now, safe in their illusion of unanimity, but the empty moments between when I had only myself to fall back on, waiting silent in line to receive a hot dog off the grill from one of the grown-ups, sitting alone in darkening light on some stranger's lawn with a paper plate in my lap to catch the relish that spilled from the end of my bun. It was these most usual things that seemed furthest from me, that people had barbecues at all, conversations, back yards, that they took so much for granted; and perhaps what I most wished for finally was not the transcendence of belief but simply to feel at home in this strangeness, this ordinariness.

XIII

With the new greenhouses finished and planted our lives at home had finally resumed their familiar rhythms after the disruption of the fire. There was the first false spring after planting, the promise of it, the earth smell and the heat, the greening rows stretched out in their newness though outside the ground was bone-hard and piled high with snow; and then the work, unrelenting, the silent bustle of hands, the endless tedium. The added help of my uncle's family seemed to balance exactly the added work of the new greenhouses as if by some law, our time always filled as before; what seemed to matter was not the work itself but simply that it should go on as it did without pause or slack. Jobs circled back on themselves as the plants grew, waiting always to be begun again: I passed whole weeks at the same chore, knew only its small, endless repetitions, just the animal part of me present, my knees, my chafed hands.

We worked cut off from each other, lost in the separate hush of the walls our rows formed, the greenhouse sounds reaching us there like jungle static, the crack and hiss of the steam pipes, the tinny background drone of the old car speakers Rocco had connected up to a radio in the boiler room. Aunt Teresa and Tsia Taormina did the winding and suckering, keeping pace with one another as if they drew some solace from each other's presence though their silence was broken only by brief, abrupt exchanges like the failed beginnings of conversations, Tsia Taormina's voice tentative, neutral, Aunt Teresa's dismissive and curt; Domenic and I spread straw, pruned leaves, pruned again. Sometimes Rocco joined us, sometimes Tsi'Umberto, a sort of foreman to us, the disembodied conversations he had with his sons reaching me then across the rows like a kind of familial shorthand, sporadic and arcane, having nothing to do with me.

Tsi'Umberto seemed humbled by the new responsibility of the farm. We looked to him to be told what to do but he in turn always consulted, in his way, with my father, making declarations to him, needlessly grave and considered, which my father corrected or contradicted or simply concurred with with a dismissive shrug; he seemed most content, most himself, exactly when he was just working among the rest of us without any special authority. There was a hint of deference in him toward his sons now, toward Rocco especially, that was almost touching, a grudging yielding to them as if they'd freed him of all his past unforgiving hardness by simply becoming themselves: they were competent, self-sufficient, assured, had somehow weathered all the years of their father's anger to become what his abuse of them had seemed all along to deny they were capable of.

His deference extended to me as well, but differently, more abstract somehow, less directly earned, based perhaps exactly on what distinguished me from his sons, my separation from the life of the farm. At some point it had been decided that other hopes resided in me, other possibilities; I understood this distinction but not its genesis, whether it was the source of my distance from the others or a symptom, how they had come to make it at all when I showed them so little of myself. It seemed self-fulfilling, with its half-deference and half-condescension, the assumption I wouldn't fit in, that I could be given only the simplest, least essential jobs, had somehow to be accommodated; and I both used it and resisted it, uncertain any more where my real life lay, both home and school now merely two limbos I moved between, each a waiting for an ending, for an opening into some truer other life.

My father worked apart from us, caught up in his own silent, mysterious arrangements and preparations. He spent a week building storage niches along a wall of the boiler room, labelling them in his cryptic phonetic script; he arranged careful settings for our tools on a board behind the workbench; he hung numbered squares of painted plywood in each of the greenhouses, 1 through 6. There was something at once frivolous and grand in these projects – they seemed to flow from a vision of things imperfectly grasped, aspiring to a kind of North American modernity and perfection but revealing always in the end a makeshift immigrant crudeness. He'd furnished his office with a sleek metal desk, a filing cabinet, a swivelling armchair, maintaining a small professionalism even down to the store-bought lettering on the door. But then he'd covered the chair with a tattered blanket, had installed a rusting second-hand fridge, had bolted a two-by-four to one wall and attached to it handfashioned wire hooks, sharpened to a point on the grinder, that he poked bills and statements through to file them; and soon the room had lost all sense of its first businesslike spareness and newness, become merely clutter and crude improvisation, just as the storage niches, with their careful, misspelt labels, had soon become simply random catch-alls for whatever odds and ends came to hand, and just as the tool board, after a brief pristine newness, had soon fallen into perpetual disarray, the holders and pegs my father had placed there merely ghostly reminders of the first order he had tried to impose.

He and Rocco looked after the watering and spraying, took loads in to Longo's, did repairs. When one of the pumps broke down Rocco took it apart piece by piece to fix it, a kind of miracle, not simply that he built it up again, functioning and sound, but that he had dared risk the chaos of scattered parts in disassembling it; but my father seemed to take this competence in him for granted, seemed almost to call it up in him by his unthinking reliance on it. There was an equilibrium in their relationship, in its neutrality, its detachment, that made my own relationship with my father seem so fraught by comparison. He seemed to expect at once more and less of me than the others did – over a little thing he might rebuke me with sharp impatience, but then for some more serious transgression, a broken plant, a steam pipe left wrongly closed, show suddenly a grim indulgence, souring with his inturned anger yet saying nothing, seeming somehow to take the blame for my mistake on himself. There was a constant tension between us like the brooding, mute avoidance after an argument; but there had been no argument, only this tension without beginning, the instinctive darkening in him in my presence.

On nights I'd had bible classes Tsi'Umberto had always assented to my early departures from work with an unquestioning solemnity, probably assuming they had something to do with school; but my father from the start had seemed to hold them silently against me, never quite daring to challenge me on them yet for that all the more suspicious of them.

"Where is it you have to go, always to these classes?" he said finally.

"It's part of a church group I go to."

I thought he should be pleased, knew he wouldn't be and yet was surprised by his anger.

"What church group, what is that?"

"It's bible classes," I said. "We study the bible."

"*Sì*, you and your aunt, all that garbage she reads, now she wants to rot your brain as well –"

But already he'd drawn his anger back, made a grudge of it, though afterwards he seemed to imagine some conspiracy between me and my aunt, with her magazines and programs, some complex challenge to the order of things he represented. I sensed his hovering gloom whenever I left for my meetings, felt a defiance in the face of it but without conviction, knew how little he'd understood, how much I would have welcomed from him the excuse of his forbidding me to attend. And yet we'd simply gone on like that for weeks, his unspoken anger, my unwilling defiance, as if this was the only way we knew to communicate at all, this mortal conflict between us without purpose or source.

Riding silent with him on Sundays to mass, feeling him there shadowy beside me, I had the sense sometimes that what divided us wasn't our anger or our hate but merely this silence, my being unable to make the simplest offhand comment or begin the simplest conversation. There seemed some common ground between us I couldn't break through to though I could sense every subtle motion of his mind as if he were a thing I myself had created, some need in him I couldn't give myself over to though I couldn't bear the pressure of it on those Sunday drives, his dark, hunched silences beside me. If I could have found the way to do these things then we might have entered perhaps into a clarity, become simply father and son, begun to take for granted how such roles unfolded. But instead it seemed he was the child and I the parent who had refused to indulge him, whom he kept his better moods from as if to protect them, the person in him who laughed too loud, was generous, went about his small private jobs on the farm, who at a wedding once at the end of the night had locked arms with some men at the bar and begun to sing, the group of them bellowing out like drunken soldiers to the near-empty hall in their quavering baritones.

XIV

One Sunday shortly after I'd started grade ten I came out from mass at St. Michael's to find Elena waiting at the bottom of the church steps, her eyes catching mine and then shifting darkly away to avoid my father beside me.

"My mother said to ask if you wanted to come to lunch."

There was a car idling across the street, an older man in spectacles sitting eyes-forward in the driver's seat, a woman beside him in a hat, the barest silhouette of Rita in back. My father had already taken the car in, seemed to have gathered at once who Elena was, who had sent her.

"What does she want?" he said, in Italian, though as if he'd understood her, was merely seeking some sort of contact with me.

"They want me to go eat with them."

"*Mbeh*, go on then."

And already he'd turned in shadowy retreat, seeming to draw a curtain between us.

I hadn't seen Rita for more than a year, caught a flash of her like a dream image as the car door swung open to let me in, her hair sleek as Elena's now, cascading like hers in gentle curls that seemed to contain the oval of her face like a picture frame; but then once in the car I acknowledged her only in my silence, my instinctive subordination of her to my awkward introduction to Mr. and Mrs. Amherst.

"We're so glad to meet you finally," Mrs. Amherst said, surveying me in the back seat like a chaperon. She had the trace of an English accent, the plain, heavy set of her features seeming granted a sort of dignity by it. "We thought what a shame it was you hadn't seen your sister."

There was an air in the car of Sunday formality, Rita and Elena in their knee socks and Sunday dresses, Mrs. Amherst in her hat; I imagined them all fresh from the Amhersts' other church, its unknown peculiarities.

"Mother, can we show Victor our bicycles?" Rita said.

I felt a kind of revulsion at her addressing Mrs. Amherst as Mother.

"We'll see, dear, maybe after lunch."

At their home my mind seemed stretched taut against the unfamiliarity of the Amhersts' world, registering only vague impressions like low reverberations, the glow of wooden surfaces, the glint of cutlery and plates, Mrs. Amherst's bright, brittle energy filling the kitchen like a glare. I watched her with Rita, with Elena, her not quite convincing displays of affection as if they'd remained for her other people's children.

"Now girls, make a place for Victor there, he's the guest."

Next to his wife Mr. Amherst seemed inconsequential, shambling and rumpled and slight, boyishly deferential to her, seeming to see where she was merely a misty glow of positive qualities.

"It's Mother who keeps the house together, what with the girls and everything, you can't count on an old bachelor type like me for that sort of thing."

He referred to Rita and Elena as the girls just as Mrs. Amherst was Mother, a kind of affectionate disowning of them, hardly ever addressing them directly but seeming to take a distant, shy solace from their presence.

I followed Rita to the garage after lunch to see her bicycle, our small charade of sibling affection.

"We're not allowed to ride them on the street, only in the driveway or when Father takes us to the parking lot at school."

There was a plastic wading pool propped up against a wall, an electric lawnmower, an assortment of garden tools, the small accoutrements of this mysterious other life she'd been assumed by.

"It's very nice," I said.

Mrs. Amherst drove me home. In silence she seemed to revert to a strange stolidity, pale and imposing and hard as a statue, her energy seeming then a shell beneath which her body remained inviolate. But then some switch would click on and the life would flow into her again.

"It would be so nice for your sister if you came over every Sunday." She'd stopped the car at the foot of our driveway, seemed to resist the further intimacy of driving into the court-yard. "You know the way now, don't wait for an invitation, just walk over from church whenever you'd like."

At home no one mentioned the visit. My father seemed chastened by it, a kind of perverse integrity in him, showing me a muted deference as if in silent acknowledgement of my familial rights in this matter. At church the next Sunday I noticed his glance across the street as we came out, felt emboldened somehow by this tiny evidence of vulnerability.

"They said I should go over every Sunday." Then the sinking in me, the thought of his dead retreat.

"If they'd wanted you to go they would have come to get you."

"They said I should walk. It's not very far."

It was understood afterwards that I'd go to the Amhersts' every Sunday after mass. My father never offered to drive me, seeming to relinquish at the church doors any claim he had to me; and the few blocks I walked to the Amhersts' was like a chasm I crossed from our world to theirs, coming into their street as into a different country, the trees and front lawns and dappled light, the air of town calm, the houses with their windowed porches and gravelled drives huddled up intimately one next to the other. Amongst them the Amhersts' house sat comfortably indistinguishable, solid and two-storeyed and square and then with touches of ornamentation like timid afterthoughts, false leaf-green shutters framing the windows and an eye of stained glass staring out from the gable.

Inside, the house had an air of sunny invitation, all blond wood and tidy furnishings and polished surfaces. There was a sunroom in back, lush with plants like a greenhouse, a dining room off the kitchen bright with lacquer and crystal. Yet the promise of these things seemed to remain never more than a backdrop to our kitchen meals, mysterious like a sudden glimpse of a home through a window, the play of light, the lives suggested and withheld. Going upstairs to the bathroom I'd cast sidelong glances into the other rooms there, the Amhersts' bedroom with its curving dresser, Rita's and Elena's with its two narrow beds, its pink comforters, its smell of sleep. There was one door normally closed that I finally discovered ajar once, nudging it further to find a room filled with an odd assortment of old toys, jack-in-the-boxes, wind-up soldiers, dolls of every sort.

"So I see you've found my little room."

Mr. Amherst had soundlessly come up behind me. He had a way, for all his shambling awkwardness, of drifting through the house surprisingly nimble and quiet, disturbing nothing.

"It's just some things the family's collected over the years that I put out here. Mother likes to keep them out of the way. Mostly my great-grandfather's, I guess, he used to make them as a sort of hobby."

We stood a moment as if sharing a secret, Mr. Amherst in sheepish pride and me in silent awkwardness beside him. Arranged as they were in the room's curtained gloom the toys had a peculiar formality as if all along they had never been intended as playthings, their chipped and fading colours seeming the last shimmer of a promise that had never been fulfilled. There was a doll set apart on its own special shelf, bright-cheeked and stiff in its ballooning dress; there was a train with each car carefully sculpted through to its windows and seats. In a small glass-topped cabinet a tiny village had been set out, with inch-high people and small red-roofed houses, a church and a stable, skinny, intricate trees, every object infinitely detailed and frail, the scene they formed heartbreakingly placid and hopeful and pure with its tiny intimation of life; I imagined Mr. Amherst carefully setting out its fragile pieces, wondered what small private contentment would have taken shape in him then.

Our meals unfolded amidst the controlled relentlessness of Mrs. Amherst's kitchen bustle. There seemed always some task to be tended to, some moment's lull to be averted. She'd ask me questions about school, about home, veering toward dangerous ground and then away, with hidden motive perhaps, though afterwards she'd confuse things as if she'd merely been being polite, forget names and relationships, ask questions I'd already answered; and then just when it seemed we must taper off into silence she'd find some way to draw in Mr. Amherst, seeming to have at the ready an index of his anecdotes and thoughts.

"You know, David was in Italy during the war, wasn't it Sicily you were in?"

And Mr. Amherst would be off on one of his stories, timidly loquacious, rambling through a haze of detail and digression toward some little insight or joke.

"I guess we're all immigrants here in the end, I've always said that. There's my own family – the first Amherst here wasn't an Amherst at all, he was an Amsel, I guess the British brought him over from Germany to help fight the Americans. I always say that at least we had the good sense to change our name – that's how I managed to trap Mother here, she thought I was good British stock."

"I'm sure Victor doesn't want to hear about all that."

Though something yielded in her whenever his stories came around to her, seeming to reveal for an instant a surprising softness in her.

They'd met in England at the end of the war. I tried to picture their coming together, their younger selves, his bumpkinish soldier's charm, her bustling Englishness, how they bridged the disjunction between them. What the names might have meant to her, Mersea, Essex County, their familiar ring; and then the arrival, the falling away.

"She didn't much like it at the start, our Canadian ways, she won't admit it, I know, but it's true. But she made a way for herself I guess. She was the president of the IODE in three years, I guess if it wasn't for her the hospital here might never have been built."

"David, you know that's not true."

There were moments at these meals, the group of us gathered intimate at the kitchen table, the room warm with cooking around us, when I seemed to enter into some different idea of what a family was, held safe there and accepted like an honoured guest, even Mrs. Amherst then appearing transformed, fussing over me maternal and staunch as if she had truly made a place for me in herself.

"It's so nice to have a young man in the house, just us girls and old fogies all the time."

Yet in the end something seemed always held back, a question never posed, an unease never quite broken through; and sometimes the meals lapsed into a strange, deflated silence, broken now and then by cryptic shreds of conversation between the Amhersts like a kind of code and then the silence again. I imagined some revelation in those moments, some truth slitting the fabric of us, what Mrs. Amherst seemed to armour us against with her rallies of bright, forced enthusiasm. But there was only the silence, a lingering emptiness without nuance, and it seemed uncertain then whether any of the warmth I'd felt had been real, whether all that happened there wasn't simply a matter of getting through.

My visits began to stretch into the afternoon. Until then Rita and Elena had remained merely peripheral blurs at the edges of our meals, always outside the focus of them, Mrs. Amherst serving them with a brisk suppressive efficiency; but now the three of us were left alone in the basement rec room, Mrs. Amherst plotting activities for us, television, tutoring, reading aloud. I thought some disguise would drop away from us then, that we'd somehow acknowledge among ourselves how out of place we all were in the Amhersts' world. Yet Rita and Elena merely continued on in their demure poised politeness, the obedient children, seeming to see in me merely another grown-up, to be guarded against and pleased. Whatever separateness they had didn't include me, was only theirs, safeguarded in the furtive glances that passed between them, in their whispering asides; I remained the outsider, in need of instruction.

"We're only allowed to watch TV for an hour, then you have to help us with our arithmetic."

There were always these rules that Rita protected the sanctity of, impersonal and absolute, so different from at home, where rules about what was acceptable, what should be done, seemed merely the expression of the house's shifting moods, haphazard, to be guessed at; she seemed to hold them over me as in some elaborate game of make believe of which she was the master, the small contempt for me in her then the only sign that she remembered our past familiarity. I had the impression when I was with her that there was some logic I hadn't quite penetrated, her world of Father and Mother like television appellations, her little rules, her picture-book curls; and then her dry, sibling kisses when I left her, our careful ritual of emotion, Mrs. Amherst supervising it with a tight-smiled discretion.

"Say goodbye to your brother now."

At the end of these visits I felt always the same disappointment, the sense that some elusive pleasure or reward had been kept from me; and then there was the strange mood I had to come home to after them, my father's shamed sufferance, his surrender of me to them as to an obligation he could neither participate in nor oppose, Aunt Teresa's enigmatic detachment, her small buoyancy as if she approved of the visits and not, sympathized with my father's hurt yet was pleased with it. After a while the visits had begun to seem a kind of penance our family paid that I both owed and reaped the benefit of, continuing on exactly through this ambiguity of emotion, the subtle equilibrium of it; and I could neither feel I'd had a choice in them nor escape the guilt of them, began slowly both to dread them and to dread they would end.

At Christmas the Amhersts came unannounced to our house. Even they themselves seemed thrown off balance by the enormity of what they'd done, by the air of sudden lull in our kitchen, the sight of our half-finished Christmas meal; and they stood an instant in strained expectation, fresh with cold from the outside, Mr. Amherst stooped and apologetic, otherworldly, Mrs. Amherst burgeoning with the unspent brightness of greeting as if interrupted in mid-sentence. She had undone the buttons of her coat to reveal a dress all in satiny floral, seeming ready if necessary to offer herself to us like a gift.

"I hope we're not disturbing you, we just thought we'd bring by Victor's present."

They'd removed their shoes at the door, standing there now on our yellowing kitchen floor in their stocking feet; and that detail more than any other made them seem vulnerable suddenly, cast adrift.

"Get them some chairs," my father said, in Italian.

There were awkward introductions, handshakes, Mrs. Amherst's pained cheerfulness counterbalanced by our gloom. Tsi'Umberto introduced himself as Bert, a name I'd never heard him use before, seeming offered to the Amhersts now as an odd sort of concession or apology, for the room's hot closeness, our dirty plates, the raw inelegance of our immigrant disorder.

Mrs. Amherst had handed me a small wrapped parcel.

"It's nothing, we just wanted you to know how much we've enjoyed your visits."

Then a silence, a lapse. They'd remained standing – no one had moved to bring them chairs. Mr. Amherst fiddled with the hat in his hands, staring into it; Mrs. Amherst smiled waxenly, at a loss.

"Go on, Vittorio," Aunt Teresa said, impassive, conceding nothing. "Open your present."

Another silence while I tore through the wrappings – a watch, elegant and expensive-looking, weighty in my hands.

"Thank you," I said.

"I wasn't sure about the band, if it's too large Mr. Amherst can take a few links out at the shop –"

Then silence again.

"Let me make you some coffee," Aunt Teresa said.

"Oh, no, please don't trouble yourself, we really can't stay."

For all the shame I felt when they'd gone, still it seemed we'd somehow got the better of them, had given up less ground than they had. But afterwards the tension surrounding my visits seemed to grow more acute, my father more moody, the Amhersts more inscrutable. I felt a change in how I was received now, a subtle shift like a modulation in a room as a cloud passed, some familiarity I'd begun to take for granted suddenly withdrawn from me, pulled back with the unthinking wariness that came after a humiliation or hurt. Mr. Amherst grew more ghostly and awkward, always mumblingly distracted around me now; his wife grew more painfully solicitous and bright. Then driving me home one day she seemed flustered suddenly as with some embarrassment between us, forcing a few minutes' conversation but then lapsing into strained silence.

"Victor, I think you should know we'll be asking to legally adopt your sister," she said finally. She'd tried to put it as a pronouncement but there was a question behind it, vaguely touching in the power it seemed willing to grant me. "We just think that's the best thing for her. We hope you'll keep seeing her, of course – it's not a matter of that, it's just that we thought you should know."

There seemed no question to me of their right in this matter, no objection I would have ever have thought to put into words. Yet some line seemed to have been drawn now that I had to fall on one side or the other of. My visits grew afterwards increasingly more awkward, the pressure of pretending that nothing had changed more intense; and Rita herself seemed more and more inaccessible, withheld somehow like the beckoning luminescence of the Amhersts' house.

"Elena says you're only my half-brother," she said once, and it was as if she was making known to me where her own allegiances lay.

Then in the deepening gloom that had followed the Amhersts' visit to us my father's stomach ailment began to bother him again. There seemed something convenient in this, the way he began to make us always aware of his pain now with his constant grimaces, his sudden sharp intakes of breath. Our doctor put him back on a special diet and prescribed an array of pills, but my father only grew more morose, more sullenly distrustful, seeming determined to be ill. He had me drive him one night into Emergency at the hospital; the doctor came from home, angrily good-humoured, bundled in a parka against the cold.

"Mario, *paesano*, what's the problem?"

He had my father checked into the hospital for tests. Sunday came and he hadn't returned home; I called the Amhersts to explain that I wouldn't be coming, though I had my licence now and could have driven over on my own.

"I hope it's nothing serious," Mrs. Amherst said.

But somehow I regretted having admitted this vulnerability in us.

The tests apparently showed nothing; but my father looked truly ill now, lying listless and dulled when we went in to visit him. Aunt Teresa brought him food from home but he hardly touched it.

"It's in his head," she said to Tsi'Alfredo. "This thing over the girl that woman wants to do, you know how he is about that."

But in the end he was transferred to a hospital in Windsor; more tests, then finally an operation. Aunt Teresa was at the hospital the whole day, and then in the evening Tsi'Umberto and Tsi'Alfredo and I went up as well. My father was still recovering from the anaesthesia when we saw him, hardly aware of us. A nurse came in to change his intravenous, then a doctor, closing himself off with him behind the bed's square of curtain. Through a gap I caught sight for an instant of my father's belly as the doctor removed his bandage, the scabby outline there of the incision they'd made like a flap cut in cloth.

"The glue seems to be holding," the doctor said afterwards, oddly jovial. "We got him just in time, he was half-rotten in there."

"They said before there was nothing wrong with him," Aunt Teresa said.

"Oh, well, sometimes you can't tell with these things till you open someone up and take a look around. Anyway in a few months he'll be as good as new."

But my father seemed unwilling to recover from the first drugged stupor of his operation, remaining for days in the same state of restless half-sleep, fading in and out of awareness and mumbling odd imprecations like someone gripped in the delirium of a fever. Aunt Teresa condescended to him as to a child, impatient, overloud.

"What, Mario, what is it?"

He complained vaguely of headaches, of stomach pains; then when he was taken off his intravenous he refused to eat, and had to be put on it again. As his stay in hospital dragged on a quality of shame began to attach to it, our visits growing increasingly more strained and subdued. Nurses would come by to check on him, administering pills and making quick notations on the clipboard that hung at the foot of his bed, their grim smiles revealing nothing.

"Just something to help him sleep."

"It's the same story," Aunt Teresa said. "The doctor says there's nothing wrong, who knows what to believe."

In the meantime we'd begun to have problems in the greenhouses. Some of the plants had contracted mosaic disease – Tsi'Alfredo noticed a patch of it when he came by one day, the upper leaves of half a dozen or so plants coming up gnarled and rough like lizards' skin. Tsi'Alfredo was livid.

"Is it possible no one noticed anything till now? You've probably spread it to half the crop already."

Other patches began to appear, small islands of plants here and there with heads stunted as if by frost. We had to mark off the infected areas and wash our hands and change our clothes after we worked in them. Since the disease affected only new growth it could be checked by clipping the heads off infected plants, thereby saving at least the few sets of fruit the plants had already put out. But every day new cases appeared, within a couple of weeks the greenhouses become a disconcerting patchwork of gaps as the healthy plants dwarfed the diseased ones. Our work was marked by a growing sense of futility: with no new growth to keep them thriving the infected plants had soon begun to look sickly and old, their remaining fruit maturing wrinkled and small and our production already beginning to fall off though we were not yet in mid-season.

It was over a month after his operation before my father returned home. He was visibly shrunken, seemed to have shed a layer of himself like a suit of clothes. For several days he stayed in the house, still in a fog, shuffling out stoop-shouldered to the sink to take a handful of coloured pills, shuffling back to his room. Then the Saturday after his return he finally came out to work.

"What happened with those plants?" But he'd remained dim and morose with fatigue like someone resisting being roused from sleep.

"Disease," Aunt Teresa said. "You can see for yourself."

And afterwards she had to sort through the tomatoes he'd picked to remove those he'd picked too green.

Sunday morning he prepared for church. A look passed between us, seeming to contain in it his sulky determination that things would go on as before, my visits to the Amhersts, his martyr's hurt; yet the whole time of his illness I'd not been to see them, felt the resistance rise in me now at this drugged stubbornness in him, at being forced to choose.

He waited for me in the car while I finished dressing. The instant we'd set out I could see he shouldn't be driving, the whole of him seeming mired in a dreamy slow-limbed torpor. Yet somehow I couldn't bring myself to stop him, to try to reach him, took instead a strange angry pleasure at the danger he was exposing us to. Then at the town's four corners he failed to stop at the light.

"*Papà*, there's a car –"

We were into the intersection. There was a screech of tires, a horn, a dark blur of motion beyond my father's window; and then miraculously my father had wheeled through to the cross-street and pulled to a stop at the curb. The other car was sitting in the middle of the intersection, aslant from its sudden stop, the driver already jumped from it and coming toward us red-faced and seething. But the sight of my father seemed to sour his anger.

"Asshole!" he shouted out, then climbed back into his car and sped away.

The whole thing was over in a matter of seconds, and in a minute more the few other cars that might have seen what had happened had driven on their way and the intersection had assumed again its Sunday languor; but in the becalmed silence that opened up then, my father and I still stalled there at the curb-side, my heart still pounding, it seemed we'd just come through some prolonged ordeal, a chasm dividing the moment when the crash had seemed inevitable, the terror and the hope then that my father would die, from this awkward moment afterwards.

"I guess I better drive," I said finally.

I came round to the driver's side. My father had slid across to slouch against the other door; with the movement his coat had hiked up his back like a child's. He shifted beside me as I moved the mirrors and the seat, trying to arrange himself, an instant's painful exertion.

"Maybe you should just turn around and go home," he said. "You can go back on your own after."

He seemed as close as he'd ever come to asking me to stop seeing the Amhersts.

"It doesn't matter," I said.

For a moment some more certain concession seemed possible, some way of reaching him that would take away from him the guilt of the visits I wouldn't make, make a gift of them to him; but finally I simply swung onto the road in silence, turning up the next sidestreet to circle toward home.

XV

With the end of my visits to the Amhersts my father and I appeared to reach the point of a final silence between us. Some juncture had been crossed like the moment that passed between strangers when an overture was no longer possible; and then the longer the silence went on the more unbridgeable it seemed. Days went by, then weeks, when not so much as a word passed between us: it was as if we'd had a language once that had been slowly withdrawn from us to its last syllable, had left us now with only the animal sensing of impression and mood.

At school I'd become friends with a Sicilian, Vince Lasala. He'd come to Canada around the same time as I had, and had remained, like me, a year behind in school. At first he had played up these similarities with a kind of public camaraderie that seemed intended less to join us than to measure out some distance between us; yet in the end we'd become friends exactly through the pretence of that first forced gregariousness, through my going along with it till we'd slowly been propelled by it into the habit of each other's company. Afterwards, when things were more taken for granted between us, this exaggerated Italianness began to seem merely a kind of mask he wore, exploiting it with his mafia jokes, his Sicilian swear words, but then quietly contemptuous when people were taken in by it. I walked home with him sometimes after school, expecting at first to discover some mark there of his being Sicilian, some cruder or more exotic version of Italianness, but finding instead a sedateness, his house nestled, with its low, brick modernity, its carpeted rooms and back patio, amidst a dozen like it in the quiet green of his subdivision, always the peculiar air of leisure there that came from not living on a farm. Sometimes I'd linger in his living room with a beer until it was too late to go back to school for the bus and I'd have to wait for Vince's father to return from the fishery with the car, seeming then to try on Vince's home like some more comfortable suit of clothes before returning to my own.

Weekends we went out with Vince's friend Tony Peralta. I kept awaiting some change in my life then, some sudden, belated entry into adolescence; but our evenings quickly took on a predictable sameness, the endless cruising and cigarettes, the pinball games, the parties we crashed at the Italian club. For the first while Vince reserved a special deference for me, introducing me to the other friends of his we ran into like a new, honoured acquaintance. But then more and more it began to seem that both Tony and I were merely a sort of audience to him, to his small successes at the arcade, impressive and poised when his turn came to play, quietly conscious of seeming better than we were if others were watching, to his long aimless conversations with other friends at the club while Tony and I stood by getting silently drunk. Sometimes he danced, ungainly and stiff with his narrow, immigrant's body but still keeping up a kind of dignity, in the slower ones putting a hand on the small of the girl's back and casually drawing her to him, now and then her smile opening over his shoulder at some comment he'd made in their whispering closeness. Tony and I would stand hardly speaking at the edge of the dance floor then like Vince's attendants, me wondering at the ungrudging way Tony simply took Vince for granted, at this untroubled silence in him when we were left alone. At school sometimes Tony would pass me in the hall with merely a nod and a crooked half-smile as if in acknowledgement of some unspoken complicity between us, the only sign in him then of all the wasted hours in which our friendship with Vince had forced us together.

I grew to hate these evenings, their monotony, their frustrated expectation, the deadness in me when I was home again and in bed, numbed from liquor and cigarettes, the sense I had then that I'd found nothing else in my life to put against its other emptinesses. But nights when neither Vince nor I could get a car, or when Vince didn't call, there'd be his stories to put up with on Monday, the other friends he and Tony had gone out with, the sense that his real life always happened apart from me.

"I thought about calling you, eh, but it was kind of a last-minute thing."

I saw through these stories he'd have ready and not, saw how even our own evenings out seemed unrecognizable in his retelling of them, in the aura of significance he'd imbue them with. Yet still I felt a kind of rage at my exclusion, at his power to wound me when I wanted to think of myself as somehow his better.

We spent our lunch hours at the arcade. At that time of day it was nearly deserted, sometimes only the two of us there with the run of the machines, George, the Portuguese man who looked after it, cooking up greasy hamburgers for our lunch on his tiny grill while his attention flitted to the small television he kept near the cash.

"You boys, you're good boys, you never make any trouble for me."

Without other people around Vince seemed diminished somehow, all his other friends, his other possibilities, coming down then to only the two of us, our friendship seeming then merely a kind of shared aloneness, promising nothing more than itself, the cigarettes we shared, the laconic conversations, the mute tense endless games of pinball. Yet there was a sort of intimacy in these lunch-hour excursions, the silent walks together down the gloomy sidestreet that led from the school, the air sickly sweet with the smell our cigarettes made in the cold, the sense the arcade gave in its dingy spareness of a covert delinquency, of a world set apart from the normal routine of our lives. Something fell away from us then, our tangled need to best one another, the two of us together in our small common enterprise while George sat hunched shadowy in the background before his TV like our silent guardian. What I felt most then was simply the fear that I disappointed Vince somehow, not casual enough, not sure, not able to enter the world of unthinking poise he seemed to inhabit; but afterwards he'd still find stories to tell of our time together, not lies so much as a subtle heightening, the different mood things seemed to have happened in, perhaps how he really saw things though nothing we did then ever seemed to me much more than simply killing time.

In the spring the arcade grew more popular, groups of boys beginning to drift in from the high school, slowly taking it over with their noisy playing and talk. Some understanding between Vince and me seemed to break, Vince growing canny again, conscious once more of an audience, always finding his subtle means of drawing attention to himself, seeming to create at each instant the person he wanted to be seen as. His confidence then was like a weapon, something I could only stand in the shadow of, like his stories a kind of pretence yet still working for him, winning people over, enviable not so much for its truth as for his ability to carry it off.

At some point Johnny Elias began to come into the arcade, my old nemesis from St. Michael's, he and his friends playing pool for four dollars a game at the table at back, Johnny dressed always in the same slim jeans and the same boots with their three-inch heels, his hair grown out to an Afro now to crown the long lean trunk of his body like an exotic bush.

"Vic-tore, my son, how's the *zubbrah*."

But he seemed to invest no special energy in me, only his usual offhand indifference.

He came over once after he'd finished a game to where Vince and I were playing pinball, casual, seeking distraction, propping his pool cue against a machine to watch me play.

"Victor, my boy, you've gotta put more English on the ball." Almost friendly, paternal. But he began to jiggle the machine as I played, trying to force the ball up to the extra-points hole at the top.

"Come on, Vic, push it up there."

The ball dropped in.

"All right, rack 'em up there, buddy," Vince said.

The scoreboard clicked upward and the ball popped back into play, Johnny beginning to work the machine again.

"Just leave it," I said.

"Come on, buddy, we're hot."

It seemed for an instant that things could go either way, that if I could just bring myself to go along then what was happening could almost pass as if there were no humiliation in it.

"I said just leave it."

I'd made the choice; Johnny gave the machine a final shove and tilted it.

"Too bad, my son, game over."

Vince was still standing to one side of me. I expected some sign from him but he seemed perfectly neutral, unreadable.

"Fucking asshole," I said, under my breath.

"Eh, buddy?" Johnny flicked the back of his hand hard against my cheek. "Did you say something?"

I was trapped now, wished for some easy return to the dull normalcy of a few moments before but there was no going back.

"Tell me again what you said, buddy, I didn't hear you."

"Asshole," I said.

He shoved me hard against the corner of a machine, my back crunching up against metal. But my eye had gone to his pool cue: I reached for it and wrapped my hands around it, all instinct suddenly, swung out. For an instant as the cue arced toward him, sank finally into the cushion of his hair as he tried to duck away from it, I felt a delicious power surge in me, the fullness of my anger, its drunken single-mindedness. But then the cue hit bone and all my will to fight seemed to drain from me like some stranger that had fled, and it was a kind of surprise afterwards to see Johnny loom up still large with his resolve, still intent on prosecuting this violence I'd given licence to by striking him. In an instant his foot had swung up hard into my groin; then the searing pain, its slow sudden blooming like an explosion in me. I fell, screaming perhaps, my mind emptied, felt another blow on my face like a dull aftershock and then voices, Vince's and Johnny's, George's shouts.

"Bums! Get out of here, all of you. Like animals!"

Afterwards I found myself sitting on the toilet in the arcade's tiny washroom, still dazed with the memory of pain. Vince was holding a bloodied paper towel to my nose, a warm trickle seeping into it almost pleasant somehow, reassuring.

"You all right?"

It took an instant to find my voice.

"I think so."

"I guess you must've passed out."

I took the towel from him and we remained a few moments in awkward silence, crammed close in the washroom's smallness.

"Fucking asshole," Vince said finally. "You got him good, though, that first hit."

We skipped class for the rest of the day, wandering into town through spring sun and then down greening sidestreets to the lake. What had happened seemed strangely distant already, a kind of role I'd played, my mind emptied now as after a fever. I wanted only to guard the stillness in me, felt far from any sense of grievance or hurt but was content to let my silence encourage Vince's solicitude.

"In Italy the water would be hot enough to swim in by now," he said. It was the first time Italy had come up like this between us, had assumed a physical presence and shape. "Our place was right by the beach, eh – the people who stayed are making a shit-load now from the tourists, my old man would be rolling in it by now if we'd stayed there."

I had an image of his village in Sicily, the fishing boats and narrow streets, the stone houses rolling down to the sea, of some other person he might have been there if he'd stayed, the incarnation somehow of his village's sun-bleached familiarity.

"It was different there," he added strangely. "Everyone knew each other. Here they're just in their own little groups."

We were walking along the beach, picking our way through the winter flotsam built up there, the reeds and driftwood and rotting fish. For an instant a single mood seemed to wash over us, pull back.

"I guess we better get going," Vince said finally.

And it was only now that I began to regret my fight, what it would cost me, that our friendship wouldn't be strong enough to erase the residue it would leave between us after these moments of grace though Vince was merely alone and vulnerable like I was, trying to make his own way.

It was odd that for all the hours Vince and I spent together in the elusive pursuit of our adolescence the times that most lingered with me were the ones at his home, after school or invited in if I came to pick him up for an evening out, left then with a beer to wait while he dressed, or simply sitting with him for a time in the placid intimacy of his living room. Some distance between us seemed clearer then, what our obligations were, what respect we owed each other; and I'd feel a quiet status settle around me there as a guest, his parents and brothers soberly attentive in the background, the whole house seeming to adjust itself to allow me a place in it. A different person came out in Vince then, adult, secure in his role, the eldest son, exercising an unthinking authority over his brothers, left free to smoke in the house; he might have been some aging gentleman inviting me into his home, his life, like a cherished friend, saying come, come, all things are possible between us here. What seemed to wreck us in the end was the world, our need to fit it, what we sought there and what we missed in the seeking, who we might have been to each other if we could have allowed in ourselves some unfolding of what seemed merely a waiting, these islanded moments alone, their small respectful calm.

XVI

In the summer our nights out took on new dimension, bars in Windsor and Detroit, house parties Vince heard about, late-night drunks with other groups of Vince's friends along deserted sideroads or on the Seacliff beach. We ran car races sometimes on the town line, terror pressing down on me the whole time like the darkness our cars hurtled through; there was nothing in me that was true to the sort of bravado we put on then and yet the fear seemed to hone a violence in me, focusing it like a pinpoint on that single sudden rush through the dark.

At the end of these evenings I felt always the same recoiling, the numbness and self-disgust; and then the following day there'd be my father's useless unspoken anger at how late I'd come in, at the signs of drunkenness, at all the contempt toward him he imagined in me in our silent unknowing. In one of his odd, sudden gestures of veiled generosity he'd bought a new car and turned his old one over to me and Aunt Teresa; but now I took it out at the smallest opportunity, to go to school, to smoke, for my joyless evenings out, felt the resentment in him at my abuse of it, at the endless tanks of gas I used from our pump, and yet was somehow unable to make any concession to him. I seemed to be playing some pointless game, stubbornly resisting him, always doing the thing that was most an affront, and then punishing myself for it afterwards with his silent anger.

We stopped in at Diana's sometimes at the end of a night out. There was a waitress there who began to be friendly with us, just the noncommittal disdain of recognition at first but then each time lingering an instant longer at our table when she served us.

"So what do you guys do every night anyways, coming in here at one o'clock in the morning."

"Oh, you know. Drink, look for women."

"Well I guess you're still looking." Then an instant's pause and her laugh, as if she were laughing at someone else's joke.

She'd somehow picked us out as being Italian, seeming to see something strangely exotic or amusing in that.

"That's right, nice Italian boys," Vince said, playing her up. "That's Vittorio and Antonio over there and I'm Vincenzo."

"Vittorio, that's nice," she said, slurring the name back into twangy English. "I seen you sometimes at school."

But her picking me out like that brought out a strange aggression in me.

"That's funny," I said, "I've never seen you."

Vince and Tony laughed.

"We only just moved down from Michigan last spring." Matter-of-fact, speaking directly to me. Then, as she was leaving: "My name's Crystal, since no one's going to ask."

"Hey, Crystal," Vince called after her. "Nice name."

"*Migna*, she's a big one," Tony said.

"Victor, my boy," Vince said, "I think she's got the hots for you."

"Yeah, right."

There had been that, the energy that had passed from her for an instant like a code, though some kind of mistake, some wrong impression she'd formed of me that she'd see through in an instant. But then the next time we came in she seemed to brighten at the sight of us, coming over to our table with an unabashed familiarity.

"I was wondering when you guys would come in again."

"Did you miss us?" Vince said.

"Not you."

"Maybe Victor then."

"Victor? Who's that?"

"My good friend Vittorio, don't you remember him?"

She laughed.

"Victor, yuk, Vittorio's much nicer."

I was surprised how her laughter cut me, how much I'd invested in the possibility she might like me. But Vince seemed certain of her.

"She's yours Victor, I tell you."

"She doesn't even know me."

"What's there to know? In the dark we all look the same."

Crystal came back with our orders.

"You must get kind of bored working here," Vince said.

"Talking to guys like you, sure."

"What about Victor here, you seem to like him all right. Maybe the two of you should get together some time."

Tony laughed. I ought to have made some remark then, something funny and sharp, dismissive, but merely sat there in flushed silence.

"I gotta go," Crystal said finally.

But when she brought us our bill she'd written a phone number on the back of it.

"I'm off tomorrow night," she said, then was gone.

Outside, both Vince and Tony seemed infected by my own euphoria.

"All right, Victor!" Tony shouted, strangely energized, then put two fingers into his mouth and whistled loud and long into the empty street.

I called the next day from the phone in my father's office. Now that the thing was before me I felt only the dread of it, its nagging reminder of how wretched I was: I was nearly eighteen, had never dated a girl, made love to one.

"I didn't think you'd call," Crystal said, disarmingly frank.

"Well here I am."

We made arrangements to go to a drive-in in Windsor. But already I felt something go dead in me, the conversation perfunctory and strained as after some argument.

"I guess I'll see you around eight," I said.

"Sure."

She lived at the town limits, her house part of a last straggling row that stretched out past St. Michael's before the town gave way to open country. The house had the look of an old farmhouse that had been slowly hemmed in by the encroaching town, narrow and ramshackle and tall, its Insulbrick siding warping from the walls and its porch leaning precariously. A painted wind toy, a cartoon-faced fireman with revolving legs, stood endlessly running at the foot of the driveway, oddly hopeful and bright there against the house's fading red.

Crystal was waiting in a weather-greyed chair on the porch,

springing up at once when I drove up the lane and coming toward the car with a lumbering girlishness. She was dressed in a short, sleeveless sun-dress that seemed incongruous over her big-boned shoulders and hips after the trim fullness of her uniform. Her hand went down instinctively to pull her hem toward her knees when she settled into the car.

"Hello, Victor."

"I thought you didn't like that name."

"Oh, that, I was just making fun."

She laughed, this time her laughter seeming to betray a vulnerability like a window into her, something in me brightening at the sound of it.

We drove through the town, the wind swirling warmly through the open windows, blowing Crystal's hair back into a tousled fullness. There was a quality in the air, a peculiar, late-summer mellowing though it was only early August, that filled me suddenly with a sense of promise like the first pleasant haze of drunkenness or half-sleep; we sat several moments without speaking, seeming joined in that mood, Crystal murmuring along with the lyrics of a Dylan song on the radio.

"Do you like Dylan?" I said.

"Oh, is that who that is?"

But then once we'd passed through town to open highway and the wind forced us to close the windows the world seemed to fall back, leave us stranded there together in the car's intimacy.

"So how was it you ended up moving here from Michigan?"

Though I had the sense now I'd missed some opportunity, that the moment when the right tone might have been struck between us had already passed.

"I dunno, my mum's sister's down here and my folks are getting divorced and all that."

"Oh. I'm sorry about that."

"It's all right, it's not your fault."

She laughed but I couldn't seem to pick up on her humour.

"I guess it was kind of hard moving here and everything."

"I dunno, it's all right."

And already a panic had started to build in me, a heaviness I took for boredom beginning to creep into her voice.

Less than halfway to Windsor we had lapsed into unbroken silence. In the thickening gloom of nightfall the silence seemed a pit we'd fallen into, drawing us in more deeply each moment it went on. I thought of the long evening still stretching before us in the car's silence-poisoned closeness, how impossible things would be, of the vision I'd had of some better self, light-hearted and full of confidence and grace, who might have slipped an arm casually round Crystal's shoulders, kissed her, won her over.

At the drive-in I asked if she wanted popcorn, desperate to free myself from the pressure of our silence.

"Sure."

But when I returned from the concession she'd moved perceptibly toward the centre of the seat. I didn't understand, our date already ruined in my mind, didn't see how she could continue on in the charade of it.

"Are you angry or anything?"

The question jolted me.

"No, do I seem like it?" But she was right: something in me was hard with anger, my jaw stiff with the tension of it.

"I dunno," Crystal said, awkward. "You just seem so quiet and everything."

Her candour seemed to strip some veil from between us: I felt aware of her suddenly, human and real beside me, as if for the first time.

"I'm just shy, that's all," I said, though the word left a taste in my mouth like bile. "I'm always quiet."

"Yeah, I thought so," Crystal said. "That's how come I noticed you when you came into the restaurant and everything, because you seemed different like that."

And though her compliment only seemed to point up what I most disliked in myself still I was glad to have it, to be able to protect myself in this image she had of me.

The film came on. It was a trashy horror film but Crystal seemed drawn by it, growing animated now, making fun but also oddly involved. There was a character, a detective of some sort, punctilious and sceptical and cold, who made her bristle with animosity.

"God, he's such an asshole, he's such an asshole!"

I sat during the whole film in my own corner of the seat, never felt there was a moment when I'd earned any intimacies. But on the trip home Crystal remained squarely in the seat's centre, the heat of her tangible there beside me. In her driveway she leaned toward me suddenly and grazed my lips with her own.

"I'm off work tomorrow too, if you want to call or anything."

We began to see each other regularly, within a few weeks moving almost imperceptibly from the awkwardness of our first date into a kind of habitualness, one date simply leading on to another until it seemed hard to remember when things had been any different between us. I spent two or three evenings a week at her house watching TV with her in the comfortable clutter of her living room, her mother and sisters, Rocky and Kate, seeming to accept me there with an odd indulgence, Crystal

189

locking her arm in mine on the sagging couch as if displaying me before them like a prize.

"It looks like Crystal's got her hooks on a handsome one this time," Kate, the eldest, said. "You should have seen some of the ones she dragged in back home."

There was always this sense of being held in esteem there, in the tired, sad pleasure Crystal's mother appeared to take in me, in Rocky's tomboyish lingering near me as if to await some moment to bask in my attention; and I seemed to have entered there as by a kind of inevitability, this house of women I'd somehow become the man of, there to complete its half-familyness with my own.

Yet even in that first flush of acceptance there was already the doubt. It was the quickness of things I couldn't understand, how I'd earned this ready entry when I'd shown them all so little, remained forever awkward and inarticulate with them for fear of contradicting whatever image it was they had of me; and then the longer things went on the more I felt torn between my relief at the effortlessness of it all and my unease at how much appeared already taken for granted. For Crystal it seemed that whatever it was that had formed between us had become already immutable: she talked often of the future, of the things we would do, the next week, the next month, the next year, obliviously constant in her affection for me even through my own moods and silences, silences that more and more became charged with an unfocused resentment. But for my part I seemed never to have reached the point where I'd made a choice, had somehow merely given in to her own attraction to me as if it were something I had no right to oppose. We usually ended our evenings now necking in the car or on the couch, some grim urgency underlying this contact for me, pushing me on like a separate will; and yet the further it took me the more the rest of me withdrew, refusing to give itself over, seeming then the proof of the wrongness between me and Crystal, this sense I was furthest from her when I should be most close. Rubbing up through our clothes once against the hard muscle of her thigh I came suddenly, for an instant all my insides seeming to liquefy and flow out of me; but even in that instant there was the same withholding in me, not so much shame as a failure of emotion, and afterwards it was that failure that I seemed most anxious to hide from her in keeping from her what had happened.

School began. In that context we seemed so unlikely suddenly, with our different worlds and interests and friends. I'd formed a life at school now outside of Vince and his group in which she seemed incongruous; and slowly a kind of partitioning began, a turning from her there as if to hold intact the different images of myself I'd splintered into. I imagined at first that Crystal didn't notice this tension in me and yet gradually an understanding developed that things were somehow different between us at school; she stopped waiting for me outside my classes, stopped coming up behind me in the halls to slip an arm silently into mine. I couldn't see her there now without feeling a mix of shame and contempt, for what I was doing to her, what she let me get away with, her sudden brightening at the sight of me and then her instinctive restraint. Yet somehow we went on in that way as if there was nothing unnatural or strange in it, though outside school we'd meet and at once revert to our other selves.

Weekends Crystal had off we went out sometimes with Vince and Tony. The group of us formed an odd, ill-sorted family in our differences and incompatibilities, Crystal already beginning to seem more a part of Vince's and Tony's world than of mine, perhaps simply because I'd met her with them or because together they formed now this separate, other life I led, my real life in a way yet provisional, leading nowhere. Away from Vince, Crystal spoke of him with a disdain that secretly pleased me, doing mocking imitations of his walk, in her version of it a strutting swagger.

"He think's he's such a big man."

But then I'd be envious of the way they played off one another when they were together, Vince bringing out an energy in her that made her seem oddly strong-willed and desirable. It must have appeared then from a distance that she was merely part of a casual foursome we formed that Vince was the leader of.

"Yeah, I seen you guys the other night with that American girl, what's her name," one of his friends said once, asking after her as if she were some common property we shared. "I had a little thing with her last spring at the show, eh, not too bad."

A leaden pause.

"Victor here's been going out with her a few months," Vince said.

"Oh, Christ, man, sorry about that. It was no big deal, eh, just necking and shit, no offence."

The incident left a residue in me like grit. I never thought of Crystal this way, had to twist my mind to imagine her as part of this teenage delinquency, this quick furtive contact in the dark. I felt a kind of protectiveness toward her but also something else, the need to hold this thing against her in some way, to break her with it, as if in breaking her I could somehow prove my right to be free of her.

"What're you thinking about?"

"Nothing."

"You're sure giving nothing a lot of thought. I can hear the wheels turning up there in that big brain of yours."

But though I could see that I was the one, that she held herself out to me like some fragile thing I'd been entrusted with, still I couldn't find the way to stop the quiet seething in me when I was with her.

It seemed in the end that I was no different from Vince and his friends, no better, had wanted only my stories to tell, the groping in theatres, the normalcy of that, the conquests, had wanted some relinquishing in me of the fever my body was; and what seemed to keep me from these things wasn't choice but simply that I lacked some lightness necessary to carry them off. At home I lay in the bathtub sometimes envisioning Crystal spread naked before me, her imperfections strangely arousing then, the bulk of her hips, the pale dwarfed insufficiency of her breasts, every flaw a kind of sanction of my freedom from her; and stroking myself beneath the water I'd imagine sinking into the liquid heat of her until I came, bleeding into her then in the safe intensity of imagination what I could find no place for between us, my cold loveless desire.

In March, Crystal's sister Kate got married. The wedding seemed oddly impromptu to me after Italian ones, with its single bridesmaid and usher, Kate's simple trainless dress, the quick ceremony at the church; and then the reception at the Moose Lodge in Goldsmith, the hall tawdry and domestic and close as a living room, the food served in one quick onrush of vegetables and meat and the bar offering only soft drinks and beer. After the meal a young ruddy-faced disk jockey set out rock and country songs on a scratchy phonograph.

"This one's for the young folks, let's see you shaking it out there."

Crystal's father had come down from Michigan. At the church he'd towered over Kate with a grim composure as he'd led her down the aisle, his face creased with fatigue like something chiselled out of stone. But at the reception he grew animated, a small crowd lingering at the bar in the circle of energy he seemed to have formed there. He took my hand with a smooth, reassuring aggressiveness when Crystal introduced us.

"So you're Crystal's young man, is that it?" His speech was pure as glass, had none of the twang of Crystal's. "She's said some very fine things about you. That's a pretty high recommendation as far as I'm concerned, Crystal's always been very fussy about her men."

"I guess he'll do for now," Crystal said.

But she seemed so vulnerable before him, so awkward and adoring, seemed to miss entirely the edge of forced enthusiasm in him. I saw him dancing later with Kate, Kate distant and independent and cool and he with the same grimness he'd had in church, more himself somehow, more defeated; and it was suddenly clear to me that Kate was the daughter he cared about, something crumbling in me then at the thought of all Crystal's innocent need.

Crystal and I danced. Through the fabric of her dress I felt her hips sway beneath my hands. For a few moments there amidst the loud rough exuberance of the other guests we seemed to form an island, held safe in our aloneness as we danced out of rhythm in drunken slowness.

When we left, around two in the morning, there was a mood of pleasant relinquishment between us. In the truck, which I'd had to take because my aunt had needed the car, Crystal slipped her legs under the gearshift with a low hiss of nylon and pressed up against me, her breath like steam in the cab's damp cold. For the first time I felt my body give itself over to her. I began to kiss her, leisurely and deep, moved a hand over her belly and hips, between the warmth of her thighs.

"That feels nice," she said, beery and guileless, and it seemed the first time there'd been this acknowledgement that what we did was somehow intended for pleasure.

For a moment my desire for her seemed to reach an absolute fullness. I tried to ease myself around on the seat but the cramped closeness of the cab made any comfortable position impossible. A car drove by on the highway, its flash of headlights casting up for an instant the cab's farm-engendered squalor, the dust on the dashboard, the paper scraps, the ragged wad of bills and receipts my father clipped to the visor.

"We should go somewhere," I said, wanting some sign from her of common intent. But she settled away without speaking, squeezing back past the gearshift to give me room to work it.

I pulled onto the highway, struggling to formulate some plausible scenario for bringing the evening to what had seemed for a moment its inevitable conclusion, the small mundane steps that would lead us there. But already my desire seemed debased, made unsavoury, in my having to plan its fulfilment.

We began to come up toward Mersea. At the last instant I flicked my signal and turned down my concession.

"Where're we going?" Crystal said.

"I just wanted to show you something," I said, wanting to make a joke of it but hearing the words come out awkward and flat.

At the driveway to the farm I put out the headlights and downshifted only to third before turning in to keep the sound of the engine low. The house lights were out, my aunt's car parked at the side of the kiln; but the garage door was closed. It was possible my father hadn't come in from the club yet, but I didn't have the nerve to stop to check, driving on to the boiler room and then cringing at the rumble of the overhead door as its tiny motor slowly rolled it up to let us in and then down again. I felt panicked now at having brought Crystal here, and yet some compulsion pushed me on, the sense that there was some line I had to cross, some burden I needed to free myself of, wouldn't let me simply back the truck up again, take Crystal home.

Crystal and I had climbed down from the cab. In the darkness the boiler room was all dim shapes and cavernous shadow. A single pin of orange light shone out from the boiler's tiny viewing hole, bright in the dark like a cat's eye.

"Where are we?" Crystal whispered.

I realized suddenly that she'd never been to the farm before, knew as little of my life here as my family did of my life beyond it.

"I live here," I said, awkward. But Crystal laughed.

"Nice place you got," she said. "Pretty big."

Her laughter seemed to dispel for an instant the strangeness between us.

"At least it's warm," I said.

In darkness I led her toward the door that opened into the greenhouses. I'd thought of grabbing a blanket or some old clothes from my father's office to lay on the ground yet still couldn't bring myself to make obvious my intentions.

Inside the greenhouses moonlight dappled the plants like frost, luminous as in some magic place.

"This is wild," Crystal said. "It's like Africa or something."

But it occurred to me that she might have taken me at my

word earlier, thought now I'd brought her here merely to share this with her, this other life I led. I'd handled things so badly, bringing her here, trying both to hide my intentions and gain her approval of them. The moment of feeling between us in the truck seemed already impossibly distant, Crystal merely a sort of impediment now, at once infuriatingly passive, appearing ready to follow my lead without resistance, and yet still stolidly herself, living out her own version of what was happening between us, refusing simply to dissolve into the fantasy version of her that I'd reserved for this moment.

I led her up into the darkness of one of the rows, thinking we might lie on the straw there. But I couldn't muster the deliberateness it would have taken to have us stretch out there in our good clothes on the straw's spongy dampness.

"Where're we going?" Crystal whispered, amused or merely bewildered.

We stood hemmed in now by the wall of plants around us, the air musty with the stable smell of manure and straw.

"Just here."

I began to kiss her where we stood, moving my hands over her awkwardly, trying to regain my earlier arousal but wanting only to be past this moment now, away, outside and driving or already home in bed and alone. I heard a sound like a distant engine, had an image suddenly of my father opening the greenhouse door, flicking on the lights, coming to stand there at the end of our row; but then everything happened very quickly. Somehow in the darkness I managed to draw Crystal's panties to her knees, to drop my own pants as well; and then in a confusion of hands and flesh I tried to enter her and came almost at once, not certain whether I'd withdrawn from her before the first throb of my coming or whether I'd entered her at all.

Then at once the familiar failure in me, the awkwardness as we pulled up our clothes, our silence. I felt the sinking hopelessness of dreams I'd committed murder in, the sense of no going back.

"Are you all right?"

Her voice in the dark, the whole of me turning from her at the sound of it, needing to blot her out.

"I'm fine." A dead pause. "What about you?"

"Yeah. I guess I wasn't expecting that."

We didn't speak again until I dropped her off at her house.

"You're kind of quiet," she said. I could hear the question in her voice, the need to know more about what had happened.

"Sorry," I said.

"That's all right."

She leaned toward me to kiss me but our lips met awkwardly.

"Will you call me tomorrow?"

"Yes."

But I awoke the next day with the same hollowness in me, what had happened eclipsing my thoughts like a haemorrhage at the centre of them. From bed I heard my father preparing for mass, the dull sound of his movement, the clink of pots and cups as Aunt Teresa prepared his coffee.

"Where's Vittorio?" Leaden, accusing.

"I don't know, he's in bed, go see for yourself."

"We'll see how long this goes on, out every night until three."

Though when he came back from mass he said nothing to me.

Around one o'clock Crystal phoned.

"Hi, stranger."

She sounded oddly lighthearted, some version of the previous night different from my own seeming to be playing out in her.

"I guess Kate must've got to sleep around the same time we did," she said, then her laugh.

"Yeah," I said.

"You're a big talker today."

"Sorry. I guess I'm just hung over or something."

"Out drinking again last night?"

A pause, then her voice dipped.

"That was the first time for me."

I felt my heart sink, knew she was telling the truth though I'd assumed all along there'd been others.

"For me too," I said dully.

"Yeah, right," she said, laughing. "I know you Eye-ties."

Another pause.

"I guess it wasn't very safe," I said.

But Crystal seemed unconcerned.

"I think it's all right."

"How do you know?"

"Oh, a girl knows, that's all."

She laughed again. I gave myself over to her own unconcern as to a kind of magic, afraid to question it lest its protective spell be broken; but my first thought was that I was free now to break with her.

"Why don't we go for a drive or something," she said. "I'd like to see you."

When I came by for her she leaned into me in the car to kiss me and take my arm, content and proprietorial like a bride though my whole body screamed at her touch.

"I feel so close to you today."

I drove out to the dock. It was cold out, the dock and the boardwalk beyond it deserted; though out on the lake the ice had begun to clear, heaved up into great jagged mounds like frozen waves near the shore but giving way beyond the break-water to open blue.

I couldn't find the way to break the silence burgeoning between us.

"Is anything wrong?" Crystal said.

"I dunno."

"What is it? You're so quiet."

But my thoughts seemed to crackle in my head like static.

"I dunno. I guess I feel a little weird, that's all."

"About what?"

"I dunno. About us, I guess."

Then an awkward silence.

"What're you saying?" And already there was an edge in her voice, a retreat. My mind strained for a response but I couldn't find the right way to avoid the truth.

"I guess things don't feel right between us for me."

"What're you saying?" The edge, harder. "What do you mean, they don't feel right?"

"I don't know what I mean. It's just a feeling, I don't know."

A strangeness had fallen over us. Outside, the lake, the white rocks of the breakwater, the snowy heaps of ice near the shore, had a hard, sun-brightened clarity, reassuringly real and inhuman; next to them we seemed anomalies, amorphous, on the brink of dissolving into this shapelessness we were drifting in.

"You're such an asshole," she said finally, and already she seemed transformed, completely outside me now, my enemy. "You think you're so much better than me, don't you. It kills me that everyone thinks you're such a nice guy. You're not like that at all, you're just an asshole."

I couldn't bring myself to answer her. Her hatred seemed so

certain and hard; I felt ruined in the face of it, saw the sum of me reduced to the simple truths she'd seen into.

Crystal's eyes were bright with tears but she wouldn't give in to them.

"What a *fucking* asshole."

We sat silent for several minutes. It had taken so little to strip away her mistaken impression of me: I couldn't imagine now how we'd gone on so long, what had kept her attracted to me. I wanted to offer some reparation, wanted both to hold this sudden clarity between us yet somehow make things better again.

"I'm sorry," I said.

"For what."

"For everything, I guess."

A silence.

"So I guess you're sorry you ever got involved with me, is that what you mean?"

But beneath the edge of sarcasm in her voice there was the invitation to contradict her, as if she were still offering, even though she'd seen through to the truth of us, a way out, a way back.

"That's not it." And already I could feel myself retreating. "I just meant I was sorry if I hurt you or anything."

Crystal didn't respond.

"I guess I was just nervous, that's all, with last night and everything. I feel like everything's happened too fast, that's all."

"It was your idea," she said.

"I know."

She shifted, still stony but seeming buoyed for an instant by the point she'd won against me.

"Maybe I made a mistake," I said. "Maybe we should go more slowly for a while."

But I was merely spinning words out now, was surprised when Crystal responded to them as if they'd had meaning.

"If that's what you want I guess I don't have much choice, do I?"

We drove back to Crystal's house in silence.

"Do I still get to call you? Or is that too fast for you?"

I went home with my mind in a haze, uncertain what had been decided between us. There had been the moment of terror, of exhilaration, during her anger when it had seemed some certainty had crystallized between us; but it had flashed and then gone, untenable like an unstable element, had left merely this bad feeling between us without gain.

But then at school the next day Crystal came up behind me in the hall as if nothing had happened.

"Hi, stranger."

And she smiled at me so instinctively that all the awkwardness of the previous day seemed an aberration suddenly.

"You must've had a rough weekend, you look kind of hungover," she said, and laughed.

We seemed to return for a few weeks then to the first timid stages of our dating, careful and courteous and attentive, our argument like a shadow looming at the limit of us that we didn't dare approach again. But some difference between us had been made clear now, both of us seeming slowly to slip back into our separate lives even as we carried on in the pretence that nothing had changed; and it was only now that I seemed to see her with any clarity, as someone separate from me and our relationship, made poignant already in my memory of her through this quiet giving her up, in her small, familiar gestures, the life she lived there in her house on the edge of town. From the window of an upper classroom I saw her once after school walking away from the front exit toward town, alone but oddly buoyant, heart-breaking, lost in her thoughts, swaying her shoulders as she walked with a girlish exaggeration; and I felt a closeness to her then in this fleeting secret glimpse of her without me like some darkness I'd touched at the bottom of myself.

The end of the school year approached. I seemed to be concluding some phase in my life, still a year of high school remaining for me but unspoken decisions having been made now, in how we'd been streamed, about who we were, what was possible for us. Weekends I continued to go out with Vince and Tony but they seemed now like some vestige I was no longer sure of the use of; and the less I made Crystal a part of our evenings together the more separate from them I felt, become merely an observer among them, a guest.

"So what's happening with you and Crystal, are you guys still together?"

And for all Vince's own stories of girls he'd met or picked up it was the first time since I'd started seeing Crystal that the subject of her had ever come up between us.

"It's just casual I guess, we sort of broke up."

"Just casual," Tony said, laughing suggestively, but I let the matter drop.

But that summer it fell out by chance once in the last-minute rush of filling a Friday night that Vince and Crystal and I went up to Windsor together to see a film, the group of us seeming joined like fragments from different pictures and yet oddly intimate for that, somehow put on the same level for once by our mutual abandonment.

"Long time no see, big shot," Crystal said, mussing Vince's hair as she climbed in between us in the front seat of Vince's car.

"I guess you must've missed me."

"Yeah, right."

Then on the way home Vince took a short cut through some of the back roads and came out on Highway 76 just above my concession.

"I might as well drop you first, eh, if that's all right."

"Sure."

I had the premonition of some betrayal as he dropped me off, even took a certain righteous pleasure in the thought, and yet the next day felt as if a fist had struck up against me when Vince recounted this fantasy of mine to me as fact.

"She started rubbing my leg and shit, eh, but I figured you guys had broken up and it was no big deal."

I could hardly make sense of this story, that it had happened or that Vince would tell it to me now, with his usual subtly boastful tone, as if it had nothing to do with me, that he'd be so foolish as to grant me this clear grudge against him. But then suddenly he seemed to twig.

"No offence, eh, I mean it was no big deal. If I'd thought you guys were still together I wouldn't have gone for it."

"No offence," I said, muted, accusing.

The following day Crystal called.

"Maybe we could go out or something tonight."

"Why?"

"I dunno, do I have to have a reason?"

In her driveway I killed the engine and waited for her to come out, uncertain yet what to do with this knowledge against her, this need in me to feel betrayed.

"Hello, Mister Victor."

We sat in the car a moment in silence.

"Is there anything wrong?"

"Should there be?" I said.

I could go on or not, felt the falseness in my tone yet couldn't bring myself to let the matter drop.

"What do you mean?"

A silence.

"What happened when Vince brought you home on Friday?"

"What're you talking about? Nothing happened." But there was an edge, an instant's hesitation.

"That's not what Vince told me."

"What did he tell you?"

"I dunno, you tell me."

"What did he tell you? I can't believe it, what did he tell you? He's a fucking liar."

"Is he?"

"What did he tell you?"

"He said you came on to him."

"Do you believe that?" She was practically shouting. "Do you believe that?"

"I don't know what to believe."

"He's so full of *shit*."

"He's my friend."

"Some friend, he's a fucking liar. Do you believe him?"

"I don't know."

"You're just as big an asshole as he is, I don't give a *fuck* what you believe."

And she was out of the car, the door slamming behind her and then the screen door of the house.

Something had happened, probably not as Vince had described it and yet real enough for me to use her uncertainty against her, her not knowing what I would find acceptable. Yet at bottom I didn't believe she had wronged me in any way, that our argument had been anything more than the lingering need in me to escape her. For an instant I wanted to go to her and explain these things, console her, show her how I'd failed her. But I couldn't see any way from there to the real truth of how things were between us, couldn't bring myself to give over this single, hard grievance I could hold against her.

With Vince it was the same. As the summer went on I saw less and less of him, using what had happened with Crystal like a wedge, putting him off until we both seemed to have acknowledged at some level the arbitrariness that had marked our friendship from the outset. In the fall he went on to community college in Windsor and we stopped going out together entirely, occasionally running into each other in town and agreeing to call, though we never did; and within a few months he'd begun to treat me whenever we met with the same special deference he'd shown me in the first tentative stages of our friendship, and it was hard to imagine then that we had ever dared hold each other in contempt, had ever been close enough for that.

Crystal and I didn't speak for several weeks after our argument. But then one evening she phoned.

"Hi, stranger."

My heart sank at the sound of her voice, at the thought I'd somehow come round to starting up with her again.

"Don't worry, I'm not going to make any moves on you, I just wanted to see how you are."

She'd given up her job at Diana's and was working full time at the Fotomat now, having decided not to go back to school in the fall.

"It's so cliquish and everything there, everyone's such assholes. Anyways I'd rather make money."

Afterwards she never called again. But driving through town I often passed her in her little Fotomat booth at the Erie Mall, went out of my way sometimes to catch a glimpse of her there, looking staunch and mature in her uniform and her pinned-back hair and still brightening then at the sight of me, waving and shouting out as I passed as if nothing unkind had ever happened between us.

XVII

We had built another two greenhouses on the farm, joined to the
ones from a few years before like reflections, their spreading lake
of glass now filling the field that edged Tsi'Umberto's house.
Together the group of them formed a space exhilarating in its
vastness, with its long vistas of posts like colonnades, its network
of wires and pipes and machines, its glint of metal and glass; and
the farm now had the modern, efficient feel of a factory, of
something that had dwarfed us, made us irrelevant, grown
larger somehow than the sum of our individual histories. One
evening the lawyer came by, Mr. Newland, and set out a thick
sheaf of documents on our kitchen table which my father and
Tsi'Umberto and Rocco and Aunt Teresa set their signatures to
in turn, Mr. Newland talking to them the whole time in an oddly
casual way about taxes and shares and assigning them titles,
president, vice-president, treasurer, as in some children's game.

"I'd keep an eye on Teresa if I were you," he said. "She's the
one with the real power in this organization, make no mistake
about it."

And in the sanction of these documents and titles and seals some new final order seemed to have taken shape among us, fixing us like the last coming together in a story or film.

My own role in this order seemed defined exactly by my exclusion from it, by how little I'd known of these changes and plans before they'd come to pass. Even Domenic, who had impressed me with his stubborn commitment to his small, private aspirations, doggedly finishing out his grade twelve and getting accepted into carpentry at the community college in Windsor, had finally instead been quietly drawn back into the family, going to work full time on the farm, morose but also grown larger somehow, more estimable, as if he'd compressed into a single chosen future the force of all the others he wouldn't have; and this, too, had come to pass as from some natural rhythm in the family I'd lost touch with, a silent cryptic molecular working I remained unassimilable in. We'd recently bought a new stake truck, the inscription that had been on the doors of the old one, "Mario Innocente & Son," so familiar that I'd long ceased to think about it, replaced now with "Innocente Farms Ltd.," shadow-lettered green, white, and red on each door in a wide rainbow arch; and it struck me how far my father and I had remained from the simple promise of that original inscription, the vision in it of some inevitable working out between father and son.

But I saw these things now as from a great distance, my father, the farm, my life there, felt only my imminent parting from them, the sanction my outsideness gave to my release into some new, unknown, uncontaminated future. I saw my father sometimes working alone in the conservatory we'd built off the boiler room, tending the vines and fig saplings and orange trees he'd planted there, kneeling like a child to build small protective basins of earth around each plant that shimmered blue with fertilized water like tiny oceans when he filled them; and it seemed possible then to imagine him grown old and calm and contented, pottering secretive amidst his vines and trees like some country gentleman. I wanted to leave him like that, safe in the small space of his private projects, had the sense seeing him there that things could be all right with all of us, that our histories, what we had wrecked and what we had lost, hadn't crippled us beyond redemption.

Yet it was odd when we'd so clearly prospered that my memory of our years on the farm till then was only of setbacks, the constant sense that we verged always on the brink of ruin; and still now in the perpetual arguments among my father and uncle and aunt there seemed the continuing need in us to remain forever vigilant against the brunt of whatever catastrophe we'd shouldered upon ourselves, even Rocco now drawn into this grammar, his demeanour changed, underlain with a hard weary restraint as if he had failed at some important thing. All along we'd seemed caught in this tension between initiative and retreat, bravest exactly when the worst had happened, as if we found in our ill fortune a kind of absolution, and then afterwards clutching our fear again like a talisman, living our lives with the same frugality, the same sense of threat, as the peasants in Italy who'd wondered from one year to the next if their harvest would last the winter. When I thought of us there on the farm, it was always with this feeling not so much of having moved forward as of having struggled to remain the same, forever stranded as on an island within the tight logic and rules of what was acceptable, how far we could reach.

We'd taken a trip once with Tsi'Alfredo and his family, had

packed our cars in the dead of night and driven through a chill October dawn to Niagara Falls. The trip had lasted just that one day, unfolding from our cars like a circus, all our provisions, food and pop and beer and sweets, pulled from our trunks at parks and roadside rest stops and then packed away again, our tiny caravan already wheeling back through the deadened streets of Mersea by midnight; and we'd seemed summed up in the trip like a parody of ourselves, in our avoidance of restaurants and motels but then this bounty we carried with us like gypsies, in our taking a trip in the grey cold of late October when the time for holidays had long passed, half the sights by then already closed down for the season and even the falls themselves seeming hopelessly remote in their autumn desertion. Self-contained as we'd been, the world had seemed to flash past us like some foreign planet, a place we visited but didn't belong to, dazzled briefly there by daylight and then our cars fading back again like satellites into the night.

The summer before my departure for university I began to visit the Amhersts again. At some point I'd started including their street as part of the route I took on my weeknight drives, instinctively slowing near their house as if to glean some secret from it though it presented always the same blank façade, the same glow of curtained light, the aloof nighttime calm; and then finally one night I found myself at their front door being ushered in by Mrs. Amherst, all their world suddenly as vivid before me as if I'd just left it although over three years had passed since I'd last been there.

"Victor, what a surprise! Come in, come in, I'll call your sister for you. Look how big you've gotten, almost a man now."

But the awkwardness was plain on her at seeing me again, something in her seeming to want to repel me even as she led me in.

I was left to wait in the living room, Rita appearing a moment later in the arched entrance. For an instant I didn't recognize her, so much had she grown, her body seeming stretched like a cartoon character's, long and adolescent and thin, small breasts forming cones in the cloth of her dress and her hair cut into a page-boy that made her face appear haughty and gaunt like a model's. But then her small, childish shrug of awkward greeting brought her suddenly back to me and I felt a stab of emotion, surprised somehow at the sight of her, as if she were someone I'd ceased to believe in.

"Hello, Rita."

Though already I felt some gap open between us, whatever possibility or hope I'd sensed in the instant of recognizing her seeming to vanish before I could name it.

"Hello."

Mrs. Amherst set a glass of Coke out for me on a coaster and then left us, Rita sitting across from me in an armchair. She had pulled up toward the front of it with her feet on the floor and her hands on her lap, at once childlike and primly mature, her every gesture seeming caught in this contradiction, as if some younger, more familiar Rita had been trapped in the body of this awkward, guarded stranger.

"How have you been?"

"Okay, I guess."

"How's school going?"

"It's okay."

We talked uncomfortably like that for a few minutes, Rita fidgeting in her chair, kicking idly at the floor an instant or biting a nail but then suddenly reverting to a gloomy self-consciousness.

"How's Elena?"

"She's all right, she's just upstairs. We're sisters now and all that." Though at the mention of Elena her eyes had darted towards me for an instant with a bright, guileless animation. "But I guess you already knew about that."

"About what?"

"You know, so we have the same last name and all that, Mom and Dad had to go to the lawyer and stuff."

We parted clumsily, standing in the hall a moment a few feet apart.

"Maybe I'll come by again."

"Okay."

I returned perhaps half a dozen times in what remained of the summer, in the evenings usually, wanting somehow to avoid recalling the Sunday familiarity of a few years before. The Amhersts for their part seemed to oblige in this, remaining always shadowy in these visits as if they'd relinquished Rita to me now, Mr. Amherst out in the garage half the time at work on some project, the light shining hazy above his workbench there to the dull sound of his sanding and careful hammering, and Mrs. Amherst ushering me in and afterwards out again all bustling energy and hospitality but only the sense of her present in between, her muted sounds from the kitchen as we watched TV in the rec room, her muted voice from some upstairs phone. But without their earlier rituals my visits seemed to give way to a kind of formlessness, simply these dead, aimless hours that Rita and Elena and I spent hardly speaking watching TV, shaped only by the parentheses Mrs. Amherst enclosed them in.

"All right now, girls, up to your room."

I'd expected something more from Rita and Elena, not this adolescent inarticulateness and inertia, the sense I had of simply being an adult among children. Elena seemed always to sit in sullen resistance to me, broodingly, reprimandingly pretty and watchful and lank; I could hardly bring myself to address her, had the sense always that she was seeing right through me.

"So I guess you and Rita have it pretty easy in the summer, just hanging out and watching TV." Always a hardness in my voice despite myself, a failed nonchalance that came out as accusation.

"We have swimming lessons and all that. We don't get to watch TV much except when you come."

I imagined that if I could only get Rita away from Elena during these visits then some shadow between us would fall away, that we'd grow suddenly familiar to one another with a simple sureness and rightness. Yet alone with her there was only a deflated awkwardness between us, almost a boredom, Rita's attention wandering from me then as if I were a sort of haze she couldn't fix on. Whatever line of force there was between us seemed to need other people to pass through, as in the loud, theatrical childishness she'd put on sometimes around Elena, always a contempt in her then in the way she'd play on Elena's earnest going along with her that seemed a twisted deference she showed me because I was the outsider, less familiar now than Elena, less certainly won. I thought at first it was only when I was around that this unlikeableness came out in her, this way she seemed to glance off the world as if at once to control and evade it; but then more and more I noticed how Elena catered to her with the hurt tentativeness of being used to her rebuffs, how Mrs. Amherst always spoke to her with an edge of forced indulgence.

"Rita, you know you shouldn't be wearing those shoes in the house."

Once I arrived after there'd been an argument of some sort, sensed at once the house's tension, the embarrassment in Mrs. Amherst at being caught out. But there was something else in her as well, the need to make clear to me what Rita was, as if to remind me where she'd come from.

"You'll go directly back to your room when your brother's gone."

In the rec room Elena and I sat in gloomy silence, Rita on the floor cross-legged and stiff-backed in front of the TV, closing us out.

"What's your mother angry about?"

"I dunno, some plants Rita broke or something."

"Does she get angry much?"

"I dunno. Not really. Sometimes."

Rita turned up the volume of the TV. We sat silent in the noise, Rita's back blocking our view.

"It's too loud," Elena said. "Mom's gonna get angry."

But Rita gave no sign of hearing her, continuing to stare into the screen as if we weren't there, holding us in thrall even while she shut us out. For several minutes we sat silent in our places and she hardly moved; walled up like that in her wilfulness she seemed dangerous suddenly, seemed to have taken some hard malevolence into her like a changeling.

"I guess I better go," I said finally.

Mrs. Amherst saw me out, still tense with the pressure of concealing and disclosing.

"Mr. Amherst's just watered the lawn, you'll want to stay off it on the way out."

And before I'd stepped out the volume had already died on the TV downstairs, Rita's shadow disappearing an instant later up the stairs toward her room and then her door closing with a hard controlled thud, ceding nothing.

When the fair came to town at the end of the summer I offered to take Rita and Elena to Children's Day. They were dressed in blue jeans and Bee Gees T-shirts like uniforms when I came for them, seeming made small again in their girlish suspense at appearing in their public incarnations.

"This is all they're allowed," Mrs. Amherst said, handing me two five-dollar bills. "Don't let them force any more out of you."

But in the car Rita pulled quarters and dimes from her pockets, a few crumpled dollar bills, and began to sort through them ostentatiously.

"Where did that come from?"

"Just allowances and stuff."

Canny, evasive.

"Well you're not allowed to spend it."

But she continued her silent counting, carefully folding the dollar bills, carefully slipping them back into her pocket.

At the fair I quickly grew bored in the noise and heat, the crowds of children, my embattled waiting while Rita and Elena made the rounds of the rides; I'd imagined some sort of sharing with them like a parent's indulgent husbanding of possibility but was merely the half-forgotten chaperon, visibly out of place amidst the midway's tinselly forced excitement. As a child I'd awaited the fair each year as I had the feast days in Italy, the din of it audible from our back field, its skyline of rides and lights seeming to turn the rest of the town into merely the fair's dingy outskirts; but then each year it had seemed to grow smaller and more tawdry, the island it formed like an illusion whose spell was broken once you'd sensed the edges of it, and it was hard to remember now in this onrush of children and noise what wonder had ever coloured it for me. Once I'd wandered alone into the barns beyond the midway where the competition animals were housed, the midway blare giving way to the murk of barn light and to straw-hushed animal sounds, and it was that image of the fair that most stuck in my memory now, as if I'd discovered then some older, truer fair still going like a spectre at the midway's edge.

Rita and Elena met groups of friends as we went along, forming tentative congregations with them.

"You guys should try the Whirl-a-Wheel, it's wild. We're going to go on it again later."

"I dunno, I think I'd throw up or something, it looks scary."

But there was just this sidelong appraisal and then they moved on, this coming together and drawing apart. Rita would seem to need to impress herself on the others but then after some first boastful assault she'd lose interest suddenly and retreat into listless silence, attention slowly shifting away from her as from a threat.

"Well I guess we'd better go."

Around three we joined the flow of the crowd as it moved toward the grandstand for the show. A helicopter sat discordant in the far corner of the oval the grandstand's track formed, distracting like an irritation. I had seen it circling above the town during the course of the fair on its twenty-minute expeditions, though now its station seemed deserted.

"Dad said maybe he'll let us ride in it if we come on Saturday night," Rita said.

But from the furtive look Elena gave her it seemed she'd lied, had simply pulled the thought from thin air.

We threaded our way through the crowd into the bleachers, Rita leading. There seemed a kind of violence in the air, the shrill, amorphous energy of children. A stage had been set up across the track from the grandstand, its backdrop, propped up behind it like a false front, showing a yellow brick road winding toward a distant Emerald City, the image seeming to merge without division into the yellowing corn field that stretched out behind it beyond the edge of the fairground. In our seats Rita leaned back theatrically into Elena.

"There's no place like home, there's no place like home."

A young woman sitting next to us with two small children, her thin knees exposed beneath the hem of her dress, smiled over at me at this as at another parent.

The show was a spoof of *The Wizard of Oz*, beginning with a small brass band's slow, out-of-key rendition of "Over the Rainbow" and then taking twisted shape around the original, with a moustached magician in coattails and top hat named Professor Marvellous and a Dorothy-like character named Dotty in a skin-tight dress and high heels. My attention wandered, to the crowd, to the pale awkward knees of the woman beside us. The day seemed wrecked for me somehow by her smile, its simple acceptance of Rita when all day I'd felt only my irritation with her, my disowning of her though I could see now her tangled need. It seemed I had looked all along for these signs in her of some sort of rebellion but now that I had them would have preferred simply to see her whole and well and in place, not to feel this residual lingering of responsibility for her like an accusation. In a few days I would be gone, the whole of me focused now on this escape as on some last desperate hope; and from all my years in Mersea it seemed I'd take away only this sourness in me, this sense that nothing that had ever happened there had been untainted or complete.

For a few years we'd come to the fair as a family, watching the shows together from the twilight hum of the grandstand and then dispersing into the midway, lingering sometimes near a booth where a barrel-chested hawker made outrageous bargains with the passing crowd to draw them in. Once my father had taken up the hawker's offer to pay fifty-five dollars for a fifty-dollar bill, poising himself for the inevitable joke as he handed the bill over and then laughing louder than the rest when it came.

"Now I'm going to take *your* fifty-dollar bill," the hawker said, slipping the bill into a pocket with a magician's flourish, "and turn it into mine."

Though true to his word he then peeled off fifty-five dollars for my father from a wad of bills in his hand.

"I used to see those same guys at the fairs in Trivento," my father said when we'd moved on, seeming more knowing now than he had in his laughter. "Once they've got people taking their wallets out they can sell them anything."

And I'd had an image of him then, young and unburdened and canny, his life all potential, visiting the fairs in the high wind-swept towns around Castilucci in some life I'd never known him in. It had seemed the first time that I'd ever envied him anything, holding inside him this other unencumbered past, his memories of this mountain freedom I'd imagined for him.

XVIII

From the mass of calendars and forms and brochures my possible futures had been laid out for me in, I'd chosen a university in Toronto, Centennial. It sat on the outskirts of the city, the vast square of its campus hemmed in like an island by the sprawl of suburb that surrounded it, the long rows of highrise apartments, the strip malls and endless bungalows; though it shared with its surroundings a treeless brick-and-concrete newness, its outcrop of buildings seeming like some landscape of the future from a film or television show, a future where even the natural world had been stripped down and modernized, set out in its own careful symmetry like so much more concrete and steel. To the north, at Steeles Avenue, the city ended suddenly, the highrises on the south side of the road there walled up against the corn and wheat fields across from them as at a coast; and riding the bus along Steeles I'd get a sense what an arbitrary thing a city was, how imposed and artificial, though from the inside it gave the impression of a hard immutability and rightness, its stores and streets and office towers seeming the very meaning and soul of the space they filled.

I'd chosen Centennial because it had offered a scholarship, and was new, and was in Toronto, though as it turned out the long trip downtown by bus and subway seemed to keep the city always at one remove, merely a distant place I visited from time to time; and I'd chosen it because I knew of no one else from Mersea who had, and going there seemed an escape from what I'd been, from what others had seen me to be. But in my first months there I felt as if I had stepped out suddenly into empty space: I had nothing, finally, that defined me, not even the dull routines that had made up my life in Mersea, what I'd thought of then as encumbrances, obstacles in the way of some freer, better self, but that seemed now all that had kept me from the brink of this emptiness I felt impelled into. Waking my first morning in residence to the clean, comfortable newness of my room, its seventh-storey view of the fields north of the campus, its privacy and self-containment, I felt a kind of awe at my sudden freedom, the whole day, my life, stretching before me to be filled as I wanted. But already at breakfast, sitting alone in the residence cafeteria, watching the other students sift into their groups and alliances, I felt the panic build in me at being thrown again into the strangeness of another beginning, at having nothing more to bring me through it finally than myself.

Classes started. I waited for the time when I might enter the university's world, when my own life there might begin; but there seemed some rhythm I couldn't quite catch, some crucial moment I'd missed when a decisive action or word could have brought me suddenly inside of things. Everything about the university gave the impression of a fixed but impenetrable order, everywhere taken for granted and nowhere explained: people came and went, alone or in groups, purposeful, self-sufficient; in the lecture halls they whispered together, made notes, showed every sign of understanding and competence though the lectures were thick with names and references I knew nothing of. In the main complex's large indoor square, groups of students formed daily around tables where people distributed pamphlets and flyers or in a small amphitheatre where musicians sometimes played or speakers held forth, the sense palpable there of what I'd imagined a university to be. Yet even these groups, continuing on in their places day after day without clear purpose or end, attracting every day the same crowds, the same long-haired young men in bandanas or pigtails, the same women in loose, flowered dresses or torn jeans, had an air of exclusion about them, of enclaves already complete and fully-formed.

It might have taken so little to step out of my isolation: in my residence, in my classes, other students spoke to me, were friendly, seemed willing to take for granted my normalcy. But somehow I couldn't strike the right tone with people, felt I'd lost myself, could only impersonate, had to make up instant by instant who it might be acceptable for me to be; and the people who were friendly with me were exactly the ones I afterwards avoided, afraid they'd finally see into this falseness in me. Day by day the world seemed to narrow, its possibilities falling away, tapering down to the litany of my small failures, what I added up to, the true word that hadn't come to me, the people I hadn't met. I began to eat at odd hours or not at all, to keep to my room, sought out always the back corners of classrooms to be close to the safety of exits; for whole days at a stretch I spoke to no one, emerging from my room only for my two or three hours of class and my erratic meals. Yet the more I cut myself off the more conspicuous I seemed, felt eyes burrowing into me always. Every venture outside my room seemed to carry a threat: if I heard laughter near me, or whispers or shouts, my body tensed instinctively against some expected humiliation.

I started sleeping incessantly, twelve, thirteen, fourteen hours a day. My lethargy seemed to feed on itself, irresistible, taking me over like a kind of possession: I sat for hours reading over and over again the same paragraph or page, stumbling through the thickness of words, their dreamy fading into gibberish; I began to nod off in the middle of lectures. For the first few weeks I attended every class, so frightened by my own ignorance, by what might be required of me, that the idea of skipping one never occurred to me; but then one morning I slept through my alarm and missed a lecture. I felt so panicked by what had happened that for the next few days I awoke with my heart pounding at the sound of my alarm. But my panic seemed exactly the fear that I might lose the one imperative that still gave some shape to my life, that my lethargy had understood now that there was no final authority to stand in its way and would slowly overwhelm me.

I began to think seriously of killing myself. It was my first thought now when I awoke every morning, my last before I slept; it was the shadow behind all my other thoughts during the day. I'd often thought of my suicide before, had a thousand times planned out its every detail, taking a strange solace then from the idea of it; but there was something different in me now, a sick sense of its inevitability. I didn't will myself to think of it, merely found the idea present in my mind at the end of every train of thought, forcing itself on me with what seemed a clear and inescapable logic; I didn't plan for it, only cast around each time the thought formed for the most immediate execution of it, a passing car, the window in my room; I felt no pleasure in imagining what others might think of it, felt only the shame of it, wished instead that I might simply vanish into thin air like some character in a science-fiction film, all history silently shifting like water to efface every memory of me.

The world began to take on the strangeness of a place that I would soon be leaving. Every quality of it seemed a mystery suddenly, the shapes of things, the colours, the odd liveliness of people, continuing in their ways as if some secret energy propelled them, as tireless and as certain as machines. But already a dozen times when I felt close to the thing, went so far once as to remove the screen from the window in my room, stood for a moment, my heart pounding, against the window's square of empty space, it was the thought of my family that seemed to keep me from it, of the monstrousness of it for them, so far from anything that would make sense to them – they were what I'd wanted so much to escape and yet all that seemed to connect me now to the world, resurfacing out of the murk into which I'd tried to consign them to hold over me this final tyranny, the slender grip of home.

I'd go into the common room sometimes late at night to watch TV, furtive like an intruder, sitting there in the dark through endless late movies trying to lull myself into self-forgetting. Coming in once, I found a group of other people from my floor just lighting up a joint; and before I could withdraw, one of them, Verne, his knees spread with a newspaper bearing a tangle of browning stems and leaves, had pulled to the side of the couch he was on and motioned me to sit beside him.

"Do you toke at all, Vic?"

In the inevitable crossing of paths on our floor in the wash-room and halls Verne had always been oddly, reassuringly friendly toward me, seemed with his ragged clothes and his long centre-parted crimp of blond hair to have the benign, distracted look of a prophet or saint. But now his earnestness made me fear he was setting me up for an insult.

"Not really," I said.

"Not into it?"

The first joint was still passing from hand to hand; Verne had begun to roll another one, casually intent, some small part of him precisely focused on the work while the rest of him floated free, still attentive to me, still awaiting a response.

"I guess I've never really tried," I said, flushing.

"A virgin," someone said, and laughed. But Verne was still all sincerity and respect.

"You should try a hit," he said. "Anyway you don't get much off it the first few times."

He lit the second joint, the twist of paper at the end of it flaring for an instant as he drew in, then fluttering into ash. Keeping back his first long draw he held the joint a little away from his lips and drew in several more quick bullets of smoke, unthinkingly expert, then still holding his breath offered the joint to me, his eyebrows raised in question and his head nodding to answer, reassuring.

I took a long drag as Verne had done, tried to hold it, coughed it up. Verne finally let out a long thin shaft of smoke.

"You'll get the hang of it," he said. "Give it another pull."

I drew in again, more gently, then again.

The others had begun to talk. I followed the thread of what they were saying, drifted, came back, the joint passing from hand to hand and then to me again. The conversation had somehow come around to Verne's dog.

"Between my dog and a person I'd shoot the person, no second thoughts."

"Yeah, right."

"I'm serious. My dog never hurt anyone."

The joint continued to pass. My head seemed to have taken on the inflated hollowness of a balloon.

"How does it feel?" Verne said.

"It feels pretty good," I said, and laughed, strangely, not certain why I'd laughed at all. But some of the others were laughing as well.

"I guess he's getting the hang of it," one of them said.

Afterwards Verne seemed to adopt me in some way, taking me on like a novitiate, stopping by my room now whenever he and his friends got together to smoke to invite me to join them. Everything in me resisted at first taking any pleasure from this new friendliness – it seemed too paltry a thing, too tenuous, to abandon all my hopelessness for. But despite myself a small feeling of well-being began to take shape in me. I kept waiting for Verne to turn against me in some way yet he merely continued on in his unquestioning inclusion of me in his world, seeming to require nothing more of me than that I be myself; and somehow this little thing was enough to pull me back, day by day the darkness I'd been in growing more distant till it began to seem a memory of some younger, more troubled self.

Verne smoked up almost daily, a changing assortment of his male friends from the residence gathering in his room late at night and stretching out there on his bed or floor while he rolled joints under the fluorescent hum of his desk lamp; and though I spoke little during these sessions, retreating into the high, mellow hollowness of my stone, the conversation of the others then seeming to swell and die in odd fits like a kind of code, still I felt comforted by being there in the cluttered intimacy of Verne's room, by his own mute acceptance of me, the sense of having entered somehow into the residence's secret life. Verne liked to talk about dope, guilelessly erudite in his arcane knowledge, how it was grown, how its different products were harvested. But I'd think then of the countries it came from, the fields of it slung over jungled mountainsides or tended in the desert like gardens, the greening rows of it, of the sandalled workers who harvested it like coffee or grapes knowing nothing of us or our rituals, only doing a job every day like any other.

In a matter of weeks I'd become a regular at Verne's sessions. Slowly I began to take on the look of a smoker, let my hair grow, then my beard, started to keep my own supply which I'd steal a few quick hits off in the mornings to get the first subtle luminousness of a high before class. Yet it seemed that what kept me smoking wasn't pleasure but a failure, the unrealized promise of its first newness, some cataclysm of vision I'd expected that hadn't come; and more and more the time I spent stoned appeared simply lost to me, with no aftermath but the dull lethargy it left in me the next day. I began to have the sense that weeks of my life had passed as if they'd been lived by somebody else: once, returning stoned to my room from Verne's, I stared into my mirror and for an instant couldn't recognize the image I saw there, saw someone who looked like Verne and his friends but who seemed to bear no relation to the person I thought of as myself.

Then as we approached the end of fall term our smoking sessions dwindled in the face of impending deadlines and exams. A slow panic began to build in me at all the work I'd deferred. But when I tried to sit down to it my thoughts refused to focus, humming in my head like droning insects. I started to smoke up alone in my room, hoping at first to simply quell the roil of my thoughts but then inventing a thousand different excuses, though once I'd smoked I'd merely lie on my bed in a kind of paralysis, unable to work, to go out, to do anything. Finally I bought a dozen bennies from one of the residence dealers, the drug seeming to clear my mind like sun lifting a fog; and afterwards I began to sleep days and work nights, bringing myself up at night with the bennies and then down in the morning with a hit of pot or hash. The world seemed to fall away: there was only my work, the dead calm of the residence at night, the adrenalin rush of the drug coursing through me. One night we had our first snowfall, the snow swirling like a mess of phantoms outside my window and then laid out unbroken in the grey of dawn as if in forgiveness, the campus and the fields north of it stretching white and placid and still to the horizon.

But when I'd finished, my body raw with the memory of its overexertion, I felt only drained and despondent. I spent long hours in the common room watching TV in a kind of daze, its flow of images mesmerizing after my isolation. The news from the Buffalo stations was full of the Watergate hearings, of Chile, of the oil embargo, of Spiro Agnew and Gerald Ford; the stories seemed to follow the same logic as television shows, had heroes and villains, aroused the same sense of an impending climax. Coming into them like that out of nothing I felt a strange disorientation, surfacing to them as from the mind-emptied clarity after a fever. The previous months seemed a dream I'd been through now: I'd come out to discover the world and yet still it eluded me, remote as these flickerings I watched in the common room's late-night dark.

When Verne had finished his last exam he invited me to go downtown to a place he knew, a college of some sort, where we could pick up some dope. We took the Steeles bus to the subway, then rode down to Bloor and across. At Bloor there was a palpable sense of the nearness of Christmas, people milling on the platform clutching shopping bags and parcels and Christmas carols playing tinnily over the loudspeakers.

We emerged finally into the slushy wet of Bloor Street, coming a little farther west to what seemed an apartment building, tall and plain and new like the buildings at Centennial, of the same grey concrete. A forecourt in front held the huge huddled statue of a man or boy, two leather-jacketed men loitering idly in the shadow of it, eyeing us as we approached, both holding German shepherds like extensions of themselves at the ends of short leashes.

"We're just here to see a friend," Verne said to them. "Tom, on the third."

And one of them looked us up and down with a kind of bored amusement, then nodded us through.

Inside, the building lost all trace of the grey conformity of its exterior. There was a large, careful mural in the lobby, portraits in different hands of various musicians from the sixties; but beside it someone had spray-painted LONG LIVE ELVIS in a crude fluorescent pink. The surrounding walls, the elevator doors, were thick with similar graffiti, much of it indecipherable or merely random slashes and swirls of colour. There was an air to everything of prematurely decayed newness, the carpeting worn and spotted with burns, the ceiling tiles stained and pitted. In a corner, amidst cigarette butts and paper scraps, was what looked like the hardened stool of a dog or child.

We waited at the elevators for several minutes.

"Let's walk," Verne said finally.

We went up a dim stairwell to the third floor and came into a long corridor, at one end of it a small child sitting naked on the floor fumbling with a set of large coloured rings. As we watched, a woman emerged from an open doorway nearby dressed only in a flowered sarong, breasts and belly exposed, and bent to pick up the child, her breasts swaying. She caught sight of us as she turned and stared at us indifferently an instant, then disappeared again through her doorway.

"This place is wild," Verne said.

Verne knocked on a door toward the other end of the corridor and was answered by a tall, muscular man in jeans and a brown leather vest, his hair tied back in a long pony-tail like an Indian's.

"Verne, my good man." His voice had the hint of an American drawl. "It's been a long time."

He shook Verne's hand firmly, seeming to distinguish himself from the decay of his surroundings by his air of robust well-being. But when Verne introduced us his energy closed me out, remaining fixed on Verne as if I weren't there.

"Another one of your converts?"

We passed through a large, gloomy living room or common room of some sort, the windows papered over with newsprint and the furnishings sparse and institutional and worn. From a corner another German shepherd lay glaring at us out of a wicker crib, his low growl rumbling like distant thunder.

"What's with all the dogs?" Verne said.

Tom grinned.

"How long has it been since you've been down here, my son? There's nothing like a German shepherd to prevent the in-fil-tra-tion of criminal elements."

But his humour seemed oddly cryptic and private.

He led us down a dim hallway and into a room at the end of it whose door-frame was edged with strips of foam, the door closing behind us with a soft hiss of forced air like a hermetic seal. Inside was a desk with a scale on it, a bed, a few book-shelves; on one wall hung a mask in dark wood, African or Indian, its face contorted into what seemed a shout or a scream. Tom opened a cabinet to reveal a phalanx of sleek stereo com-ponents, setting an album rolling on the turntable there with a reflexive efficiency; and then with the same instinctiveness he pulled a baggie from a drawer and began to roll a joint.

There was a bookshelf near where I'd sat, and I began to look through it idly, the titles there as cryptic as Tom's humour.

"I see this one reads," Tom said to Verne. "I thought that was going out of style these days."

"Yeah, Vic's a real brain."

But I couldn't have said how Verne had formed that impres-sion of me.

We smoked a few minutes in silence, Tom meanwhile meas-uring out baggies of dope on his scale. Stoned, I felt a heightened sense of menace, from Tom, from the dogs, from the building's otherworldliness. There was something here I couldn't quite make sense of, some former fundamental upheaval and then its falling away.

Before handing us our bags Tom pulled a vial from a drawer and knocked two tiny pills from it into his palm.

"Purple microdot," he said to Verne. "On the house. A little Christmas gift."

He wrapped the pills in a piece of foil and dropped them into one of the bags.

"I dunno, I'm not really into that stuff," Verne said. "Why don't you give them to Vic?"

Tom shrugged.

"Suit yourself. Just don't accuse me of corrupting our youth."

He handed the baggie to me and took the money I offered him.

"Take it easy on that stuff, my boy," he said, speaking directly to me for the first time.

Outside the cold had turned cutting with the approach of night.

"Can you believe that place?" Verne said. "It was different before when it was just students and that. Christ, did you get a load of those dogs?"

But I had the sense we'd been diminished somehow by our visit, carrying on in our own small delinquencies with no project beyond the simplest one of getting stoned. I wondered now what had ever connected me to Verne, how we'd spent so many hours in this illusion of shared purpose, how I'd imagined him so much on the inside of things when in the end his life was as small as my own. And yet there was a kind of perfection to him, to his generosity, his essential normalcy, and I would have given anything to live as he did, with his sense of being at home in the world.

I rode back to Mersea the next day on the bus. There was a changeover in London from the express to the local, and I had time to go down a sidestreet near the station and smoke a joint. Afterwards I caught a glimpse of myself in the station window, long-haired and bearded and stoned, and panicked suddenly at what I'd become; and back on the bus, single-minded with urgency, I pulled my razor and foam from my suitcase and locked myself in the windowless stench of the washroom to shave, bracing myself against the bus's bumps and swerves like an astronaut fighting weightlessness. My beard came away in small creamy tufts I had to wash from my razor with each stroke, careful and methodical and slow; I watched my face, my older, younger self, emerging in the mirror like an image slowly brightening in a Polaroid, felt the same sense of some strange temporal leap, of hovering briefly over the chasm that divided present from past.

When I emerged, my face raw, it was twilight already, the bus gliding through a shadowy dreamscape of barren trees and flat, greying snow-puddled fields. An older woman in an overcoat and flowered dress had been waiting to use the washroom, sitting tentative in a seat near the washroom door; she averted her eyes when I passed as if ashamed to be discovered there, waiting. There were a half a dozen or so other passengers, a few older people up toward the front, a young woman, two long-haired teenagers in back – it struck me how little I could say about them finally, where they came from, what they thought. I had lived in this flat countryside for most of my life but still entered it now like a stranger, knew little more about the lives unfolding here, on this darkening bus, in the one-store towns, behind the farmhouse windows we passed along the highway's gloom, than if I were entering for the first time into a foreign country.

I drifted near sleep in my seat, lulled by the warmth seeping up from the heating vents, by the last mellow lingering of my stone. I remembered a television show I'd seen once where a man fell asleep on a train and awoke to find it had stopped at a town in the past, Willoughby, light-filled and rustic, remembered how the show had filled me with boyish hopefulness. At the end, when the man decided to get off the train, to step into his dream, we discovered he'd hurled himself to his death; but in the dream, in the past, he'd walked on into town as if his death had been merely a shifting off of his other life, the small token price of his entry to a world more familiar even than home.

XIX

My father picked me up at the bus station. I felt awkward at finding him waiting there, hunched against the cold at the side of his car like a footman. Some lightness, the anticipation of greeting, seemed to fall away from him at once when he saw me.

"*Come nu bum*, with your hair like that." And already I'd ruined things, could hear in his tone his lost good intentions, his desire, his inability, to get along with me.

We held a gathering at our house on Christmas Eve. A tinselly Christmas tree had been set up in a corner of the living room but there were no presents beneath it, only a plastic manger scene with a tiny cloth-diapered Jesus laid amidst bits of varnished straw.

"Oh, *mascalzone!*" Gelsomina said. She had three children now, had put on weight and carried herself with a smooth adultness, aggressively good-humoured. "You look like a Beatle with that hair."

But there was a wariness in people, a forced friendliness I felt deadened in the face of. I tried to bring up the person in me who'd fit in with them but couldn't find the right gesture or word that might conjure him, even speaking Italian seeming to require a hopeless exertion, my mouth resisting it like a lie.

"*Come va*, up there in Toronto?"

"Okay, I guess."

And though I wanted to despise them all I knew I was the one who was lacking, that I'd found no better world to put against their own.

On Christmas morning my father gave me a cheque for five hundred dollars.

"And if you ever come back with your hair like that you can sleep on the street."

I thought of returning the cheque but couldn't muster the strength, the outrage, to do so, could see only how far from the point my father was, how he'd misunderstood, how above all he wanted only to be good to me, for me to allow that. In the end I locked myself in the bathroom and cut my hair, Aunt Teresa joking afterwards that the cut had cost my father five hundred dollars.

"Next time he'll come home with a beard on top of it, and it'll cost you a thousand."

"*Sì*, we'll see about that."

But my father had darkened with emotion at Aunt Teresa's teasing, seemed as afflicted by my capitulation to him as he might have been by my continued resistance.

It seemed pointless now to have come home at all. I'd imagined some vague pleasure in returning, some coming back to myself, yet felt now unsolid as air, without contours. I called no one, could think of no one from high school I wanted to see, instead sitting holed up in front of the television till late into night like someone in hiding. During the days I worked with

235

Rocco and Domenic on the farm – we were steaming the greenhouses to prepare them for the winter crop, spreading long plastic strips down their lengths that blistered like heaving monsters as the steam fed under them. But our conversation was stilted like that of strangers, dwindling finally to silence as the hours of work wore away the obligation we'd felt to speak.

The Sunday after Christmas I visited Rita. I'd bought her a gift, a portable radio, what I'd imagined appropriate for someone approaching her teens.

"That was very thoughtful," Mrs. Amherst said, but she took it up along with its wrappings almost at once after Rita had opened it and disappeared with it into the basement.

I was left alone with Rita in the living room, sitting across from her like a suitor. I could hear television sounds from the rec room, sensed Elena silently watching there.

"How's school?"

"Okay, I guess."

But already I could feel the familiar deadness in my voice.

"I guess you're in grade seven this year."

"Yeah, Mrs. Miller, what a drag, she's so strict."

We talked a few minutes and then she grew restive, shifted in her seat, pulled down the hem of her dress, shifted again. She seemed burdened, evasive, seemed to sense some expectation in me she couldn't meet.

"So I guess I'll see you again at Easter or something. I just wanted to bring your present."

"Thank you."

At home I lay on my bed in a kind of stupor, tried to read, decided to take a bath. For a long time I lay perfectly still in the water, letting it smooth out till it held the pale inertness of my body like glass.

I decided to take the morning bus to Toronto the next day, New Year's Eve.

"*Ma come*," my father said, irritated, thinking perhaps I only wanted to get out of work on the farm. "I can't believe school is starting already."

"I have some work I have to finish."

And in the morning we parted as darkly as we'd met, only the silent ride to the station and then I was gone.

I arrived back at the residence in mid-afternoon. The building was deserted, the halls empty, the cafeteria closed. I walked through an arctic cold to a mall near the campus and bought some lunch meat and bread at the Dominion store there, but back in my room left the food in its bag and smoked a joint instead, then smoked a second one.

Afterwards I went to the common room to put my food in the fridge there and watch TV. But some of the Chinese students had gathered there to cook supper, come out of the shadowy existence they'd had during term to take over the common room now like squatters, the air bright with cooking sounds as I came in and with the quick lilting tones of their conversation. At the sight of me there was a hush as if they'd been caught out in some embarrassment or crime; I put my food in the fridge, then retreated at once to my room.

I decided to drop one of the hits of acid I'd got from Tom. When after fifteen minutes or so I felt nothing I dropped the second one as well; and then almost imperceptibly my blood began to quicken. There was a hum in my teeth like the metallic aftertaste of electricity: it promised some slow revelation if I would wait for it, the gradual unfolding of each tiny path and step that led on to the end of things.

I put on my coat and went outside, walking through a blanket of unbroken snow toward the tiny lake at the front of the residence, the cold splitting like water to let me pass. On the lake the ice groaned beneath its cover as I walked, cracks splintering away from each step – I imagined following their jagged progress, imagined being the thin nothing of a crack as it shot through the ice. Then in the centre of the lake I lay down spread-eagled in the snow, staring up into the star-spattered dark of the sky. The snow seemed neither hot nor cold, the sky neither empty nor full. I closed my eyes, floating, and remembered a poem from high school about an old Indian woman left to die in the cold, remembered the teacher describing the slow dreamy warmth of freezing to death.

I lay with eyes closed for a long time, bits of my body seeming to fall away like breakage from an ice floe. Then there were sounds, dream noises; from somewhere a light winked over me.

"Are you all right, son?"

I sat up. There was a man with a flashlight standing at a distance.

"It's just the snow," I said.

"What's that?"

A security guard. I grew aware of where I was, the snowy bushes around the lake, the looming shapes of the university, buildings beyond.

"I just came out for a walk," I called out, too loud perhaps and yet lucid, pleased for an instant at this picture of reasonableness I'd presented.

"I think you'd better be getting back inside now."

I slept in the next day, New Year's, until three. My head felt blasted, hollowed out; I imagined it blown apart like John

Kennedy's, the back of it scooped out like so much meat and bone. I needed to eat but lacked the will to, nibbling on some of the food I'd left in the common room but then smoking a joint and passing the rest of the day in stoned half-awareness in front of the common room TV. A couple of the Chinese students came in at one point but at the sight of me simply removed some food from the fridge and retreated. I wished they'd return with their cooking sounds and talk, imagined them taking me in as in some Christmas story about the sudden unexpected brightening of a life at the brink of despair.

The next day I decided to go downtown to buy more acid from Tom, the prospect of a goal heartening me. But when I reached Tom's building there was a crowd gathered in front: someone had jumped. The body still lay there on the pavement, lumped like a sack in the circle of space enclosed by the crowd – a woman perhaps, or a girl, though someone had draped a parka over her and only the back of the head showed, a mat of black hair with a line of pale scalp at the parting. A smudge of blood had coloured the pavement near the head, frugally though, hardly visible against the pavement's wet brown.

There was a strange tension in the crowd, a muted, gloomy excitement.

"There's one or two every New Year's," someone said.

This was not how I'd imagined it, at once so mundane and so chilling, the crowd, the strange tension, the body crumpled anonymous on the pavement as in a scene from a movie, as unreal, as distant from me, as that. Yet she had had a life as I did, had moved, thought, been human, and still had managed to cross the gap that kept the thought from the act, been able to open the window, to lift herself over the sill.

The police came, then an ambulance.

"Just move along, folks, the show's over."

I walked away from the building toward downtown. It had begun to snow, the flakes swirling in the halos of streetlights in the twilight chill; I wanted only to be warm, inside, alone. I stopped to eat at a Harvey's, the man in the booth beside me unfolding a wrinkled picture of Jesus, smoothing it meticulously, carefully folding it again.

The next day Verne returned from the break and stopped by my room.

"Hey, Vic, how were the holidays?"

"All right, I guess."

But I couldn't bear the deadness in me when I spoke. The line between present and future, who I was and who I imagined I'd be, seemed dissolved; I saw only the endless perpetuation of things as they were, my small illusory rallies, my steep descents.

I thought: I will do it. There seemed nothing between the thought and the act now but empty space; I would come to the point where I'd crossed it.

There was a notice in the residence lobby for the university's counselling clinic. I had seen it a hundred times, had somehow assumed it had nothing to do with me; but now its message stuck. For several days I circled around the idea as around an enemy, trying to find its weakness; and then one day I was simply there in the centre's office.

The receptionist was cheerful, condescending.

"What can I do for you today?"

I had to fill out a form. I imagined the impression I made, a mental case, gloomy, unshaven, my hair spiky and uneven from the crude cut I'd given it.

I was assigned a young woman in a loose, flowered maxi and a muslin blouse, a hippie type.

"Hello, Victor, I'm Marnie."

I followed her down a narrow corridor, then another. She walked with a slow, long-strided tranquillity; with each stride her thighs shimmered briefly into shape against the fabric of her skirt.

"You'll have to excuse the office," she said. "I have to share it with another student. Very *straight*."

She gave me a smile of complicity. Her candour made me uneasy, made me feel she'd assumed some affinity between us that I had to live up to now.

The office was small and cramped, institutional; two metal desks had been lined up against the walls as if stored there. I sat on a black vinyl couch and Marnie across from me in a large desk chair, her legs pulled up beneath her.

"So. What would you like to talk about?"

I had rehearsed a hundred different responses but they all struck me as false now exactly because I'd rehearsed them.

"I dunno. I guess I haven't been feeling very good and stuff."

"Emotionally or physically?"

"Emotionally, I guess."

Marnie nodded, slow, reassuring, seeming a careful impersonation of what a counsellor was.

"How would you say you felt? Sad? Depressed?"

"Depressed, I guess."

"Was there something that happened, something that made you depressed?"

"No, I dunno. It's just that things didn't go very well last term, I started smoking up and stuff."

Everything had started wrong. I'd made her think I was inarticulate, simple-minded, had the sense I was inventing some other person, not me, as I spoke. We went on to talk about school, about friends, about doing drugs, and yet everything I said seemed at once true and beside the point. Mirrored back to me through her my problems appeared unambiguous, two-dimensional: I was merely lonely, merely shy, merely depressed.

But at the end of the session she reached out and set a hand on my knee.

"It sounds like you're pretty bummed out," she said, and there seemed even through her sad-eyed counsellor's earnestness such a bald recognition of how I felt that my throat tightened with emotion.

I began to see her every week. After the first few sessions the hope of some sudden impending change in me began to fade: I'd expected her to take me up through my life as through a film of it, building toward some final resolution, but each session seemed a new beginning, brought out the same inarticulateness in me, the same evasions. Somehow I couldn't strike the spot that would crack open the truth of things, felt always a swerving, the instant I came up against what I couldn't put into words and took refuge in what was merely acceptable, a second-guessing of what Marnie might expect from me. What kept me going at first was only the relief at each session's end: I muddled through, hardly speaking sometimes, hardly able to string together two honest words, and then came out at the end as into fresh air again, seeming somehow to leave the worst part of myself in Marnie's office till the following week.

We talked about my wanting to kill myself. I held back at first, afraid of exceeding the bounds of what Marnie might find acceptable; but then when she reacted with her predictable calm I felt a kind of disappointment.

"You have the right to decide to kill yourself. Some people make that choice. But I want you to promise you'll call me first if you ever feel close to it. Anywhere, any time. I'll give you my number at home."

Something in me shrank from taking on this responsibility to her, felt as if in a breath she'd acknowledged my right to kill myself and then made me surrender it to her. And yet the instant obstacle now of that imagined call seemed to serve its purpose, already making the thing seem unlikely as soon as the thought came to mind.

There was a mat-lined room around the corner from Marnie's office where we did body work. I'd stand on one leg, one hand lightly holding Marnie's for balance, and let myself fall when I grew tired; I'd get down on all fours, Marnie's hand on my belly like an ember at the centre of me, and let the muscles relax in my belly and groin. Marnie seemed to think of the body as an extension of the earth, talking about reconnecting with the earth's gravity; and there was something comforting in this vision of things, its animal freedom, the mind seeming a tiny place within it, merely the last refuge of the body's slow self-forgetting. But while I could grasp the sense of her theories, somehow I couldn't muster the faith to surrender myself to the truth of them. In the exercise room once, Marnie had me crouch on the floor and then without explanation draped herself over me like a sack, her breasts, her groin, pressing into me, the weight of her slowly closing me down; and though I could guess her intent, knew I ought to heed my body's slow scream for release, still I couldn't find the true moment in me when instinct and thought overlapped.

243

"I think it would be a good idea if you tried to get me off of you."

There were other exercises, word associations, role playing; and then the grittier work of looking at my week, my life, the slow haphazard foraging in the past. I wanted to dredge to the bottom of me, bring up all my anger and hate, everything that was missing in words like "lonely" and "shy"; but echoed back through Marnie my reactions to things seemed at every point understandable, predictable, sane.

"What I'm hearing from you is you didn't feel you had the right to break up with her, that you felt trapped because of that, that that's where your anger was coming from."

And in the end these statements seemed not so much solutions we'd groped towards as a coming back, the discovery merely of the shape I'd arranged things around from the start, always the sense in me afterwards of some darkness I hadn't stepped into, a line I hadn't crossed.

She asked about my mother's death. It was the issue we'd seemed to circle around from the start, that I could feel Marnie drawing me back toward with a textbook determinedness. But though I'd thought I could simply set out all the facts with a spare, unsentimental concision, recreate whole the slow unfolding of my mother's disgrace, of her death, now that the matter sat clearly before me there seemed a lapse in my memory like a hole in it. I could hardly call up an image of her, could remember only flickering details like the lingering fragments of a dream, the echo of footsteps in a hall, two eyes staring out from a stable door. I had the sense for an instant that I'd mistakenly thought of as real some story I'd only imagined.

"I dunno," I said finally, "I guess I don't really remember much, I was pretty young and stuff."

Marnie was sitting straight-backed across from me, intent but also oddly self-contained. I thought of her thinking of me, trying to make me out, and felt a throb of affection for her like a pain.

"Victor, look at yourself, how you're sitting."

I had huddled into a corner of the couch, my knees up and my arms wrapped around them, a parody of withdrawal.

"The few times you've mentioned your mother it's been the same, your whole body just closes right down."

I expected some gloss from her, some pointing out of the obvious, but she let the moment hang silent between us.

"I guess our time's up," she said finally.

Then already we'd begun to approach the end of spring term. We continued on as before but something had changed, the sense of working toward any revelation. I seemed under the full tyranny by now of the image I thought Marnie had formed of me, the complex dynamic of wanting her good opinion and not believing in it, of silently holding her in contempt for it and yet daring less and less to expose it to any risk.

And yet I'd got on with my life, had felt from the outset of my visits a kind of temporary reprieve as if the final question of my worth had been suspended for the time being by them; and then slowly I'd begun to make friends, to do well in my classes, till gradually the largeness of my despair had seemed to dissolve into the everydayness of things, into my small, familiar frustrations and hopes. Nothing had happened and yet everything after all had changed, not the making over I'd hoped for but the subtle shifting of things that made them once again bearable.

We came to our final session. Marnie was just finishing a Master's and would be leaving the university at the end of term, but she suggested I call her at home when I got back in the fall.

"I'd like to see you again," she said. "As a friend."

"Okay. That would be nice."

There was an instant's awkwardness when I got up to leave and then we hugged.

"I feel kind of teary," Marnie said, and laughed. She seemed genuinely moved, her eyes glistening. I hadn't expected this from her, saw our whole time together skew as if it had grown suddenly real, as if I'd missed till then some crucial element in it, some crucial possibility.

"I guess maybe we'll see each other in the fall," I said.

"That would be nice."

But already walking back across campus I'd let her slip from my mind, felt only the niggling residue of her, the strange lingering pleasure and guilt of parting.

XX

At home that summer I had the sense I had to be accommodated like a visitor, a new formality in how the others treated me as if I couldn't be expected to understand any more how things worked there. Only Aunt Teresa seemed comfortable around me, casual and confidential, speaking to me in an unusually colloquial English and calling me Victor instead of Vittorio, something I couldn't remember her doing in the past.

There were tensions. We were building more greenhouses, three of them, running south from the boiler room to the irrigation pond, and my father and uncle were in the midst of some argument. All the familiar patterns, the familiar displacements, Tsi'Umberto's sharp condescension toward his wife and sons, my father's silences, the sense when they were near each other of two shadows, two glooms, silently hovering. Domenic had been brought in as some sort of partner in the new greenhouses but appeared grim with the new responsibility, his old rebelliousness still smouldering in him. He had a girlfriend from

Detroit now who he brought down once to a wedding, a strawberry blonde with wide hips and pasty skin, and all night long he and his father seemed dark as if with the unspent resentment of some long, festering conflict.

A strangeness had formed around Aunt Teresa like a force field, something to do with her lingering odd religious inclinations, never talked about though the evidence of them was plain enough now, in the magazines she still received, in the meetings she went to every Thursday. But there was more to it than that, or less – the religion seemed merely a marker she used to distinguish herself, to make clear to the rest of the family, to other Italians, that she wasn't one of them. There was nothing of the smug benevolence of faith to her, only the old cynicism, but backed up now by the threat of an unspoken moral prerogative; she was friendly with people, ready to laugh, to joke, and yet the threat was always there. At the beginning of the summer I was drawn to her because she appeared the one person with whom I could be myself, have a normal adult conversation; but it grew clear finally that her cynicism took me in too, whatever weakness I showed her seeming only to buoy her up in her own superior view of things.

My father had been elected president of Mersea's Italian club that year. I couldn't fit this fact into any image I had of him, had always thought of him as irredeemably crippled, outside of things; and yet he'd got by, made a way for himself, was to all appearances the very figure of success. He was the president of the Italian club; he had built up a prosperous farm. The new greenhouses would give us nearly four acres under glass: only a few *inglesi* and Dutchmen and four or five of the older Italian families had more. At parties at the club he was the one now to whom people came, whom families passed by to greet before supper, whom the men, weighty with confidences, sidled up to at the bar. What had seemed before a child's sullenness had become in its consistency a kind of dignity – that was what people appeared to honour in him, that he had remained always true to his misfortune, his shame, respectful of it as to the memory of the dead. His very sinew and bone seemed shaped now by that struggle, since his operation his body having taken on a tawny muscularity like something slowly worked down to its essence, with none of the look of well-fed complacence of other Italian men his age.

Yet there remained something shambling about him, a creeping disorder at the edge of his life that might have been simply a comfortable indifference, the last secret retreat of his truer, less driven self, but that struck me as sad somehow, a failure of will, the threat against which everything else had been precariously won and held. He'd bought a new car recently, a cobalt-blue Olds, whispery with comforts, all hydraulics and murmurs and whirrs, an uncommon indulgence for him. But he treated it with the same mix of crude immigrant carefulness and neglect that he showed anything new, covered the front seat with a stretch of old, flowered tablecloth to keep it clean but left bills, church programs, cigarette packs, to collect on the floor, left the body spattered with insects and mud; and he seemed to repeat in it the tension in him between some dream of completion, some belief in himself, and the small apathy that slowly undermined it, just as after his first boyish ministrations he'd let the new boiler room slowly resolve itself into burgeoning islands of clutter, and just as he'd let the farm itself, despite his occasional sudden bouts of cleaning, slowly decay along its edges, the ramshackle barn, the garbage-strewn slopes of the pond, the chaos of brambled junk and rusting implements that lined the path to the back field.

Our house as well had surrendered itself to a slow deterioration, the walls discoloured, the floor tiles yellowing and worn, the kitchen counter rotting with damp around the rim of the sink. Loose tiles on the stairwell and in the entrance hall had been crudely tacked down with nails; tears in the vinyl of the kitchen chairs had been covered with electrical tape or simply been left to gape, wads of stuffing protruding. Aunt Teresa cleaned haphazardly, had the lassitude of a mother who'd just seen her children leave home; my father complained to her but there was a tiredness in his anger, something blunted or broken by the years of Aunt Teresa's belligerence, her refusal ever simply to yield herself to the notion that they shared a household she was the woman of.

"Don't think you'll have me to look after you the rest of your life."

And there was a hardness in her threat that made it sound plausible, made me think she'd seen through the waste of the life she'd had with us and was silently plotting her escape.

In the bathroom creeping moisture had begun to erode the plaster around the edge of the tub, chunks of it fallen away to reveal metal mesh and empty space behind. Taking baths I thought of my father, my aunt, sitting naked and alone there as I was, all the years they'd done that while the room had slowly decayed around them. I began to cry once, slow, heaving sobs that came up from my belly and chest – there seemed a darkness in things too deep to contemplate, a grief so endless that no crying could ever exhaust it. For perhaps the first time since school had ended I thought of Marnie, of all the things I hadn't told her, wanted to render up to her now the whole of this moment, the cooling water, the crumbling wall, the room's strange quality of light, amber and unreal like an autumn twilight after rain.

I worked together with my father a few days on the new greenhouses, the two of us setting rafters in place on the purlins while Rocco and Domenic followed behind to clamp them down. There was a tentativeness in him that seemed to want suddenly to include me in things, that hung in the air between us like a question.

"The young guys now it's different, with school and everything, you can learn the right way to doing things." His English made him seem vulnerable, rustic. "Half the time we just take a chance, we don't know if it's gonna help. You just learn every year. I thought if Rocco or Domenic did some course but their father just wanted them to work, that's his business."

But it hurt me to see him so shyly loquacious, to feel his need: I had nothing to offer him, wanted to be on good terms with him but only to disentangle myself from him, to define more clearly the line that divided us. In my vision of the future he had no place, was simply a liability to be gotten beyond.

I didn't see Rita until the end of June, half-expecting some invitation that never came, then appearing impulsively at the Amhersts' one evening gloomy with resentment; but afterwards my visits took on their old regularity. Certain details in the Amhersts' house stuck out suddenly, idiosyncratic, the cow figurines on the window-ledge in the kitchen, the crocheted doilies in the bathroom, small touches of domesticity I hadn't noticed before, that seemed out of place in my memory of Mrs. Amherst. But beyond these petty observations I seemed to take away from my visits nothing that was pleasurable or new. If there was any logic in the visits at all, what drove me to continue them despite their awkwardness, their tedium, the guilt I felt on returning home, afraid my father could read in me my skulking betrayals of him, it was only in the vague belief that my persistence would somehow be rewarded: Rita was all I had in Mersea, nothing else left there to hold me, not my family nor my abandoned friends nor the place itself, which had never seeped into my marrow, become home, my visits now merely a kind of waiting, some claim I was laying on Rita's future.

I came over once or twice a week, arranging myself around Rita's and Elena's schedules, music lessons, Girl Guides, swimming. Their lives seemed endlessly leisured to me yet they talked about their various extracurricular activities with a bored dismissiveness, seeming happier simply to watch TV in the rec room. The rec room remained their enclave, where they seemed to live some secret other life, stripped of the privileges the Amhersts bestowed on them down to their realer, more common selves, merely bored adolescents as I'd been, awaiting some change that could transform them.

Rita had turned thirteen in the spring, the suggestion of a bra beneath her blouses and dresses giving her an air now at once solemn and slightly comical. There was a fraught, suppressed urgency in her, her movements childishly impulsive, tomboyish, but then reined in at the last instant as if she'd remembered suddenly this new, adult body beginning to take shape around her. Her hair had begun to grow long again, and she had a habit of reaching up with both hands to flick it back but with her elbows in tight at her sides like folded wings, seeming at once to display and to shield herself, like the young girls in Italy who'd cover their mouths with a hand when they spoke to hide their lipstick. We'd grown more awkward with each other, avoided contact, our bodies seeming charged like the like poles of magnets; but then sometimes she'd brush up against me or lean into me suddenly on the rec room couch and some message would seem to pass between us. She and Elena shared their hermetic jokes, sealed themselves off in their arcane adolescence, yet I had the sense that the two of us were always aware of each other, that the room hummed around us with that awareness like static.

I glimpsed once by chance through the sleeveless opening of one of Rita's dresses the stiff lace of her bra, the pale mooning curve of the flesh that rimmed it. I avoided looking at her after that, realized that I had long avoided looking at her, had trained my eyes not to rest on her for more than a few fleeting seconds. But now each glance at her seemed more forbidden, etched in my mind like the quick furtive lines of a figure sketch. Images of her would flit past my mind's eye, be suppressed, then be there again, the round of her shoulders, the hollow her throat dipped down to. I grew more distant with her, more fatherly, more severe, trying to retreat into a gruff, indifferent adultness. But some screen between us had fallen – we seemed to have become too familiar to each other again, to have reverted after the years of formality our separation had imposed on us to the brutal unspoken intimacy of siblings. She'd mimic love scenes from TV, aping their hackneyed dialogue, swooning into me on the couch; but there was a knowingness in her that chilled me, a kind of contempt, some dim awareness of the power she had over me. Every engagement between us seemed a tiny battle of wills, Rita drawing me in and then suddenly, pointedly, ignoring me, one instant all attention and the next casually oblivious.

She and Elena and I were watching TV the day Nixon resigned: the show we were watching cut out, a newscaster came on, then Nixon.

"This is boring," Rita said.

We watched a few minutes longer, and then Rita got up to change the channel.

"Leave it," I said.

But she'd begun to turn through the channels. Every one of them showed Nixon; but she continued to turn.

"I said leave it."

She turned finally to UHF, found a station there in the midst of a movie, returned to her seat.

I was seething. I thought for an instant I'd strike her, felt the urge shoot through me like a spasm. Elena cast a furtive glance toward me from her seat, then we simply stayed as we were in charged silence.

I got up a few minutes later without speaking and left the house. I sat for a moment in the car, my blood pounding, then began to back out of the Amhersts' driveway, heard a screech of brakes, hit my own: an oncoming car had swerved to a stop. It wheeled around me now, the driver leering.

"Asshole!"

I pulled into a parking lot on Talbot. My hands were trembling; I felt tears coming, didn't want to stop them but felt too exposed there to allow them. In my sudden frailness I thought for an instant that I touched something true about my feelings for Rita, deeper than all the distortions, than my anger, than my need; but I wouldn't give in to it, couldn't bring myself to relinquish this clear instance of hurt I could hold against her.

I returned to the Amhersts' only twice more that summer. The first time I sat watching TV again in the rec room, stuck in a sullenness which Rita feigned indifference to but seemed to circle around at a distance as if seeking the spot that would break it. It might have taken so little then to make things right between us, some small magnanimous gesture, adult and for-giving, a gesture the brother I wanted to be, light-hearted and winning and mature, would have been capable of. But instead I had only my sullenness to offer, which I could pass off at least as anger, was at least a language of sorts, more bearable than the mere confused awkwardness that seemed its alternative. Then toward the end of my visit there was a moment when she and Elena were joking together that I seemed genuinely forgotten. I saw myself for an instant as Rita might, with her child's mixed sense of what people were, of what they might want from her, saw how she'd instinctively turn from me finally as from a ques-tion that couldn't be answered.

My last visit, at the end of the summer, I had supper with the Amhersts. There was an air of finality about the evening, of the relieved beneficence that came before a departure. It was odd to be reassembled again in our old formality, to see Rita and Elena revert to respectful silence, become small again: for the first time at that table I had the sense that they were more strangers to the Amhersts' world than I was, less comprehending of it, something in their containment making me feel suddenly the full measure of their outsideness, perhaps simply the dis-tance that separated child and adult or something more, the strangeness of being here in this house they didn't belong to.

"You'll want to make sure you come out of school with a profession," Mr. Amherst was saying to me. "That was my mistake, taking over the business. I've done all right, I can't complain about that, but there's no soul in it. After a while it's just counting nickels and dimes."

"Don't be silly, David, you just did what you thought was right. It's different now, kids have more choices."

"Yes, well, all the same."

But it was odd to hear him speaking so plainly about himself, to hear that note of disappointment, of self-awareness.

Before serving coffee Mrs. Amherst sent Rita and Elena upstairs to do homework. Rita said goodbye to me before going up.

"So I guess you're going back to school and stuff."

"Yeah, on Monday."

"I guess I'll see you at Christmas or something."

"I dunno, maybe I'll come back before that."

We brushed cheeks. I caught a whiff of the hot, milky smell of her breath.

"Well, goodbye then."

And there was something different in her now, a shyness, a capitulation, as if we'd passed safely back into the separate spheres of younger sister and older brother.

Afterwards I lingered. Mrs. Amherst served sherry in the living room, bringing out an ashtray to allow me to smoke. In this air of adultness the Amhersts seemed transformed, less perfect somehow, more human. Mrs. Amherst filled and refilled her glass until she was subtly but definitely drunk, her face taking on a surreal, leathery quality like a mask and her speech edged with a small hysteria, slowly thickening from its learned flat Canadianness into a British burr. I could see her suddenly in another life sitting contented around some kitchen table in England with her family or friends, not the abstraction of Englishness I'd seen her as but merely at home, in her element.

"Do come again soon," she said at the door, hugging me, an unheard of thing. "You're practically part of the family."

She seemed truly drunk now, Mr. Amherst standing beside her flushed with embarrassment.

"Maybe at Thanksgiving," I said.

Riding home I could still feel the impress of her arms against my sides. I was glad to be leaving, to be spared a few months the awkwardness that would hang between us the next time we met because of that drunken moment of feeling.

The next day, rummaging through the trunk in our basement for boxes to pack my things in, I came on the corduroy dress I had bought for Rita years before, folded away beneath a stack of old linen. I felt a throb of shame at the sight of it: it seemed such a shabby thing now, though Rita had only worn it a few months before outgrowing it. I remembered having hidden it here, childishly possessive, to keep Aunt Teresa from turning it into rags or throwing it out, wanting somehow to prolong the value of it. I held it up to myself, amazed at the smallness of it, couldn't imagine now the person Rita had been when she'd first worn it, the brief furtive pleasure she'd taken in it then, not daring either to revel in it or take it for granted. For the first time I felt a relinquishing in me, a turning over of her to her other life, though still with a child's guilty instinct I carefully refolded the dress, set it back in its place.

XXI

In my next three years at Centennial I felt a slow coalescing in me, some essence of what I was seeming gradually to distill itself from the mess of all that I'd been. That seemed what a life was in the end, not, as I'd imagined, a suspension the future intruded upon, precipitously, making you over, but merely this slow accumulation of things, what you woke up to find had been going on like some stranger's life while you waited.

I began to feel more at home in my aloneness. It was the thing I'd most fought against, most hated, yet also what made me most clearly myself, what I'd always clung to as the last refuge of what I was, and it seemed enough now merely to learn how to carry it with some dignity. There were people whose spheres I passed into for a time as I had into Verne's, briefly part of their worlds, though like Verne they somehow remained always outside the true flow of my life – what I seemed to need was only the idea of them, the constellation they formed in my mind like a map of familiar territory. And there were a few women as well, relationships that entered my life like dreams and then faded like them, that quickly took on an oppressive intimacy while I was in them but that afterwards seemed strangely implausible. None of them ever lasted more than a matter of weeks or months, winding down with a deadening predictability from the first imagined closeness and promise to a strained awkwardness and then a parting.

What seemed to sustain me in the end was my work, the sense of knowledge taking shape in me, assuming patterns as if building toward some final truth about things. I majored in English literature, becoming the expert now in this strangers' language; though what drew me to literature was that it seemed to leave nothing out, to hold the whole world, and invariably I gravitated toward courses that crossed into other disciplines, psychology, religion, philosophy, more interested in the haze of meaning texts threw off than in their subtleties of structure and style. The world, its slow progress of ideas, took on a history and a logic; within them I looked always for ruptures, the hard sudden reversals when truth was turned on its head, nothing taken for granted but the brute random fact of existence.

In the time it took me to finish my degree I had almost no contact with my family: I saw them for a week or so each Christmas, sometimes at Easter, perhaps a weekend or two in the summer; there were no regular phone calls, no letters, merely a tacit lapsing into estrangement. Summers I worked painting houses in the northern suburbs of Toronto, taking sublets in the graduate residence on campus and working twelve- and thirteen-hour days, six days a week, catching the bus at seven and then not home again till nine or ten at night. At bottom there was no compelling reason to work myself like that: I had a scholarship still to cover tuition; I had government loans I'd simply banked, wanting to have the money ready there when the loans came due;

I had my father's occasional handouts, his apparent readiness to help out if I should ask him to. But instead I behaved like an immigrant, asking for nothing, filling my life with work until it seemed a vessel I no longer occupied, merely set out every day then reclaimed at night for my brief dead hours of sleep.

Weekend dances often drew groups of Italians into Centennial from the surrounding suburbs, usually slick-haired boys in platform shoes and tight shirts whom I felt nothing in common with, strutting and tough, seeming to wear their Italianness like a challenge. But there were few Italians who actually attended the university, those of us who did seeming like quiet interlopers within the university's tidy enclave of privilege. There was an Italian in a satire class I took in second year who began to grow friendly with me at some point, Michael Iacobelli, a few years older than I was, the two of us seeming to come together with the same unspoken bond of forced difference and sameness that had joined me to Vince in high school, gradually gravitating toward one another in the after-class gatherings a group of us held in one of the residence pubs. Michael talked little at these gatherings, visibly set apart, balding and wiry and small like a wizening construction worker; though he remained true whenever he did speak to a peculiar iconoclasm, swerving always from the expected as if to subvert at once any thought people had that they were better than he was.

"It's not the oil crisis that's going to bring the world down, it's the humour crisis. People don't laugh any more. Make a joke, for Christ's sake."

But then when the group thinned down to just the two of us, as it usually did, there'd seem a silent, almost bored complicity between us as if a disguise had just fallen away.

He lived with his parents still, in a subdivision not far from the campus, his street dwindling from the malls and highrises of Jane Street into a small-town decorum, spruce-treed and brick-bungalowed. The first time I visited him there I registered only an indifferent blur of familiarity, the vine bower out back, the pictures of Christ, the baroque excesses of furnishings and flowered ceramic and swirled plaster. People came and went: siblings, shadowy in the background, so that afterwards I couldn't remember how many I'd met, what their names were; his mother, in apron and hairnet in the kitchen, greeting me with a curt, silent nod and a look of suspicion. Before going down to the rec room we sat a few minutes in the living room with his father, burly and gruff, enshrined in his armchair there like a monolith.

"We live down St. Clair before, is better. Too many different people here now, *drogha*, black people, everything."

"Come on, Dad," Michael said, good-humoured. "What did black people ever do to you?"

But his father didn't respond, walling himself up against the edge of condescension in Michael's voice.

"He gets into his moods," Michael said afterwards. "He's like those slugs, you poke them and they roll up into little balls."

Michael had been briefly addicted to heroin a few years before. He and two childhood friends, Perry and Gus, still did what they called chipping, no longer addicted but tripping out every month or so when the urge suddenly took them. The three of them would show up sometimes at my residence subtly altered, looking for distractions the way a cat sought movement, for some object outside themselves that could give a shape to the strange floating energy of their high. Gus took on a keen, malevolent irony when he was stoned, treacherous, mind-twisting; at the residence he'd hit on women in the pub with a manic onslaught of banter and innuendo.

"Say, don't I know you? I'm sure we met at that sexology conference down in Fresno, you were with Xaviera Hollander."

But it surprised me how often women were taken in by him, attracted to his outlandishness or perhaps simply too mystified by him to ward him off.

The three of them formed an odd group, Michael the still centre around which the other two revolved like polar opposites, Gus an A-student, overbearing and articulate, Perry shambling and easygoing, a high-school dropout, grown eccentric with his unschooled intelligence. Yet they seemed to have evolved over the years into a single organism, even their differences, their marked individuality, their constant disputatious assertions of it, seeming the shift and flow of a common energy. For a time I fell under their spell, drawn into their sphere like a satellite by the collective gravity of them, part of them and not, wanting the community they seemed to offer yet feeling something in them that was meant as much to exclude as to attract, to hold the people they drew to them in abeyance like disciples. I mentioned to them once a socialist group I'd joined and felt suddenly like I'd been caught out in some betrayal of them, put on the defensive by their quick dismissal of the group though I myself had never taken it very seriously.

"So what do you guys do?" Perry said. "Sit around and plan the revolution?"

Of the group Gus was the most politicized, forever haranguing us over whatever issue had most recently caught his attention. But now he was all condescension and concern.

"Victor, I thought you were smarter than that. Can't you see, they're brainwashing you. They're as bad as the Moonies."

"You're just talking off the top of your head. You've probably never had anything to do with this kind of thing."

"I don't have to, Vic, believe me, I know what they're like – you meet in some basement room, there's the little group of them that runs things, there's the people like you that sit at the back and don't say anything and then never come back. It's like a religion for them, Victor, they're just looking for converts so they'll feel they're important. It doesn't have anything to do with politics."

"It's not that," Michael said. "It's the scope of these things. You can't change the world like that. Those are the same people that go home after and beat their wives, they don't see the contradiction."

And my meetings after that seemed to lose the one satisfaction they'd still given me, that of allowing my own scepticism to take solid shape in me.

Toward the end of third year I shot up with them once, in Michael's rec room, the rest of his family away though there seemed something purposely cavalier in doing it there, in the defiance of it, in the tawdriness, the strange disjunction between the delinquency of what we were doing and the banality of where we were. Michael helped me raise a vein and put the needle in for me, the experience intimate like sharing a bodily function, the sight of the needle's tip pricking the skin, of the blood swirling up into the syringe. Afterwards we went up to a floor party in my residence; I had the impression the drug hadn't affected me though the world had taken on an odd liquid resistance.

"Look at Vic, he's already nodding," Perry said. He made a face, a clown's exaggerated grin.

Gus began to work the room, disappearing into the crowd, while Michael and Perry went off in search of beer. Then a few minutes later Gus resurfaced beside me.

"Vic, I'm having a bad trip. I'm freaking out."

He seemed visibly shaken, his body like a single nerve.

"I've gotta stop doing this shit, Vic, I'm wrecking myself. I get it into my head and it's all I can think of."

The intensity of him alarmed me. He seemed one instant merely desperate and then the next oddly lucid, inside the experience of his own brutal honesty as if it energized him.

"Talk to me, Vic, talk me down." But he continued to talk himself, increasingly paranoid and strange.

"I get this hatred going through me sometimes, this pure hate, I think I could be one of those guys you hear about, those normal guys who start picking people off on the street from a roof one day. I've never told anyone about this before."

I felt truly disturbed now, less by what he was saying than by the responsibility for him he was urging on me.

"Maybe we should go," I said finally. "Just let me get Perry and Michael."

"Go? Why?" He looked at me suddenly in mock incomprehension. "Oh, all that stuff I was saying, is that it? I was just joking, Vic. Relax."

And he walked off into the crowd.

I went down to my room. Half an hour or so later the three of them were at my door.

"Hey, Vic, no hard feelings," Gus said. "It was just a joke."

"What, did Gus pull one of his mind trips on you?" Perry said. "You've gotta make allowances for Gus, he gets a little cockeyed when he's stoned."

But I was determined to feel betrayed, not just by Gus but by all of them, the thing they formed together.

"Are you all right?" Michael said.

"I'll be fine."

"He's okay," Michael said, as if interpreting me for the others. "He just wants to be alone for a while, it's his first time, you know what it's like."

Michael came by to see me the next day.

"Gus is a bit of an asshole sometimes," he said.

But what Gus had done seemed somehow beside the point.

"It's not just Gus, it's all of you. You close people out. You make it seem as if the world should revolve around you."

But I'd put it more harshly than I'd intended. Michael seemed genuinely taken aback.

"We're individuals, Victor. Half the time we don't even get along ourselves. You make it sound like a conspiracy or something."

"I'm not saying you do it consciously, it's more subtle than that."

But I'd lost the offensive, had wanted to seem coldly perceptive but came across as merely resentful.

"Victor, it's normal you'd feel left out sometimes. We've known each other for years, you can't just walk into something like that and understand it. I know what you're like, you like to sit on the edge of things, check them out. I respect that. But you can't hold back like that and then blame us for closing you out."

It was this reasonableness in him that was most frustrating, his ready, level-headed responses. I'd expected him to see at once the truth of what I was saying and capitulate; but finally he was the one in the right, seemed at bottom sincerely to want some connection between us while I'd simply been awaiting some clear excuse for a rupture.

In the summer, back at my endless routine of work, I had a call one night from Michael: Gus's parents had discovered he'd been using again and had thrown him out of the house.

"He just needs a place to crash for a couple of days while they calm down."

"What about your place or Perry's?"

"It's no good, our parents won't have him. You know how it is with Italians, these things get around."

But they had other friends, more indebted, seemed to turn to me now as the path of least resistance.

"We don't even get along very well."

"He's just uncomfortable around you, that's all. He thinks you don't like him. I thought this might give you a chance to get to know each other."

Gus stayed for nearly two weeks. Almost at once he made himself at home with an irritating imperiousness, his things everywhere, the kitchen littered with his mess.

"I really appreciate this, Vic, I can't tell you how much."

Yet the whole time we hardly spoke to each other, Gus only just rising from his cat's bed of cushions when I left for work in the morning and out when I came in or forever on the phone.

"Ma, it was the first time in three years, I swear it. I'm your own son, for God's sake. You send me out like this to beg off *stranieri*, it's humiliating."

But he didn't sound humiliated at all, sounded his old self, lying, conniving, manipulating, though afterwards it was more Michael I felt used by than Gus, who after all was merely being himself, couldn't help being himself.

Oddly, Michael dropped out of Centennial that fall, only a few courses short of a degree, to enrol in a college course in computer repair.

"Basically it's easy money," he said. "The younger guys there, it's a kind of mission for them. But I get into the mindlessness of it, you know, Zen and computer repair, that sort of thing."

But he seemed to have capitulated to some lesser self in him, talked about being left free to pursue other things but with a backwash of unspoken defeat. Then part way into the year Gus dropped out as well, going to work full time for his father's construction firm. I suspected some cosmetic compromise, some means he'd worked out of being able to support his habit while seeming to be drawn back into the fold; but the next time I saw him he seemed truly chastened.

"Believe me, this is what I need right now." There was the smug desperate assuredness in him of someone aping borrowed wisdom, strange for him. "They don't give me the cash, eh, they're not that stupid, it all goes right into a trust. But in a few years I'll have enough to do whatever I want."

But I sensed the same resignation in him as in Michael, the same falling back into the world they'd come out of as if they'd been held there by some limit it had set on them.

I had entered my last year at Centennial. I'd envisioned simply going on in school, but the weeks passed and still I'd made no enquiries, sent for no applications. Each time I opened a book or entered a class now I felt a resistance in me, a disjunction, the sense I'd been taking on faith some way of looking at things that finally had little to do with how the world was.

There was an information session one evening for a development organization that sent students overseas to teach. I expected political rhetoric, the unreliable earnestness of the converted, felt my suspicions confirmed at the sight of the speaker, long haired and bandana-ed and bearded. But his talk unfolded anecdotal and small like a returned vacationer's, following a series of slides like the ones Father Mackinnon had sometimes shown us at St. Mike's after one of his trips, the shanty towns, the blasted landscape, the people gravely posed before the camera as in a wedding portrait. It was exactly this unassumingness in the talk that seemed to draw me in, this sense of making a tiny, other life in some unknown place as if starting from scratch. The next week I began the lengthy process of application, and by early March I had been accepted to teach English the following fall in Nigeria, a country that a few months before I could not even have located on a map.

The next weeks I passed in a kind of dream, set now on this future that had somehow been conjured out of nothing. The world took on an impermanence, everything already compared to the future's imagined foreignness, the buildings and shops, the traffic lights, the strange organization of things, so arbitrary, roads and highways and malls, the endless civilized neatness of suburbs. Then my last day at Centennial had come: I felt no nostalgia, no remorse, only the unthinking relief at having got through again.

I'd decided to spend the summer in Mersea. Michael came by the residence in his car to help me carry my things to the train station.

"A lot of stuff," he said. But I had been pleased at how little I'd thought I'd accumulated.

After we'd checked my things we had a coffee in the station coffee shop.

"So we never had much of a chance to talk about this Africa thing," Michael said. "Maybe this is some kind of Catholic thing coming up in you, all that propaganda they used to feed us about missionaries. I remember they used to collect plastic bags from us to ship to Africa for people to put their rice in, bread bags and that. My mother would leave the crumbs in them so there'd be a little extra."

"I dunno, I'm just going over for the weather," I said.

"No, seriously, I know you were into that group for a while, I know you're serious about this kind of thing. I just don't know if this is the way. These groups always want to change people, make them think we're better than they are. I'm not kidding, my mother used to leave the crumbs, that was her idea of charity. She thought they were animals or something."

"Whatever she thought, the bags probably helped."

"That's not the point, Victor, it's the attitude people have. All this development work, it doesn't change anything if people don't change how they think. You can't do that on a big scale."

I felt my anger rise but said nothing. He'd often talked himself about going abroad but had never managed to, seemed simply to be rationalizing now his own lack of enterprise.

We paid for our coffees and walked toward the departure gates. I moved to join the line that had begun to form for my train but Michael suggested we wait in the seating area.

"There's plenty of time, these trains are always late."

We sat. Michael lit up a cigarette though a No Smoking sign was posted nearby.

"Vic, I know it's a little late but there's something I need to get off my chest."

I had feared this, Michael's need to make some gesture. I expected a sort of apology, some expression of feeling though underhanded somehow, twisted into a proof of his own deep nature. But even yet I hadn't understood him, was still awaiting some capitulation from him as if my own point of view was the only possible one.

"I dunno how to put it, Vic. I guess I've never really had the feeling there was some sort of two-way thing going on with us. It's just little things, I don't want to seem petty. Like back there at the coffee shop, you could have offered to pay for the coffee at least, just a little token like that."

It was true: he'd driven me to the station, had been willing to be here for my departure, and yet I'd felt no spirit of generosity toward him.

"Even that time when Gus stayed with you, I dunno, maybe it's just a different way of looking at things."

But now I was truly confused.

"What are you talking about?"

"Just the way you made it seem like such a big deal and all that. I mean the guy was in pretty rough shape, it's just basic hospitality."

"He didn't look like he was in very rough shape to me."

"Come on, you know what he's like. He was covering himself, that's all, he thought you were laughing at him. And then the little stuff, how you always put your food at the back of the fridge to give him a message or something. I don't want to get into the nitty gritty of it, it's just a feeling, that's all, a way of dealing with people."

We sat in silence. I wanted to mount some defence but the gap between how we saw matters had left me dumbfounded.

"Maybe it's an Italian thing," Michael said finally. "A kind of reverse prejudice, you-like-us-you-don't kind of thing, trying to work out some stuff from your childhood or something."

"I don't even think of you guys as Italian."

"I dunno, maybe that's the point."

The line had begun to move forward; Michael and I joined the end of it.

"Look, Vic, I don't want it to seem like I've been holding all these grudges against you, it's not that. I just wish we could have been closer, that's all."

On the train I felt grim. I found an empty seat, setting my shoulder bag on the place next to me to discourage anyone from sitting there but then feeling despondent at my mean-spiritedness.

"You'll have to take that bag off the seat, son, we've got other passengers coming on."

At Oakville I received my punishment: a drunk, the very caricature of loutishness, hulking and bearded and leather-jacketed.

"Hey, buddy."

Heads turned, energy homing in on us from the seats around us. A woman across the aisle smiled at me conspiratorially.

"Just going down to London, eh, got a call from the fuckin' old lady, she's in some kind of shit."

He seemed willing to talk to the air, unfocused, yet I could feel him ready to turn on me if I closed him out.

"So what's that you're reading there, you some kind of teacher or something?"

A sort of conversation started up between us, mainly his drunken ramblings and my noncommittal attention.

"The name's Ace, that's the name I took in the can." He held a huge hand out to me with drunken aggression. "Aces up!"

And afterwards he kept coming back to that phrase like a kind of mantra.

"I don't want any shit, eh, but the old lady called and I gotta go. I said to myself just three days on the wagon, that's all you've gotta do. Then halfway to the station I'm already shitting bricks."

The conductor came collecting tickets. Ace took a moment to register what was happening, began to fumble through pockets.

"Hurry it up there, I've got a whole train waiting behind you."

"Just hold your fuckin' horses, sir," Ace said, baitingly good-humoured, "I've got it here somewhere."

Heads turned again.

"What was that?"

Ace found the ticket, held it out grinning.

"Here it is, sir, got it right here."

"You watch your language, buddy, or I'll have you off this train faster than you can spit."

"Whatever you say, sir," Ace said, still grinning. "I don't want any trouble."

"Fucking a-hole," he said when the conductor had gone. "Then he's the type you get a few beers in him he's swearing up a blue streak."

When the conductor passed back a few minutes later, Ace's leg was stretched out in the aisle. The conductor stopped, seeming to be willing another confrontation.

"You mind pulling your leg in there."

"No fuckin' problem, sir."

"No, I think there is a problem here, you clean up your mouth or you're out of here. You got that?"

I could sense the anger rising in Ace, his helplessness in the face of it.

"Give me a break, man, you're the one trying to bust my ass."

"I don't think I'm getting through to you. These people paid for their tickets just like you did, they don't have to put up with this kind of trash."

"You're the only one seems to have a problem with it so why don't you just go fuck yourself?"

The hatred between them seemed close to violence now.

"As far as I'm concerned you're out of here."

The conductor headed back down the aisle, returning a few

minutes later with another uniformed man, large and broad-shouldered and calm.

"Why don't you just come along with us."

But Ace was subdued now, rising up with an air of tired defeat.

"See you around, man."

The whole episode had been so unnecessary: I ought to have interceded somehow, tried to pull Ace back. I resolved to speak to the conductor, feeling the falseness in this belated solidarity though still I made my way through the train, coming finally to a car empty except for four uniformed staff in a booth at the front and then Ace staring out a window toward the back. He caught my glance as I came in, nodded slightly but seemed either wary or confused, had perhaps already forgotten me.

"Can we help you with something?"

It was the conductor who'd argued with Ace, though he showed no recognition of me.

"I was just wondering what you were going to do with that guy."

Immediately he grew imperious.

"What's it to you? A friend of yours?"

"I just wanted to say I thought he'd be all right." I glanced toward Ace, wanting him to hear me and not, afraid I would betray him somehow; but he was still staring oblivious out the window. "I mean he's just a little drunk, that's all. I don't think he needs to be in any trouble right now."

"Don't worry, buddy, we'll look after him. Why don't you just go on back to your seat."

I'd accomplished nothing. But when I searched the platform at Woodstock to see if Ace had been put off the train I couldn't make out any sign of him.

I went back to my reading and gradually drifted into sleep, the panicky sleep of trains, its half-awareness of the world as of something left unsettled. I dreamt that someone was being put off the train, a woman perhaps, my mother or my aunt, even from within it the dream's meaning seeming strangely obvious; then something shifted and it appeared I'd made a mistake, that the woman was a stranger or I'd somehow entered the wrong dream, that while my attention was turned some more significant thing had happened elsewhere. But when I awoke I felt strangely elated, what had happened with Michael, with Ace, already fallen away: what seemed important about these things now was that there was no one I needed to share them with, distort the truth of them for, that they were simply incidents in a life that was truly mine.

XXII

I returned home from Centennial as from a kind of initiation or exile, the graduate now, some special seal set on my difference that made it a thing at once nameable and thoroughly arcane. For several days the question of what I planned to do next seemed to hang like a suspicion between my father and me, but then when my father finally came round to it there seemed no way of putting things to him in all their complexity.

"Africa?" He seemed truly uncomprehending, balking as at some outrageous whim. "I can't believe there aren't any jobs around here for teachers that you have to go to Africa."

"It's not that. It's a kind of volunteer thing. Anyway I'm not really qualified to teach here, I'd have to go back to school again."

But already I'd put things badly.

"If you need to go back to school I don't see why you don't finish now. I can't see how it can help you to go to Africa."

It might have taken so little to win him over, the single word from me that could have brought him into the meaning of what

I was doing, allayed his sense of betrayal, at my withholding from him, at my leaving, at my refusal to offer any pattern to my life he could make easy sense of, going off now to another country like an immigrant, accepting that humiliation when no logic compelled it. But there seemed no language between us that wasn't infected somehow with misunderstanding.

"It's just something I want to do. Anyway it's only for two years."

He had planned a graduation party for me but the pleasure of it seemed lost for him now in this confusion over my future. For several days he appeared to brood over the question, till finally Tsi'Alfredo offered to hold the party in the rec room of the new house he'd recently built.

"If I was his age I'd be doing the same thing," he said of my plans. Since he'd built his house a new sense of well-being seemed to have come over him. "Look at us, all our lives shedding blood in those damn greenhouses, we've never been farther than Niagara Falls."

"*Sì*," my father said, "we broke our backs and now they take it all for granted."

But he needed only to see there was no shame in what I was doing to begin to relent, seemed almost ready to take some pride in me, to admit whatever unrealized part of himself, his own lost freedom, he saw taking vicarious shape in me now.

Tsi'Alfredo's house had been built in the preferred style of Mersea's Italians, long and white-bricked and ornate, sitting raised on a small knoll of bulldozed earth next to his old one, where his son Gino now lived with his wife, as in some before and after picture in a tale of immigrant success. Upstairs the house was a mausoleum of useless rooms, unlived-in, the walls left unpainted while the plaster set, and the sparse new furnishings, with their islands of sudden extravagance, seeming lost in the house's immensity. But the rec room was a clash of old and new, with a built-in bar at one end and a full kitchen all in gleaming ceramic but then aging furnishings brought over from the other house like a re-creation of it, the old fridge and gas stove, the sagging old couch and armchair, the old black-and-white TV. It was as if this part of the house had been saved as the truer refuge against which the upstairs remained merely the idea of what was possible, the promise we held out to ourselves while continuing on with our in-between lives.

Tables had been set up at one end of the room for the meal, dense now with cutlery and dishes and glass. People showed me an odd good-humoured deference, handing me envelopes stuffed with cash, seeming ready to believe that some sort of transformation had taken place in me. At the beginning of the meal Tsi'Alfredo proposed a toast to me, making some suggestive allusion in dialect about African women that I couldn't quite follow.

"Anyway he's spent half his life in the jungle working in his father's greenhouses so I guess he should be all right in Africa."

I had the sense briefly of what it might mean to be accepted by these people, these half-strangers, my family, how it might feel to see myself as the flourishing of their collective will, the one their hopes resided in, instead of being so far from them, going out from their alienness now as toward some return to my truer self.

"Maybe when you come back you can bring some of that sunshine with you," Tsi'Umberto said.

But I didn't think of myself as ever really coming back, ever being held again within the sphere of their static world.

Then after my few minutes of their attention people settled back into their usual languid incuriousness. I was sitting next to

Tsi'Alfredo's daughter Nina, remembered watching her when I was younger whenever we'd worked together, the curve of her body against her clothes, the mist of sweat at her temples in the greenhouse heat, remembered the small hatred in me toward her then for her air of normalcy and disdain when she wasn't so unlike me. But now she might have belonged to a different generation, unquestioningly in her place here, still enviable in a way in this at-homeness though I could hardly understand any more how my blood had quickened once at the sight of her.

"So I guess you won't be coming home or anything while you're over there."

"I dunno, I doubt it."

"I always thought I might want to do something like that, just go away, maybe not for two years but maybe for a year or something."

But there seemed no real envy in her voice, merely the moment's interest in something she considered outside the true realm of her life.

The meal wound down, slowly disintegrating in its last courses into the inevitable movement of children, the sated pulling away from the table, the women's bustle of cleaning up. In this slow unfurling of ourselves we seemed almost a normal family, almost thriving, comfortable in the day's excesses, the food and the liquor, the noise of children and conversation. But I caught sight of my father at one point sitting alone at the end of a table looking suddenly old and forlorn like some forgotten patriarch; and in the gloom that flickered through me then I felt my continuing connection to him, the sameness, after all, that had always joined us but also my wish to have him approve now, an impossibility, of my need to escape him.

I worked for a couple of weeks on the farm. We'd recently built several more greenhouses, in plastic, as people were doing now, hunched narrow constructions of purlins and hooped steel that rolled out like dunes beyond the last of the glass greenhouses. Yet for all this ongoing expansion there was an unfamiliar air of leisure on the farm, the more monotonous work done now by the workers we brought up from Mexico every year on contract. Offshore labour, they were called, which conjured up in my mind a vision of them parked in houseboats off a coast and rowing in to shore every morning to work; and this image seemed to fit the reality of their lives, their long unrelieved hours of toil and then their retreat every night into the tiny private world of the trailer my father had set up for them near the boiler room, their muted voices sometimes drifting from there late at night to my bedroom window as across a lake.

The Mexicans and I greeted each other every morning when I came out to work with a deferential half bow and a *buenos días*, courteous and timid like lovers. I kept resolving to try to strike up a conversation with them, but the days passed and we never got beyond our smiling greetings. They were our past, what we'd been when we'd first arrived here, with their low wages and their subservience, their insistence on working twelve- and thirteen-hour days to make the most of the few months every year that they were allowed in the country; and yet there seemed no clear way now of bridging the distance between us, of avoiding the inevitable habit of mind of merely thinking of them as our workers. They held quiet parties sometimes on Sundays outside their trailer, friends coming by on bicycles from other farms carting six-packs of beer, and a ghetto-blaster perched at the screen of one of the trailer windows playing tinny cassettes of guitar and quavery vocals, the group of them seeming there in the sun, with their rickety table and chairs, like a backdrop in some American western; and though my father occasionally joined them then for a beer, speaking to them in his pidgin Spanish, still there was in his indulgence of them always a boss's condescension, the hint that next to his own complex life theirs was simple and rustic and innocent, how he himself must have seemed to the *inglesi* years before playing cards some Sunday afternoon outside his little barnyard shack.

In our living room there were two aerial photos of the farm, one taken not long after my father had bought it, with only the old boiler room, the old greenhouses, the barn, and then a wide stretch of flat green field, the other taken the previous fall just after the plastics had been built; and what struck me most about them was how each so clearly belonged to its different era, the first like a film set's recreation of the past, its few buildings worn and domestic and pastoral, dwarfed by the lush expansiveness of the landscape that surrounded them, while the second was staunchly, impressively modern, all concrete and glittering metal and glass. The trees around the house had been cut back or down; the irrigation pond, which in the first photo was an oasis of plant-and water-green, had been stripped down to a haggard earthen grey, its banks nearly barren except for the odd sapling or clump of weeds cropping up through the years of garbage that had been poured down them. It was as if the natural world had been slowly colonized by the greenhouses, made internal, as if against the momentary idyll, sun-drenched and impermanent, of that single summer day in the past we had built up instead this fortress of perpetual summer, while what was outside it, what was changeable and unfixed, slowly wasted away in its irrelevance; and perhaps all our progress had been no more than that, this attempt to hold time in place, free ourselves from it, to somehow arrive again in the new leisure all our work had afforded us at the simplicity we imagined we saw now in our Mexican workers, longed for in us like a memory of some sun-filled afternoon, without crisis or threat, that seemed as if it must stretch on to time's end.

XXIII

I saw Rita toward the end of May. She was sixteen now, tall and lithe and womanly except for the downy adolescence of her complexion, her blue eyes set off like opals against the raven black of her hair. A new restraint had gradually taken shape between us over the previous years with the growing scarcity of my visits and with her own rapid maturing, her old childishness gone now like some possession cast out of her and little pretence remaining of a generational distance between us, with the strange decorum and licence that that had brought. Our new decorum was more adult and hence simpler and more oppressive, around me Rita seeming to close down some essential part of herself now, retreating into a dutifully cheerful sociability as if changing into proper clothes for a guest.

"Africa, that's wild! Sort of like a missionary or something."

"Not exactly. There's no religion involved or anything."

"Anyway that sounds great. I'd love to do something like that."

But finally she seemed as incurious about my plans as my family had been. I felt a kind of revulsion at her forced agreeableness, the hint in it of Mrs. Amherst.

"So how are things with you?"

"Okay, I guess."

It came out that she and Elena would be spending the summer in England with Mrs. Amherst and her family.

"It's just to see family and stuff," she said, downplaying the trip as if in deference to my own. "I guess it'll be pretty boring."

"I dunno, it sounds great."

The visit left me with a familiar dejection. Away from Rita I would go days, weeks, without a thought of her, felt guilty then at how small a space I left for her in the daily unfolding of my emotions. Yet each time I saw her some nerve in me was touched, some old rawness, as if all along the shadow of her had lain at the back of my consciousness.

She was leaving in a matter of weeks; by the time she returned I'd be gone. I let a week pass without seeing her, vaguely imagining she'd eventually call, then feeling resentful when she didn't, even though I realized how I must seem to her, merely this moody half-stranger who suddenly appeared in her life from time to time as out of nowhere. Finally I called and arranged to see her the following Sunday.

"I just thought we should have a chance to talk before you go."

"Sure. That sounds nice."

There was a wariness in her voice on the phone, but then when I arrived on Sunday she seemed genuinely pleased to see me.

"Hi, stranger, I thought you'd forgotten about us."

She was dressed in a short, pleated skirt with legs bare beneath and a large pullover that puffed her upper body into formlessness, an odd mix of pale, exposed flesh and bundled warmth.

"I guess I've just been busy on the farm and everything," I said.

I suggested we go for a drive. I wanted her alone for once, outside the roles we seemed consigned to in the Amhersts' house.

"All ready for your trip?"

"I guess so. We went shopping in Windsor yesterday for clothes and stuff."

"Maybe I'll come to see you off at the airport."

"That would be great."

We drove a few minutes in silence. Rita seemed lost in her thoughts, unmindful of me, of the car's intimacy, my silent awareness of her sitting there beside me.

"Where're we going?"

"I thought maybe we could drive out to the Point or something."

"That's where people go to neck."

"Is that where you go?"

"Haw haw. Anyway Mom won't let us start dating till next year, what a drag."

We talked a few minutes more, then lapsed again into silence.

"So is anything up?" Rita said finally.

"What makes you think that?"

"I dunno. It just sounded like something important when you said you wanted to see me, usually you just come over."

"I just wanted to make sure you'd be home." I felt uneasy suddenly at the claim I'd made to her attention. "Anyway we might not see each other again for two years, I thought we should have a chance to talk."

Rita dropped her voice to a mock-portentousness.

" 'The time has come,' the walrus said, 'to talk of many things.' "

I was surprised by this sudden literateness in her.

"What's that supposed to mean?"

"I dunno, it's just a line from some poem, it just came into my head."

"Since when did you start quoting poetry?"

I hadn't quite been able to phrase it as a compliment but still she flushed with awkward pleasure.

"Maybe you're not the only one in the family with brains."

We'd come to the tollbooth at the entrance to the park. I recognized the attendant from high school, one of the popular boys then, even now radiating the same sheen of blithe unthinking self-confidence. An instinctive shame pulsed through me, my mind doing a rapid inventory of the things that might compromise me; but he showed no sign of recognizing me.

"Have a good day, sir."

We drove into the park in silence, the car engine echoing hollowly beneath the canopy the trees formed over the road and the air growing heavy with the smell of humus and lakewater. A dejection passed through me like a chill – the woods seemed to reduce us somehow, with their gloomy chaos of growth and rot, spindly sumachs and beeches and maples struggling up like abandoned things through the twilight of vines and fallen limbs. On a school field trip once we'd gone out to the very tip of the Point, the land tapering down into the lake there like the last draining away of a continent; and I'd thought then of the first explorers arriving at that tiny foothold centuries before, of the tangle of endless forest confronting them alien as another planet.

Rita was staring through her window into the trees; something in the angle I saw her at, half-turned in her seat, only her cheek visible and then the long sleek black of her hair, made her seem a stranger suddenly.

"I guess I should come out here more often, people make such a big deal about it," she said. "Watch the birds or something."

"You could come swimming."

"Yeah, right. Mercury City."

I turned off the main road onto the gravelled one that led to the West Beach. There was a couple sunbathing there in the early-June chill, then a family picnicking at one of the tables set along the beach's length as at some lakeside café; I drove beyond them to the far end of the parking area and parked facing out toward the lake. To the left the shoreline curved gradually round to the Mersea boardwalk, distantly visible in the afternoon glare; but ahead of us there was only the lake, stretching out a steely northern blue as endless as the sea.

I took out a cigarette.

"Could you spare one?"

Rita had turned on the seat and bent a leg onto it.

"You shouldn't be smoking," I said, but held one out to her.

"I only smoke when I'm nervous."

"Are you nervous now?"

"I dunno." She looked away toward the beach and let out a thin line of smoke. There was a woman in baggy shorts and a bandana spreading a towel out there; as she bent to straighten it, her blouse sagged for an instant to reveal a patch of ruddy cleavage. "I guess when you called I figured you wanted to talk about our mother and all that."

I was caught off guard. The suggestion seemed so unlikely I couldn't think how to respond to it, pre-emptive somehow, premature. At some level I'd long imagined beginning this conversation with her, passing on to her this trust; but now the moment seemed lost even as it was offered, ruined by her having suddenly thrust it before us in all its awkwardness.

"What made you think that?"

"I dunno, I just figured that was it."

"Do you know anything about her? I mean about what happened?"

"Yeah, I guess so. I mean, this and that, I guess you know a lot more than I do."

But that she knew anything at all seemed somehow to worsen things, to make it impossible to speak now in anything but the vaguest terms.

"How did you find out?"

"I dunno, here and there, I guess it's not such a big secret really. Mom told me some stuff, not very much, and Elena's always asking kids at school, the Italian ones, I guess their parents say things sometimes. And then Aunt Teresa."

"Aunt Teresa? What, when you were little?"

"No, I mean since she's been coming to see me."

"What are you talking about?"

She grew reticent, seeming afraid she'd given away a confidence.

"I thought you knew. She's been coming sometimes, the last couple of years. Not much, I guess three or four times. She hasn't come for a while now."

For some reason it burned me like a betrayal that Aunt Teresa had been seeing Rita, that this had been going on without my knowing. It seemed just like her to meddle like that, to have to always bring things within her control.

"What, was she trying to convert you or something?"

"No, why? Convert me to what?"

"So what did she tell you exactly?"

"Just the story of what happened and stuff."

"How did all this come up? Did you ask her about it?"

"I don't think so. I mean I can't remember really, I think she was the one that brought it up. I guess she didn't want me to think she was a criminal or anything, from what other people said about her."

We sat silent. Rita shifted and drew in her leg, instinctively tugging the hem of her skirt over her knee.

"You're not angry or anything are you?"

"Why would I be angry?"

"I dunno, you just seem – I dunno."

The discomfort between us was palpable now. I hadn't imagined this moment like this, the insufficiency of it, the inarticulateness, yet somehow I couldn't bring myself to compete with whatever version of things had already taken shape in her.

"So how do you feel about all this?"

"It's sort of strange, I guess. At first it was like a kind of game to find out but now I don't really feel anything about it, it's like it has nothing to do with me. I mean it's not as if I ever knew her or anything. Is that weird?"

"No, it's not weird. It's pretty normal, I guess."

But there seemed a rift between us now.

"Anyway if you ever want to talk about it again –"

"Sure."

But there was such a relief between us at dropping the matter, such a tangible drawing away, that it seemed unlikely we would speak of it again.

We took a walk along the beach. The detritus of spring had not yet been cleared away there, the driftwood and garbage that the storms had thrown up, giving the beach an air of abandonment, despite the picnickers and the sunbathers.

"It's weird how things happen," Rita said. In our silence I'd imagined her hopelessly lost to me, was surprised now at her note of timid intimacy. "I mean how I came to live with the Amhersts and all that, it all seems so unreal now."

"Anyway it looks like everything worked out in the end."

"Yeah, I guess so. It's just, I dunno, I feel like I've been two people or something, it's been so different."

But I could feel myself withdrawing from her, resisting this intimacy though it was what I'd thought I wanted.

"Do you remember much? I mean, from when you were living with us?"

"I dunno, not really, I guess I was pretty young. I remember what's-her-name, Tsia Taormina, she was nice, I guess I thought she was my mother or something. And Aunt Teresa, going into the greenhouses and when she used to read to me and stuff, though the first time she came to see me I didn't even recognize her."

But her memories seemed strangely uncontaminated – she might have been recalling some calm, pleasant childhood, light-filled and unremarkable.

"I guess I must have been a real brat," she said.

"No. You were pretty quiet, really."

"It's funny, I don't remember it that way. I always think of myself as being really noisy or something, I don't know how to describe it."

We'd come back to the car. I offered her a cigarette, and for a few minutes we sat silently smoking, Rita staring out, oddly composed, toward the lake.

"God," she said finally, "remember that time we got called down to Pearson's office, I thought for sure you were going to tell him I'd been lying. I guess everything would have been different then." She wagged a finger in the air in imitation of Mr. Pearson. " 'No dawdling in the halls, now, girls!' "

I searched back through my memory of that day, could remember only the buzz in my head as from the sound of a fingernail scratching a blackboard.

"Lying about what?"

"About the bruises and stuff."

I felt myself redden.

"I didn't say anything about them. What did you expect me to say?"

But I'd misunderstood.

"I dunno, I guess I thought you'd tell him the truth, that I'd gotten them playing and stuff."

"What do you mean?"

"You mean you didn't know? All those bruises and stuff – not the first ones, that was just what started it. But after that, the ones I got playing, we used to tell the Amhersts I got them from your father. It was Elena's idea, she thought I'd be able to stay with them then. I thought you knew."

A small rage had taken shape in me.

"How would I know?"

"I guess I just thought you'd figure it out."

She'd presented the story so innocently, like some harmless delinquency we could laugh at together, feel complicit in.

"You're not angry are you? I was just a kid."

"No I'm not angry, I just don't like the idea of everyone thinking he was some kind of a monster."

We sat a moment in charged, awkward silence. I'd ruined things now; whatever fragile understanding we'd established seemed broken.

"Look, I'm sorry," I said finally. "Anyway I guess everything worked out for the best."

We drove back to the Amhersts' without speaking. My anger had vanished, had left now only the awkwardness of our silence, though each moment it stretched on seemed to make reconciliation more impossible. When I pulled up to the Amhersts' it was Rita who was the first to speak.

"So I guess you'll be gone when we get back." Tentative, probing; she seemed to be inviting me to offer again to come out to the airport and yet somehow I pretended to myself to have understood the opposite, that she preferred me not to come.

"I hope you have a good trip and everything," I said.

"You too. Maybe we can write or something."

"That would be nice."

She leaned forward awkwardly and brushed her lips against my cheek.

"Well, goodbye."

And though a hundred times in the following days I ached to call her, still each passed until finally the day of her departure had come and gone.

XXIV

I had taken a job for the summer when it had grown clear that I wasn't needed on the farm, hired on by a group calling itself the Italian Historical Committee that had received a government grant of some sort to research a history of Mersea's Italians. They had put in a notice at Manpower requesting four students to do the work; and though the whole notion had seemed suspect to me still I'd applied, been asked in along with several others for an interview, been finally taken on as the project's co-ordinator.

The committee was vaguely attached to the Italian club, our interviews held in the boardroom there and the club secretary, Colomba, quietly managing things in the background, reassuringly competent and efficient. But the other members of the group were an unlikely assortment of aging farmers and brassy, middle-aged women and a few younger, better-spoken people who seemed held up as the committee's veneer of credibility.

"We're still working out the details of how this is going to work," one of them said. "There's a professor up at the university who'll be helping you out with that."

The committee's chairman was a man named Dino Mancini, round-faced and round-bellied and suave, his own comments always in an ostentatiously casual English, easing themselves into the discussion now and then like innocent afterthoughts. He reminded me of the self-styled *galantuomini* who used to sit out on the terraces of the bars in Rocca Secca, full of pretence and condescending camaraderie, vaguely powerful though only some dubious, half-forgotten distinction or parentage made them so. During my interview he'd eyed me the whole time with a kind of paternal magnanimity as if making allowance for some obvious flaw in me.

"I'm sure you speak *abruzzes'* and all that from home but maybe with the *sciusciar'* or the Sicilians you'll have to speak a little Italian now and then. Do you think you can handle that? Just enough to get by, I mean, I know you were born there and that, maybe you studied it in school."

"I think I can manage all right."

But then when the interviews were done he seemed to grow more expansive, instinctively deferring to me as the only male among the students they'd hired.

"You guys, you've been to school, we got the idea but you kids gotta decide what's the best way to do it. We thought it might just be about the first ones who came over but it doesn't have to be just that, we should talk about what we've done, the club and all that. Whatever way you can find to do it, that's good. All those houses on the lakeshore, for instance, when my old man came over before the war it was one hundred per cent English there and now it's all Italians."

"What we have in mind," one of the younger men said, as if interpreting, "is the sort of book the town put out for the centennial, you know the one. A history book, the first people, photographs, that sort of thing."

"But you don't expect us to write the book as well?" I said. "It takes years for that kind of thing."

"We realize that," Dino said. "That's the professor's job, he's gonna be doing the book – you guys, all you have to do is the research."

I hadn't mentioned the job to my father but somehow he'd found out I applied for it, finally coming round to the subject sullen with suppressed curiosity.

"You don't want to get mixed up in all that book business," he said heavily. "It's all politics, you don't understand it, that damn Dino Mancini and his gang there."

But I hadn't sensed any conspiracy; the group had seemed too unfocused for that.

"I dunno, he seemed all right."

"Yah, those guys, they make everything sound nice, they always want to make it seem like they're doing such a big thing for the Italians. I don't say Colomba's like that but the others, they don't know, they just do whatever Dino says."

It seemed I'd ignored the obvious, had once again stumblingly, wilfully, set myself against him, taking on a project that given his own past he could only regard as a threat. Yet the topic had animated him, as if he were grudgingly pleased at this common ground that had opened up between us, this opportunity to instruct me.

"Anyway it's too late now, I already said I'd do it."

"*Mbeh*, you'll find out how these things work. I said from the start they have to involve all the Italians in a thing like this but Dino's got his own ideas, he just wants to make a big deal that his family was one of the first."

And finally his resistance appeared less a personal thing than simply his usual scrupulous fidelity to his own peculiar code of what was right.

The group of us that had been hired met at last, along with the committee, with our elusive advisor, Professor Mariani, just back from a visit to Italy and seeming still caught up in the first flurry of return. I had expected some thin-faced pedant, oozing condescension the way people of status in Italy had; but Mariani gave off the air of a broad, chaotic vitality, all emotion and single-mindedness.

"It's a different world over there now, completely different, never mind all the problems about the south. Fashion, technology, art, it's at the front of everything. And the amazing thing is it's a socialist country, free medicare, everything. The workers get free resorts in the mountains, for God's sake, hotsprings, everything paid."

"I don't know," Dino said, "I can't see that. Every time you open the paper you see the government's changed again over there."

"But that's the point! It's the bureaucracy running the country, not the politicians. Here you have a government in for five years, they want to change the whole country around. There's no continuity!"

It was Colomba who finally steered us round to the subject at hand. But there was a confusion now about the nature of the professor's involvement.

"Maybe there's some mistake, I never said for sure I could do it. It's a wonderful project, it needs to be done, but we're talking maybe years of work if you want to do this thing right. I'll need funding, I'll need to take time off of teaching –"

"It was my understanding," Dino said, "that this was all settled."

"No, Dino," Colomba said. "Maybe that wasn't clear. The professor said he would help the students to get started on the research, that's all. The book, that's another thing, we have to get the money first and then we'll see."

We began to talk about how to proceed with the research. My father's suspicions seemed unfounded now: the professor wanted us to interview every Italian in the area, even down to the second and third generations.

"If they start doing everyone they have to finish that way," one of the committee members said. "We don't want people saying we did some and not the others."

"We can't say that. Maybe there's some people who don't want to do it."

"Then that's their problem, we can't force them."

"I don't know, we gotta be careful," Dino said. "We don't want the Sicilians for instance saying we didn't include them."

"What, have they said something already?"

"Not that I heard, I'm just saying."

"That's what I'm telling you, we have to make an effort. But how can we force them?"

But we seemed no closer to a plan than we'd been at the start.

"What we need to know," I said finally, "is what exactly you want us to ask people."

"Everything," the professor said. "Not just about here but what it was like over there, how they lived, what they ate, who ruled over them, the *padroni*, the government, Mussolini."

"What is he telling us?" one of the older men said, in dialect. "What does Mussolini have to do with it?"

But the professor had understood.

"Ah, ah, don't tell me the people didn't like Mussolini, he was a hero in the south! Most of those villages had never seen a schoolhouse until Mussolini."

"Look, Professor," Dino said, "it's all right to talk about the old country and all that but we don't want a thing like that show they did on the radio a few years back, about the life in the village and that sort of thing. There was a lot of people upset about that, you know all that stuff about going to piss in the stable and so on. I don't deny things were different there, but it's not the kind of thing we're trying to do."

"What we gotta decide," Colomba said finally, "is what the book is gonna be. Maybe a chapter on each thing, like the centennial book, on the old country, on the trip, maybe something about the religion or the culture, something like that."

"What culture?" someone said. "There's no culture, they're all farmers."

"What do you mean there's no culture?" the professor said, mischievous, triumphant. "What about *agri*culture? We're talking about the most basic form of civilization!"

It grew late. It was decided our research team should come up with a list of questions on our own and then discuss them with the professor before proceeding.

"Call me at home. Any time after Wednesday is fine."

In the meanwhile I looked up Mersea's centennial book at the library. It consisted mainly of photos flanked by thumbnail profiles and old newspaper clippings, the world it chronicled seeming at once familiar and utterly foreign, the rows of sober faces, the hard Presbyterian names, the buildings and vistas, changed over time or the same, in each case predictably, it seemed, as if the town had contained from the start its own future. At first glance the book struck me as a hodgepodge but

297

then I began to discern a sort of story-line, beginning in the anonymous past, the Indians, the bush, and then moving through profiles of the town's founding fathers and entrepreneurs toward an increasingly anonymous present, grey-bearded individuals giving way to groups, groups to institutions, the tone one of slow, inevitable progress toward the perfection of the present day. It was as if the vision of Thomas Talbot, who a century before had ruled over the vast wilderness Mersea was carved from as over a private fiefdom, dreaming of establishing some personal paradise there, had slowly come to a kind of fruition, the present in its bounty the symbolic return to the first Eden that Talbot had imagined he'd stumbled on.

Yet ultimately the book seemed an anachronism, might have been portraying some bucolic hinterland town untouched by any history but its own, had been unable to accommodate in the simple line it drew from the past to the present what seemed to me the essential thing about the texture of life in Mersea, its mongrel heterogeneity. On a whim I searched through the book's index: apart from the odd exception the names there flowed like an uninterrupted stream from the Anglo-Saxon ones of the first settlers, Armstrong, Baker, Campbell, Curtis, Drake. The discovery gave me a perverse satisfaction yet seemed too easy finally, too opportune, was perhaps less the sign of a bias than of a self-exclusion – the Italians thought of themselves as owning the town and yet they'd never elected a member to the municipal council, to the provincial legislature, to parliament, had hardly involved themselves in the town's civic life beyond organizing their clubs and saints' feasts. Even the business directory at the back of the book showed a dearth of Italian enterprise: there was a barber-shop, a grocery store, a gift shop; there were three or four construction firms; there was Longo's

Produce. It was enough, merely, for a kind of self-sufficiency, the comfort of passing one's life outside the sphere of the *inglesi*.

A photo toward the end of the book showed the sleek new public library that had replaced the more august one, an old white-pillared and white-corniced building in stately Renaissance style, torn down to make way for it. It took me an instant to realize what the photo left out: the fountain that the Italians had had constructed in the library's triangle of front lawn as part of their own observance of the centennial, no doubt not yet begun at the time the photo had been taken though it stood now, just across the road from the new municipal hall, like the town's centrepiece, perhaps not so much a sign of the Italians' contribution to the town as simply a monument to their irrefutable presence there. The Lebanese, too, had built their monument, a great shrine to the Virgin that towered over their club at the town's outskirts, its cone of concrete spiralling up three or four stories to the light-haloed figure at its peak like a beacon at the town gates; and somehow these things seemed part of a different story, discontinuous, as much removed from the carriage works and the fire brigades and the town councils that formed Mersea's founding mythologies as these had been from the Indian history they'd erased. It was as if a new, more subtle colonization was taking place, self-contained and self-protective, not so much replacing the dynasties of the town's grey-bearded fathers as slowly rendering them irrelevant.

Yet the story was not so dissimilar after all: the town's first settlers had had the same unillustrious roots, had fled the same hardships, been thrust into the same foreignness that they'd forever held themselves hard against; and perhaps the motive to tell it now was also not dissimilar, the desire not so much to reclaim the past as to redeem it, all its meanness and ignominy, to recast it as the ennobled source of the present's happily-ever-after.

I met with Professor Mariani in the small, steamy office of the newspaper he ran, *Il lavoratore*, The Worker. He pored over our list of questions from behind a tiny desk piled high with files and old newspapers, his jacket draped haphazardly over a chair, his tie loose, his sleeves rolled; he seemed a cliché, a caricature of himself, the socialist professor toiling in the dingy office of his socialist paper.

"This is great, Victor, perfect!" Yet always there was a surprising genuineness in his enthusiasm, a true generosity. "Everything's there, the whole story, beginning to end, the war, discrimination. Don't be shy when you ask them these things, dig, dig, get down underneath. Ask them everything, about their mortgages, how much they make, how much they own. That's the amazing thing, this incredible wealth in a single generation. Do you know how many hundreds of years they lived exactly the same, with their few little plots of land and a few goats?"

We started our interviews, beginning with the half-dozen or so men who'd come over in the 1920s. They were a mixed lot but I sensed among them all the more fundamental rupture they'd lived through, that in their years alone in Canada they'd been forced to remake themselves in a way that later Italians, more secure in their own little worlds, never had. Yet there was a spirit in them that drew me, an entrepreneurial largesse: most Italians slaved for years simply to pour all their savings in the end into the needless extravagances of their houses, but these earlier ones had been more expansive in their ambitions, had built up businesses, dynasties, enterprises. One had turned his greenhouse farm into a tourist attraction, sold flowers and tropical plants, had a petting zoo with sheep and rabbits and deer, pony rides, a llama, a yak, had built a domed conservatory that served fast food beneath palms and orange trees.

"People back home, they said it was just bush out here. 'Don't go out there,' they said, 'you'll die out there!' But I had to do it. I'll tell you the truth, the only reason I stopped here was because it was close to the border, I thought I would sneak across some night the way people did then. But now it's the other way, the Americans come up here to see my sheep."

But then almost at once we ran into a snag: we had assumed from the outset we'd simply transcribe every interview and reuse the cassettes, but five hours into my first transcription I was less than halfway through the tape. I met with Colomba, our liaison with the committee.

"At this rate we'll only have a few dozen interviews done by the end of the summer. The best thing would just be to save the cassettes."

"There's no money for that."

"What about the club?"

But I'd sensed from the start that the club wasn't behind this project.

"It's too compli-cate with the club," she said, "it's all politics. The board this year, anything Dino Mancini he's involved in, the board doesn't like it. Already they say I spend too much time with the book when it's not the club's business. I'm not saying your father's like that, but the other ones."

But I hadn't known that my father was on the board that year.

"Call the professor," Colomba said. "Maybe you can just make a summary instead of to write the whole thing."

The professor, though, seemed surprised that we hadn't been planning to save the cassettes all along.

"Do you realize what a historical record that is? It would be a sacrilege to erase them, it's absolutely out of the question."

"Maybe you should explain that to them."

"Okay, tell them this, tell them I can't possibly do the book without those recordings. It's true, those are source documents, without them the book would be meaningless."

I met with Colomba again.

"We'll have to go the club," she said. "Try to make up some kind of report to give the board, why we need it, how much it's gonna cost."

I prepared a report, careful to stress the professor's involvement, that we'd be trying to interview all the Italians; there was no subterfuge in what we were doing, were no villains, and yet somehow I'd allowed myself to be pitted directly against my father again, had been drawn in on the wrong side of old rivalries and grudges as if it were ordained that he and I should be perpetually in conflict. But when I brought the matter up with him in private he seemed strangely unaccusing.

"As far as I'm concerned I don't care, if you think you need it. But I don't know that the other guys are going to go along with it."

I hadn't been prepared for this trust in me. For a few minutes there seemed a quiet solidarity between us.

"Anyway, Dino's hardly involved in the thing at this point," I said. "I don't see what everyone's got against him."

"Oh, you know, all those old fights and things, stupid things, it's always the people from Castilucci are one way and the ones from Valle del Sole are the other."

The board met; the funds were approved. I thought of my father closed up in the boardroom with the others, making my case.

"So you got your money," he said afterwards.

"Yeah. Thanks."

And perhaps all along he'd wanted no more than this, the simple chance to show me he believed in me.

All that remained now was the work, almost anticlimactic after the manoeuvring of getting going. With the time we'd lost there seemed no chance of finishing our interviews by the end of the summer. But Colomba was calm, reassuring.

"Just do whatever you can, we'll try again next year to finish it." Beneath her brisk efficiency there was always this warmth, a kind of shambling physicality like some secret message her body gave. "Anyway you guys did the hardest part, to get it started."

We began our interviews in earnest, moving up chronologically by year of entry into the country. I was surprised now at how gruelling each interview seemed, precarious and never quite satisfactory, never quite seeming to break through to the truth of things; and then after the first dozen or so they began to take on a tiresome sameness, as if a single collective mentality governed the whole community, a single story had shaped their experience. Whatever eccentricity there might have been seemed levelled by our recorders – the mood changed at once when they clicked on, people putting on a stiff formality like a mask, distrustful and impressed at this importance we granted them. The recorder itself became a presence, a silent official in the room that we were in collusion against. People would catch my eye sometimes trying to find a way to speak around it, to silently contradict, to seek approval that they'd said the proper thing. More sensitive questions had to be thrown out from the start, on the matter of finances for instance: at the first hint of this subject people seemed to gird themselves as for some expected humiliation, a reserve that struck me as odd at first, a Canadian trait, out of keeping with the ostentation Italians showed in their homes, their weddings, their cars; but the unease was too palpable to be an adopted one, might have gone back to the belief – as perhaps it did with Canadians, for all I knew – that numbering one's possessions invited fate to take them away.

There were three distinct groups among the people we interviewed, the *molisani*, my own group, still known as *abruzzesi* from when Abruzzo and Molise had formed a single region, and then the *ciociari* and the Sicilians; and with each year we moved up, the task of interviewing the *molisani* fell more and more to me since I spoke the dialect, English becoming less common among them the later they'd arrived and standard Italian bringing out in them a second level of strained formality. Even their dialect was so riddled now with unthinking anglicisms that it had perhaps lost any reference point outside the small colony they belonged to in Mersea; I imagined ethnographers in years to come going through our tapes to chart the contours of this new language, respecting it like a relic, but to me it seemed no language at all, merely the tattered, imprecise remnants of one, a gradual dimming of the world that words lit up until all that remained was the pinprick of consciousness their own community formed. But these interviews awakened memory in me like a prod, through the bone-familiar inflections of people's speech, the lingering Samnite stolidity of their features. The small unease I'd felt since the start of the project grew more insistent: there was always now the moment of recognition, when people drew me like a witness into their pasts.

"But you were born there, you remember what it was like."

But I wasn't part of their pasts, I wanted to say, not the official ones they constructed for the machine, that left out somewhere the essentials, the flies, the heat, the colour of evening light, some texture of things that could hold what wasn't spoken between us. Then one evening I interviewed an old couple from Valle del Sole who had come over only a year or so before I had.

"I remember your mother," the old man said, so ingenuously that for a moment I was certain he'd made a mistake. "She used to come around to get milk from us when she was little."

"It was a shame what happened," his wife said, "*cchella disgrazia*. It was hard for your father, too, I remember that, but he did the best he could, no one can say anything against him."

I could hardly fathom what they were saying, couldn't wrap my mind around the thought that all that had happened, the whole horizon of my past, could be reduced in others to such small innocuous observations, that people could be as simple-minded as that, as forgiving. *Cchella disgrazia*, that misfortune, that disgrace – the two seemed never far from each other in people's minds, every tragedy a kind of humiliation, a punishment of the gods; and yet they'd brought up the matter so casually, had made it seem such a distant, manageable thing. Perhaps I was the one, after all, who had never seen the matter clearly, continuing to carry the thought of my mother's crime and death with a seven-year-old's sense of affliction when for others these things had long been made benign by the passage of time.

It was just this once that my mother was mentioned to me, though perhaps only because of the distance I instinctively took on now with people who knew me. But all summer long she seemed the spectre that haunted me, the unremembered thing in the memories my interviews stirred, what inserted itself like a shadow between people's predictable stories and some uncertain admission or truth I wanted to prise from them. Then once, interviewing a young woman just recently brought back from Italy as a bride, some casual gesture of hers suddenly brought my mother back to me with a sharp fleeting clarity, not merely a ghostly notion of what she might have been but someone for an instant as solid and as real as the woman before me in the present moment. And yet what I felt most strongly in that instant was a sense of loss, the sudden realization that all the rest I knew of her, what I'd somehow imagined still lay whole and intact in me, vivid as life itself, had long ago faded away to mere shadow.

XXV

As the end of summer approached a small euphoria began to take me over, the relinquishing that came at the end of things. I drove around to my interviews pleased with the world, Mersea seeming spread out sun-filled and simple and benign like a town from some old television show. It was as if I was creating for myself a stranger's memory of the place: this was what the town was, would have been, without me in it, a place without pain or humiliation or threat.

One of my final interviews was with an old man from Castilucci who lived with his son along the lakeshore. The house was set back from the road like a Roman villa, and seemed to aspire, with its pillared entrance and arching balustrade, to the pretensions of one; I had seen a hundred variations of it over the summer, this confusion of flourishes, intended somehow to recall Italy though they had nothing to do with the plain stone dwellings people had lived in there. Behind the house long rows of greenhouses stretched toward the lake, blocking a view of it though it seemed held in the sky's hollowness like a reflection, a breeze wafting in from it laced with subtleties of texture and smell like forgotten words.

A small boy answered the door, curly-haired and elfin and stern, staring up at me in silent appraisal.

"*Chi è*, Car-men?" An older voice from inside, faltering against the truncated English sounds of the boy's name. "*Chi è?*"

"It's a man."

Coming from the boy the judgement sounded oddly solemn and complete.

The old man had come into view.

"*Vieni, vieni*, you must be the one from the book, aren't you the one I spoke to? Mario's son, I remember, I used to chase him out of my grapes down in the Valley of the Pigs."

Inside, the air was distilled to a comfortable coolness. There was a large family room, surprisingly tasteful and inviting, off the side entrance, but the old man led me instead up a few steps into the kitchen. The boy followed behind, still gazing at me circumspectly, trying to fit me into whatever order of things my arrival had momentarily fractured.

"Your grandson?" I said.

"My grandson's son! They bring him over sometimes to keep me company. We get along well – with my five words of English and his five words of Italian we never argue."

He invited me to sit.

"So. What can I offer you? A beer, a glass of wine?"

"Please, nothing, thank you."

"Well I'll have one for myself then."

He went to the fridge and tremblingly withdrew a bottle of wine from it, tremblingly poured himself a glass.

"The young and old," he said, "they always get left behind. One in a crib and the other in a casket. My son already bought a place for me, up there on the highway so I can see the lake. Just next to my wife. She died five years ago now, maybe you remember the funeral. Your father was there."

He was dressed as my grandfather might have been for a trip to Di Lucci's bar, cuffed corduroy trousers wrinkled tight at the waist by his belt and a white dress shirt whose sleeves were held up by silver armbands, his body shrunken and stooped with age but seeming to hold in itself an old dignity like a memory. But there amidst the kitchen's gleaming modernity he appeared an anachronism, made merely quaint, nothing in his surroundings reflecting back who he was. Little Carmen, who'd retreated to the front entrance hall, seated on the marble floor there amidst a cornucopia of toys, at home again and content, would never know this man: there in his plenty he seemed the final oblivion in a slow forgetting, taking this world, this house, this luxury, utterly for granted.

I began to set up my recorder.

"Do you mind if I use this?"

"Suit yourself. The truth is the truth, whether you record it or not it doesn't make any difference."

It came out that he and one of his sons had lived in Abyssinia briefly in the thirties, settling there after the Italian conquest.

"Not that I wanted to go off into the bush, mind you, I wanted to go to America like everyone else. But in those days you couldn't even cross the road without the government's permission, so I said I'd go wherever they sent me. Then we found out the land they'd given us was even worse than what we'd left behind."

I told him about my own upcoming trip to Africa.

"Well, maybe for a young man like yourself it's all right. But I already had one toe in the grave by the time I got there, I had nothing but bad luck there from the start. We farmed a bit, did this and that, tried to send a little money home; but then the war started up again and my son was killed. I could understand that, he was a soldier. But my other son, my youngest, when I came back to Italy, that was hard for me. It was a little thing – some of the boys found a plane that had fallen and started to play with the guns, and a bullet got him. I thought I couldn't go on after that. But it was hard for everyone then."

His eyes had begun to tear; he pulled a handkerchief from a back pocket to wipe them. I'd heard so many stories like his over the summer, had each time sat through them in the same awkward silence – there seemed no adequate response to them, no way of assuaging a pain that was so general. But the old man recovered in an instant, as people did, this gift they seemed to have, to be able to touch the bottom of a painful thing and emerge from it whole a moment later.

"*Mbeh*, you didn't come here to watch an old man cry."

The rest of the interview unfolded more predictably, his life in Canada seeming in comparison to his past like a retirement in some pleasant holiday country, comfortable and uneventful. Canada was his home now, he said, was the only place he fit in.

"I've been back to Italy twice now, but no more. I stay with my daughter in Rome and she won't speak to me in dialect, she says I sound like a peasant. And in the village it's just as bad. Everything has changed there – Italy has progressed but here we still think the way we used to twenty years ago."

I asked if he had any old documents or photos we could use for the book. Older people were often reluctant to lend us these things, fearing some danger to themselves if their photos were reproduced; but the old man disappeared with an air of pleased intent into the house's gloom and returned a moment later with a yellowed shoebox tied with string. He'd put on a pair of glasses; one by one he went through the items in the box, scrutinizing each from a distance through narrowed eyes and then handing it on to me. His old Italian passport; an identity card from Fascist times; three or four packets of photographs; a medal his son had earned in the Abyssinian war. A glint of silver at the bottom of the box caught my eye – a coin, an old one *lira*, I recognized it at once. I reached for it and a thrill passed through me like a premonition: the coin was the same as the one I'd been given years before by my mother's friend Luciano, the same year, 1927, the same nick in the eagle's wing that he'd said had stopped a bullet from entering his heart during the war. For an instant time seemed to falter and warp.

"I had a coin like this once."

"*Mbeh*, they were common enough once, before the war, a *lira* was still worth something then."

"No, I mean exactly the same, the same year, the same mark like that on one side."

"Oh that, of course, it sometimes happened like that back then. One year all the twenty-cent pieces had the king's ear missing. You couldn't spend them to save your life, people said they were bad luck. With this one it was different, it was good – people made up stories about it, that Mussolini made it like that to protect himself from the pope, all sorts of things, you know how people thought back then. I never believed in all that foolishness – I kept it like that, as a souvenir. You can take it if you want, I don't have any use for it now. If I gave it to Carmen there he would lose it in half an hour."

I weighed the coin in my hand. A child's acquisitiveness stirred in me, an old belief in the magic of possessions.

"You don't mind?" I said.

"Not at all, please, take it. Maybe it'll bring you better luck than it brought me."

But when I had pocketed it I felt peculiarly burdened, as if something until then chimerical, evanescent, had become suddenly mundane; whatever meaning I might attach to it now would be merely a kind of conceit, an indulgence.

Carmen followed us to the door, slipping past the old man to look up at me still vigilant, still unconvinced. I imagined him having seen me pocket the coin from his great-grandfather's box, having followed me now to bare his silent resentment. I had robbed him of his story, whatever fiction the old man might have spun out for him in passing on to him the coin. But in the thrill of departure even Carmen forgot himself, waving goodbye, goodbye, as I backed down the drive.

"*Buona fortuna in Africa!*" the old man called out, holding Carmen's tiny hand in his trembling one like a flower.

XXVI

I spent my last week in Mersea preparing a final report. At home I'd carefully labelled and filed all the materials we'd put together, interview tapes and notes, photos and documents, index cards. Sorted like that they seemed an impressive archive, weighty, official, so much more orderly than the work that had gone into creating them, than the community they represented. I wondered what truths or fictions the professor would draw from them; or perhaps they would merely sit gathering dust in some office of multiculturalism, having no value beyond their official one, simply a proof that the government had given its sanction to an ethnic community.

But when I came to write up the report it seemed impossible not to leave out what mattered most, the countless things that were known but never discussed, the truer, finer, more vulgar things, the garish furnishings in people's homes, what they might say over supper, how they held in their hearts' fonder remembering until the moment the machine was turned off and they'd sat back in pleased relief at their careful deceptions. The most interesting interviews, the atypical ones, were the hardest to use, didn't fit any pattern; and the very act of summarizing seemed to steer me toward exactly what I wished to avoid, a kind of panegyric that sifted and levelled all differences into a bland, harmonious whole. I was reduced finally to a sort of doltishness, to stating the obvious, to charts and statistics and glosses that left out a haze of impression and nuance that couldn't be put into words.

I worked in my room, conscious of being there at a desk while outside my father and the others worked on the farm seeming at once the fulfilment and contradiction of my report. I had set their own tapes apart, Tsia Taormina's and Tsi'Umberto's, my father's, feeling a vague obligation to listen to them, though the days passed and still I kept putting the task off. When my father's turn had come up in our interviewing I had assigned him to one of the younger workers, Filomena, had half-expected, half-hoped, that he'd decline to be interviewed at all; but then in the cassettes that Filomena had turned in to me at week's end my father's had been there, so innocent-seeming among the rest that I couldn't bring myself to disturb it.

Ultimately it had been Aunt Teresa who'd refused to be inter-viewed, something that seemed both in character for her and not, simply her usual perversity or perhaps something else, a sort of integrity. She'd refused a platform to speak, to contradict, to call attention to herself, had chosen instead simply to hold her tongue, as if she'd understood how little place there was in this sort of thing for the truth. Perhaps all along I'd underestimated her, had never been willing to concede to her this strength of character. Even her visits to Rita, what she'd told her: seen dif-ferently they seemed to fit the pattern of a long, quiet manage-ment of our family's emotions, of the self-denial that had lain always just beneath the surface of her, what might have been the only thing, finally, that had saved us from ourselves.

It was only after I'd finished my report that I listened to the tapes. Tsi'Umberto's was predictable, the reasonable man, the persona he took on with people, his bad English straining for authority, for the idiomatic, only a small sullenness showing the wariness beneath his responses, the care he was taking to keep them unremarkable. Tsia Taormina's, done separately in dialect, I almost gave up on, put off at first by her plodding literal-mindedness; and yet there were things that surprised me, perceptions I couldn't account for.

"It was hard for the kids at first, because of the language and everything. The oldest one was all right but for the younger one it was harder, he said the kids at school made fun of him and things like that. He wanted us to buy him clothes like they had but we didn't have any money for that in those days."

But I was amazed she could have known these things, that her sons had had that closeness with her; we had all lived together then and yet I couldn't fit these moments of intimacy into the strange foreboding gloom that was all I remembered from then.

My father's tape was an agony. There was none of Tsi'Umberto's forced reasonableness in it, his voice throughout raw with humility, a single note hanging in it like the hollow after-throb of a bell. The contrast to Filomena's was almost comical at times, as if their voices had been spliced together afterwards for a gag, Filomena resolutely buoyant and automatic, my father's responses like a sea she skipped across to reach the safe haven of her questions. There was a palpable warmth that came through when my father spoke about Italy – he grew almost voluble then, almost expansive, a nostalgia I'd seldom seen in him, that didn't fit the image I'd somehow developed of his having left Italy coldly, without remorse; but then Filomena asked about his family.

"My son came over in sixty-one with my wife, but my wife, she died on the trip."

A pause.

"I'm sorry, you said your wife died?"

There was a catch in my father's voice, a stillness.

"Yep."

Another scratch of empty tape.

"How did she die, was she sick, did she have an accident?"

"She died in childbirth."

Filomena's awkward earnestness enraged me, that in a community as small and claustrophobic as ours she hadn't known these things; and yet I'd chosen her to do my father exactly because she'd seemed the least likely of our group to know.

"I'm sorry about that," she said, then returned with a quaver to her usual list of questions. I had the impression that if she'd continued to probe, my father would simply have gone on like that to tell the whole story, would have answered every question with the same humbled sense of obligation to the truth.

I thought of removing my father's tape, his entire file – there was an intimacy in his answers I couldn't bear, something laid open, not so much in what he'd said as in his simple inability not to speak, that made my mind ache. Yet perhaps in speaking he himself had already made peace with himself, could see his life more whole than I did, less out of the ordinary. There were a hundred different tragedies in our community, and beyond them a hundred scandals, infidelities and betrayals, illegitimacies, an ancient murder; and yet the earth had never split open in the face of them, the people they touched carrying on with their lives, accepted, marked only by the lingering gingerliness others showed around them as if out of respect for human frailty. In the end I put the tape back in its proper place, feeling my father was owed that or perhaps simply wanting to see it there, so innocuous, among the others, apart from its few awkward moments telling, after all, the same story they did, as if time had finally levelled our lives to a comfortable normalcy.

XXVII

The morning of my departure my father drove me to the depot. He had dressed, though it was a work day, in his after-work clothes, a loose summer shirt, old suit pants, his good shoes, the two of us alone again as in our old Sunday rides to church in the car's intimate closeness.

"Does this bus from here going to take you all the way up to Ottawa?"

"I have to switch in Toronto."

"Ah."

He had a habit of leaning into the steering wheel as he drove to cradle it like a child, with the gesture now the sleeve of his shirt hiking up to reveal the flesh of his biceps, pale against the tauter bronze of his forearms, vulnerable and unformed like a teenager's. I had the sense suddenly that in all the years I'd known him I'd never once dared to look at him squarely, to hold him whole in my sight, even now feeling merely this impression he was beside me, this peripheral blur, his arm on the wheel, his weight pressing down the cushioned velour of the seat.

"Do you have some kind of address or something if we have to write to you?"

"I don't really know exactly where I'll be yet. I left a phone number for the people in Ottawa with Aunt Teresa – they'll know how to find me if you need to."

A pause, the small tensing of resentment in him.

"It seems funny to me, you don't even know where you're going."

"It's not that, it's just I don't have the exact address yet. Anyway I'll send it to you as soon as I have it."

But I hadn't imagined writing to him, had thought of this departure as somehow complete, no lines leading back.

At the bus stop there were a half dozen others waiting on the sidewalk, a few teenagers, a young man with a crew cut in a university jacket, two women in the stiff skirts and high-collared blouses of Mexican Mennonites, their baggage two bundles wrapped in blankets and twine. My father helped me lift my bags from the trunk, a duffel bag, an overstuffed backpack, what I'd whittled myself down to.

"You don't have to write only every six months," my father said. "My English isn't that good to write, you know that, but I can manage all right to read it. Maybe your aunt can write in English."

"You can write in Italian, I'll understand it."

We stood a few minutes in silence. My father looked at his watch.

"Looks like it's late," he said.

But a minute later the bus rolled around the corner. My father, wallet in hand, went up to the driver as he stepped down.

"How much for Ottawa?"

"Hold your horses, buddy," the driver said, moving past him. "Let me get these bags on first."

His insolence stung me but my father seemed oblivious. When the driver returned my father peeled off a few bills for my ticket and then handed a sheaf of wrinkled fifties and hundreds to me.

"Something for the trip."

I wadded the money awkwardly into a pocket.

"Thanks."

I was the last to board. I wanted only to be gone but sensed the emotion welling in my father, the need for a gesture. I had only to embrace him, to brush my cheeks against his, the usual ritual of parting; and yet I had never done such a thing, couldn't bring myself to do it now though my whole body felt impelled to.

"So I guess I'll see you in a couple of years," I said.

"Yep."

And then I was already on the bus, without so much as a handshake, a touch. As the bus pulled away I had a last glimpse of him lingering there on the sidewalk, a lonely figure I'd never known, seeming still the sad stranger I'd sat beside years before on a Halifax train.

XXVIII

My first vision of Africa, as I surfaced from afternoon sleep to gaze from the window of our plane, wasn't the endless bush I'd expected but a city of sun-baked mud on the desert's edge, moulded out of the rusted earth like some child's creation. Then the wall of heat as we stepped from the plane, the ramshackle airport, a cinder-block shed merely, alone in that blasted landscape like a final outpost; and finally the bus ride into Kano, the road alive with a human traffic like a refugee trail, on foot, on bikes, on tiny scooters and motorcycles that chirred away from the path of our ancient bus like swatted insects, everything suspended in the blaze of desert heat as in a dream.

Our in-country orientation was held in a government teaching college just outside the city, the group of us sequestered there in our whiteness as in some holiday camp. All the rhetoric we'd heard in Ottawa about development work seemed to fall away now: there was no global perspective here, only the nuts and bolts of getting by, basic language training, how to work a kerosene fridge, how to select and slaughter a chicken. There'd been talk in Ottawa about a boycott against Nestlé but here their products were used unthinkingly, the powdered milk and the biscuits, even the coffee, Nescafé instant, imported from Belgium though Africa abounded in coffee.

Some of the older volunteers led groups of us into the city. The heat there, the mud barrenness, gave the sense of a perpetual aimlessness or repose, of a world still awaiting the decree that would set it in motion. Taxis – battered blue Datsuns and Beetles, white Peugeot 504s – barrelled through the narrow streets like rockets, from another planet, the calm splitting open to let them pass and then closing again. We came on a bar, a warehouse of a place in yellow stucco, where a dusty juke box was playing the latest Rolling Stones; but outside you had only to walk a few minutes, into the maze of crooked lanes the city was, to feel that time hadn't moved for a thousand years.

In the old market the gloomy alleyways hummed with quick activity, narrow mud stalls leading back into mysteries of secreted goods. The traders, tall and sharp-featured and dignified, haughty, called out to us in Hausa, *bature*, white man, then gave the air of not caring to sell to us if we approached them. At prayer time, prayer mats were unfurled, activity ceased: we seemed made invisible then by their indifference, irrelevances they toyed with, then blotted out.

Some fifteen of us out of the eighty or so volunteers who had come had been posted in the southwest. On the fifth day we set out before sunrise in an old plywood-floored bus whose back seats had been removed to make way for a large metal drum, of oil or kerosene or petrol, I was never clear which. The drum was part of some private transaction of the driver's – the field officer who'd come up from Ibadan to accompany us, Richard Harmond, blond and pink-skinned, seeming to exude still the dying glow of a suburban complacence, had made a show of arguing with the driver before our departure; but the drum had remained. The road was pocked with great potholes, craters really, two, three, four feet across; the driver, never letting up speed, careened and swerved to avoid them, though sometimes a wheel caught the edge of one and the drum at the back gave out a liquid groan as it shifted with the jolt.

As we moved south the landscape grew greener, resolving itself finally into a tree-studded savannah; small mud villages and Fulani encampments glimpsed distantly from the highway gave way to towns of more modern appearance, the buildings of sun-faded stucco, the roofs a sea of corrugated tin. At Kaduna we stopped to eat at a lorry park, a great dusty square ringed round with chop houses and traders' stalls and crowded with taxis and minibuses and mammy wagons. The older buses seemed cobbled together from scraps of old metal and wood, each one distinct, painted in yellows and blues and inscribed in florid lettering with strange slogans, "No condition is permanent," "God is God," "Water be for sea."

Beyond Kaduna the land grew gradually more hilly, the vegetation more dense; here and there abandoned lorries lay toppled at curves in the road like felled monsters. The towns we passed seemed like settlements in the Old West, dusty and becalmed, provisional, the buildings sitting at odd angles to the road as if someone had wrenched the country out of square.

The checkpoints grew more frequent. In the north we'd encountered them only at the outskirts of towns: the soldiers would step up into the bus, officious, then their eyes would glaze at the sight of us and they'd wave us through. But now the checkpoints appeared without warning in the middle of the bush, makeshift, simply planks laid over metal drums to block the road and little shanties of corrugated tin at the roadside where two or three soldiers milled, rifles slung languidly over their shoulders. Sometimes they didn't bother to rise up from the little benches they sat on, merely gazed unimpressed at our faces in the windows and called the driver out to them, joking or condescending, going through his papers indifferently or with a painstaking thoroughness, unpredictable; then sometimes they boarded the bus.

"*Oyinbó.*" The Yoruba word for white man; we were passing into the south.

At one of these stops a soldier came on and strutted idly to the back of the bus, prodding some of the baggage there with the butt of his rifle and then tapping a finger against the top of the metal drum.

"Driv-uh!" The driver came to the back; the soldier made a cursory inspection of his papers, then put them ostentatiously into the pocket of his shirt. He tapped the drum again.

"Na be safety hazard, not so?"

There was a brief exchange in Yoruba and then the soldier left the bus; the driver followed. Outside, a long discussion ensued in mixed Yoruba and English, the soldier's voice growing increasingly more peremptory, more adamant, the driver's more pleading; the words "safety hazard" repeated themselves amidst long stretches of Yoruba like a catch-phrase. Finally the soldier crossed back to his shanty and the driver boarded the bus – but only, it turned out, to pull it off to the side of the road. The soldier hadn't returned his papers; they could be seen bulging still in his pocket.

"Welcome to Nigeria," Richard said.

The driver resumed his pleading. But the soldier seemed to have lost interest in him now, busying himself with other vehicles passing through or simply sitting at his bench talking idly with the other soldiers, closing the driver out. A few of us got out of the bus to smoke; ten minutes passed, then twenty. Richard kept apart, explaining nothing – he seemed to be awaiting some inevitable conclusion, though time passed and the driver appeared no closer to winning the soldier over. His pleading seemed a ritual merely, the two of them like characters in a masque, the driver perpetually playing the penitent, lean and diminutive in his ragged pyjama clothes, the soldier perpetually feigning indifference.

"Leave me now!" the soldier said finally.

The driver came over to Richard.

"*Oga*, I beg you, make you give 'am dash."

"No way," Richard said, but with a kind of smugness, of put-on authority. "It's your drum, it's your problem."

"No be so, *oga*, they dey see so many white man, they think na big big money. Why you wan' make palaver for these people, na be all night we go sit here."

One of the older volunteers, David, had gone up to them.

"Look, why don't you just give them the dash. You were the one who wanted to do the trip in a day."

Richard shrugged.

"We're not that far behind schedule." But he seemed put out at the opposition, tried to make light of it. "Anyway you wouldn't want me to set a bad example for our new recruits."

"It's the way things work," David said. "They might as well get used to it."

Richard pulled a bill from his wallet and handed it to the driver.

"Then just don't accuse me of corrupting you guys."

And in a minute we'd set off again.

A few miles past the next town one of the front tires gave out. The bus veered wildly for an instant but then the driver righted it and brought it expertly to a stop. I expected some complication, some tremendous delay; but the driver pulled a spare, balding but sound, from somewhere under the bus and in a short while we were back on the road. At the next town he stopped at the lorry park to repair the flat. The mechanic was not in his stall; someone was sent to fetch him. We bought some suya from one of the Hausa stalls, some greasy pastries, a few bottles of Fanta and Coke from a barefooted boy who hawked them out of a water-filled bucket. The boy lingered warily at the edges of our group while we drank, anxious that we not leave without returning his empties. Other children gathered, stood staring at us from a distance; one, a small girl, came toward me, put out a tentative hand to touch the whiteness of my skin.

"*Oyinbó.*"

The mechanic arrived; again I expected some delay.

"Is not possible," he said, looking over the damage; but then he and the driver argued, discussed, and finally he set about things, efficient and quick, bringing his tools out from his stall into the open and squatting strangely as he worked, exquisitely balanced. But when he went to inflate the tire his compressor failed to start.

"No NEPA," he said.

"NEPA," David explained. "No Electrical Power Anytime."

"Just leave it," Richard said. "We'll stop in the next town."

The NEPA was out in the next town as well. We found a mechanic with a hand pump; it took several minutes of effort, the driver and the mechanic alternating, to fill the tire. Twilight came while we waited, the town seeming to take on a strange frenetic energy, taxis calling out for final passengers, the stalls around the lorry park closing up; and then almost at once it was night, the darkness falling like a blanket, complete, punctured only by the flickerings of scattered hurricane lamps, tiny winks that moved disembodied through the dark like fireflies. Overhead a million moonless stars glittered distantly – I had never seen such a thing, such a night sky, at once so black and so light-filled.

In darkness we crossed the Niger, a stretch of inky black hemmed in by shores of shrouded bush like wading phantoms. It seemed shabby somehow, unimpressive, not the vista I'd expected but merely a trickle lost in the heart of a continent; and yet I had a sense of having crossed over, of having arrived. Just beyond the river lay another town, larger, but like the one before it already beginning to close down for the night; the few taxis still plying the streets there beat their horns in endless staccatos like drums and flashed their high beams as they passed as if in welcome.

Past Ilorin we hit another checkpoint, more official-looking, more entrenched. A soldier came onto the bus and ordered us out.

"Make you come now," he said, good-humoured. "*Oyinbó* go sleep here this night."

A dozen or so other vehicles had been pulled over, their passengers milling along the roadside and soldiers picking through their scattered baggage under the narrow beams of flashlights. But at the sight of us gathering there among the others a tall, muscular figure in crisp khaki, the commander perhaps, came toward us from the station-house.

"Where to?" he asked Richard.

"Ibadan."

"It's not possible." Yet there was something comforting in his voice, an unexpected humility. "Go back, go back to Ilorin, the roads are not safe at this time of night."

"We need to get to Ibadan," Richard said. "These people have postings to get to."

There seemed a petulance in his insistence – I had a sense of him trying to blot the country out, intent only on having things unfold neat and on schedule, on getting back to whatever comforts awaited him in Ibadan. Yet the commander seemed to consider what he'd said, turning finally toward the station-house.

"Olushegun!"

We were assigned a soldier to accompany us into Ibadan. He sat at the front, his rifle propped casually against the floor; at each jolt of the bus I expected it to go off but the soldier seemed oblivious, gazing silent into the funnel of light the headlights formed on the road. At some point he and the driver began to talk, in mixed pidgin and Yoruba, warily at first but then with increasing animation, gesticulating, telling tales. Their voices had a lilting buoyancy, every syllable stressed, important. The air of belligerent authority the soldier's uniform gave him fell away – he was no more than a boy, really, perhaps eighteen or so, seeming to revert now that he was away from his post to some truer, more human self.

Somewhere beyond Ogbomosho the bus broke down: the engine choked, regained itself, then choked again and died. The driver pulled a flashlight from a toolbox, descended, lifted the hood.

"Na be engine trouble," he called out.

"No shit, Sherlock," someone muttered.

The driver worked under the hood while the soldier held the flashlight for him. Snatches of conversation passed between them peppered with bits of English like sudden luminescences, "fuel line," "carburetor," "distributor cap." The rest of us milled listless at the roadside, worn down now by the trip, the constant delays, the bus's rattling uncomfortableness.

"Maybe we'll have to sleep in the bush after all," Richard said.

The darkness rose up around us like a wall, tangible, broken only by the small glow of light from under the hood; and yet we seemed protected somehow, not so much by the soldier as by our own inconsequence here, by our whiteness. There was no sense of crisis: the driver and the soldier tinkered away at the engine, absorbed in their work; even Richard, who had retreated back into the bus, had the air again of having withdrawn himself to await some inevitable solution. In every instance during the day when we'd encountered some obstacle I'd sensed this strange passivity just beneath the surface of his stubbornness; I had thought of it as weakness but now it began to seem simply a benign resignation, a capitulation to an order of things too large to struggle against. All day long a certain rhythm had been working itself out; we were merely caught up in it oblivious, riding it like bodies riding a stream over rapids.

Time passed. A taxi went by, then a minibus, but no one bothered to hail them. Finally the driver tried the engine: it caught. We let up a cheer, spontaneous, all relief and goodwill; for the first time that day the driver seemed part of us.

"Fuel filter na clog," he said, basking. "I dey say so na first thing, na be fuel filter, not so?"

It was not yet eleven when we came into Ibadan: we had made good time after all. We dropped the soldier at a check-point off the ring road and then made our way into the city. In the dark it seemed a vast village, endlessly repeating itself, the dusty buildings and streets, the nighttime hush, the dim haloes of light from windows and streetside stalls and shacks. In the flash of the bus's headlights I caught a glimpse of a man, his hair a clump of matted dreadlocks, sitting stark-naked atop a smouldering heap of garbage, calm and dignified there like some silent guardian of the city.

Our hostel was in the Government Reservation Area. The streets there were more kempt, almost suburban, the houses tidy bungalows set back in the dim inviting glow of porch lights and vegetation. At the hostel a groundskeeper or watchman of some sort came out from his shed at the edge of the compound to open the gate; and within a few minutes we'd unloaded our bags, briskly efficient, re-energized now that we'd arrived. The hostel had the air of a summerhouse, set on a hill amidst palms and hibiscus and banana trees; from its island of normalcy, of calm, the day seemed a kind of fiction suddenly, purposely, predictably exaggerated like some amusement put together to keep us at a remove from the real life of the country.

Richard left with the driver to return to his own home after we'd settled in. A group of us sat up a while on the back patio, the city distantly glowing in the background, a hundred thousand scattered pins of light. The older volunteers told horror stories, of travelling, of the bureaucracy, of the conditions at their schools.

"It's a country everyone loves to hate," one of them said. "My friends thought I was suicidal or something at first because my letters sounded so negative. But I was having a great time."

At some point the lights went out; all around us the city went black, seeming to retreat in an instant into the night. We lit a hurricane lamp, the group of us huddled there within its intimate haze as around a campfire, made small suddenly by the darkness. For the first time I had the sense of a country stretching unknown around me, the wonder of it. Out in the dark small lights like ours had begun to appear like tiny greetings; for a moment the earth seemed to mirror the sky, with its profusion of stars, to join it, a single canvas, the same blackness and light, the same slow coming forward out of nothing as at the beginning of things.

XXIX

I was assigned to a boarding school outside the town of Ikorita. "Crossroads," the town's name meant, though only a single road passed through it; dusty and prosaic and slow, it was like a hundred other towns in the region, shambling toward modernity, not so much the clash of old and new as some uncertain hybrid between them, the TV antennas that sprouted above its tin roofs seeming as natural to it as the ju-ju stalls in the market, with their monkey skulls and dried rats and small bundled pouches of unknown charms. The market followed a non-weekly rotation I could never keep straight, forever shifting to accommodate holy days and feasts; though it seemed now merely a sort of lingering habit, offering little more than what could be had at the shops that ringed the lorry park, onions and shrivelled tomatoes, cassava root, dirty rice, canned tomato paste from Portugal, canned mackerel, Geisha-brand, from Japan.

Outside the town the jungle rose up, the tiny fields hacked from the wall of it here and there seeming merely moments' irritations in its continuous slow burgeoning. Our school,

Mayflower Secondary, lay in the midst of it like a secret clearing, an arched gateway at the main road bearing its name and its motto, "Knowledge Is Light," and then a steep gully-scarred lane leading up to its little village of buildings and outbuildings, vaguely ramshackle and crude but still giving an air, amidst the flame trees and irokos and palms, of a tropical elegance. I had a bungalow secluded behind a wall of hibiscus bush at the edge of the school compound, its windows barred with metal grilles because of the danger of thieves there, the far side looking out toward guava and citrus and bush and the back opening onto a small plot of rock-hard earth that I worked a few months then abandoned, unable to hold it against the ravages of insects and weeds and heat; during the rains the house was a mess of leaks from the stones students threw to knock down guava but otherwise it was comfortable enough, with its warps and odd angles, its smoothed concrete floors, it generic furnishings, slightly shoddy and sparse but enough to give an illusion of home. Shortly after my arrival an important chief died in a nearby town, for days afterwards the drums sounding long into the night to mourn him; and from my place there at the edge of the bush, with the crickets chirring outside in the brilliant dark and the vines creeping up through my windows, they seemed an ironic welcome, like the distant drums in some movie about darkest Africa.

There were four of us there at the school, four white people, "Europeans," beyond myself an Englishwoman, Kate Townsend, who'd been there for years, and two Americans on a one-year exchange their university had set up; the rest of the staff were mainly Nigerian and then a mix of Ghanaian and Indian and Pakistani. In my first weeks some of the native teachers came by my house to greet me, wandering inquisitive from room to room, leafing through my books and magazines, establishing their presence as if laying a claim on me; but amidst the ceaseless blur of school work it seemed after a few months that little had come of this contact aside from the brief exaggerated friendliness of greeting when paths crossed between classes, that it had remained no more than a haze of indistinct possibility at the edges of my aloneness. There appeared an assumption in most of my dealings with people there that beneath the surface gestures of fellowship there was a chasm that couldn't be bridged, so taken for granted that every exchange seemed a kind of evasion, a circling around some truer version of things that was never named; and there was perhaps less the lingering of a colonial distrust in this than simply the belief that whites couldn't be expected to understand how things truly were, our notions no doubt fine for the efficient mythical world we came from but merely quaint, inessential, misguided, in the grittier, more complex reality we now found ourselves in. Inevitably I fell in more and more with the Americans – we were united, at least, in our whiteness, our newness, had less work to do to understand one another; though even then there remained always the shadow of difference between us, if only in the quicker, more expectant intimacy others assumed with them because they were Americans, known quantities, emissaries from the centre of the world.

Our school had been founded in the fifties by a Nigerian reformer in protest against the forced teaching of religion in government schools. Hence the school's name, though it seemed to me a strangely innocent choice, conjuring an image of American slave ships plying the African coast; and hence also its continuing distinction, its founder become a legend of sorts, he and his students having carved the school from nothing out of the bush and built it up as a kind of monument to self-sufficiency. But by my time the school had passed into government hands and a creeping decay had set in. There was evidence still of a former glory, in the tiny world it still formed with its bakery and piggery and farms, the lingering ethic of a well-rounded self-reliance; but always there was the gap between the rhetoric of how things should be and the reality of how they were. Perhaps the school had never been as illustrious, as efficient, as the collective memory of it portrayed it; but my whole time there I was dogged by the sense that we were a waning, that the country outside us, with all its disorder and contradictions, had slowly begun to contaminate the tiny enclave we formed.

I taught fourth-form English and literature, preparing the students for the O-levels they'd write the following year. As a teacher I was adequate perhaps in the simplest things, dogged, methodical, but finally never comfortable in a classroom, never sensing with the sureness of instinct the thing that was needed, the moment that worked. Mr. Tsikata, the portly Ghanaian who headed the English department, seemed to extend to me at once an infinite forgiveness.

"There is a syllabus, I have it," he said, smiling, amused, embarrassed, "but you could say it's a kind of Platonic construct. It bears little relation to our own sublunar reality here."

But still I began every day with the same small despair, did my teaching as best I could, took on extra duties, arranged extra lessons, yet never shook the feeling that every effort was provisional, incomplete. Short of starting from the beginning, what a noun was, what a verb, of re-creating from scratch the whole edifice of a language, it seemed possible only to keep up a panicked salvage of whatever the students had, all that I knew appearing sometimes to recede into the protean haze that language had been when I myself had first learned English years before. Ultimately my teaching became simply a matter of getting through: I longed every day for the final bell, the silence the classrooms took on then, the crooked rows of empty desks, only in that calm the fear lifting from me of some impending chaos that my own insufficient grasp of things would be responsible for. The school was more the students' world than mine, with their regimen of meals and prep and physical labour, their prefects and officers, their societies, their understanding of the hundred shifting rules and the thousand shifting exceptions that governed the rhythm of their lives there; and early on I simply conceded to them this greater authority, accepting the role of innocent that my whiteness allowed me, the token reverence that came with it and its reverse, a kind of invisibility.

That invisibility seemed in the end what most defined my stay in the country. If I'd fought against it, refused to obscure myself behind my difference, I might have broken through to some truer level of exchange with people, become real, an individual; but there seemed always a risk in the transition, a challenge to the accepted order, always the line to be walked between this innocuous thing I was seen as and the darker history I might cross back into. In my first months in the country I made an attempt, though English was common enough there, to learn the rudiments of the native language; but when I moved from simple greetings to phrases, to catching now and then some word of conversation, there appeared a subtle shift in people's reactions to me, no longer the first exaggerated praise but a twinge of unease and a kind of boredom, as if I'd undermined somehow the game established between us.

What I seemed offered finally in my encounters with the

country, or what I was able to see, were always its most obvious elements, what was folkloric, colourful, quaint, the face prepared for the foreigner, for the white, what instinctively served to mask from outsiders the truer life that went on beneath. But that truer life, the complexities that informed it, seemed accessible only by a kind of indirection. The country cried out for caricature, all garish surfaces and excess, the noise and the heat, the oppression, the endless soldiers manning the endless checkpoints, the poverty and the wealth. Every journey out revealed some new contradiction, the elaborate rites for the dead and then the bodies left rotting at the roadside because people feared being implicated in their deaths, one that I'd seen on the Benin road flattened into the pavement like a decal, the contours still visible of hands and legs, a face; every month revealed some new fad, the tennis rackets strapped to the front grilles of Peugeot 504s, the sudden appearance of Coca-Cola in cans at the tollbooths off the Lagos expressway. The newspapers gave out a wealth of bizarre incident, riots in Lagos spawned by the stealing of genitals, human heads found in shoeboxes to be used to redeem the souls of wealthy chieftains; and everywhere there were the signs of a rampant mongrel spirituality, the *babalawos* and the brothers, the churches and the shrines, the thousand different sects, from the Hare Krishna to the Adventists to the ghostly luminousness of the Cherubim and Seraphim, who could be seen on Sundays dancing single file along roadsides in their gossamer robes. But these surfaces seemed to play against one another like mirrors, revealing only in what they obscured, some more secretive life going on beneath them, more magical, more mundane – the life of the school perhaps, with its prefects and prep, its adolescent hopes, its essential normalcy, or the quietness Ikorita took on after nightfall, the stilled market stalls then and the smoky courtyards, the calm domestic ordinariness of meals and sleep.

Yet even as I stood outside it the country seeped into me, grew familiar as if I'd remembered it from my own past. There was a way people were there that brought up in me the sense that they were my secret, truer allies who I'd defected from to the whites: with students sometimes a gesture or tone of voice, the contour of a face, would bring back suddenly some class-mate from Valle del Sole, the ramshackle classroom there, its uneven walls and stone floor; in the lorry parks the market women, mocking and independent and fierce, seemed to hold in them a familiar fire. And I was happy there finally, unreasonably so, felt a contentment at the core of me that seemed to have little to do with the daily texture of my life, its frustrations and ten-sions, its occasional satisfactions, was more the sense of the smallness of these things, tiny blips in an energy too large to take the measure of. Being there made the world seem suddenly without horizon, without centre, like the surprise of discovering life on another planet: here was a place going on so far from anything I had known, with its own history and rules, its own sense of importance, the thought filling me sometimes with a wonder that made of the simplest things tiny perfect revelations, the smile of a girl in the market, the signs over shops, the odd names of my students, Bunmi Benson, Lola Leigh. Or perhaps the wonder was simply in feeling fall away from me all the foreign world I had never quite entered into at home, to be in this place without expectation that I should ever have to find the way to fit in.

In the full moon there, bright enough to read by, the world was lit like an enchanted place, all silvered and phosphorescent

338

as from some cool inner glow. I wandered into the bush some-times to revel in it, down the paths cut there like secrets by the local farmers to reach their tiny patches of hidden field. Even in daylight those paths were like some inner dreamscape, with their gigantic vegetation, their huge unknown flowers, their scattered evidences, the potsherds and blackened gourds, the ashy remnants of a fire, of whispered midnight rituals; but in that haunted moon I had the sense that I might step at any instant into the miraculous. It seemed a kind of redemption to be reawakened like that to the world, attuned to every possibil-ity, to feel at every breath the blood's quickening, the heart's hollow thrum.

XXX

The mail truck came out to Mayflower twice a week, its blue hump surfacing like a tiny whale from out of the bush that lined the steep climb to the school gates. I grew attuned to its comings and goings, always the instinctive glance toward the gates on mail day mornings from the windows of classrooms, the small tensing of anticipation when it arrived; and then the trek to the administration block between classes for the quick furtive glimpse at my mail slot.

The school secretary, Mr. Johnson, sorted our mail with a painstaking slowness, squinting down at each envelope to silently sound out the name there and then seeking out some correspondence to it on our cubbyholes with the circumspection of someone seeing their foreign array for the first time. When there was nothing for me he'd avoid me, grow irritable, seeming to take my barely veiled expectation as a sort of affront, ready to defend himself against the accusation of it; but then finally something would come.

"Ah, Mr. Victor! I'm thinking you must be having a girl-friend in Canada, isn't it?"

This anticipation in me seemed at first merely a kind of reflex: there was nothing of special import I had any reason to expect, no lover on whose words I hung, no final answer on which my future depended. The few correspondences I kept up, with people from university mainly, were little more than a matter of form – a letter or two to Michael, a few others to people who'd passed on their addresses in the last months of school in the quick, shallow intimacy that came before a depar-ture; I wrote to these people at all, it seemed, only for that first fleeting pleasure of finding something more in my slot than the endless circulars from the Central Schools Board. Yet always there was the small unreasonable hope of some crucial message or change; or perhaps it was simply that I couldn't abandon the proof some arriving letter gave that I'd existed before, that I'd come from somewhere and would one day return there.

Letters came from my family as well, from my father, from Rita. At bottom I hadn't expected to hear from them, had imag-ined I had only to subtract myself from their lives and that would be the end of it, a sort of reverse insensitivity, the belief I could cease to have any meaning for them simply by leaving them; and yet I had written to both early on. To Rita I'd sent a postcard, falsely blithe and urbane, when we'd stopped in London a day on the way to Nigeria, making a joke about our planes crossing in mid-Atlantic; then a few days after I'd arrived at my post I'd sent a letter as well. I'd begun in the same false casualness, still trying to find some way around the strangeness that had marred our last parting; but then finally I seemed to find the right voice, the right distance, ending up with five closely written pages, a diary of sorts of all that had happened since I'd left Canada.

Her reply, when it came, even written double-spaced in her billowing script, barely filled a page.

Thanks for the letter, it was great! Africa sounds *wild*! It must be really different there, it sounds like it anyways from your letter.

It went on like that, breathlessly adolescent, saying nothing – its tone made me think of the girls in high school who I'd loved and despised from a distance, had nothing in common with, who talked about dates and played on school teams and struggled each term to get their marks into the seventies. The Rita I'd written to, with all my careful analyses and descriptions, seemed now merely a fiction I'd conjured up: each time I read her letter through I felt more irritated, each time more baffled, kept coming back to it as if some revelation I'd missed lay hidden in it as in an artefact, in the slope of the letters, the paper smell of the page.

"Gotta go," it ended. "Elena says hi."

I was almost ready then to cease writing to her at all, put off replying for a month, then two; but toward Christmas a card arrived from her.

I thought I'd send this off early to make sure you got it –
I guess you won't be getting much snow for Christmas!
Write soon. Rita.

She'd included a school photo of herself, an odd gesture, inscribed "Hot Stuff!" on the back though she seemed imbued in it – posed awkward and smiling before a swirl-patterned backdrop – with an unfamiliar pathos, her eyelids drooping against the camera's flash and her forehead scarred with acne. I felt a small crumbling in me at the sight of her, at this tentative handing over of herself, off-putting almost in the need it showed: it seemed once again I'd misread her, shifting from one imagined extreme to the other when she was merely this simpler, more complex thing in between, a sixteen-year-old, my sister, guarding her own unknown fears and half-formed hopes.

We began to write more regularly, exchanging responses every two or three months, about as much as the erratic mails allowed. Rita's letters grew slowly more sophisticated, more thoughtful: what had struck me at first as simple-mindedness seemed now to have been merely a kind of probing, the first evasive manoeuvres of intimacy. Even now she remained forever gingerly, made concessions, kept always to what was neutral between us, adopted a cynicism toward things that seemed not so much a true bitterness as her instinctive deference to me, the deprecation of her own life to make mine seem the more interesting; but it was exactly in this, in the subtle texture of what went unsaid, that emotion seemed to take shape between us, piecing itself together like a puzzle whose definitions were in what was left out. At the back of my mind now there was always the thought of our letters like a tiny secret retreat in me; the weeks would pass after I'd sent my own and then I'd feel the slow pleasant mounting of anticipation at the imminence of her reply.

My father's letters were more sporadic. I'd sent a brief note home a few weeks after my arrival, the barest facts of my situation delivered in plainest English, addressing it to both my father and aunt, listing their names in full one beneath the other,

343

"Mario Innocente," "Teresa Innocente," reluctant somehow to link them more intimately. I half-hoped there'd be no reply, but then a few months later one came from my father.

Son, I write to you five line in Inglish but you no my inglish is imperfit I hope you will understand it. At the moment evriting is OK overhere. I wish you could spend a week at home and teste the wine that we made is real good. The grinhaus crop is almost finish but maybe thats the last year were gona do a fall crop, its not much money in it.

Then part way through the letter switched to Italian, grew denser, more obscure. There were words, whole phrases, I couldn't make out, lost in his script's whorling sameness: he thought of me, had been happy to get my letter; then an uncertain stretch and the phrase "*ti voglio tanto bene*," literally "I wish you well" but more expressive than that, the equivalent, really, of "I love you very much." It was a ritual phrase and yet it stung me like an accusation.

I sent off a reply in my same impassive tone, saying nothing really, merely filling the page; but then his next letter followed the same pattern as the first, began with his rote greetings and wishes and then veered abruptly into wrenching emotion. There seemed something generic in these sudden declarations to me, without basis in any knowledge he had of me; and yet still the same despair flickered through me at them. I thought of him sitting at his desk to write these things out, his hand against the pen, against the page, and couldn't bear somehow then the brute existence of him there in his close far-away life, still connected to me though I had gone.

A sort of correspondence developed between us then for a

time, a strange fretwork of engagement and avoidance. His own letters, all in his careful schoolbook Italian now, continued on in what seemed a twisted candour, honest and not, agonizingly raw and yet still seeming to be circling some unstated thing; and for a while I simply went on with my same empty replies, in my simplified English at first but then switching from time to time to Italian, borrowing his own rote phrases to try to forge some illusion of a common language between us. But he seemed to be trying to will some more direct confrontation.

"It makes me sad to think you've gone," he wrote once, "and to know you don't value the life I tried to make for you."

I tried to respond to him directly then, careful and unambiguous, expressing my pride at what he'd accomplished, my gratitude at the possibilities he'd allowed me; but he seemed to miss the point, glancing from what I'd said still intent on his own trajectories.

Son, you say you value what I have done and I wish to God I could believe you but right now I wish I had never come to this country, it was the biggest mistake of my life and I have paid for it for twenty years and I am still paying for it. There are many things that have happened that you don't know about and some that maybe you do, but I pray to God that when he takes this suffering away from me you will forgive me and remember that I tried to do my best for you but I was only human and that whatever happens I will always be your father.

In the end these swells of emotion began to wear on me. The reproach implicit in them, that I'd abandoned him, seemed beyond crediting, ignoring as it did all the intricacies of unspoken emotion between us; and even what was genuine in them, his pain, his regret, seemed diluted somehow by his excess. If he could have said these things to my face there might have been dignity in them; as it was they seemed more and more simply self-indulgent, as if the pain he'd held in all his life had begun to lose now the one thing in it that had given him stature, the restraint he had borne it with.

Then at some point I made the mistake of mentioning these letters from my father to Rita. "Perhaps we've been a little unjustly harsh in our opinion of him," I said, or something to that effect. "Apparently the man has been tortured for years by self-pity and remorse." But Rita's reply made no reference to him. I began to think I'd been accusing, cavalier: there was a tone in her letter that seemed new, a certain hollowness, a restraint. I compared it to previous ones but couldn't put my finger on what had changed, decided to let the matter pass; but then my next letters seemed always to be skirting this unmentioned thing, her responses to be skirting my skirting.

Our correspondence began to falter. The gaps between letters lengthened; the letters themselves grew slowly more falsely amiable, more superficial. There was no clear point at which I could have said things had changed definitively, irrevocably, just this slow estrangement, this gradual turning away, so instinctive that it seemed what I'd said about my father wasn't really the point, had merely revealed a distance that had always existed, been what had punctured the illusion of intimacy that had first buoyed us like the moment in a relationship when it grew clear suddenly that the other person was a stranger. The whole course of our correspondence seemed to skew: what we had shared, it seemed now, had been not so much our lives as each other's absence from them, the careful stripping away of

346

any implication they intersected, she with her instinctive discretion and I with the distance she appeared always ready to let me fall back to, the worldly older brother, the mentor, recreating myself in the written word in the persona I lacked in life.

But by the time I'd seen these things, admitted to myself the change between us, the small perversity in me that had taken a kind of relief in it, we seemed already to have drifted back into separateness, forever more cautious and controlled. Already it was hard to remember the first timid promise of our early letters, the sense then of moving toward some imminent culmination, each letter now like a new beginning, taking nothing for granted, seeming to strain for a perfect neutrality. Rita's were mainly litanies now of the trials of life in Mersea, the backwardness and the boredom, but she herself abstracted somehow, merely striking a pose, the disaffected adolescent. What had served before as the tissue of self-revelation, her sarcasm, her careful evasions, now seemed merely to obscure; and it struck me finally how much the voice in her letters had begun to resemble that in mine, ironic, detached, committing to nothing.

It happened one morning that I found a snake in my kitchen. It seemed to have come in through the window, had somehow crawled in under the shutter and draped itself over one of the crossbars of the window's grille; and in the shuttered dark I didn't notice it until a flicker of movement caught my eye, inches from me, as I poked a stick through the grille to prop the shutter open. I drew back, my heart pounding, the snake outlined now, a long, slim green, in the window's light, a mamba perhaps, deadly. I seemed to process a thousand thoughts in an instant, seemed to need to kill it and yet take away from it some uncertain advantage or blessing, as if it had come like a messenger out of my own past; but the snake remained where it was, placid but alert, its tapered head flexed in calm tensed awareness of me. For a moment an absolute stillness seemed to settle over the room, I at my end and the snake at his, staring; and then finally the snake seemed to reach a decision, slithered an instant, and was gone.

Later, composing in my head the story I'd tell, I grew aware that the first audience I'd imagined for it was Rita, realized how she'd become for me over the course of our letters this constant inner companion, how then every event in my life seemed always to lead back to her as its final referent. For perhaps the first time I felt a genuine sense of loss at how I'd mismanaged things between us, of plain regret. Somehow I'd missed the simplest things, the simplest possibilities, that we might somehow have shared our lives, been human, that it would have cost us so little to be simply ourselves.

XXXI

I'd chosen to extend my contract into a third year. I was allowed a paid trip home but took a cash equivalent instead, spending the summer stretched out beneath a scorching equatorial sun on a tiny island off the Kenyan coast, the last destination off the muddy coastal road that went north from Malindi; but when I returned to my posting at summer's end a great lethargy overtook me, the country having grown too real somehow through my having chosen to remain there, seeming ramshackle and gritty and wearing now beyond endurance. There was an election that fall, a transition to civilian rule, though for all the pomp and promises the only thing that seemed to change once the election had come and gone was that the soldiers at checkpoints were gradually replaced with civilian police; and yet finally my malaise seemed less the result of the country's ills than of my own continuing detachment from them, the sense of the randomness of my presence there, the mistake I'd made in not reckoning how much my contentment had depended on the illusion there was some real life I'd be returning to. In early September I'd helped with the orientation of a group of new volunteers and they'd seemed from a different race, fresh-faced and curious, earnest, ambitious, still reeking of their robust northern lives; and I'd been confronted in them with the fact that life at home had continued on in my absence, that I might be a stranger there when I returned.

At Mayflower the first Americans had come and gone, replaced by another who'd slowly grown bitter and strange, then another again; and each of these new arrivals seemed to strip me of some of my own sheen of newness, made me seem less the transient, less the innocent. I sensed now in how taken for granted I'd come to be that I had been a disappointment somehow to the rest of the staff, leading my quiet life there at the edge of the bush, never quite living up to whatever first false promise they'd seen in me when I'd arrived – there was perhaps nothing but the normal indifference of familiarity in this, and yet it disheartened me to see the early sense of possibility I'd felt whittled now down to a kind of everydayness, my students, my work, the few teachers on staff whom I felt some rapport with. I tended to gravitate toward the other outsiders, the Ghanaians, the Indians, the Ibos, recognizing in them the subtle embitterment of the migrant at being out of place; but even then there was always the small lie at the bottom of our friendliness, the small wariness, the fear of exposing some sudden embarrassing chasm between us.

I'd formed by then an acquaintance of sorts with Kate Townsend, through her gaining an entry into the world of white expatriates, the limbo I seemed to accede to as my stay in the country lengthened. Kate was known at the school for the roster of men she kept, mainly wealthy alhajis and businessmen, every now and then one of their Volvos or Mercedes parked discreetly for a few hours or days beneath the plane trees that shadowed her house and afterwards Kate reporting on whatever gifts had been bestowed on her. She'd had a son by one of them, round-faced and olive-skinned, his hair blondish like his mother's but coiled into supple cherubic curls; though the father was the worst of the lot, Kate said, didn't visit for months at a time, borrowed money he never returned. She seemed comfortable with this arrangement, one that was perhaps merely the extreme of a fluidity of family arrangements that appeared fairly common in the region, women often raising their children apart from their husbands, with their own incomes, their own lives; yet in it seemed to reside most clearly the contradiction of her life there, at once exotic and mundane, resolving itself around a whiteness she both exploited yet held in no special regard, that had ceased to have any connection to the elsewhere it drew its power from.

There were others like this, teachers mainly, seeming, like Kate, to stay on simply through a sort of inertia, earning only the usual meagre government wage, without special prerogative or power except what came to them randomly through their whiteness; they seemed a perverse sort of emigrant, coming to where they'd be privileged rather than scorned for their difference and yet more hopeless for that, always outside, without prospects. There was a Canadian I heard about at some point who'd come to the country as a volunteer years before and stayed on, the stories people told of him giving the sense of some fabulous eccentric; but when I'd met him finally I'd been surprised at how common he seemed, how predictable his insights, how undramatic and small his daily life, his only distinction the inconsonance of his Canadian ordinariness lost there without context or purpose in a world that reflected nothing of him.

In a sense it was easier to understand the other whites, the ones who held themselves apart, came strictly for the money, their instincts seeming more basic, their motives more pure. There were a number of them who worked for a cement factory outside the town, their housing compound tucked away behind high, glass-studded walls well off the main road; and entering there was like arriving at some misplaced North American suburb, with the tidy brick bungalows and landscaped lawns, the smell in the buildings of an air-conditioned newness, the group of them secluded there as in a throwback to colonialism, all evidences of the country held out. The few times I accompanied Kate to the club there the conversation veered always toward an aggressive racism, people anxious to establish where I stood, to have me on side; and what seemed to drive them in this was a fear, the constant need to reaffirm what they were, what they imagined they stood for, like an immigrant's holding hard against the threat of some creeping assimilation. Kate was always quick to condemn these people when we came away from them but among them remained evasive, anxious perhaps to preserve her small privileges with them; and what disturbed me was how quickly I began to grow like her among them, how my own resistance to them seemed made merely sullenness and petulance in the face of their monolithic certainties.

In the end it was only with Mr. Tsikata, the head of English, that I had formed what might have been called a friendship. From the outset I'd been drawn to him, to the sense he gave of some complicity he was willing to enfold me in; and that first instinctive bond carried us through the initial carefulness and false steps, the arabesque of awkward deference we seemed in the first months to circle each other with. Early on I'd searched out his house once with some question or problem, finding it in a ramshackle block that appeared to be a sort of ghetto for the Ghanaians, merely rooms really, arranged like barracks around a dirt courtyard with a blackened fire pit at its centre, Mr. Tsikata seeming in that setting in his faded after-work Kente-cloth tunic like some spry village elder, from another world.

"Ah, Victor, come in, come in, so you've found me out!"

But I could feel his beaming embarrassment as he ushered me in, the hopelessness in him as he made a few helpless gestures to rearrange the disorder of his tiny sitting room; and it was several months after that before I could bring myself round to asking him over for supper, afraid of putting him in the awkward situation of having to reciprocate. He seemed so elaborately pleased, so touched, when I finally did so that I thought I'd made a mistake in delaying. But then the day he was to come he sent a message to me through one of the students: there was another obligation he'd forgotten, he was terribly sorry, hoped he could make it up to me by instead having me over to his own home the following evening. Some shadowy ritual of hospitality seemed to be playing itself out – it was as if in finally signalling that invitations were possible I'd also somehow shamed him by having been the first to offer one.

When I arrived at his house the next evening I found a woman and small boy with him: his wife and son, visiting him from Ghana, though he'd never mentioned a word to me about their coming, seemed awkward again at this new self-revelation, this seeing him at home, in his element. All evening long his wife hovered in the background hardly involved with us except in her sullen brief asides to Mr. Tsikata in what I took to be Ashanti, in Mr. Tsikata's gruff replies; and it was only toward the end of the meal that I gathered these asides had formed a sort of terse running translation of our own conversation, that all the while

I'd been imagining his wife's resentment at my intrusion she'd been quietly directing toward me this carefully focused attention. When I finally conveyed a compliment to her on the food through Mr. Tsikata her face lit in a smile like sunlight.

"She says it's the guest that makes the meal good," Mr. Tsikata translated for her, "not the cook."

After a time, Mr. Tsikata and I had become cohorts of a kind, forever joined now in the ceaseless trials and demands of the school's extracurricular activities. Our first politeness gave way to a deeper one, more instinctual, each of us seeming to see in the other a sort of mentor, I in his competence and humility, he in whatever arcane knowledge or power he imagined I brought with me from the world I'd come out of. He began to come to me with various private projects and schemes, boyish and hopeful though there was almost always the hint of a swindle in them, a creative writing school in England that offered tutoring by correspondence, a university in the States that offered Master's degrees.

"I dunno, these kinds of things usually aren't very reputable."

"Ah."

And then his smiling abashment, the small dwindling in him as another possible future slipped away.

In the summer following the second year of my placement he had returned to Ghana, hopeful that elections there might bring some improvement that would make it possible for him to remain. We exchanged addresses, promised letters, future visits; but then a few days before fall term began he returned. I happened to be in the lorry park in Ikorita on some errand when his bus came in, saw him from a distance as he stepped from the bus's undignified closeness, his travel-dirtied clothes, his tattered suitcase, the patch of sweat that darkened the back of his shirt; he seemed suddenly lonely and old like some road-wearied pedlar, reduced like that by the humiliations of African travel, by the prospect of returning again to his twilight life in this strangers' country. I thought of skirting him but then he caught sight of me, seeming for once to forget his awkwardness at being caught out.

"So you see I've come back after all, you thought you'd got rid of me!"

And when I came up to him he wrapped an enfolding arm around my shoulder in spontaneous affection, caught up in the fullness of his sad pleasure at seeing me again. I sensed the heads turning around us, the smiles, for an instant all the lorry park seeming to focus in on this single odd moment of feeling as if to confirm it in its rightness.

The letters from my father had eventually begun to dwindle. All along they'd seemed to suffer more than most from the mails, months elapsed sometimes between their Canadian postmarks and their arrival; and now it had begun to grow difficult to discern any continuity from one to the next, any accumulation, each seeming merely a kind of repetition, working out the same formula of greeting and complaint. He'd had some argument with Tsi'Umberto, he didn't say over what; he was considering selling out his share of the farm to Rocco and Domenic; he'd been in hospital for a pain in his chest, he didn't say what had caused it. At one point in my second year he'd written at length about a heavy snowfall that had caused some sort of breakage in the greenhouses.

By the grace of God we were able to save some of the crop before it all froze but how much damage we had we won't know until the end of the summer. I hope the insurance will pay for some of it but so far we haven't seen a penny from them, in the meantime we had to pay all the costs from our own pockets.

I'd had the impression from his tone that the farm was on the verge of imminent collapse; but then his next letter had made no reference to what had happened, moving on to other matters, other complaints. These lapses made it seem as if his problems had little reality outside the first moment he wrote of them, perhaps true in all their intensity in that instant, in the blunt insistence of the written word, but then dissipating afterwards into the general flux of his life.

What had remained consistent was only his tone, the constant sense of upheaval, its underlying inducement to guilt – it often seemed to me that that was the point, not some new honesty between us but this other veiled language of accusation. Out of the blue once he mentioned he'd gone in for confession: "I made my peace," he said, "but there are some things the priest doesn't know, only God knows." But all this seemed melodrama somehow, the lurking ominousness, the implication that his life was on the brink of some dissolution – a single crisis might have caused me concern, but this steady stream of them suggested he was simply carrying on with his life much as he always had, selecting from it for me only what fit some unspoken working out of old grievances and pain.

Then toward the last months of my third year at the school I got a letter from him that truly unsettled me. He'd begun in the usual way, greetings and family news, then gone on to some sort of conflict he'd had with the Italian club board; yet there was a strange buoyancy in his tone, a sort of hovering remove from things as if he himself were absent somehow. I grew aware of a creeping incoherence, shifts of thought I couldn't quite follow, that seemed to slip for an instant into a kind of darkness – he went on for nearly a page about this problem with the club and yet I couldn't grasp the essence of it, all his referents secretive and sly as in a whispering, boyish plot, "those people," "the others," seeming to wind toward some vague final coming together that was never reached. Then at the end no formal closing, untypical, his last sentence simply dropping off into empty space without so much as a punctuation mark.

I had a premonition then of his death, the idea he'd seemed to be urging me toward all along, then discounted it at once as something that couldn't come true exactly because I'd imagined it, was merely my reflex attraction to doom, my reaching always toward the simplest most dire solution to a problem. But the sense of his absence lingered, the feeling that the person who'd written his earlier letters, who might have been reached, had crossed over now into some new remoteness. I began a letter to him in English but was afraid of some misunderstanding, began one in Italian but felt reduced in it to the merest commonplaces – we hadn't so much as a language between us, had always been forced, especially in our letters, to some compromise, my simplified English, his careful Italian. It occurred to me, exactly now when it seemed already too late, that perhaps all along I'd misread him, missed some crucial clue, had mistaken for maudlin what had been merely a lack of skill, such a little thing as that, the uneasy forcing of emotion into the unwieldiness of an unfamiliar idiom.

In the end I wrote back to him in my usual tone, careful and bland, thinking somehow to anchor him with my own normalcy, touching on some of the things he'd said as if to make him, myself, believe in the sanity of them; yet I sent the letter off without any faith that it would have effect. I thought of writing to Aunt Teresa as well but then reasoned that there was no point, that I would be home soon, that if something had happened I would have heard, though at bottom I was vaguely afraid of the letter's falling into my father's hands; and afterwards, when the worst had happened, I guarded the strange illusion that it was somehow best that I hadn't written after all, that to have put the thing into words would have been a kind of incrimination, proof that it had been foreseeable and yet we'd done nothing.

The next news I had of my father was in fact of his death: I came home from class to find Richard Harmond waiting for me on my verandah, so transparent in his awkwardness that I thought again my first expectation must be wrong, that bad news couldn't come in so obvious a package.

"It's your father." He was unable to bring himself to say the actual words, letting his flushed silence stand in for them. "They said they would try to hold the funeral until you got back."

I had the strangest feeling afterwards, not of relief or inevitability as I'd expected but a kind of disorientation, a nausea as at the thought of something unnatural or evil. Richard sat with me an hour or so in my house, touchingly solicitous, volunteering information though I asked for none, was uncertain what I was permitted, what could pass under the circumstances as normal.

"It was your aunt that called Ottawa, I think. They didn't really say what had happened."

"Ah."

"Was he sick or anything that you knew?"

"I dunno, he had some pains in his chest."

"Maybe that was it."

There was a flight through London the next morning; Richard had already made the arrangements. I had only to pack, to take whatever I needed and leave the rest for him to ship home afterwards. He offered to stay to help me with my packing and then bring me back to Ibadan with him for the night.

"You could use the phone there, if you wanted to call home."

I wondered how reasonable it would be for me to refuse these things, felt reassured at the small relief that seemed to pass through him when I did.

"I guess you probably just want to be alone for a while."

"Yeah, I think so."

"I wasn't sure if you wanted me to speak to anyone at the school. If you want I can wait till after you're gone."

"Okay."

I spent the evening alone. I ought to have been going around, taking my leave, the adult thing, ought at least to have spoken to Mr. Tsikata; but I couldn't bring myself to disturb anyone, be disturbed, wanted only to hold the still quietness at the centre of me till I'd understood what it seemed to be urging me toward.

In the morning Richard came before dawn. The students had already begun to rise; I could hear their distant morning sounds from the dorms, the sleepiness of voices, the dull patter of a thousand hurried feet as they moved toward the exercise grounds. In the sky the stars had only just barely begun to pale in the morning twilight: I seemed to be leaving as I'd come, from dark to dark, stealing away like some scuttling sea thing beneath the wrinkling surface of the day.

XXXII

My father had drowned in our irrigation pond. No one mentioned suicide and yet it seemed the word behind every other one, every condolence, every silence. The silence was the oppressive thing, at our house, at the funeral home, the long procession of solemn mourners before the closed coffin, reduced to a mute, awkward restraint in the face of our humiliation. I learned only the barest facts of what had happened, that he'd gone missing one day, that Rocco had found him several days later in the pond.

He had begun to build a new house. The old wooden greenhouses had been levelled and a pit hollowed there for the basement, trenches and poured concrete already sketching out its ghostly outline. He'd never mentioned the house in his letters and yet obviously he'd planned for it, set money aside, imagined a future in it. Already weeds had begun to crop up in the yellow soil that had been dug down to, a skid of blocks tottering there at the edge of a trench in abandoned waiting.

At the funeral Aunt Teresa wore black. She cut a stern figure, anachronistic, staunch and forbidding like the dark widows of

Valle del Sole; but she was the one in control of things, who seemed to hold us together dignified and whole, coolly efficient and restrained as if my father's death had been merely another of his childish excesses. It was Tsi'Umberto who appeared most stricken, his face a perpetual grimace as if his pain were a physical thing, unremitting – I'd never seen him like that, so broken, seemed to see my father in him suddenly, the same rawness of emotion, the same humility.

Rita was there, alone: I saw her emerge from the church as we were being arranged into cars for the procession, didn't recognize her at first and then felt a start when I did at the instant's transformation she underwent from young woman to sister. She was dressed in a grey suit, elegant and severe, dark nylons leading down to the small adult rise of her heels and her hair pulled back into a bun, a few loose strands hanging free from it over her brow as if in last girlish dishevelment. Now that she was there live before me the veiled complexities of our letters seemed a kind of indiscretion.

"I'm sorry about what happened and everything."

There was still the familiar tentativeness in her voice; yet something had changed, some old deference been diminished, her adolescence seeming to have been peeled away to reveal this self-possessed adult underneath, with her stranger's blue eyes, the intimation in them of all the things about her I couldn't know.

"Maybe you could call me in a couple of days or something," she said. "If you wanted to talk or anything –"

"Okay."

But the following day I came down with malaria, my body still remembering the distant life I'd been leading a few days before. It hit hard and swift, a sudden drop into the darkness of it, seemed to have been coiled patient inside me awaiting this moment of weakness; I grew delirious, the world become a single dizzying pain, was aware of people moving around me but couldn't shape an identity for them, was aware of speaking but as out of a dream. I couldn't find the place in my mind that divided nightmare from waking; and then finally I slipped into a kind of sleep but my mind continued to race, seeking not a solution but a question, an equation whose answer was zero, an infinite series of numbers that would slowly collapse on itself till it came to nothing. In the morning the fever broke, my mind slowly groping back toward clarity; and then the symptoms began again, the creeping chill, the sudden drop again into the fever's darkness.

I went on like that for days, lost track of things, was aware only of the landscape of my illness, my islands of sudden clarity and then my descent, the awesome pain there, the strange dreamy urgency of my thoughts. I had the sense people had turned against me, was relieved every time I grew aware of Aunt Teresa bringing in food, fresh clothes, wiping the sweat from me with a careful, undeserved humanity; but then the moment she'd gone I'd begin to suspect again some abandonment. Several times I was taken out to the hospital for injections, seeming enfolded then in the bright friendliness the world had put on to hold me; but afterwards I played out the scenes of what had happened as if to find in them some smiling duplicity, the moment that was wrong.

When the fever broke, definitively, I came into a strange euphoria, surfacing to it as into sudden daylight. For a day or so I went on like that, my mind scoured, without contents, a transparency merely for the world to pass through; but then slowly a structure of things began to take shape there again, my first buoyancy giving way to a gloom as if I'd awoken from a dream of calamity only to find after the initial relief that the calamity was real.

"Your sister called," Aunt Teresa said.

It was the first time I could think of that she'd ever called the house.

"What did she say?"

"She just wanted to know how you were, that's all. I told her you were sick."

But I put off calling her back, wanting only to close out the world, to be sound again.

Aunt Teresa and I began to talk. She would be at the kitchen table in the morning when I awoke, sipping her coffee there, seeming to wait for my company as out of the lingering habit of not being alone.

"You know how he was, he was never happy, he could never forget what had happened. That's how he was made."

And yet his death seemed to have remained outside her, left her unimplicated, what she wanted now not an expiation but simply the tired sorting out of things after the inevitable.

There'd been the problem at the Italian club that he'd alluded to his in his letter, a small thing it turned out, ambiguous, some accusation by Dino Mancini's board that a committee my father had been part of had misused funds; then in May his mother had died in Italy of a stroke.

"He'd never been back, he couldn't forgive himself for that. It was hard for all of us, your uncle at least had been back the year before but I hadn't seen her since I came here. But to your father it was the end of the world."

"But how did he seem, before that, I mean? There must have been something, some sign." Though I couldn't bring myself to mention his letter.

"You know how he was when he got into his moods for one thing or another, he went on like that for months. Who knew it was any different this time?"

Yet still I couldn't think my way into his death, couldn't find the essence of it in these explanations, couldn't quite bring myself to believe in the truth of it. It seemed the important questions remained unanswered, the anatomy of his death, the small thoughts he'd had, the small steps he'd taken, how he'd climbed down the bank of the pond, how he'd stepped into it, how he'd held himself under. What he'd looked like, a few days later, floating there on the surface of the water.

If he'd carried on, it seemed now, remained whole, there might have been some meaning in his life, the virtue at least of persevering; but his suicide negated him somehow, seemed a line drawn through his life like a cancellation. He'd brought so little pleasure into the world, to others, to himself, had brought only unease, even now in his death.

Aunt Teresa said she'd found him crying once in the kitchen over one of my letters.

"You can't understand what passes between a father and son, he said."

When I finally tried to reach Rita she'd gone, off on a French immersion program with Elena in Quebec.

"I'm very sorry about your father," Mrs. Amherst said. "I would have come to the funeral but I wasn't sure, with your family and everything –"

She seemed truly distraught, had perhaps all along felt the guilt of our exclusion of her.

"I understand," I said.

She gave me a number for Rita. I put a call through and got a voice in a thick Quebec patois; then finally Rita came on the line.

"Hi." Hesitant, gingerly. "I tried to call you before I left, I guess you were sick or something."

"Yeah."

There was laughter in the background, the clink of cutlery.

"We're staying with a family here, it's pretty wild."

She asked about my plans.

"I don't know, I guess I'll probably be back up at school in Toronto again." But I felt reluctant somehow at saying so, knew from her letters that she would be there as well. "I applied up there anyway."

"That would be great. Maybe we could move up together or something when Elena and I get back."

"I'm not sure I can last that long here."

I could hear myself trying to play on her sympathies.

"Yeah, I guess it must be pretty rough."

But at the end there was no suggestion from either of us that I call again.

I began to work on the farm. My life seemed without direction suddenly – I wondered now what exactly I'd intended for myself, had vaguely envisioned continuing on in school and yet that plan had seemed always provisional, the mere background to some other larger, as yet undetermined fate. I remembered a story, "The Beast in the Jungle," about a man who saved himself all his life for a destiny that never came to pass.

There was a new, second office in the boiler room now, bright with computer screens and lighted panels, part of some government pilot project; a researcher came by once a week to monitor it, Rocco and Domenic huddling with him in the office all seriousness and intent, caught up in their arcane new technologies and systems. They were clearly in charge of things now, knew how they worked, what needed to be done; and I wondered how I'd ever imagined that I was any better than they were, their own lives seeming now so much more purposeful and solid than my own.

Domenic had married, to a young dark-eyed woman named Marisa, the two of them living now in the family's old house next to the new one, a modest bungalow in white brick, that Tsi'Umberto had built on the adjoining lot. Marisa had been sent over from Italy after some scandal there, a failed tryst of some sort, a family connection with Tsi'Alfredo having finally steered her toward Domenic. Their marriage seemed the last logical step in Domenic's domestication; but the flaw in it, its convenience, appeared to bring out in him a gruff protectiveness. Perhaps he simply realized how fortunate he'd been after all, how precious Marisa was, lively, attractive, intelligent; for a few weeks my conversations with her were the only things I looked forward to, the sight of her in the mornings in her mannish working clothes, the wisps of hair that fell over her temples from under her kerchief. When she spoke of Italy there was a suppressed longing in her voice like the lingering heartbreak of early sorrow, a resignation too old for her; and it seemed she was the one who had made the sacrifice, catapulted as she'd been out of her youthful promise into the narrow islanded gloom of our farm.

Toward the end of July we gathered at Tsi'Umberto's to read the will. Tsi'Umberto by then was returning to his old self, putting on a careful solemnity in the lawyer's presence; but the lawyer himself, still Mr. Newland though he'd begun to grow old now, appeared almost lighthearted, elegant and trim and spry in a pin-striped suit, skimming over our own sombreness with a practised efficiency. The terms of the will were quite simple finally: my father had left me everything, his savings, his share in the farm, every cent. When Mr. Newland began to go through the figures I was staggered, the totals quickly rising well into the hundreds of thousands. Against these amounts my father had owed toward the farm only forty thousand dollars, the principal on the original loan he'd taken out twenty years before to buy it, and coming due in full at the end of the year.

This was my father's legacy to me then, these unreasonable sums, this excess. Somehow I hadn't expected it, had always imagined the farm heavily mortgaged, its profits slim, had hardly even considered I could have much of a stake in it when I'd been so removed from it all my life. Suddenly there amidst people who'd given their lives to it I'd become from nothing the principal – for the first time since my father's death I had the sense what it meant to be his son, the gravity of it. It seemed there'd been a mistake, that somehow the strict rules of inheritance shouldn't apply here; and yet already as Mr. Newland began to explain complications, monies that belonged to the company, taxes that had been deferred, I felt the resistance in me to any whittling away of this unhoped for birthright.

Later I met with Mr. Newland privately, at his office. There was a matter of life insurance, fifty thousand dollars, with double indemnity for accidental death.

"There's an exclusion clause, of course. The death was listed as accidental but the company might do its own investigation, you should be prepared for that. Or they may be willing to settle for just paying the principal."

There was also a codicil to the will he hadn't mentioned: it expressed a wish, simply, that proceeds from my inheritance be provided at my discretion to Rita should she ever suffer financial hardship.

"It has no force in law, it's only a wish, nothing more. If and when and how much is entirely up to you."

I hadn't reckoned on these lingering obligations, these ambiguities: I had the sense my father had simply handed his life to me whole, his responsibilities and his guilt, the onus of coming to grips with what he was worth, how he had died. His financial affairs were a tangle, all his assets somehow tied up in the company, a substantial tax due on them at once because of his death and then a further one due if I should choose to remove them from the company, as much as two-thirds of their value at stake; and then there were the conditions set on the sale of company shares in the company charter, Byzantine, the protections and balances, the contingencies. What I wanted was just to have what was mine laid out clearly before me, whole and intact, without entanglements; but it seemed my inheritance had meaning only within the context it arose from, that the only way to derive benefit from it was to step full into my father's place.

For a few days I actually considered this possibility, began to see the farm in the light of it, what I'd have there, an income, a purpose, a structure to my life; and when I looked at my life as it was I seemed to have little in it to oppose to these things. What most surprised me was how readily the others appeared willing to grant me a place among them, the deference in them as if they truly believed I'd taken on my father's authority along with his assets; and being among them in their new respect seemed somehow to draw me back into their world, perhaps more known to me now, more instinctive, exactly in having been forgotten. But at bottom I knew I would go – for a month, perhaps a year, I could define myself within the bounds of what was possible there, the profits and the work, the small predictable promise of the future; and then my estrangement would begin again, whatever it was that was alien in me would grow large again.

I met with Mr. Newland once more and then with the accountant, Mr. Dirksen, ghostly and grim in his Mennonite pallor.

"A little planning could have avoided these problems, I told your father that. But you know how the older immigrants are, my own people are like that, they still act like before when they used to hide their money in a sock."

Another meeting was arranged with the family, the options laid out; what we arrived at, after more meetings, more discussions, was an arrangement that on paper involved the creation of various company shares but in practise amounted to a kind of mortgage the others would pay out to me over the next ten years to buy me out. Of my father's savings not much remained after taxes and various bills, his outstanding loan; and what I was left with was this intangible, not so much money as time, these ten free years like a hole in my life, a kind of slow penance, what I would owe him, would pay him, for all his own years of sacrifice and work.

We seemed far by then from the reality of my father's death: it had been possible, after all, to extract him from what he had been, but only at the expense of losing him in these abstractions, sums of money that didn't exist, neat red-sealed documents, obfuscations. There'd been an envelope in his safety-deposit box stuffed with some five thousand dollars in worn Canadian and American bills, hidden income, probably proceeds from the junk cucumbers we sold to a Lebanese trader from Detroit; and there'd seemed more of my father in those tattered bills, the feel of them there in my hands, than in all the hundreds of thousands he'd been worth on paper. I felt tempted briefly to press a claim on his insurance, wanted that hard sum of money, perhaps less for itself than for its tangible proof, conspicuous and large, that I'd taken something from his death; in the end what kept me from doing so was a sense of filial respect, not merely the threat of an investigation but that I ought simply to do what was right, what my father would have done, though afterwards I could think of a dozen contradictions of this image of integrity I'd formed of him.

I signed documents and waivers; I opened a current account; I sorted my father's papers, what ought to be kept, what could be destroyed. Then finally nothing remained to be done: there was only my father's absence, my life, the freedom stretching before me blank as the sea.

XXXIII

I prepared for my departure, going through the house to shore up what was mine. Boxes of my things had begun to arrive from Nigeria, sporadically, one or two every week; I thought of Richard carefully packing them in the mouldy damp of my house at the edge of the bush, placing this thing here, that knick-knack, these books. He'd included things that weren't mine, that I'd found in the house when I'd arrived; but there were a few I wasn't sure of, an old tie-dyed shirt, a Hemingway reader, had to search my mind to place them as if reconstructing out of arte-facts some other person I'd once been.

I went through my father's belongings. He'd had so little finally, so little that was truly his, his clothes, an electric razor, an old watch. I found a shoebox in a drawer in his bedroom filled with black-bordered funeral cards, small glossy sheets with prayers on one side and grainy photos on the other. There was some jewellery there, a gold chain and cross, two rings, one an unadorned gold band – his wedding ring. I tried it, found a finger it fit and left it there.

I went down to the pond, for the first time. There was no sign there of anything, of any breach, the banks grown thick with saplings and weeds, the water thick with algae. I threw a stone and the algae briefly retreated to let it through and then reformed, the water heaving an instant beneath its blanket of green, then stilled.

The torpor among us that had followed my father's death had begun to pass. Rocco, I found out, had been engaged for some time to a local Italian girl; the wedding had been put off but now already quiet plans were being made again, a date chosen, bridesmaids and ushers picked out. To allow them to live in our old house after the marriage Aunt Teresa decided to continue on with a more modest version of the new one for herself; and already it seemed that the family had begun to shift to accommodate my father's absence, to fold themselves over it. There was no one to mourn him really, no one whose world had crumbled with his death – without the blemish of him the aspect our family presented seemed more one of soundness than of affliction. I thought of Tsi'Umberto's daughter Flora, in teachers' college now, a young woman, affable and respectful, with her mother's dark heaviness but attractive in her way, the attractiveness of being unremarkable: she seemed such a miracle now though I'd so long disliked her, content and unrebellious and on her path, the ideal immigrant's child. There was no explaining her, how she'd emerged from our family so undamaged by it, become truly her namesake, the flower now of what had appeared merely a slow desolation.

I left home for Toronto in the last week of August, a Sunday, my birthday, anxious now simply to be alone again, to be away. I was to take my father's car: in the contamination of his death it had sat in the garage unused the whole summer. I felt the ghost of him still there when I got into it in the position of mirrors, of the seat, the place arranged to hold him, felt a strange sensation as I altered things as if erasing him.

Then I had loaded my few belongings and was gone. Home, the farm, fell away in the anonymity of the road, its first pleasant moments of suspension when it seemed possible never to have to arrive. It was a brilliant day, the air crisped with the intimation of autumn, in its glassy clarity the landscape seeming charmed, the tidy white farmhouses, the silos and fields, the clusters of trees in the distance. As a child, remembering some story I'd heard, I'd sometimes imagined those endless clusters of trees as flying islands, wondrous and grand, quietly touched down there in that flat countryside in their beckoning magic; things then had still harboured secrets about themselves, like the first strangeness of my father's farm, the promise and the threat of unknown things before they turned mundane.

Past Chatham I saw an amazing thing, fantastic like some trick of sunlight: a field full of hot-air balloons, dozens of them, blooming in the distance like a strange fairy-tale crop, still and multicoloured and huge. I pulled over to the shoulder, still uncertain whether I'd understood – some sort of festival seemed to be in progress, the field alive with movement, cars and concessions, people, strains of music. Then as I watched, the balloons began to lift off, one or two at first like tests and then more, a slow growing flurry of them, elephantine and graceful, drifting their weightless way with a languorous patience, goodbye, goodbye, until they filled the horizon. For an instant it seemed the world could not bear the magnificence of them, must suddenly make itself over, become childlike and bright and unreal as they were to hold them; and then slowly they began to disperse and fade, small dots of colour like candy against the realer, stranger hue of the sky.

ACKNOWLEDGEMENTS

For their contributions to this book I am grateful to the following: Lee Robinson, for her ongoing advice and encouragement; Janet Irving and Peter Robinson, for their patience and support; Peter Day, Jan Geddes, and Greg Kelly, for their helpful suggestions; Veronique Naster for her expertise in childrearing; Alex Schultz, for his scrupulous eye; and Ellen Seligman, for editorial assistance above and beyond the call of duty.

I would also like to thank Mary Di Menna, Rosella Mattei, Lily Policella, and Elizabeth Puglia, with whom I worked in 1979 researching the history of the Italian community in the Leamington, Ontario, area, and Professor Walter Temelini, who oversaw that research and from whose writings I drew one of this book's epigraphs.

The epigraph from *Crime and Punishment* follows the Constance Garnett translation (Modern Library).

For their financial support over the seven years in which this book and the trilogy it forms part of have been taking shape I thank the Explorations Program of the Canada Council, the Multiculturalism Directorate of the Secretary of State, the Ontario Arts Council, and the Arts Award Service of the Canada Council.

Rafy

Nino Ricci was born in Leamington, Ontario, in 1959. His first novel, *Lives of the Saints* (1990), won the Governor General's Award for Fiction, the SmithBooks/Books in Canada First Novel Award, and the F.G. Bressani Prize. The novel was also a long-time national bestseller, and was followed by the highly acclaimed *In a Glass House* (1993) and *Where She Has Gone* (1997), which was shortlisted for the prestigious Giller Prize. Ricci holds a B.A. from York University and an M.A. from Concordia University. He is a past president of PEN Canada.

Nino Ricci lives in Toronto, where he is at work on his next novel.